THE FAE NEXT DOOR

THE FAE NEXT DOOR

FRIENDLY NEIGHBORHOOD WIZARD BOOK 2

SmilingSatyr

Podium

*To Mom and Dad,
for giving me the break I needed
to explore Faerie at my leisure.
This one's for you!*

All rights reserved. No part of this publication may be reproduced, stored in a retrieval system, or transmitted in any form or by any means electronic, mechanical, photocopying, recording, or otherwise without prior written permission from Podium Publishing.

This is a work of fiction. Names, characters, places, and incidents are either products of the author's imagination or used fictitiously. Any resemblance to actual events, locales, or persons, living, dead, or undead, is entirely coincidental.

Copyright © 2024 by SmilingSatyr

Cover design by Kittra McBriar

ISBN: 978-1-0394-5414-9

Published in 2024 by Podium Publishing
www.podiumaudio.com

THE FAE NEXT DOOR

CHAPTER 1

The Unseen Roads

Back when Wil McKenzie was a child, his parents used to tell him stories before bed. In these stories, there would always be monsters and beasties and brave young men who could fight them off and save the day. He didn't know until later that these stories had been based in part on the truth. There were indeed monsters and dragons and other dangerous creatures that had disappeared as Calipan had been tamed. But there were also the fae.

These were never the stories Wil liked best or even really cared about until he was already an adult at Saint Balthazar's Academy of Magic. There, he had learned about the elves and brownies and goblins and ogres that used to inhabit the land, and that had been that. They were curiosities, nothing he would ever have expected to deal with. And why would he have? The fae had disappeared years ago.

And now he found himself blinking as he stepped from his world into another, through the gap in the mushroom ring. His girlfriend, Darlene Johnson, stood at his side, her body tense. They took in their surroundings.

Not knowing what to expect, Wil had imagined an ambush, or a greeting, or *something* waiting for them in the land where the kidnapped citizens of Harper Valley were being held. But there was nothing other than trees and mushrooms and big green beanstalks of some kind reaching above the tree line. He wondered if he would find a castle if he climbed to the top.

The closest thing to life was birdsong—and a rabbit the size of a large dog running past them in the clearing, down what looked like a well-trod footpath.

"That was big," said Darlene, adjusting her magic-detecting spectacles and watching the rabbit retreat until it was out of sight. "Think we could find one big enough to ride?"

She and Wil exchanged a glance before laughing, restrained and tense at first before they both relaxed a little and gave into it.

"Maybe," said Wil. "Carpets and sleds not good enough for you? I'll see what I can do, but damn, Darlene."

His girlfriend's face lit up with amusement before she remembered why they were there. "So, where do we go from here?"

Wil's smile dropped. "Um . . . good question." He looked around again.

The doorway to Faerie behind them, they stood at a crossroads of sorts, a clearing from which five paths led through the woods ahead. Any one of them could take them where they needed to go—or none of them. Their gnome captive, Declan, had said that all roads led to Oakheart Spiral, so maybe it didn't matter.

"This one," Wil said, pointing at the path closest in the middle of the clearing. Darlene shot him a look, as if she could read his mind and wasn't sure she approved of him guessing the direction, but she shrugged, and they set off.

The path took them through a thick tree line Wil couldn't see through. The farther they went, the thicker the trees became, until they had to step over logs and squeeze past a half-fallen elm tree. Wil had to tilt his staff to get it through the gap. He listened intensely, keeping his eyes on the road while Darlene looked all around through her spectacles. They kept on, until one more curve brought them back to the clearing. They stood on the same path they'd initially chosen.

"Did we just go in a circle?" Darlene asked, wrinkling her nose. "How? There was only one path and it brought us here!"

Wil stepped into the middle of the clearing, looking around. "Faerie magic, I imagine. They're known for things like this. I once read a story about a man who got lost in the woods for a week and when he came out, twenty years had passed."

Darlene shot him a look. "Gee, I feel so much safer. Thanks, Wil. What now?"

Wil unshouldered his pack and dug in for a magic wand and one of Bram's handkerchiefs. He tied it to the wand and took a deep breath. He cast a searching spell, and the wand spun in lazy circles in his palm. It continued to do so until Wil stuck it back in the pack.

"Right, so, I'm guessing we're in a stretch of forest made to keep people lost. I'm going to be honest with you: I'm not sure how to deal with this other than just . . . trying more paths until we find the right one."

"Well, I guess we don't have much choice, huh?" Darlene sighed. She rested a hand on the iron bar at her belt for comfort.

Wil picked the next path at random. Unlike their first choice, this path took them down a wide, open stretch of forest. Birdsong still followed them wherever they went, but the farther they went, it more it sounded muted and distant, like something heard through a closed door. Soon after, though the trees were spaced apart, darkness crept in.

By the time Wil noticed the light dimming with each step they took, it already looked like nightfall. He looked around wildly, stopping in place. Darlene continued for another few steps before she noticed and turned around.

"What's wrong?" she asked.

"It's getting dark, but it's too early to get dark, isn't it?" Wil looked up. He couldn't see the sun, or any light, in the sky, only dim blue, tinted black. "We've only been here for, like, half an hour."

"It's not dark for me," said Darlene, looking around. "It looks perfectly lit up."

"Take off your spectacles."

Darlene lifted them and did a double take. "Oh. Whatever's causing this, it just glows through these and I can see through it." She placed them back down. "Do you think we're in danger?"

Wil shrugged. It was genuinely hard to say. They were supposed to be safe, but Declan had promised him safety from his people, not the environment itself.

"Let me try something." Wil channeled through his staff and conjured a ball of light. It lit up everything within about ten feet but the rest of the world remained dark. Good enough. He motioned for Darlene to continue.

The darkness pressed in on Wil as they went, swallowing the world outside the radius of his ball of light. And then, before too long, that radius shrank. The only things Wil could see were himself and Darlene, and he worried how much longer that would last. "Are you sure you can see just fine?" he asked.

Darlene nodded. "Yeah, this is just a normal path. I don't see anything objectionable here. It's just been a straight line for— Wait a second, I think I see a side path." She stopped. Holding tightly to his hand, she led them off the road.

Wil tried not to flinch as branches scraped his face and clothes as he and Darlene snuck through the trees. The light in his hand faded until it was pitch black entirely, with only Darlene to guide him forward. Panic gripped him like a bucket of cold water dumped over his head, shocking every part of him awake. He swallowed it down, trying not to shake as he imagined everything that could potentially attack them.

And then, fast as a blink, the light came back and Wil could see. The two of them froze at the sight of civilization. The forest opened onto a massive clearing where dozens of tiny homes were scattered about. Mushrooms stood like short trees, five feet tall, with doors and windows built into them. Even some of the trees along the sides had ladders leading up to homes inside.

More importantly, there were at least a hundred Wee Folk there, just as frozen as Wil and Darlene. They stood at about a foot and a half tall each, wearing clothes made of plants and bark. They looked like miniature people, but wildly alien and different.

"Um . . . , hello!" Wil called out. "Don't be afraid!"

The next thing he knew, a bloodcurdling scream sounded in the distance and chaos broke out. The entire village panicked and ran around in circles, some of them too scared and surprised to do much more than keep moving, heading toward any available door. The smart ones got inside their mushrooms and trees and closed up their doors and shutters, leaving a few scared fae outside and trapped with the humans.

"Well, this is a good start," said Darlene. Louder she called out, "We're not here to hurt you, we're just a little lost!"

It didn't make things better. Wil sighed and stepped forward, looking down at the little homes. The aroma of cooking meals wafted up through tiny chimneys. He came up to one of the little people, towering over him. The little man looked up, quivering in place.

"Mercy!" he cried. "Please don't smash me! I didn't do nothing to no humans, I swear!"

"Relax," said Wil. "I have no intentions of hurting any of you, unless you hurt me first. I promise."

A little tingle crept through Wil's veins and went to his heart and head. He remembered that promises had real power here among these people. The little man relaxed, stroking a short brown beard.

"You should ask our chief," he squeaked, pointing to the biggest tree in the back, a massive oak tree that towered over the nearby trees.

"Than—" Darlene started before Wil magically silenced her. She looked at him in annoyance.

"Be careful what you say around the fae," he said. "If you thank them for anything, they may think you owe them for something." He turned to the small man and said, "The direction is welcome. You may go in peace."

The little man scampered off, finally finding his right mushroom and diving in through an open window rather than opening the door. Wil couldn't help but smile at the sight.

"You really gotta stop doing that," Darlene muttered when she could speak again, but she didn't seem all that mad. Mostly just embarrassed she'd nearly made a mistake.

The door to the chief's tree stood at Wil's eye level, complete with a balcony. Wil brought his staff up and gently tapped the tip of the dragon horn against the door three times. "Excuse me," he called out. "We seek directions to Oakheart Spiral, but we seem to be lost."

"Go away!" a gruff, squeaky voice said. "We don't want nothing to do with humans!"

"But that's a double negative," said Darlene, with a wicked smile. "So you *do* want to deal with us. Come on out."

The door burst open and an older man with the physique of a potato came out with a gnarled walking stick. He came up to the railing of the balcony and jabbed the stick in Darlene's direction. "Get out of my village! You don't belong here!"

Wil opened his mouth, but Darlene was way ahead of him. She turned up the charm, smiling and saying, "We're terribly sorry for the intrusion. We came in from the human world and found ourselves near here, lost. If we had directions to Oakheart Spiral, we'd have no reason to be here. I think we'd leave pretty quickly and probably never come back."

The chief looked between them with narrowed, suspicious eyes. "Is that true, Wizard?" he demanded.

Wil bowed his head in acknowledgment. "We seek no quarrel with you, good chief. We just want to be on our way. But if we don't have a safe direction to go in, then . . ." He looked around the village and then back to the chief with a smile. "Your home is beautiful, and looks like a nice place to stay while we get our bearings."

"Bah. You want to get to the capital? Go back the way you came. Right back through the ring you stepped into." Then he scowled and went back inside his tree, shutting and locking the door behind him.

Wil and Darlene looked at each other.

"Well," said Darlene, "that was useless. What path do you think we should try next?"

Wil shook his head. "I think we should do exactly what he said. We go back to the ring. If need be, we find another way into Faerie that won't get us stuck in the forest. You *can* lead us back there, right?"

Darlene tapped her spectacles.

The way back was, as always, much faster than the way there. Wil stayed close to Darlene through the darkness, and breathed a sigh of relief when they made it back to the original clearing. There was no telling where the path might have led them if they'd tried again, but Wil guessed it would have been another dead end or trick, all to help keep the village hidden.

They looked at the ring of mushrooms. As one, Wil and Darlene stepped forward though the gap, expecting to return home to Harper Valley. Instead, they found themselves outside of the forest, in a large meadow. A sea of green surrounded them, broken up by wildflowers of all colors and sizes, some as big as Wil himself. Off in the distance was the largest tree Wil had ever seen, rising and piercing the sky. Try as he might, he couldn't see the top through the clouds.

"Is that it?" Darlene said, pointing at the tree. "Oakheart Spiral?"

"I think it is," said Wil. "Looks pretty far away. We should probably get moving. How're you feeling?"

Darlene snorted. "Why? Going to offer me one last chance to go home if I want to? Screw that—we're getting Bram and the others back."

Wil smiled and put his hand on Darlene's shoulder. He squeezed reassuringly. "Then let's get moving, shall we?"

The path rose from the faerie circle across the meadow and over rolling hills, heading in the direction of the great tree. The way was long and this detour was proof they didn't understand how this place worked or know what to expect, but Wil was still confident.

Nobody was going to keep him from setting things right.

CHAPTER 2

The Wampus Cat

Of all the things Wil expected from and dreaded about Faerie, unparalleled beauty wasn't one of them. He supposed it made sense that a collection of magical people who avoided industrialization would have great natural beauty where they lived, but it was different seeing it for himself.

The path leading to Oakheart Spiral took them over rolling emerald hills covered in bright flowers, with the occasional pond or stream as far as the eye could see. Now that they were no longer stuck in the enchanted forest, they were not alone. Unfamiliar, brilliantly colored birds flew across the sky in formation, singing and diving to snatch flowers, or fish from the ponds. Groups of what appeared to be especially shaggy goats frolicked, grazing on the grass.

"I can't believe this place," said Darlene in a voice little more than a whisper. The sun seemed to shine clearer in a sky of deep azure. A rainbow passed between the few clouds.

"I know what you mean," said Wil, in just as much awe. He stepped carefully, still getting used to walking with a staff. As lovely as the fae countryside was, he wasn't forgetting how dangerous this place could be, and having a new staff was a great comfort. He found himself angling closer to the goat-looking creatures, curious.

"I'm still amazed this doesn't look like Harper Valley at all, or anywhere in the basin," Wil continued, still looking around. "Part of me expected something like a mirror of our world, especially after parts started bleeding over. This is its own land, and I bet it's at least as big as Calipan!"

"Is getting closer safe?" Darlene hung back. "What even are those?"

"Good question," said Wil, grinning. "Hey, what are you guys?"

The not-goats turned and looked up at him. Then, to Wil's and Darlene's surprise, they exchanged looks with each other and bleated. They turned around and ran clear in the opposite direction, cloven hooves stamping out a muffled beat against the thick grass. Before long, they crested the next hill and disappeared.

"Was it something I said?"

Darlene nudged him. "You're enjoying yourself too much."

Wil opened his mouth to protest, then realized she was right.

"I'm not trying to," he said, looking around the vivid meadow. "This is just something I never thought I'd get a chance to do. I know we're here for a reason and have to get our people back home, but . . . just look at this place!" He gestured with his staff.

After a few seconds of keeping an impossibly straight face, Darlene gave in and nodded. "It's beautiful. But we need to keep our guard up, right? We should maybe not approach any creatures, and instead assume that everything is out to get us."

Wil hesitated. "That's probably smarter, but . . ." How should he put this? "I get almost nothing but a good feeling from where we are now. My stomach's not getting weird. And if it helps, I can reach out and get a feel for the land and how welcome we are."

Darlene raised an eyebrow. "What, talk to the meadow and see if you can make friends? Is that something you can do?"

"Kind of." Wil shrugged. It was complicated, but a wizard's sense of the world around him was greatly enhanced compared to that of normal humans. When one opened themselves up, they could feel the magic around them, and it told them so much—the health of the land, echoes of its history, and a sense of what intelligence left its mark. It wasn't perfect and it wasn't entirely intelligible, but it made sense to him.

"Well, go for it then," said Darlene, shrugging.

Wil took a long, deep breath and let it out. He closed his eyes and opened his mind. The land of Faerie dwarfed him, bigger in all directions than he could comprehend. There could've been terror in that sense of smallness, but Wil took comfort in it instead. The land was old and rich and had its own personality and humor. He could feel the goatlike animals, still running off. The birds in the sky, the worms in the earth, and the richness of the soil—all were one.

It soothed him. On and on his senses stretched, to the edge of the forest they had come from, which had a closed-off feeling. Over the base of the mountain, where things were less soft and a little tenser. Not malicious, just the wariness of the wild. Down to a swamp in the southwest, and a shadow that—

Wil opened his eyes suddenly.

"What?" Darlene asked, watching him closely.

"I'm not sure," he said, reaching out again. It had almost felt like another powerful magic user, someone slipping into their *wizardsense* and seeing him just as he saw them. Whatever it was, it was gone now, a momentary shadow in his mind.

"I think we're okay. This place feels good. We should just follow the road, and every so often, I'll check again."

Darlene smiled and motioned for him to lead the way. "You're the expert. I'll keep an eye open too."

The path to the great tree led them northeast. There was no actual road, just a worn groove in the earth by who knew how many hundreds or thousands of years of travelers crossing from Faerie to the capital. And for a while, it was as uneventful as either of them could hope for.

Sure, there were signs of life in strange creatures and the occasional sighting of tall, ethereal, beautiful people in the distance who looked like they wanted to stay far away. Nothing bad happened for the next hour of walking. Maybe it was inevitable that Wil would let his guard down. He was too caught up in looking at the landscape to notice the creature stalking them.

"So Declan said we'd be gone for three days our time, which means three weeks here, right?" Darlene said.

"Yeah, I think so," Wil said, his stomach twisting a little. He looked around, but everything seemed fine. "Why?"

"Because if that's the case, does that mean it's going to take us over a week to get there, and then over a week to get everyone back?" Darlene made a face. "Please tell me you think Declan is erring on the side of slow."

It was something Wil had thought about more than once since they had first agreed to come to Faerie. "I think it might take up to a week. This is about more than just getting Bram and the others back. If we're going to diplomacy each other into a peace agreement, it might take some time." He looked behind them, but there was nothing. Still, the twisting continued as if his stomach were seconds away from dropping.

Darlene snickered. "'Diplomacy' each other?"

Wil grinned. "I don't know the proper term to convey that I will be engaging in diplomatic relations with a possibly hostile foreign nation. Diplomify, maybe?"

"'Diplomify'? That just sounds si—"

Wil's gut wrenched. He whirled around, swinging his staff. It collided with a long, sleek form. Wil exerted some power and flung the creature away from him. The beast landed hard and rolled, coming up into a ready, crouched stance.

"Well, well, well," he purred. "You're not as oblivious as you look, Wizard." The creature looked almost like a mountain lion, but bigger and with six powerful legs instead of four. His feline face had only one green eye, but it glittered with malicious intelligence. One long, crooked bottom tooth stuck out from his lower lip. A stubby tail flicked behind him. "You'll make for good prey."

"What the hell are you?" Darlene demanded, showing no fear or hesitation. She drew the iron bar and held it up, not a threat so much as a promise of violence.

"Me? I'm *hungry*," the cat said, letting out a harsh, hissing laugh. "But only a little hungry. Run along, little girl, I prefer the taste of wizards. No need for you to die too."

Before Darlene could take a swing at the beast and maybe get hurt, Wil stepped forward. "What name may we call you by, creature?"

The big cat stalked to the side, slinking low and keeping his eyes on the two of them. Wil and Darlene rotated with him, not letting him anywhere near their backs.

"You can call me Isom," said the creature, bowing his head in a clear greeting. "Wampus cat."

"Oh, crap," said Wil, fear suddenly crashing against him like a wave.

"A what?"

"Wizard eater," Wil said. He'd barely finished speaking before Isom launched himself at Darlene.

Wil cried out as the big cat almost collided with her but vanished at the last second. Before Wil could even register the disappearance, Isom appeared in front of him, all his momentum stored up and released on the wizard. The two crashed and fell to the ground, the wampus cat savagely snapping his powerful jaws.

The first snap came within inches of Wil's face, making him flinch and jerk away. He brought up his staff just in time to shove it into Isom's mouth. The wampus cat's teeth dug in, but the empowering runes on the staff held and kept him from chomping the wood in half. Wil held on for dear life.

Darlene came from behind, swinging her iron bar down on the back of Isom's head. It connected with a satisfying thud and the wampus cat violently jerked, steam hissing off a black line in his tawny fur. He released the staff and dove away before Darlene's next hit could land Once more, Isom circled the two of them.

"Bad move, little girl," Isom said, shaking his head sadly. "Now I'm going to end you first. I'll eat your entrails in front of the wizard!"

Wil's heart raced. The cat tensed his muscles, preparing for a pounce. Wil focused and channeled power through his staff. A dark blue cloud billowed out as he shouted, "Run!"

Darlene did as he said and ducked out of the way. Wil could see through his own cloud, and he gambled on the fact that Darlene could, too, through her spectacles. The wampus cat landed where she had been and whirled around. He sniffed the air deeply, letting out a frustrated growl as he took in the scent of cotton candy, making his nose useless.

Wil threw himself in front of Darlene, staff held out and ready. The cat looked around for a second before he turned his head in Wil's direction. Then he vanished from sight. Wil dispelled the cloud and looked around wildly. "Where did he go?"

"I don't see him," said Darlene, frantically whipping her head around. If Isom was under an illusion, she should've been able to see him.

"Of course you don't see me." Isom's voice came from no discernible direction. It might as well have been above their heads, for all Wil could tell. "I don't want you to. Poor, poor wizard and human girl. You've never faced such a predator as I! Your lives are mine to play with."

"Getting a bit tired of your crap," said Wil, leveling his staff and rotating slowly, extending his senses out. "How many wizards have you eaten, Isom? You seem to have picked up a few tricks."

A deep, growling chuckle echoed from all directions in a way Wil couldn't help but appreciate as an illusionist. It was just as unsettling as the wampus cat could've hoped for. "Four. You'll be the fifth. What is your name, morsel?"

"Call me Wil McKenzie," said Wil, pouring his power into the staff. The storm inside it stirred. The runes carved into the wood crackled to life with a pale purple light. "Know that you cannot win here, Isom."

"Wil," Darlene whispered, holding up her iron bar. "Are you really that confident?"

"I am," said Wil, almost believing it. He felt powerful, more powerful than he could ever remember being. It wasn't just the staff. Something had changed.

"I'll be the one to end your hunting spree!"

Again, the wampus cat laughed. "I wonder what new ability I'll get from you, Wil McKenzie. Shall we find out?"

His laugh rose into a roar that turned Wil's insides to liquid. Wil moved reflexively, turning and facing the six-legged snaggletoothed monster as it leaped in his direction.

Time seemed to slow down. Hunger and triumph shone in the wampus cat's green eye. Isom was fast, fast enough that Wil knew he couldn't hope to aim well. But now that he was in the air, coming his way, there was no way for the cat to dodge. Wil grinned and unleashed the power he'd been building up. He blasted Isom in the face with a bolt of lightning.

It was too late to stop the predator's momentum, but for a long, shining second, Wil got to enjoy the look of surprise and uncertainty on Isom's face. The bolt hit the cat with a thunderous crack that left Wil's ears ringing. Isom's body convulsed violently before crashing into Wil and sending them both rolling along the ground.

To Wil, it was like being run down by a runaway train with claws, and the red-hot pain of his skin being pricked was dulled by the impact after. He rolled over and got back up on shaky feet, staff tightly in hand. He pointed it at Isom and charged up.

Darlene stepped in, slamming the bar down on Isom's head, again and again. Each strike left a smoking black welt and earned a pained yowl. Isom disappeared from view and reappeared ten feet away. He took off running, shimmering before fading into nothing.

"This isn't over, Wizard," the cat hissed from right behind Wil's ear. "Your heart will be mine!"

Wil said nothing, looking around. He almost expected the retreat to be a feint, just a way to get him to lower his guard. Darlene's gasp shook him from his paranoia.

"You're bleeding!"

Wil looked down. A line of claw marks across his chest bled slowly. Distantly, they hurt, but mostly, Wil's senses were on high alert. He was too jittery to care about the pain. "Huh. I guess I am. Darlene?"

"Yes?" Darlene reached for his chest and then thought better of it.

"I think I appreciate how dangerous this place is now."

CHAPTER 3

Faerie Tour Guide

By the time they got off the road and found a nearby stream, the wounds on Wil's chest were screeching in pain. A quick inspection showed that the wampus cat's claws hadn't dug in too deeply. Two hours into their adventure and already Wil had an injury and a new enemy. A bit faster than he'd expected, but he supposed it could be worse.

"How're you feeling?" Darlene asked for the sixth time.

"Like an apex predator landed on me claws first," said Wil. "It hurts, but I'll live."

They stopped before the water, Darlene holding Wil back. She looked around carefully, straightening her spectacles. Wil found her care endearing, but the water looked cool and he knew how soothing it would be to wash his wounds.

"Alright, it's clear," said Darlene, motioning for him to come forward.

Wil dropped to his knees at the river. Gingerly, he peeled his shirt up and off, wincing at the way it clung to his torn skin. Some of the blood had already dried and hardened, leaving streaks of muddy brown crust. It looked worse than it was, but Wil wasn't used to real injuries and found himself distressed.

In the time it took him to get his shirt off and sit down, Darlene had already grabbed a pitcher and sponge and was in the process of digging through Wil's pack for a potion. She pulled out one of the bigger bottles and bit the stopper off, letting the cork drop into her lap.

"This is going to hurt, right?" she asked.

"Probably," said Wil with a sigh, trying to keep very still and not tremble at the sight of so many lines in his skin.

"Then I'm really sorry about this." Darlene tilted the bottle over his chest and poured lines of viscous goo over his wounds.

Immediately, the wounds sizzled and hissed, and Wil's entire chest felt as if someone had poured oil over him and lit a match. That was just the powerful potion clearing out any potential bugs or bacteria and priming the body to heal faster. It wasn't the kind of potion that healed immediately, but it sanitized and promoted healing.

It was one of the last potions Bram had brewed before he'd been lured into Faerie, and Wil couldn't help but think of their friend and hope he was doing better than they were. The thought made him laugh, and he blinked away tears at the pain. When he looked back down, the wounds weren't closed but were no longer bleeding.

There was a high-pitched sound Wil took too long to realize came from himself before he cleared his throat and fell silent. Darlene patted his back before filling the pitcher with water from the stream and pouring it over the potion on his chest. He slumped in place as the cool water washed away the burn.

She dipped the sponge in the river and worked at some of the dried blood, cleaning around the spots carefully.

"So . . ., wampus cats?" she asked.

Wil laughed, but it hurt. "Big six-legged cats who are smart and can talk, as you may have noticed. They'll hunt and eat anything, and whatever they eat, they gain something from it. If their prey is powerful enough, at least. If they eat an ogre, maybe they'll grow stronger. They eat a wizard, they might be able to cast one of that wizard's spells. They're incredibly dangerous."

"Maybe," said Darlene, lips quirking up in a smile, "but he also made a very satisfying thump when I hit him."

"With the two of us, we're probably okay," said Wil, wincing as Darlene came close to one of his wounds.

She kept at it, gently scrubbing the blood away. Cuts like this deserved stitches, but Wil would probably make do with an alchemically treated bandage. It'd scar, but they didn't have time to take it easy.

"Just gotta be careful," he said.

"If it's going to take us a week to get to Oakheart Spiral, that's a lot of opportunity for that thing to jump us again," Darlene grumbled, dipping the sponge in the stream again. "I don't like it."

"Not sure what else we can do," said Wil. He looked around, suddenly feeling weird. Nothing had explicitly changed around them, but there was a certain quiet, a stillness, that didn't feel right with how loud and lively this place was. This stream seemed too . . . alone.

Darlene saw the look on his face and tilted her head questioningly. Wil motioned for his staff, a few feet away. She quietly handed it to him, then slowly turned to look behind her.

Wil got to his feet, considering what to do. He imagined a ring forming around him, and he filled it with his intent, summed up in two words: *seek life*.

When he let go, he was flooded with sensory information for every bug and flower and worm and mole in the dirt around him. Hundreds and hundreds of little lives gave him a mental map of the streamside thicket around him. What interested him wasn't what showed up, but the gap where no life whatsoever appeared to be. Smiling, Wil released the spell.

"I'm giving you a chance to come out now," said Wil, motioning for Darlene to stay calm. "I'm going to assume you mean us no harm. Please don't make me regret it."

Silence. Then, right where Wil predicted, a bestial man appeared. He was half human, his bare chest and arms and most of his face that of a man. His legs were hairy, spindly things on cloven hooves. His nose was flat and goatlike, as were his golden eyes with their horizontal rectangular pupils. His sheepish smile was framed by a short, sharp beard. Twin ram horns rose out of his head, spiraling outward.

"Hello, there," said the faun brightly, in a gently lilting voice. "I not only mean you no harm, but I actively have an offer for you, Wizard." He held up his hands to show he was unarmed, wiggling abnormally long fingers playfully. "Syl of the Woodlands Association, at your service."

Darlene looked at Wil in disbelief, then back at the faun. "We've already been lost and attacked today. Forgive us if we're not feeling especially charitable, but who the hell are you and what do you want with us?"

Syl wiggled elongated ears. He bowed his head and swept his arms up in a grandiose motion. "I offer to heal your wounds and guide you to Oakheart Spiral safe and sound. The land of Faerie can be dangerous for the unprepared, even the safer areas such as this. As you have already discovered yourself. How is that wound treating you, Wilbur McKenzie?"

"Call me Wil," he said automatically, less to avoid his name and more to avoid the odd discomfort that came from the fae knowing and casually using his name in front of him. He'd felt a light pull at his name he didn't care for.

"Of course, Wil." Syl stood to his full height, almost seven feet tall. He towered over them both, but Wil didn't sense anything malicious in the man. *Of course, that's what the fae were supposed to be good at—making you trust them, and then taking advantage of you.* But then, a dark voice in Wil's head whispered, *That's exactly what my people did to the fae.*

Smiling apologetically at Darlene, Wil decided on full manners and friendliness. "My wounds sting but aren't life-threatening. Your offer is a good one, and that scares me. What do you ask for in exchange for this aid?"

The faun let out a bleating laugh, gently clutching at his stomach as he gave in to amusement. "I cannot fault you, Wizard. Our kind are slippery and crafty, and your people don't trust anyone anyway. All I ask is that you answer me three questions truthfully, your word bound to your power."

"What does that even mean?" Darlene asked, her hand remaining on her iron bar.

"It means either I tell the truth or I face a magical backlash," said Wil. It seemed an easy bargain, but he knew damned well Syl could ask him an intimate, personal question or get him to either reveal secrets about the town or risk losing power permanently if he lied.

It wasn't without risks, but the benefits were worth it. They could use a guide, and if Syl had healing powers, that could be invaluable if Isom attacked again.

"Okay," said Wil, bracing himself for the worst. "I agree to your terms. Ask your questions."

Syl held up one brown, knobby finger. "What is your favorite color?"

Silence.

"What? Seriously?" Darlene scoffed.

"Dead serious," intoned Syl gravely. "An inaccurate answer or a fib will weaken you. Choose wisely."

"Well," said Wil, giving it more thought than he ever would have expected, "I've always had a special spot in my heart for green. Green grass, leaves, frogs. Green's a good color." He shrugged sheepishly, unsure of what more he could say.

Syl nodded slowly. "An excellent choice, and one I share. Very good. Second question. Who do you love most in the world?"

"Oh, jeez," Wil groaned, face already reddening. Darlene raised an eyebrow at him, amused. "That's not an easy question," he said.

"The best ones never are."

"Fine. I do have an answer. My mother, Sharon." Wil was glad no one else was there to see his credibility as a big, bad wizard disappear with the admission that he was a mama's boy, but he wasn't about to deny it. "Satisfied?"

The faun shrugged, grinning once more. "Every nugget of information I get about you helps," he said. "Which brings me to my final question. What are your intentions toward my people, Wil McKenzie?"

For a second, the only sound was the gentle rush of the stream beside them. Syl stood there at his ridiculous height, looking tranquil and pleased with himself for his question. Wil knew his face betrayed surprise. Darlene searched it for a hint of what his answer would be. The problem was, Syl had caught him off guard. And now he needed to answer truthfully.

"My intentions toward your people are peaceful," said Wil carefully, "provided my people are unhurt. My intentions are diplomacy and compromise to find a way to live with each other."

"And if we can't live with each other?" Syl pressed, leaning in closer for the answer.

"Then," said Wil, going with his gut, "we figure out how to stay the hell out of each other's way so we don't end up fighting again. The last thing I want is a war on my doorstep with people I don't have a problem with. Outside of, again, kidnapping my neighbors."

The faun looked satisfied. He turned to Darlene. "And what about you, human? What are your intentions?"

"My name is Darlene," she said, "and that wasn't part of the deal. He answered your questions, so you are going to heal his wounds and then guide us to the capital. Right?" Her voice had iron in it, a toughness and suspicion Wil appreciated, caught up in the situation as he was.

Syl bowed low, horns almost scraping the ground. "You are absolutely correct, Darlene. The questions have been answered, and I am satisfied well enough with the answers for now. Congratulations, you two have purchased yourself some magical healing and a tour guide!" The faun did a funny wiggly dance that involved a great deal of shuffling his hooves and wobbling his knees.

Darlene stared at the faun as if he had two heads, then looked at Wil, who shrugged. As far as he was concerned, they were in a better position than they had been just before the wampus cat attack, so they might as well be grateful for it. Most important, Wil decided as Syl clapped his hands and moved closer, was to keep an eye open. Just because the faun seemed friendly didn't mean he was.

"Alright," said Syl, golden eyes bright and odd pupils boring directly into Wil's. "Hope you're not ticklish!"

CHAPTER 4

The Lay of the Land

Wil had been excited to see a bit of fae magic that wasn't an illusion being used against him, but ended up disappointed when it appeared to be as normal and natural as his own. Syl put his spindly hands on Wil's chest and let out a low, rumbling sigh. Immediately, Wil's chest itched, which quickly turned into the promised tickling sensation as his flesh knit together and his nerve endings went crazy.

"Stop, stop, stop," Wil said, laughing and slapping Syl's hand away. The faun pulled his hand back with a flourish, looking pleased with himself.

"Of course," said the faun. He turned to Darlene. "Did you get hurt in any way?"

"Are you really asking or just looking for a reason to put your hands on me? I know stories of your kind." Darlene crossed her arms over her chest. She didn't look upset, just amused. Her smile only grew when Syl held up his hands in surrender.

"Can I not have multiple reasons? I'm here to be helpful!" He let out a bleating laugh.

Everything in Wil told him not to trust Syl, but the faun made it difficult to dislike him. Everything he said and did seemed to be a performance to show just how friendly and trustworthy he was. It came off so naturally, Wil wanted to believe it.

"And why have you chosen to be helpful to us? What do you get out of it?" Wil asked. Without really paying attention, he put his hands on his torn shirt and poured a bit of power into it. The sundered threads found where they'd parted and mended themselves in seconds.

Syl's smile froze on his face. "That's an excellent question! And we have plenty of time to talk about it on the road. You bought my services as a guide, and I intend to get you there safely. Shall we?" He motioned with long arms in the direction they'd been going before detouring for water.

"Fine," said Darlene, slinging her pack around her shoulders. "But we expect real answers out of you."

The three of them got moving, walking parallel to the stream. The land of Faerie was no less beautiful than it had been before, even after the attack and impromptu deal that made Wil suspicious. At least Darlene was on the same page and probably trusted Syl even less than he did. With that in mind, Wil let himself relax just a little, though part of him kept scanning the area around them for any signs of homicidal cats.

"So, you ask what I get out of it?" Syl asked after a few moments of silent walking. He kept his strides short so they didn't fall behind. It gave the impression he was going for a casual stroll, while they had to try to keep up. "For starters, I get to keep my head. My presence here was ordered by King Martinus the Silenus."

"And what does this king care about Wil?" Darlene asked. As the shortest of the three, she had to fight the most to keep pace.

Syl looked over his shoulder, then rotated his body so his strange goat legs walked backward, without stumbling, as he spoke. "I asked Wil's intentions, and they mirror the king's. Not all of Faerie is happy to see you, but the Woodlands Association sees an opportunity. The chance to reconnect and make trade and communicate."

"Who isn't happy to see me?" asked Wil. "Actually, rephrase. Who is actively unhappy to see me?"

The faun made a face. "Well, Grimnar's Ogre Federation actively wants to invade your land and take it back for themselves, torching every human settlement they encounter and sticking your people on spikes as a warning. They're mostly ogres, trolls, and other big nasties who have more might than mind."

"Yeah, that's pretty unhappy," said Darlene with a grimace. "What're the odds of running into any of them on the road and getting into trouble?"

"With me around? Not likely at all." Syl sounded confident. "You're much safer with me than without. Even without adding my knowledge or good company to the mix!"

Together, they crossed a small bridge and continued east. The ground sloped upward and their view of the massive tree in the background disappeared behind a hill.

"Who else is unhappy I'm here?" Wil pressed, using his staff to help brace himself as they continued uphill.

"Hmm. Grimnar's the big one," said Syl, scratching at his pointy beard. "But I think Timothy Twist at least wants isolation and to not have to deal with you. He leads the Wee Folk, and they're a mischievous sort but not especially dangerous. You're more likely to get pranked than seriously harmed."

Darlene nudged Wil. "We had a problem with nasty pranks before coming out here," she said. "You're saying it's because of this Timothy Twist and his people?"

"Could be," Syl allowed. "Couldn't say for sure. When the doorways began opening back up, a lot of different folks went out to explore and report back what they'd found. How the land's changed under the charge of humans. Some of us were worried you'd leave it a barren wasteland of metal monstrosities, spewing smoke and destroying the land. Imagine our surprise when your home turned out to be a beautiful land of plenty, just as we left it."

They went over the hill, and Syl seemed to know they needed a break. Darlene wiped her forehead. Wil grabbed water from his pack and took a drink, passing it over when he was finished. It gave him time to think and consider his question well.

"Do you hate us? My people, I mean."

Syl made a distressed goat sound. "*Hate* is such a strong word. I follow my king and dream of peace and cooperation. Perhaps when I know you better I'll hate you, but for the moment? You're okay." He winked.

It was Darlene, as usual, who kept Wil on track. "So Grimnar and Timothy Twist. Who else are we going to be dealing with when we get to Oakheart Spiral?" She even managed to not sound impatient.

They got moving once more. There was an actual road here made of stone, leading through the sea of green and heading toward another forest at the base of a foothill. The road wound back and forth, seemingly without any sense of ease of travel or efficiency.

"You're on point with the questions, aren't you?" Syl chuckled. "You'll have a representative of the Woodlands Association, as I have mentioned. You'll meet up with Grimnar and Timothy Twist for sure, and the two others who make up the council. One is Princess Arabella, who is likely to be there on behalf of her mother, Aria, queen of the Fair Folk.

"Arabella's not too bad, if you don't mind them as spoiled as they are beautiful. Her mother wants peace more than my—" Syl made a sound and coughed. "Apologies. More than my king does. You can expect to treat well with her. Just flatter her a lot and make her feel special. And finally, the king of the skies, the dragon Skalet, leader of the Heartless."

"Heartless?" Darlene asked. "What does that mean?"

"Unaligned fae," answered Syl. "Those without any loyalty to any of the four kingdoms of our little slice of Faerie. They can be the wildest of predators or the loneliest of souls, big or small, they handle it all on their own. Maybe a bit of help from their families but more often than not, even that's off the table. You won't need to worry about them none."

"Would a wampus cat fall under the Heartless?" Darlene demanded. "We were attacked by one just before meeting you. Funny timing, that."

"A wampus cat? Oh, yes, that'd be Heartless. And good on you for surviving. That's no easy feat!" Syl didn't sound concerned or bothered, just impressed. "If I'd been just a few minutes faster, I assure you I would've helped out. But perhaps that would've been suspicious too, eh?"

The trees grew impossibly thick then, not unlike that first bit of woods they'd found themselves in. Without pause, their guide led them forward, seemingly in a good mood despite the topic and their obvious distrust. Wil found his resolve wavering.

"Probably, but we would've been too grateful to question it, at least at first," said Wil. "Either way, I'm grateful for the healing and a way to Oakheart Spiral. What else can you tell us about the four kingdoms of Faerie?"

The faun tapped his chin thoughtfully, ducking his head to avoid a thick branch as they made their way in deeper. The light trickling through the tight treetop was dim and patchy. Wil conjured a ball of light just as Syl answered, "I'm not sure what would be most helpful to you, Wizard. You have a great deal of problems to address, and it is not for me to tell you where to start.

"However . . . , you can consider the Woodlands Association and the Fair Folk to be tentative allies. Focus on keeping them happy with you and you should be protected from Grimnar's hate and Skalet's apathy."

Wil perked up. He'd heard the name earlier, but it hadn't registered until now. "Skalet? Like Skalet Peak?"

Syl shrugged. "Possibly? I don't know your area all too well, I'm afraid. Skalet is the king of the Hearthless. A fierce dragon, mostly unconcerned with the problems of smaller creatures. You can probably ignore him for the most part. He won't vote one way or the other. Anyway, I have a question of my own, for you two."

"What is it?" Darlene asked.

"What does your town have to offer us?" Syl's voice remained pleasant, friendly, and welcoming, but Wil knew how sharp the question was. "We've got an entire world, four kingdoms here, but your Harper Valley is small and a part of a bigger nation we were once at war with. What do you bring to the negotiations?"

"Um . . ." Wil looked at Darlene for help, but she seemed just as surprised as he was. "What kind of things are you looking for?" he asked.

Syl shot him a sharp look. "Come now, Wizard, I can't give you an answer to my own question. You must have something."

Wil took his time thinking, and neither the faun nor Darlene tried to rush him. Even after Wil's fight with the mayor, it was easy to forget he was representing the entire town and had to think bigger than just their lost citizens. Thinking of his town and what it had to offer was hardly an unpleasant experience.

"We *are* fairly small in the grand scheme of things," Wil started a few minutes later, "but we're also right between three major cities, right near the center of the continent. The railroad is there and we're protected in the mountains."

"Aye, all of those are good things," said Syl with a playful lilt in his voice, "but what do you have to offer us?"

"Food, music, and good drinks," Wil said, a smile coming to his face. "A different culture and different people. Oddities, novelties, a new place to be for a little while. Harper Valley's not perfect, but we could be good neighbors, and we could share what we've got. A little foothold into our world while you get to keep the rest of the country at arm's length.

"You said your people and the Fair Folk want the same things we do. And that's what I want. For there to be peace and prosperity for everyone, and to laugh at our differences and how they used to make us behave—some of us worse than others. If nothing else, I know our buddy Bram would give up his right arm to try whatever beers and wines you have."

"Ahh," sighed Syl. "Alcohol. A good enough reason for anyone to crave free trade."

"Bram was taken from us," Darlene said loudly. "By your people. Lured into one of those mushroom circles."

Both of them turned to Darlene, who smiled in the face of the killed mood.

"Not my call," said Syl, leading them out through the forest and to the other side to a meadow, which looked to be in the middle of autumn. "Ah, I think I found us a shortcut. If we cut through the patch of spring, we can skip the summer lands and cut out two, maybe three days to Oakheart Spiral!"

"Huh. Great, a shortcut through spring." Wil looked at Darlene, who stared him down. She smiled, and in some ways, it was reassuring. Mostly though, it seemed to be a reminder: *stay focused, don't forget why we're here, and don't be too trusting.*

Who knew how many times he'd need that reminder?

CHAPTER 5

Hobgoblin Hootenanny

That first day in Faerie was the longest and slowest Wil could ever remember having. Even stopping the colossal storm and passing out for a few days had felt like a shorter time than their first trek across gorgeous meadows and rolling hills, all while their earnest tour guide pointed out the sites of big skirmishes, or a river where a battle of wits had ended with the richest gnome in town robbed blind, or told a million other little stories.

They were nice at first, and Wil had been interested enough to follow along with each of them. But halfway through the day, Wil found himself immediately forgetting details. By sunset, he and Darlene were both exhausted down to their bones and ready to call it a day. And they were soon to come to a shelter, if Syl was to be believed.

"It's right around the corner. We just gotta cut across a bridge and then shuffle sideways into a hedge, and we'll have a place to rest for the night and all the food you can eat!" Syl promised.

"Oh, is that all?" Darlene grumbled. She'd finally taken off the spectacles and given her eyes a rest partway through the day. She kept one hand on her weapon at all times, even with their tour guide's assurance of their safety. Wil supposed he couldn't blame her. "You said we were coming up to it soon an hour ago."

"Yes, well, sometimes the land changes." Syl didn't miss a beat. "And it *was* soon. Not my fault your little human legs are slow." He lolled his tongue out playfully, winking at Darlene.

Wil interjected before it could get ugly. "So tell us more about this place we're staying. Is it safe?"

"Oh, yes, it's safe," said Syl. "It's where Julietta and Roberto had their tiff over teapots a few years back, like I was telling you. Things are better now, positively bliss, and that's what we're counting on. Perfect day for it."

"Oh. Right." Wil nodded, remembering absolutely none of it.

Darlene saw right through him and didn't look impressed, but she looked past Syl. The sound of rushing water caught their attention, and sure enough, just around a corner of woodlands, they came upon a huge bridge in the middle of a wide, roaring river.

It was right out of the stories they'd been told as kids, including the massive, ugly figure standing in the center of the bridge. Wil had never seen a troll in person before and the textbooks had very differing pictures, but the creature looming over them on the bridge could've been nothing else. He looked like a very large, bulky, almost hunchbacked gorilla with yellowing tusks protruding from his bottom lip. The troll rested on massive fists pressed into the ground.

"You!" the troll bellowed, pointing at Wil. "Food or gold. Now! Or else."

Darlene pulled out her iron bar but didn't go any closer. Even hunched over like that, the troll was a good eight feet tall. And with his bulk, he made Syl's tall, gangly form look puny and vulnerable in comparison. Wil stepped forward, pointing the horn of his staff at the troll.

"Neither. Get out of our way, please. I don't want to have to blast you." After being attacked by Isom, Wil wasn't feeling very charitable about threats.

Syl put himself between Wil and the troll, holding up his hands. "Hey, hey, hey, no need for any of that. So good of you to be willing to defend us, Wizard, but we're in no danger. Why, that's Marley's girl's cousin's uncle's boy right there. Sven, right?"

The troll blinked stupidly. "Yes?"

"Ah, Sven, surely you remember me. From the last time I was around these parts, maybe fifteen years back." The faun fluttered his eyelashes up at him.

Now the troll looked uncertain. "That's a long time ago," he said. "Do I remember you? Do I?" He leaned closer and sniffed deeply, big nostrils flaring. Sven's eyes widened. "You! Y-y-your ma—"

"No, no, none of that, Sven!" Syl said sharply. "Just passing by to get to the celebrations. You keep doing a good job protecting the bridge, yeah?" He patted Sven's arm patiently.

"Yeah, no. I mean, no, yeah, of course," the troll said, bowing and scraping to get out of the way. His head dipped, he motioned for them to continue on their way. Syl bowed his head back, and gestured for Wil and Darlene to pass. They did, and this time Darlene couldn't keep her suspicions quiet.

"What the hell was that about?" she demanded when they'd crossed the bridge. "He was ready to start something until he recognized you. Why does that matter? Who are you?"

With each question, Syl shied away further. Darlene wasn't to be deterred. She pushed past Wil and nudged Syl. "C'mon, answer me!"

Syl looked to Wil for help, but Wil just shook his head. The faun sighed and said, "It's really not a big deal. I'm a man of many travels and the people around here know me well. It's just been a bit, and he knows if he started something with me he'd have my family to deal with. And, well, he may be dumb, but he's not *that* dumb." Syl let out a bleating laugh.

"Your family dangerous or something?" Wil asked.

Syl waved him off. "Most families of note are dangerous, including mine. The big thing is, Sven's a good enough kid, has an honest job protecting that bridge, and I just happen to be someone he respects enough to let me pass. Besides, rest is right around the corner. You two are tired, right? Prepare yourself for the finest of faerie hospitality!"

Before they could protest, Syl all but dashed ahead of them. The two humans ran after him, calling out his name as he disappeared through a hedge. Remembering the directions, Wil went in sideways, arms held above his head. Darlene was right behind him, growling in irritation. He had half a dozen things to say when he came out the other side, but froze. Darlene crashed into him shortly after, but she, too, stopped when she saw what was going on.

They stood before a big farm, with a massive house off in the distance. And more than that, they weren't alone—there were dozens, or even hundreds, of short, warty people in various colors, from green to burnt orange. They looked almost like a human combined with a frog-lizard thing. They weren't ugly so much as weird and goofy looking, and Wil would've found their bulbous eyes and big mouths endearing if they hadn't been narrowed in suspicion at him.

"Julietta, Roberto!" Syl called out, arms spread like he was going to grab the next person he saw into a big hug. "Am I ever glad to see you two beautiful people. How is your anniversary going? What is it, fifteen years now of marital bliss and a buried feud? You know I couldn't miss that for anything, and I brought a couple of friends you simply *must* meet."

The faun squatted low, throwing his arms around a blue man and an orange woman. He squeezed them, making their round faces puff out even farther. "Would you believe these two have never met a hobgoblin before? We're making our way to Oakheart Spiral and taking in the sights along the way, and you have a great chance to be cultural ambassadors!" Around them, hundreds of eyes stared their way.

"Err," Roberto croaked in a surprisingly deep voice, "welcome then, human."

Silence. Then Syl coughed and Roberto jolted.

"I'm Roberto, and this is my wife, Julietta. You, er . . . , you've come on an auspicious day. One of celebration and merriment." His words were pleasant but his tone was just shy of being tortured.

Wil understood what was happening. Poor Roberto was being strong-armed into welcoming them at a sensitive time. It was the last thing he wanted, but the manic grin on Syl's half-human face told him it was too late. The sun had all but set on this beautiful farm, and there was a celebration they were crashing.

"I'm Wil," said Wil, bowing politely. "And this is my companion, Darlene. It is our very great honor to share in your special day, and to perhaps perform for you all as a way to show our very great gratitude."

"Unless, of course, you'd rather we come back another time?" asked Darlene, giving them an out. She recognized it, too, and she didn't like it one bit. "We wouldn't want to impose."

Julietta's bulbous eyes slid over to her husband, and then over to Syl. She wet her lips, shuddering suddenly. "That's not necessary. We've been shown great kindness and help in the past. It's our pleasure to return the favor and pass it on. Be welcome and enjoy our hospitality."

"Excellent!" Syl boomed. "Music!" He clapped his hands.

Somewhere at the back of the party was a band, and they obediently began playing. Horns and drums and loud, crashing cymbals played gracelessly together in a bizarre mockery of music. But maybe that was how they liked it there. The wedding party turned away from Darlene and Wil after a while, and the steady buzz of chatter joined the music.

"I don't like this," said Darlene quietly to Wil, fists clenched at her sides. "It's not just me, right? Was he threatening them? It seemed like he was threatening them."

"It did seem that way," Wil admitted under his breath.

Syl remained with the host couple, chatting and laughing uproariously. They appeared relaxed now, perhaps resigned more than anything.

"But, like," Wil continued, "a distinctly nonthreatening threat. An 'I can threaten you if I want, but I don't need to' kind of threat."

"This feels like a setup," Darlene hissed. "Like a trap of some kind. He's not doing a good job of hiding the fact that he's more than he says he is. And I want to know who and what."

Just as Wil was ready to agree, a tug on his jacket made him turn around. There were three even more squat, round hobgoblins staring up at him with impossibly big eyes. Children, Wil realized. They were so ugly they somehow ended up cute.

"Uh, hi there," he said.

"Wizard?" the green hob in front croaked. "What can you do?"

Even in the land of Faerie, it always came down to this.

Wil smiled and presented his staff. With just a little focus and imagination, he conjured a miniature storm cloud floating a few feet above his head, gentle rain coming down and soaking his head and the staff. There was a tiny flash in the cloud and a bolt of lightning struck the staff, crackling violently.

Two children clapped their hands excitedly, while a third ran around in circles with his hands flailing behind him. A pink hobgoblin grabbed him by the front of his shirt and pulled him forward, wanting him to follow. Wil ran along, trying not to trip. He shot an apologetic "save me" look to Darlene, who just shook her head and laughed at him.

That put to rest any thought of talking to Darlene or interrogating Syl over who he was and what kind of influence he had. The children brought Wil around to their fathers and uncles and cousins who rested near the cooking pits, where huge sides of meat cooked slowly and the smell reminded Wil of how little he'd eaten that day. There, he repeated his performance with the storm cloud, which got some moderate applause, and also a challenge.

The hobgoblins weren't big on magic, but they were excellent at sleight of hand and conjuring and smothering fires. An especially jowly blue hob came up and juggled volatile fireballs, occasionally detonating them in midair or catching one in his mouth, where he'd swallow it, and then his big cheeks and throat would bulge from the muffled explosion, all to a cacophony of cheers and laughter.

Not to be outdone, Wil played with illusions. The fire he conjured in the center of the hobs was real enough. The shape it took wasn't: a quick sculpting of the flames and everyone's perceptions and suddenly it was a woman made of fire, dancing and swaying to the chaotic music playing in the background. The other hobs gathered around and oohed and aahed before Wil made her explode in their faces, singeing them harmlessly.

That got him a round of applause and a bottle of some murky brown liquid pressed into his hand as his new hob buddies slapped his back. Everything in Wil knew it was a bad idea to trust food and drink from strangers, but he'd been promised hospitality. And as much as he didn't quite trust Syl, he trusted him to get them to Oakheart Spiral safely. The faun wanted it as badly as they did.

So Wil gave in and took a long drink of one of the foulest beers he'd ever tasted, coughing and sputtering when he was done, to the amusement of everyone around him. He laughed good-naturedly, letting himself be welcome and join in with the festivities. One terrible beer turned into three, and then the rest of the night went by in a blur.

Wil remembered accepting a heaping plate of glazed sweet and savory meat ringed with berries, greens, and mushrooms. He devoured everything, hesitating only at the mushrooms and idly wondering if they would do anything weird to him. Later on, he'd blame the mushrooms for his decision to dance. In the end, he was glad he did, because it reminded him that he'd forgotten about Darlene.

She was already on the dance floor when he stumbled out there, dancing with a ring of admirers. Wil wouldn't exactly call Darlene a good dancer, but she was bold and fearless. Her dance was just as jerky and chaotic as the weird music, and her short, spiky hair bobbed with the motions. Her freckly cheeks were flushed with the movement, and Wil stood there for a minute, just watching his lovely girlfriend have the first bit of fun or relaxation she'd let herself have in the past week. Seeing Darlene dance lifted a weight off Wil's shoulders. He pushed his way through the ring and joined her there, dancing wildly and using his staff as a prop and something to lean up against. Even drunk and caught up in the party, he didn't let it out of his sight.

Darlene saw him and laughed and moved up close, dancing directly against him in a way that seemed downright scandalous to the hobgoblins. The gasp that went through the crowd as they moved together made Darlene snort and collapse against Wil, laughing.

"What happened to wanting to find out more about Syl?" Wil teased her.

"Oh, shut up," said Darlene, resting her head against his chest and squeezing him. "I don't trust him, but this is fun. We can interrogate him tomorrow. You said they care about hospitality, right?"

"Yeah, we should be safe."

Darlene looked up at him with a playful smile. "Then . . . maybe it's okay to have a bit of fun. Just for tonight."

CHAPTER 6

Bed and Breakfast

Every so often, Wil got a reminder of just how much he loved sleeping. Being a busy wizard, he actively dreaded having to go to bed at night, often feeling like there was more he could've done before he ended his day. But once he was asleep, it could be hard to voluntarily wake up. The dreaded fog of sleep and dreams became a protective cocoon he was reluctant to leave. Especially when he was pressed up against someone soft and warm.

That caught his attention. It wasn't as if he'd never woken up next to Darlene before. It felt perfectly natural at first, his arm thrown around her side and clutching her possessively against him. Honestly, a fantastic way to wake up, all things considered. It wasn't until he opened his eyes that he saw a reason to be startled.

Big, bulbous eyes stared into his own from a few feet away. Wil jolted away, unable to hold back a startled scream. Naturally, that made the hobgoblin child scream right back, and together, they woke Darlene. She sat straight up and looked around, blinking wildly as she put up her fists. Wil wrapped his arms around her and held her back from leaping to her feet.

"It's okay, it's okay," he whispered quickly. "I just got spooked. We're fine." Darlene's brief struggle against him ceased. "We're at Julietta and Roberto's place after their party. We're in the basement. Hi, Julio."

The greenish hob waved weakly at him from his spot near the rickety wooden stairs. Wil hardly remembered going down them, but they still seemed familiar enough. His head hurt a little. Not like the agony of a truly bad hangover, but as though he'd pushed himself and still needed more rest. They were set up on three hobgoblin beds pushed side by side, lying lengthwise. It was a tight but cozy fit, and would've been great to luxuriate in if it hadn't been for little Julio watching them.

"Gods," Darlene groaned, going limp in Wil's arms. He let her go. "I would kill for a cup of coffee and something really greasy for breakfast."

"You're in luck!" a voice boomed from the top of the stairs. Syl came down, balancing plates piled high with food on each arm and holding a couple of mugs of something brownish that Wil hoped wasn't more foul ale. The steam rising from the mug made him think it probably wasn't, but he'd learned extensively about how foul and yet still drinkable hob concoctions could be.

"We've got breakfast and a quick washup, and then we'd best be out on the road once more before the seasons catch up to us and we lose our shortcut. I trust you both slept well after having a great time?" The faun's eyebrows waggled up and down.

Darlene took a plate and mug from him without meeting his eyes, her cheeks red. "I don't remember last night all too clearly," she admitted, taking a piece of what Wil hoped was normal bacon and biting a piece off. "But I don't think I did anything to embarrass myself."

"Not at all, Darlene," said Syl, handing the other plate and mug to Wil. "You've acquitted yourself well these past few nights, and, I daresay, have made friends among the hob population. Hobulation, if you will."

Wil froze. The light, jovial tone hadn't hidden the wording from him. The hairs on the back of his arms and neck stood on end.

"What," he asked, licking his lips, "do you mean 'the last few nights'? We've only stayed here the one."

Syl's ears lowered as his head dropped between his shoulders. His sheepish smile made Wil want to scream.

"Well, kind of. The thing is, I found us a shortcut that saved us a few days, but it's draining, right? And the way things work around here, you gotta reach a balance. You saved a couple of days on the boring part of travel and got to join in as part of a weeklong party. You're actually waking up from the revelry quite well, I must say!"

"How long have we been here?" Darlene demanded, her food all but forgotten.

"This is the start of the fourth day, and we're good to go!" Syl said quickly. "We've been shown hospitality, and have given respect and presents back to the happy couple, who are quite happy with the arrangement. After that first night, things might've gotten hazy, but you kind of animated a magical guardian for their crops! Walking scarecrows that scream!"

"That does sound like something you'd do," Darlene said to Wil.

If he tried to think about it, Wil could kind of remember being hunched over in the cornfield with Roberto and a few of his friends. The scarecrow had been more adorable than anything, a children's idea of a scary face on an overly fat head. The eyes stared in two different directions and the mouth had a tongue lolling out. Wil had fought hard not to laugh and instead marked out a few runes and tied a few fallen bird feathers to the thing, and voilà.

He couldn't remember what had led up to making that scarecrow or much after it, other than the hideously adorable thing bouncing around on its pole, letting out obnoxious screams each time a bird got close to the corn. Now that he remembered it, Wil felt a deep satisfaction. It was his payment for hospitality, an act between friends made of obligation and expectation but not worded as such. The way things were done around there.

"Okay," said Wil, letting out a deep breath and rubbing his eyes. "We'll be up in a bit, Syl. I think we need some time."

"Of course. Take all the time you need," said the faun, bowing his head. "But not actually. If we don't leave in under an hour we might have to stay an extra night and help clean up before the next round. Best hurry!" He trotted back up the stairs. A long look from Wil sent Julio scampering up the stairs as well, his squat little form struggling to move fast.

Wil poked at the eggs on his plate and took a bite. If they were already affected by enchanted food, a few more bites wouldn't make things worse. On the upside, they were delicious and fluffy. That helped improve his mood. "I'm not sure how I feel about staying here a couple of days," he said, taking another bite.

Darlene sipped her drink, making a surprised but pleased noise. "I am. I'm not happy about it. This isn't what we wanted, and it's like he's always playing with us."

"That could just be fauns," said Wil with a shrug. "They're not exactly known for being straightforward, direct, or reliable. But . . . as much as I'm worried about accidentally partying for a couple of days, we're not hurt, and we're apparently on the same pace we were before. Is this really so bad?"

They ate silently after that, going from picking at their food to devouring it as fast as possible. Whatever they had gotten up to in the past day, it had worked up an appetite. When Wil tried the hot brown liquid, he found it bitter and kind of like dirt-water, but drinkable enough. It warmed him up, and soon he felt strong enough to get moving. But that didn't solve their more immediate problem.

"What do we do about Syl?" he asked.

Darlene ran a hand through her hair, keeping it the right level of messy. "I don't know," she said. "I don't know that we have any other option than going along with it. You can see the damned tree from a long way off, but apparently we went through a hole and came out the other side to another spot?" She rested her head on his shoulder. "I'm not sure we're equipped enough to know where we are or how to get there. I think we have to go along with him for now."

Wil took her hand in his and squeezed it. His gut told him everything was fine, but he didn't know how well he could trust that. Not when it would be so easy to lead them into danger or off the face of the map forever.

"We'll handle it," he said, extricating himself and grabbing his staff from against the wall. Darlene slipped her shoes on, and they went upstairs, taking their dishes with them.

Whatever they didn't remember must've been pretty good, because Julietta embraced them both when they entered her kitchen.

"Wil, Leenie!" she cried, drawing them in. "How was breakfast? You two must've worked up quite an appetite after last night!"

"Leenie?" Wil mouthed at Darlene, who made a face and shrugged.

"I guess we did," Darlene answered, sounding as chipper as possible. "That was a hell of a party and we're sad to be missing more of it, but I heard a saying once. Houseguests are like fish. After a few days, they start to stink!"

Julietta laughed, making her jowls inflate and deflate. "I like that, but you are welcome anytime. After the performance you put on last night, I think everyone will be real eager to see what you come up with next time."

Darlene hid her surprise and horror well, but Wil knew how much it killed her to not be able to remember everything they'd done.

"Absolutely," said Wil, bowing his head low. "You've been such wonderful hosts, and we'll be glad to put on another performance the next time we're out this way. It's been a truly lovely, wonderful experience." He took Julietta's hand and kissed the back of it like a gentleman.

The hobgoblin laughed merrily and put the back of her other hand across her forehead. Her rubbery skin darkened.

"You're a delight, Wizard! Is there anything else we can do for you before you get going?"

They didn't linger long after that. Syl was ready with their packs, along with freshly filled waterskins and delicious meat pasties for later. Then they were off on the road once more, taking a winding trail away from the large farm that was still filled to the brim with hobs sleeping all over the property. A group of children waved them off, becoming dots in the distance before Wil stopped looking.

"So, what did we do last night?" Darlene finally asked after several minutes of silence.

Syl looked over his shoulder, favoring her with a gleeful grin. "You sure you want to know about that, 'Leenie'?" The faun laughed maniacally.

"Leenie?" Darlene shuddered. In the end, she decided not to ask further, and Syl didn't volunteer any extra information. For the moment, they trusted him and followed his lead.

CHAPTER 7

Flowers

Their day of travel started well, despite itself. After breakfast and leaving the home of their new hobgoblin friends, they followed a winding road north, going through fields of golden wheat. Small, doglike creatures with floppy ears ran along the road with them for a while, yapping and running between their legs playfully. Wil laughed, while Darlene tried to not let them get too close.

"They're harmless," said Syl, after Darlene pushed a tawny brown pup away for the third time. "He probably smells breakfast on you and wants some."

"Forgive me for not entirely trusting your word," she said, a big sardonic smile on her face. "Things haven't exactly turned out as expected so far."

Well, there went the mood. Wil nudged Darlene, but she ignored him. Syl's face fell, and he nodded, stopping in the road. He crouched down, goat legs bending oddly to get close enough to the ground to pet the sleek doglike thing and scratch under its chin. The creature rolled over on its back, and Syl scratched its belly too.

"And I regret that," the faun said. "Definitely not my intention, but when opportunity knocks, you have to take it, no? I promise that every route I've taken you on so far has been the safest way forward and will continue to be safe, as far as I know. If we're going to forge a peace between our peoples, shouldn't we learn to trust one another?" He flashed a hopeful smile.

"Yes, I'm very much eager to trust the people who lured one of my best friends into a trap and are holding him hostage," said Darlene.

"Look," said Wil, stepping between them and ignoring a yapping little pup at his feet. "I agree, we need trust, but we also need to stop dredging up the past every time we get mad. Kidnapping our people was wrong, but we'll get them back. And while a multiday party wasn't originally planned, we're none the worse for wear, right?"

Darlene looked as though she wanted to argue. Her eyes narrowed and she took a deep, sharp breath, but then she just looked down and nodded.

"I guess," she said. Without waiting to see if Wil had more to say, she trudged down the road they'd been heading, half the dogs running after her.

Wil and Syl shared a look that was equal parts worry and exasperation. When it came down to it, Wil was more on Darlene's side than the faun's. That didn't mean he didn't see value in Syl's side of things. The goatman was hiding something, a lot of somethings, but none of them had so far gotten them in real trouble. Sighing, Wil motioned for Syl to take the lead again.

Syl did so, a few long strides closing the ground between him and Darlene. Wil ran after them and fell into step beside Darlene. The dogs barked and ran with them until Syl pulled a balled-up cloth from the pouch at his side. They surrounded him, but then abandoned him when he threw the ball off into the distance. Whatever he threw, it was enough to keep their attention long after they were gone.

The trio walked in relative quiet after that, every step taking them farther away from the farm and toward the great tree in the distance. It was still far away and still larger than life. Wil allowed himself to surrender to the road and let his mind wander, focusing on the tree and wondering how big it would be.

An hour passed without conversation. Occasionally, Wil would look at Darlene and she'd smile at him or make a face behind Syl's back, and then they'd laugh silently. Syl himself was the only one to not remain quiet. He whistled or hummed the entire time, seemingly finding the lack of noise offensive. Or maybe he just really loved music.

The road took them through another small forest, filled with birdsong and strange deer running into the distance. Wil kept alert, on the watch for potential threats or ways of getting lost. Darlene looked ill at ease. She drew the iron bar and gently rolled her wrists in circles, keeping limber. Nothing attacked them, and soon they left the forest to find a brand-new landscape that hadn't been visible from the other side.

"Gods . . ." Darlene whispered when they came to the first row of flowers. Wil's eyes widened and he gaped at the sight.

"I thought you two might like this path," said Syl, gesturing with a sweep of his arm at the clearing.

Flowers, as far as the eye could see. There were small flowers like the ones back home, but also huge ones the size of a person that seemed to turn and look at them as they got close. Reds, blues, purples, yellows, and others all collided, forming a messy explosion of color, as if someone had mixed a bunch of paints and threw the resulting amalgamation into the sky to rain down upon the land.

The path continued through the flowers, winding in and out in lazy curves around several small hills, each one topped with a massive green and red plant that seemed to be made of teeth. One of them was shut, with a skeletal arm hanging out of it. Somehow, Wil found it more striking than ominous. Darlene, on the other hand, disagreed.

"The hell is this?" Darlene asked, pointing out the big plants. "Those look pretty dangerous to me."

Syl winced. "It *is* safe. If you stay on the path and don't get too close to the hungry girls over there. And don't eat anything purple. The yellows are good, and the greens are amazing if you're backed up, but purple is a bad idea at the moment."

"Dare I ask?" Wil looked at the nearest purple flower, and the weird bell shape it had, pointing at the ground.

Syl reached over and plucked it and held it up. "This beauty and others like it put you into a waking dream that lasts for the better part of a day. And makes you want more. If you come across a garden like this alone . . . Well, chances are you end as a wretched husk and feed one of the girls."

"Why do you call them girls?" Darlene asked.

Syl whistled sharply. The nearest few toothy plants rose and their big jaws parted. Beautiful green-tinted women lounged deep inside. Not a single one of them wore clothing.

Wil's cheeks heated up. One of them saw this and grinned at him, winking and beckoning him to come closer. Darlene's hand on the back of his shirt stopped him from taking a single step.

"And why did you bring us here?" Darlene demanded.

"Well, isn't it beautiful?" Syl sounded hurt. He stuffed the purple flower into his pack. "I thought you'd appreciate seeing something few people get to. This is one of Queen Aria's private gardens. It's a beautiful and savage place, just like the Fair Folk."

"Well, I like it," said Wil, tearing his gaze away from the carnivorous plant women just as their flowers closed their jaws once more. "It *is* beautiful. It's not going to cost us any more time, is it?"

Syl shook his head. "No, it's on the way. In fact, we save a couple of hours this way. Isn't that convenient?"

"That's one word for it," Darlene muttered, but she just shrugged and motioned for Syl to lead the way.

Wil couldn't say the view wasn't beautiful. As they went deeper in, crossing into the heart of the gardens proper, the plants only became more stunning and alien. His favorite sight was a flower patch that uprooted itself and came to the side of the road, leaning in toward the group. Wil didn't dare try to touch them, but it was interesting having the flowers stop and smell *them*.

"This is pretty nice," Darlene admitted when they were almost on the other side. "I'm glad you brought us here."

"Yeah?" Syl looked over his shoulder at Darlene. His handsome face lit up as if she'd given him the best gift ever. "Fantastic! There's one other place I'd love to show you before we get to Oakheart Spiral. It's this lovely little grotto, and if we get there at sunrise or sunset and care to stop for lunch, we'll see—" Suddenly, he stopped, his long ears swiveling around. His face paled. "We're not alone."

"We aren't?" Wil looked around, gripping his staff tightly. Darlene already had her rose spectacles back on and her weapon out.

"You aren't," a deep, rumbling voice called out. From a shimmer in the air, a huge figure stepped onto the path in front of them, wielding a great bone axe in both hands. His skin was orangish and he towered over even Syl. He wore armor made from thick, smooth bark decorated with floral designs, and a helmet that looked like a red rose. It would've been absurd if not for the murderous intent in his eyes, staring out from the recesses of his headgear.

"We're here," said another figure, appearing behind them. He carried a gleaming white glaive and wore similar armor, though his was blue instead of red. The two big creatures stood about ten feet away from the trio, blocking their way on either side of the path.

"We're here for your head, Wizard."

Ogres in front and behind them, with carnivorous and hallucinogenic plants to either side. Wil took a deep breath and swore.

CHAPTER 8

Thorns

"Of course you are," said Wil, after letting it all out. To his relief, the ogres on either side of them weren't in any rush to attack. Maybe that meant they could talk it out, or at least prepare for a fight. He stood sideways, eyes darting back and forth between the two assassins as he desperately went over the combat classes he'd hated in school.

"Look, gentlemen," said Syl, getting their attention with an easygoing laugh, "he's got diplomatic immunity, yeah? We need to get to the capital and talk this out."

The ogre in red let out a deep, rumbling laugh. "There is no diplomatic immunity to humans. Not when the price is right. Get out of the way, Syl. There's no need for you to get involved."

"You know each other?" Darlene demanded. She had her iron bar out, but it looked comical when pinned in by the two hulking figures. "Why does that not surprise me?"

"I know everyone," said Syl with a dismissive wave of his hand. "The important thing is that they know what happens if they hurt me. And if I have to, I'll shield the wizard with my body!"

The ogre in blue growled. "You think we won't kill you too, goat? Our master cares not for politics, only that his will be carried out. We offer you a chance to step away, or you'll die with the humans."

"Humans?" Wil's blood ran cold. "Darlene has nothing to do with it. You want my head, fine, I'll deal with you. Leave her alone."

"Wil!" Darlene sounded shocked. "Don't you dare!"

Syl butted in before they could argue. "There's no way you'll kill me. You know who I am. You know who my father is. You do this, there's nowhere in Faerie you could hide after that. There's no way Grimnar authorized this."

Blue shifted his grip on the polearm in his hands. "He didn't. Our contract lies with another. One willing to risk it. Goodbye, Sylano."

There was a finality in those words that made every hair on the back of Wil's neck stand on end. He channeled his power through his staff, making it light up a pale purple. Blue raised his weapon, and Wil let loose a bolt of lightning from the staff. The bolt connected with the ogre, blasting a hole in his wooden armor but only making him stumble back a couple of feet.

Both ogres laughed, a slow, deep, plodding sound.

"Isn't that cute?" Red asked, amused. "The human thinks his puny human magic can hurt us."

"The puny human doesn't know what he's up against," rumbled Blue. "Shall we show him?"

"Crap," Syl groaned. He motioned with his hand and bright flowers on either side of Blue grew and snaked toward him, wrapping around his arms and holding him in place.

"Run!" Syl shouted.

Neither Darlene nor Wil ran, but they didn't stay still either. Nor did Red, who swung his axe at the faun. Syl bobbed out of the way but the bone blade bit into the meat of his arm, making him bleat in pain and stumble off the path and into the purple wildflowers. Darlene ran to him, leaving Wil to deal with the angry ogre alone.

He hadn't stopped channeling his power, reaching out to the alien land around him for the strength it could layer onto his. It felt different from Harper Valley. Wrong in some ways, right in others, but deep and potent.

Red ignored Syl and Darlene and lumbered straight for Wil, his huge, armored feet leaving shallow grooves in the dirt. He got within swinging distance before Wil lashed out.

He didn't try another lightning blast. Those weren't easy and it hadn't worked the first time. Instead, he summoned a gust of wind and raw force and threw them at the ogre, pushing high and pulling low. Wil stepped out of the way when Red's feet swept up under him as he continued forward, then fell flat on his back.

Just in time for Blue to break free of his flower restraints and charge. Wil saw the glaive coming as if time were slowed, every second an eternity. He tried to tell himself to move, but he couldn't. The glaive came closer and closer. Right before it hit, Wil shook himself out of it and threw up a quick shield.

The bone glaive hit the silver light and sent Wil sprawling off the path and into the field of flowers. Pain exploded in his shoulder and then his body as he rolled over thorns, losing his grip on his staff. He scrambled back to his feet, then had to duck again.

One of the man-eating plants snapped at him, coming within inches of taking his nose off. Wil flinched away, looking around wildly. Blue advanced on him, holding his weapon with both hands. Caught between the two predators, Wil took his chance on the stationary ones. He slipped past snapping jaws, deeper into the field.

Blue advanced, unworried about the plants. When he got close enough, he swung low and cut the man-eater down, along with a semicircle of the purple flowers. The carnivorous plant let out a wail before falling silent, a feminine hand hanging limp outside the teeth. The nearest plant women wisely drew back.

Wil chanced a glance over at the other three. To his surprise, Darlene was on

Red's back, pulling her iron bar against his throat. Even from this distance, Wil saw the orange skin blackening from the metal. Syl had a length of plant material in his hand and he wielded it like a whip, striking out against Red repeatedly.

Then Blue came barreling his way, and Wil tried one of his strongest strategies. He reached for the land with his power. It responded, though not as well as it could have. It was like ordering a cat around; it responded, but with a will of its own. One second Blue was running at him; the next the ogre was sinking to his waist in the softened earth.

As draining as that normally would have been, Wil barely felt it in the heat of battle. He let out a cheer but fell silent when Blue dropped his weapon on the ground and pulled. Dirt and plants shifted, falling away from the ogre as he ripped himself from the ground and grabbed his glaive.

Before Wil had a chance to try again and maybe sink him in deeper, the ogre swung again. Wil made eye contact. The attack cut him down where he stood, the glaive neatly bisecting his body. The two halves fell apart on the ground, blood and entrails pooling out. At least, that's what the ogre saw.

Wil huddled on the ground under a veil of invisibility. He felt ill for resorting to the magic he'd all but sworn off, but there had been no time for anything else. As far as the assassin was concerned, Wil was dead and on the ground, and could even feel the corpse if he tried. The ogre was, however, the only one who could see it.

Blue raised his weapon and let out a fierce, pants-wetting roar. Thirty feet away, the fighting stopped. Syl paused with his thorny whip held ready to strike again. Red took that opportunity to twist and fling Darlene off him. She landed on the path hard, groaning. A second later, she looked up, saw Wil was nowhere in sight, and screamed.

Well, Wil could hardly let her believe he was dead. He reappeared for a split second before going back into hiding. She understood and fell silent. Blue stormed her way, a monster on a mission.

"You killed him! You bastard, you killed my boyfriend!" Darlene yelled. She was a better actress than Wil had expected.

"And now I'm going to kill you," Blue said with a booming laugh.

Syl backed away from Red, making it to Darlene and helping her up. "You killed the wizard," he said to the ogre, either catching on or fooled, it didn't matter which. "You got what you wanted. Just leave us!"

Red flourished his axe menacingly. "Our instructions were both humans. Walk away, Sylano!"

The faun pulled Darlene against himself. "I can't do that. Don't make me hurt you." His voice trembled, but he held strong. One hand slipped into his pouch. Darlene looked scared, but also angry. Wil smiled. She knew he was going to bail them out, and he was. He just wasn't sure how.

Blue grunted. "We gave you a chance. Goodbye, prince."

The ogres moved as one, converging on the pair as they huddled together. Wil moved forward, reaching for his magic but unsure what to do other than just reveal himself. He was just about to do that when a bright white dome shone into existence over Syl and Darlene. The ogres' weapons bounced off it with a clang, the glaive's blade breaking entirely.

Wil's heart skipped a beat and he breathed a sigh of relief. The two ogres hit the dome again, making it flash even brighter, but they couldn't get through. This was Wil's chance to do something about it. But what? Ogres were resistant to magic, and he wasn't much of a fighter to begin with. And illusions? Sure, they'd saved his life but . . .

He looked at the field they were in. All along the road, the purple flowers grew, with other colors deeper inside. That was consistent throughout the garden, for reasons only the fae knew, but Wil saw his opportunity. He calmly walked through the field and retrieved his staff. Pouring magic into it, he summoned a gust of wind and blew all the cut-down flowers over to where the ogres were.

Red looked up, but Wil remained invisible. After a second of seeing nothing, the ogre snorted and turned back to the dome.

"Give her up, Sylano! You keep up like this and we'll kill you for fun."

"Already going to," Blue grumbled.

It was maybe a terrible idea, but it was the only one Wil had. He pointed his staff at the ogres and with a short burst of magical energy, he shot a gout of fire at their feet. Just enough to set the purple flowers aflame.

The ogres whirled around, but Wil was nowhere to be seen, and neither was the illusion of the corpse. Thick white smoke rose around the ogres, gathering around their faces. Blue snarled, inhaling a huge puff of smoke. He coughed, hacking and waving his hand in front of his face.

"Wizard, are you alive?" he called out. "You cannot escape us! You cannot . . ." He swayed in place.

"Brother," Red said, dropping his axe into the earth. He raised a hand in front of his face and slowly moved it through the air, head tilting to the side. Hallucinogenic smoke continued to linger in the air. Enough of it that even their bulk was affected. Blue swayed in place, letting out a deep, wordless, rumbling groan.

Wil counted to ten before dropping his invisibility. His sudden appearance made Red fall on his ass. Which gave Wil the best idea of all. Seeing what was behind the ogres, he took a few steps to his left and went with the old standby. From the earth came his favorite fake demon, fiery sword and all.

The demon roared, and the two ogres, in their daze, tripped over themselves to get directly away from it, just as Wil had planned. Still looking over their shoulder, neither Red nor Blue saw the big man-eating plants in front of them. A second later, massive green and purple jaws closed over both of the ogres, snapping repeatedly as they gobbled their prey. The plants bulged with their struggling food, but the ogres weren't going anywhere.

Wil shook his head and summoned another gust of wind, blowing the fires out and all the smoke away. He kept it up another few seconds before letting it fade. Not long after, the dome vanished, and Syl fell over, Darlene underneath him. She struggled to keep him upright but gave up and helped guide him to the ground.

The faun's left arm had a deep gash that bled freely, and blood streamed from his inhuman nose. He blinked slowly, as if in a daze himself.

"Syl? Are you okay? Syl!" Darlene shook him.

The faun groaned and said, "I'm okay, just . . . just tired. That shield's not easy."

"Sylano, huh?" said Wil, coming up to them. "*Prince?*"

Syl chuckled weakly. "I guess I have some explaining to do, don't I?" And then he passed out in Darlene's arms.

CHAPTER 9

Prince of the Woods

Darlene held Syl, staring in disbelief. "Is he okay?" she asked Wil, who just shrugged.

"That was a really impressive shield he had, and those guys were wailing on it. I think he's just exhausted." Wil knelt over Syl, putting his head against his chest. The faun's heart beat just fine and he was breathing evenly. "Yeah, sleeping. Which could be a lot worse, but given we just got attacked . . ."

A full-body shudder went through Darlene. "That was . . . I don't think I've ever been more scared!" She held up a shaking hand, laughing breathlessly.

"Did you seriously jump on that ogre's back and try to choke him out?" Wil didn't know if he was more impressed or concerned, but now that it was over, he wanted to laugh and cry.

"I think I did," said Darlene, choosing to laugh. "Can you believe that? He was, like, three times my size!"

"Please never do that again," said Wil, letting himself fall to the ground. He looked up at the sky. "He could've squished you or cut you in half. I really, really wouldn't like that."

"Oh, well, next time we're attacked, I'll hide like a good helpless girl," she scoffed. But then she ran her hand through his hair affectionately, and her tone softened. "I didn't mean to, honestly. I was so scared I could barely think, and then he attacked Syl and I went crazy. I jumped on him and held on and it seemed to hurt, so I kept with it."

Wil could accept that. He found himself laughing then, surprising the both of them.

"What's so funny now?"

Wil smiled, staring up at the clouds in a sky even bluer than the one at home. "I thought you didn't like Syl."

Darlene stirred. "It's not that I don't like him," she said, as if working it out for herself for the first time. "He's incredibly charming and pretty funny. I just didn't and don't trust him, and for good reason, apparently. Prince Sylano, huh? A few things are starting to make more sense now."

"Yeah, I know what you mean." It hadn't been an especially good deception, but Wil hadn't been willing to press the faun. It seemed good enough to have a guide who swore them no harm, who could trickle in some information. Well, once Syl woke up, he and Darlene would give him a piece of their mind. But for now?

Wil sat up and got to his feet. After blocking a couple of titanic blows, his arms and back ached, but he hadn't taken any real wounds. Unlike Syl, who aside from lying there unconscious also had a nasty cut on his left arm. It bled slowly, a deeper, brighter red than human blood.

Darlene followed his eyes and didn't need to be told what to do. She went for the pack that had fallen in the fight and fished out more of the potion they'd used on Wil. She popped off the cork and drizzled it over the wound. It hissed and steamed and sizzled.

Seconds later, Syl's eyes shot wide open and he let out a garbled cry. He sat straight up, clutching his arm and hissing. "I'm awake, I'm awake, jeez!"

"Great," said Darlene, putting the cork back in the potion. "We've got questions for you, Prince Sylano. And if we don't like your answers, Wil just might fry you."

The faun gulped and nodded. He pushed himself up to stand, and stretched. The wound stopped bleeding but remained a long red line in his skin. He held his hand to it and closed his eyes. A full-body tremor went through him, and he bit his lip and made a face.

"Feels weird to you too?" asked Wil, slinging his pack around his shoulder and making sure his staff was in one piece.

"Always," said Syl. "It's even weirder to do to yourself!" He smiled, but it faded pretty quickly. He looked around, wincing at the damage all around them. A huge section of the garden was cut down, carnivorous plants alternately killed or full of ogre, and the path a mess where the ogres had stomped around. "Maybe we should get out of here first. Before anyone else shows up who wants your head."

"Yeah, about that . . . ," Wil started, then stopped. "No, you're right, let's get out of here. For a little while longer at least, you remain our guide. Whether or not that continues is based on your answers. We're not happy with you, Syl."

The faun nodded, wincing.

It was funny: Wil had been under the impression that the fae were supposed to be good at deception and mastering their emotions to present the image they wanted. Maybe Syl was secretly a master at it and playing them, but Wil didn't think so. The faun felt about as awkwardly open and guileless as Wil himself.

The rest of the garden passed by in a hurry. It turned out they were near the end anyway. Still, the entire time, Wil kept looking over his shoulder, apprehensive about the possibility of more assassins coming their way. When he tried to think of other things, his thoughts turned to Bram, and he hoped with everything he had that his friend was okay. Things were more dangerous than he'd expected here.

Darlene kept her eyes locked on Syl. Whatever she had in mind, she kept to herself. When they got to the next stretch of woods boxing the garden in, she slipped on her rose spectacles just in case, but still stuck close to the faun. If nothing else, Darlene would be ready for a fight if somehow Syl managed to lie via misdirection.

The other side of the woods couldn't have been more boring in comparison to the garden. The land was flat, peaceful, and open. But more importantly, Oakheart Spiral stood in full view, making Wil feel incredibly small.

Never before had Wil seen anything quite so large, not even the mountains around Harper Valley. The big tree looked to be the size of a city, stretching way up in the sky. The bottoms of some of the branches peeked out from under fluffy white clouds, hanging around the tree and masking the top. A huge opening had been carved into the base, and even from this distance, Wil could see caravans of fae making their way inside.

"So, the good news is that this was another shortcut, and we'll reach Oakheart Spiral in the morning," said Syl, clapping his hands together.

"And the bad news?" Darlene asked.

"Well, I think having two assassins sent after us is some pretty bad news! And we have no way of telling if there might be more soon."

Wil grimaced. "That's a cheery thought," he said. "You said that Grimnar guy, head of the Ogre Federation, hates humans, right? Those looked like ogres to me." He continued to stare up at the great tree and the lines of tiny figures in the distance going inside, like ants returning to the nest.

The faun cocked his head to the side, staring at Wil with his goat eyes. "Not necessarily. Ogres are mercenaries. Anyone could've hired them to kill you, so long as they knew you were coming. Which could be a great many people, since my father and our court knew, as did Queen Aria and her court, and Grimnar and his, and—"

"We get the picture," interrupted Darlene. "But how many of them have the power and influence to not have to worry about killing *the* Sylano, prince of the Woodlands Association?" Her tone was pointed but even.

"Ooh, that's a good question," he said, snapping his fingers and pointing at her. "You're the smarter one of you two, I think."

Wil shrugged. "Won't hear me argue. So, it could've been anyone and we can't really pinpoint it yet and there might be more coming for us, for all we know. Fine, we'll deal with that later. What about you, Your Highness? Why did you keep it from us? Why did you come for us?"

Syl frowned, and a small shudder passed through him. He grabbed his waterskin and took a long drink, then picked his words carefully. "If you had to deal with an unknown quality, someone with a great deal of personal power who would likely bring war to your doorstep, wouldn't you want every advantage you could get?

"My father, Martinus the Silenus, sent me to try to figure you out and lead you safely to Oakheart Spiral. I owe you a debt for failing you on that mark, and for saving my life. My shield would not have held up much longer." Syl bowed his head, and a tingle passed through Wil.

Obligation and manners were key here, but Wil hadn't understood until now just how real it was. It started as a warmth, burning hot and insistent deep inside of his soul, settling into something he could easily ignore, or fully notice if he looked. Prince Sylano owed him a favor, and Wil instinctively knew he could cash it in at any time and the faun would be compelled.

"I am happy to have been able to help keep us all safe," said Wil, just as serious. "But why don't you tell me what your father and your people want?"

"Exactly what I said before," said Syl. "We'd rather have peace and trade than go back to senseless war. You have your world, and we have ours. Your home could be a place where the two meet and we can make things better. I may have kept who I was from you, but I have never lied. I'd like to call myself your ally, and even friend."

"You know what? I think I believe him." Darlene shrugged at the looks of bewilderment sent her way. "I knew you were hiding something, and if you can't tell direct lies and everything else lines up, you must be telling the truth. The thing I care most about is that you got us here fast and mostly safe, and that Bram is okay. And if Bram isn't okay, there won't be a force in the world that will keep me from holding you personally responsible." Darlene wore a smile, but it didn't reach her eyes.

Syl nodded. "I understand completely, and I will stake my life on it without hesitation. I met your friend when he stepped through, and in the weeks to follow. He's doing just fine, last I saw."

Silence.

"You mean you could've told us that at any time?" Wil asked, his voice as quiet as a dagger in the night. "We were worried about Bram, and you knew personally he was fine, and you let us worry?"

Syl's floppy ears dropped. He looked between the two of them, taking a step backward. "W-well, when you put it like *that*, it sounds bad!" he said with a nervous chuckle. "If I told you that, then you'd know more than I was allowed to share!"

Darlene drew her iron bar. Lightning crackled up and down Wil's staff.

Syl took off running in the other direction, and the two humans gave chase. "I'm sooorrryyy!"

CHAPTER 10

Take a Breath

They chased Syl just long enough to run out the remaining adrenaline and frustration. On his long, spindly legs, the faun was impossible to catch, but he quickly understood the nature of the game and stayed just ahead of them, laughing merrily the entire time. After a few minutes, they slowed to a stop, and Syl circled back.

"I am sorry I couldn't tell you everything," said Syl. He took a quick drink of water. Wil and Darlene huffed. "I was under orders from my father. And now that I haven't revealed it but you know, I don't have to keep quiet anymore. Bram is doing fine. Before coming out to meet you, I spent a couple of weeks with him and the other captives."

Darlene let out a shuddering breath and folded in half. "I really, really wish you'd told us that earlier. Do you have any idea how worried we've been?"

Wil agreed, but he understood. He didn't like it or agree with it, but he understood. "You have to realize, this is our best friend. We were investigating together when he was taken, and your man Declan came out and told me . . . told me what I'd accidentally done."

In what Wil could only classify as cowardice, he'd done his very best to avoid thinking about the torn leyline and how this entire situation was his fault and his fault alone. Now that he knew and trusted Bram was safe and Oakheart Spiral stood before them just a half-day's walk away, he couldn't stop thinking about it.

"Hey, Syl," said Wil, not quite meeting his eyes. "What are the general opinions or impressions about my little accident with the leyline?" *How bad does everyone blame me,* he left unasked. Darlene took his hand in hers and squeezed. It helped.

Syl blew out a long breath as he considered his words. "No one's happy about it, if that's what you're asking, but only Grimnar hates you for it. Timothy Twist has some concerns, but you never know what he's thinking. Skalet seeks to close the doors between our worlds, but we're not quite sure how yet. And Queen Aria tires of seclusion. Elves are capricious creatures, interested mostly in their indulgences."

"And your father and people?" Darlene prodded. "What do you all think?"

Another pause. "My father's pretty happy about it, surprisingly. The thing you gotta understand about the Woodlands Association is, we were never big on the war, or revenge, or anything like that. We're a simple people. We live with the land, we live for joy and merriment, and we don't want any trouble.

"You humans are destructive and greedy, but a lot of time has passed. Maybe you're better now. Either way, King Martinus the Silenus is tired of isolation and wants to keep the doors open. And I do too. Unless," he paused, chuckling ruefully, "the rest of you turn out to be a bunch of bastards. But I don't think anyone other than Grimnar is upset at you for it. On the contrary, it has us curious."

"About what?" asked Darlene.

Syl's rectangular pupils bore into Wil's eyes. "How powerful our wizard friend here is. How powerful all of you wizards are. When last our people knew each other, wizards were just starting to learn how to use magic. Now we have one reshaping multiple worlds."

Wil's cheeks flushed, and he shifted uncomfortably. "I'm not anything special," he said. "I'm not even close to the strongest wizard I know."

Darlene snorted. "Right," she said. "Anyone could've taken on that storm and not only survived but won. Nothing special about you at all." She shook her head at him.

"Regardless," Syl continued, "you're likely worlds stronger than the wizards my father dealt with. A hundred years for you, seven hundred for us. And you represent both a threat and an opportunity. I can't promise you what will happen at the council meeting. Just that I will stand by your side, if you'll have me."

Wil looked past Syl and up to the towering heights of Oakheart Spiral in the distance. Ever since the storm the dragon brought to Harper Valley, life had gotten to be . . . a lot. He was supposed to be a simple civil servant, doing the best for his community. Wil had never thought of himself as special. He had to work hard for everything he got. None of it was ever easy.

Now, looking at his future, the one caused by his actions and display of power, his knees buckled and Wil dropped onto his ass.

Darlene joined him in an instant, throwing an arm around his shoulders. "You okay, Wil?" she whispered.

Wil nodded, then shook his head, and nodded again. He laughed and rubbed his eyes. "Just . . . It's all hitting me." He breathed deeply. "We could probably make it to Oakheart Spiral today if we tried, couldn't we?"

"Yes," said Syl. "If we walked fast or if a shortcut opened up, we could be there by nightfall. I would recommend taking a break. We just fought for our lives, we're shaken, and the moment we set foot in the city, it'll be nonstop for a while. Let's relax for today, and we'll worry about dealing with my father and the rest tomorrow."

Darlene made a thoughtful sound. "I agree."

"I think we should just keep moving," said Wil.

"Outvoted," Darlene said in a singsong voice. "We'll set up camp here. Syl, would you be so kind as to fill up our water for us?"

The faun's face fell. "You mean on my own? They get heavy."

"Quit whining!" Darlene shot back, but she was smiling. Syl shrugged and took the waterskins as Darlene gathered them. He walked off, down the gently sloping hill to where there was a small stream in the distance. As soon as he was out of earshot, Darlene hugged Wil.

"Talk to me. What's going on?"

Wil made a distressed sound, still staring at the big tree. "I don't know how to fix things. I'm glad Bram's okay, and if he is, the other hostages probably are too. That's great, and that makes it easier to deal with. But what do I do about the leyline and the way Faerie is bleeding over into Harper Valley? When will it stop? Will things continue to merge until there's no distinction between Harper Valley and Faerie? I should know these things, but I've got no clue. I've got a decent bit of magical muscle, but I'm not powerful. Not in any way that matters. I'm still a dumb kid, trying my best."

The words came tumbling out of his mouth, and in a way, it was freeing. The entire trip here, Wil had kept everything bottled up and it had been eating at him. Now Darlene knew he was clueless and helpless.

Darlene sighed and patted him on the back. "I don't think anyone else would've been a better choice, Wil. Would you rather have had Sinclair come here? The ogres would've torn him to pieces. On second thought, maybe you should've let him come after all."

They were silent for a second, then Wil started snickering and Darlene joined in. Within seconds, they were laughing heartily. Tears trailed down Wil's face, and he wiped them away as he came to his senses.

"I wouldn't wish that on him. We've been attacked two times since coming here."

"Three times," said a rough, growly voice behind them. They turned around to see Isom the wampus cat crouched behind them.

Wil reached for the staff, but Isom snarled and made him freeze.

"I wouldn't do that, Wizard. You pick that up, you won't have time to do anything before I bite your face off. Care to risk it?"

Darlene moved to put a bit of distance between her and Wil, earning another rough growl, but Isom didn't stop her. He didn't have to look to see her reach for the weapon that had been something of a security blanket during their trip.

"What now, then?" Wil asked. It was hard to feel fear after the adrenaline crash from the ogres. "You here for a friendly chat? Maybe share a nice cup of coffee with us?"

The big cat cocked his head to the side. His one good eye flitted between the two of them. "That was good work with the ogres," he said. "You are worthy prey."

"Thanks," said Wil dryly.

Isom inclined his head in a mock bow. "I offer you an honorable death, Wizard. Just you and me, fighting to your death. Your woman can go free, and we can have a bit of fun before I eat you."

"Such a generous offer," Darlene scoffed. "You're going to lose. Again."

The wampus cat bared his razor-sharp teeth in either a grin or a homicidal snarl.

"You seem awfully confident you'll win the fight," said Wil with a smile. "I blasted you out of the air. You ran away with your tail tucked between your legs. See, I don't think you could kill me if you pounced now. You know I'd stop you and then blast you again. Look, I'm tired. Why don't you run along and try again later?"

A fluttering in Wil's stomach warned him that maybe they'd pushed it too far. The wampus cat got to his feet, and Wil snatched his staff and aimed it carefully. The world was completely still, save for the grass swaying in the breeze. Violence was seconds from breaking out, and now Wil wasn't quite sure he was even up for another fight.

A pleasant, lilting whistle caught their attention. Syl came striding up to them, carrying their waterskins. He stopped upon seeing the scene before him, his whistle sharply dropping into silence.

"Huh," he said. "Am I interrupting anything?"

To Wil's surprise, Isom's ears flattened and he bowed his head.

"Your Highness," the wampus cat grumbled, before turning around and trotting off. A few seconds later, he broke into a run and then vanished from sight.

"Well, Syl, looks like you've earned your keep as a guide," said Darlene.

"I told you I'd be invaluable! It's just about knowing the land, and also knowing the people, and being a good mediator, and . . ."

Wil shook his head as the faun preened and postured. He let himself sit back and take a minute to breathe. Tomorrow they'd face the music for what he'd done. When all was said and done, Wil just hoped he could do right by as many people as possible. He didn't know if that meant making a good deal or closing the door, but he'd do whatever it took.

CHAPTER 11

Oakheart Spiral

Wil's neck was hurting from looking up as they made their approach. By the time the front gates and the lineup to enter came into view, he'd resolved to stop craning his head to try to see the top of the tree. Not even a quick spell to temporarily sharpen his eyesight let him see that far, so he just gave up and trudged along, nerves eating him alive.

"So, to be clear," said Darlene, as they were first spotted by a trio of lithe, graceful elves a hundred yards away, "we're safe here, right? We've been attacked on the road three times now—"

"Two and a half, really," said Wil, regretting it instantly when she glared at him.

"*Three* times now, and I don't want trouble in a major city when we're going to be some of the only humans around and therefore under more scrutiny."

"Well," Syl started, brightening up, "you're under my protection and I have diplomatic immunity. To an extent. Stick with me and you should be good. Just . . . act natural, like you belong."

They got into the long, trailing line behind the trio of elves, two men and a woman. The men looked at Darlene, wicked grins on their faces. Darlene didn't notice at first but looked over when she saw Wil scowl at them. She turned back quickly, trying to hide a coy smile.

"Is there anything else I should know before we go inside?" asked Wil, trying to ignore the lingering looks of the elves their way.

Before they'd left, Syl had called a nearby bird, whispered a message in its ear, and sent it ahead of them. The rest of the walk there was spent advising Wil on what to do when they got there, what would be expected of him, and who to be wary of if security did give them trouble. After a couple of hours, Wil couldn't remember most of it and had to hope that it would come back to him when necessary.

"You mean aside from bringing a gift as a show of good faith?" Syl teased.

"Look, how was I supposed to know I should've brought a gift? I thought I was just negotiating over hostages and to *start* talks, and I've never been a diplomat before!"

Even though it was the third time Syl had teased Wil about it and riled him up, now there was an audience. The elvish trio, a couple of gnomes, and a family of rough-looking ogres who fell in line behind them all stared. The faun grinned in delight while Darlene shook her head at him.

"Relax, he's teasing you," she told Wil. "I'm pretty sure everyone cares more about the substance of the meeting than the niceties. Right, *Prince* Sylano?" Darlene had never stopped teasing him about being a prince. It was one of the few things that made their new friend wither.

"If we were meeting in the Woodlands, there wouldn't be any need for niceties," said Syl, his tone dropping to something only slightly more positive than a grumble. "We'd just have a party and negotiate when we're a sheet and a half to the wind, as nature intended."

Wil shook his head and forced himself to relax. Or at least try to. The line soon moved up a few feet, and the three fell mostly silent. Syl hummed, Darlene looked around often and seemed to be keeping track of their surroundings for them. Wil ran around in circles mentally, going over everything he could.

Little by little, they got closer and closer to the gates, if they could be called that. They were an opening in the tree itself, a place where wood disappeared and a path led in. There were still a dozen groups ahead of them when Wil first got a peek inside. The sight made his jaw drop and left some of his anxiety in the dust.

He didn't know what he'd expected. Maybe a big tree that had stuff in the center of it, but this wasn't that. Even just at the entrance, there were hallways leading down and around the edges of the tree. Once another few groups had entered, he saw there were rooms carved into the wood, illuminated by glowing moss and mushrooms hanging on the wall. Fae of all shapes and sizes milled around, constantly moving.

People lived there. Wil already knew that, but it was different seeing it in person. Oakheart Spiral, the tree, was a thriving capital with people living inside it, and in just a couple of minutes, they'd be inside too. Wil swallowed hard, leaning on his staff as they came up to a pair of ogre guards.

"Name and business," one of them rumbled. They wore armor made of wood, though far less ornately decorated than that of the dual assassins they'd encountered earlier. It still put Wil and Darlene on their guard, and Wil had to resist calling up his magic reflexively. Luckily, Syl took charge.

"Prince Sylano of the Woodlands Association and guests Wilbur McKenzie and Darlene Johnson of Harper Valley, here to see the council."

The ogre on the left sniffed. "Humans. I smell the stink of iron. You dare bring faebane into our capital?"

Darlene stepped forward before Syl could smooth things over.

"I dare. I've been attacked three times. *Three times*," she emphasized, before Wil could say anything, "by your people, so you're damned right I'm armed for self-defense."

"No iron allowed in Oakheart Spiral," the ogre on the right barked.

"I'm not leaving it behind," said Darlene.

Syl stepped forward, raising his hands placatingly. "In light of both circumstances on the road and the fact that I'm a prince and can do whatever I want, I'm afraid we're just going to walk in. Smile and nod and we'll be on our way, and you can keep doing a good job with everyone else." He winked.

The ogres growled as one, which led Wil to believe that growling was how they communicated, not unlike dogs giving a blatant warning. Syl simply stood there, waiting expectantly. After a few tense seconds, the ogre on the left gave one short, sharp nod and motioned for them to go.

The three of them proceeded in. Wil was just waiting for one of the guards to change their mind and attack as he, Darlene, and Syl walked through. But nothing happened, and then they were inside the great tree, and everything changed.

It was the air, if that made sense. Faerie in general had cleaner, sweeter air, but inside the tree it changed to an earthier, grounded scent. Right as they walked in, there was a path appearing to lead deep into the heart of the tree. Before that, Oakheart Spiral was separated into rings of rooms and clearings carved into the wood. Not far off was a staircase leading up to the next level.

It had been nearly half a year since Wil had spent any time in a populated city, and for a second it felt perfectly natural to be among thousands of people going about their day, even if those people weren't human. It was only when he realized how comfortable he was that he remembered they were in another world. A quick probe of his wizardsense nearly staggered him.

Despite so many people living inside it, like a giant ants' nest, the tree itself remained very much alive and thriving, filled with so much ambient magical energy, it was almost blinding. Wil pulled back with a muffled gasp and came away with a growing appreciation for the place. As Syl led them deeper toward the center, the hallway increasingly widened. It took a good half hour to make it to the wide, hollow center of the tree.

When they did, Wil couldn't help but pause and gape at the sight. The center of the tree was almost completely open, and rose higher than he could see. It was so big inside, it had its own weather system, and it was drizzling nearby. The inhabitants didn't care. There were dozens of little shops, eateries, and even an open section where a bunch of graceful, ethereal beings led each other in a dance with music that echoed in the cavernous trunk.

"Welcome to Oakheart Spiral," said Syl, with none of his usual playfulness. "Our beloved capital of this side of Faerie. Our destination is one of the higher branches."

Darlene made a face. "How long is it going to take us to walk up there?"

"No time at all if we use a portal," said Syl.

Wil shook out of his reverie. "Portals? You guys have real portals here?"

"Oh, did I forget to mention that?" Syl grinned at him.

"You know damned well you didn't mention them!" Wil shoved the faun playfully.

"What's so impressive about portals?" Darlene asked.

"They take a lot of really complicated, precise, potent magic to even make, let alone keep open and stable," said Wil. "Throughout all of Calipan, the only places that have portals are Cloverton and Manifee City, and even that's just because they're the ass ends of the continent. Saves weeks of travel by train, and it's reserved for high-ranking government officials and the military."

Darlene understood. "And you're saying you use these portals just to get around a big tree?"

Syl's expression sharpened. "Would you keep your voice down?" he hissed, looking around. "Do *not* call Oakheart Spiral 'just a tree.' This is the cultural and spiritual center of the land, understand?"

"Yes, sorry," she said, wincing. "But you use portals just to get around here?"

"Yes. For a few key places. Like your own portals, they're reserved for important use. And if you follow me, we can go right up to the council and announce our presence."

Wil nodded and motioned for him to continue.

Syl led them around a series of small stalls where gnomes were selling savory-smelling stews, reminding Wil they hadn't eaten yet that day. In the exact center of the tree was a guarded stairway. The faun led them through without issue, and they descended into darkness, illuminated only by a red-ringed tear in space. Indistinct images spun in unpredictable fractals.

"I should probably go first," Syl said, pausing before the portal.

There were guards here too, but without any shouts of alarm from those up top, they seemed content to just glower at the humans from afar.

"Even expecting you, I don't think they'd be happy with you two just popping in. Let me go through, wait a minute, then follow."

They could hardly argue with that. With one last nod, Syl went through. He didn't walk in, as Wil had expected of portals. Instead, he reached out and touched the edge, and those same shifting images traveled up his arm and consumed his body, bringing him in and through.

"Well, that looks disconcerting," Darlene said cheerfully. "It looks like it feels weird."

"I bet it tickles," said Wil, thinking of the healing magic Syl had used on him. "I don't think it'll be dangerous, though. Not compared to what waits for us."

Darlene nodded and put her arm around his shoulders. Wil hadn't realized how nervous he was before he felt her touch, and he was grateful for the contact.

"You ready for this? Is there anything I should keep in mind or do when we're up there?"

There was one thing, but he hated it. Wincing, Wil said, "Maybe let me do most of the talking. I value your advice and will need it, but I think I need to be seen as the representative, rather than them viewing us as a team. Just keep your eyes and ears open for anything I might miss."

"Yeah," she said, though it sounded as if it pained her. "I think I can do that. Think we've waited enough time, or do you want to wait longer?"

Wil looked at the portal. Now that they were there, he didn't want to go through it and face the music. He sighed. "Yeah, let's go through."

Darlene pulled away, letting her fingers trail down his arm until she took his hand in hers. They took a step forward and reached for the portal together.

INTERLUDE

Telegram from Cloverton

Mayor Bartholomew Sinclair rubbed his temples. He wasn't having a good day, but then, he hadn't had many good days in months. Today at least, he could take joy in knowing the subject of his ire was in danger and might not return.

The gnome Declan was trapped in a cell lined with bars of iron he couldn't touch. The frames of the cot were iron as well, and the only protection he had against the metal came by way of thick blankets provided by Sharon McKenzie. Frankly, Bart thought it was too good for the creature.

"I'm tired of asking you, Gnome. Do you want to be beaten? Our dear sheriff would be more than happy to oblige you." He bared his teeth at the creature, but Bart had never been an especially intimidating man.

Declan sniffed, unimpressed. "If you're tired of asking me, *Human*, then maybe consider not asking. I'll not answer, so really you're wasting our time. Which is fine by me, I suppose, given I've got nowhere else to be until the hostages are exchanged." The gnome stroked his beard as he spoke.

The sheriff slammed his club against the bars. Declan didn't stir. They'd tried some variation of this over the past several days, and it hadn't amounted to anything yet. Bart was beginning to think it was pointless, but that would've meant admitting he was helpless. There were few things he hated more than being helpless.

"The mayor asked you a damned question!" Sheriff Frederick hollered.

"And?"

A knock at the door stopped the sheriff from doing something stupid. Wilbur's threat of what the gnome could do if harmed lingered in the back of his mind. It made all their bluster pointless, but Bart couldn't bring himself to just drop it and let it be. That meant letting Wilbur McKenzie, that naive little pissant, win.

"Who's hungry?" Sharon McKenzie, the boy's mother, entered the jail, bringing with her a picnic basket filled with better food than the prisoner deserved. Better food than most places in town served, at that.

"Why, Mrs. McKenzie, a pleasure to see you once more," Declan declared. "And just in time! I'm pretty sure our dear sheriff was going to burst a blood vessel glaring at me. Poor fella won't think of his health. Take it from me, Sheriff, you wanna take care of yourself as you get older."

The worst part of it all was the gnome's stupid calm and serenity they couldn't seem to shake.

Sharon made her way in, pushing past Bart and going right up to the pen. She motioned with her head for the sheriff to unlock the door for her. Frederick looked at Bart for approval. Sighing, the mayor motioned for him to get it over with. Once it was open, she sat next to Declan and set the basket in front of him.

"Got you some good biscuits and gravy today. Nice and hearty, it'll stick to your ribs," said Sharon.

"If any more sticks to my ribs, you'll be rolling me out of the jail once your son gets back!" Declan let out a jolly laugh and pulled out a bowl heaped with buttery biscuits covered in savory white sausage gravy. He inhaled deeply and made an appreciative sound.

Bart turned away, fuming. Food and friendly visits had been one of the conditions Wil had placed on him. Loathe as he was to admit it, the boy's power was considerable. It wasn't that he was afraid of him. No, the soft-hearted fool wasn't someone to personally fear. It was the newfound stubbornness and defiance that made the mayor pause.

"You've got ten minutes," he said, desperate for some semblance of control.

Without looking up, Sharon said, "A pleasure as always, Mr. Mayor."

Another thing that bristled. The McKenzies now looked down on him. As if they had anything to be proud of. They ran a farm that fed them and made just enough money to keep them going, and they thought they were any better than him?

Bart took a deep breath and walked out of the jail and back into city hall. Seeing him, his receptionist, Mary, stood, smiling at him with adoration as she always did. All it took was making sure a few hospital bills for her kid went away, and now he owned her.

"Mr. Mayor, you have three messages waiting for you. Mr. Carrey wants a talk about additional protection for his land, Jocelyn Pyke wants a permit for—"

"Hold all messages for now, Mary," Bart said, motioning for her to stop talking. "For the next hour, I'm going to be focusing on . . . paperwork."

Mary's expression changed to one that was sly and knowing. "Shall I help you with that paperwork, sir?"

He thought about it. She'd been pretty once, but she was just another forty-something mother in Harper Valley. Her enthusiasm was nice, but for once he wasn't in a mood to be comforted. "That's alright Mary. I need to concentrate."

"Of course, sir," she said, bowing her head and sitting back down.

Now that was more like it. Mary, at least, had some damned respect for the position, for all the hard work he did to keep this town running. He didn't just sit on his ass all day, he spent hour after hour dealing with every little person's little problems, promising he'd take care of them all. The rest he spent networking, making important deals that brought business and prosperity to Harper Valley.

Once in his office, he poured himself some whiskey and sat in his plush chair, staring out the window. Winter was here, and with it came even more responsibilities and socialization and keeping morale up. This fae crap couldn't have come at a worse time. It was as if the universe were conspiring against him.

Snow came down gently, blanketing the valley in a coat of white. The sight helped his mood. Harper Valley was in an odd position, somewhere between a large town and a small city. When Bart looked out the window on days like this, it was like taking in a painting of the perfect quaint town.

If Wilbur managed to get the hostages, it would be good for the town, but bad for the mayor. Sometimes, when Bart thought about that, he felt a little uneasy. It wasn't as if he didn't want their citizens home safe and sound, but he had the bigger picture to worry about. Twenty years he'd spent shaping the town how he pleased. His life's work, threatened by an idealistic child.

He shot back the whiskey, savoring the burn going down his throat. He gave a short, fiery exhale and poured himself another. While Bart may not have been willing to cross Wil about the prisoner, there were other things in motion. It would mean giving up control, but it had become increasingly clear that he'd lose control no matter what. So why not go with the power that would return control to him when all was said and done?

A timid knock at the door interrupted his thoughts. "What is it?" he demanded.

Mary came in, looking properly sheepish at invading his personal time. Bart sighed and said, "I appreciate your enthusiasm, Mary, but I'm really not in the mood today."

"No, sir, sorry, sir, but there's a telegram for you. From Manifee City."

There it was. Bart jumped to his feet and snatched the message out of her hand. He didn't know how this new telegram thing worked, but a message that could've taken weeks to arrive had managed to make it across the country in just a few days. Let him handle it, the boy had demanded. Like any responsible leader would ever do that.

"Thank you, Mary. That will be all."

Ignoring her, he went back to his seat and collapsed into it. He flicked the telegram open and read it.

A mage will be dispatched to HV to negotiate on behalf of Calipan.
He speaks with the full authority of Cloverton

Perfect. A full-on mage being would be just the thing to put Wilbur in his place. It didn't matter that he'd have to work under this new wizard. Mayor Sinclair didn't need to win, he just needed Wilbur to lose. *Let's see how his bloodless idealism will last against a high-ranking magical soldier, no doubt built for war.*

Bart smiled and lifted his glass. He could drink to that.

CHAPTER 12

The Oakheart Council

As it turned out, portals were uncomfortable. When Wil and Darlene touched the swirling images, their feet locked on the ground but they were yanked forward, farther and farther until it felt as if the entirety of their beings were stretched to the breaking point. Just as it got to be too much, they snapped forward and were suddenly on the other side of the portal.

Wil came through screaming. Eyes wide, he caught himself and tried to cover it with an awkward cough.

"Sorry about that."

"Lady and Gentleman," Syl boomed, "allow me to introduce Master Wizard Wilbur McKenzie, here to negotiate on behalf of Harper Valley. And his companion and advisor, the sharp-as-a-knife Darlene Johnson. Humans, meet the Oakheart Council."

Wil looked around the cavernous room. It was bigger than the inside of Harper Valley's meeting hall and largely open, save for five thrones, two of them occupied and one of them absurdly large, meant for a being bigger than a house. That throne was currently empty.

Judging by the clouds behind open doors and what appeared to be an extravagant garden on one of the branches, they were high up in the tree. Everything decorative or furnished was built into or from the great tree itself, carved with swirling designs and letters Wil couldn't read. Illustrated poems or stories, maybe.

In the center of the room, there was a recessed circle, which Wil stepped into. He looked at the two occupants in their thrones. One of them was a three-foot-tall, black-haired man, with impossibly sharp features and an even sharper grin. He had bushy eyebrows and the kind of dapper clothing that might've been popular fifty years ago in Calipan. Meeting Wil's eyes with his bright-red ones, he bowed his head, grin widening. Timothy Twist, Wil presumed.

When he looked one seat over, he saw what could only be Princess Arabella of the Fair Folk. Syl hadn't been lying when he'd called her beautiful. She had vibrant, reddish-brown skin like fresh baked clay and hair so black it verged on blue. The elf was a tall, leggy, ethereal being wearing a vivid green dress that clung to her, and it took him entirely too long to realize he was staring. Syl cleared his throat.

Wil shook his head and cleared his throat as well, trying to ignore the amused look Darlene sent his way.

"Hello, I am called Wil. On behalf of Harper Valley, I am here to negotiate the trading of hostages and find a good resolution to . . . centuries of conflict."

Silence. Syl smiled encouragingly, but that faded after a few seconds.

"Well," said Timothy Twist, drawing out the word in his lilting accent, "that's an understatement if I ever heard one. 'Conflict.' Some might phrase it as genocide."

If he was angry about it, Wil couldn't tell. Everything he said sounded like he was holding back a laugh at a private joke.

"I . . ." Wil bit his lip. He didn't need a special sense to tell him to tread carefully here. Words mattered to the fae, and admitting serious grievances could lead to an Obligation. "I don't think anyone here would consider that an inappropriate term."

"Oh, and a coward too!" The little man laughed merrily and clapped his hands. "Such a great start from humanity's latest intrusion."

"Is that why your people came out and attacked us?" Darlene spoke up, joining Wil in the circle. Her tone was strong but not angry. Wil took her hand.

Syl stood between them and waved his hands to get everyone's attention. "C'mon, this is hardly the best way to start good faith negotiations, now, is it?" There was a goading, joking tone that almost hid the desperation.

"No, Twist is right," said Princess Arabella, looking down her nose at them from atop her throne. "Your people are little more than murderous brutes, conquering and killing anything that gets in your way."

Syl cleared his throat. "Your own people backstab each other all the time. How's your cousin, by the way? Still dead?"

The princess sniffed. "Well, that's just politics, isn't it? You play the game, sometimes you get burned. But these humans . . . , there is no game. No fun or cunning or elegance about it. They just charge on through like enraged bulls."

The worst part was that Wil couldn't argue. There was a part deep inside him that wanted to snap back about all the odd and creative ways the fae had gotten back at humans, and how many people had disappeared, never to be seen or heard from again. While neither side's hands were clean, responsibility clearly belonged to Calipan, hungry to expand after breaking away from the old world.

Wil took a deep, calming breath and just went with his gut. "I can't apologize for the entirety of my country's mistakes. I am here as a representative of Harper Valley specifically. When I get back home, I will pass on any messages you like to people above me. More than anything, I want peace and to avoid any unnecessary conflict or bloodshed."

"How many of our people have you killed since the door's been opened?" Twist sat back on his throne, playing with one of the buttons on his coat jacket.

"Three," said Wil. "*After* you stole our children and then launched an attack on the entire town. The creatures that attacked us, I believe, were largely the Wee Folk. Know anything about that?"

The infuriating man shrugged. "My people are not exactly what you called organized, Wizard. They can be spirited and bear a grudge. If a number of my people went out for a spot of mischief to blow off steam, it certainly wasn't planned. I'd say it sounds like rambunctious spirits taking things a bit far."

Darlene scoffed. "Now who's the coward?"

"Ooh, I like her," said Arabella, sitting up straight. "His woman has some *fire* to her, as drab as she is."

Syl took this opportunity to let out a sharp whistle that caught their attention. "Please, *please* consider not trading barbs for once. I know there's bad blood, *I know*. But I just spent the last five days with these two humans, and I must confess I've grown a bit attached to them. While mankind might be a bunch of murderous bastards, these two prove that not all of them are.

"Wil is thoughtful and compassionate, a trait we thought impossible in them before! And Darlene, as you've seen, is straightforward, fiery, and tenacious. But she is *not* needlessly aggressive. I think she is proof that even the angriest beasts can become tame with time. I can vouch for them."

"Thanks, Syl," Wil said flatly. Darlene squeezed his hand hard.

Arabella let out a huff and draped herself across her throne. "It's funny you think the opinions of a foolish goat can sway my opinion."

"It's funny you think I care about *your* opinion, Princess," said Syl. The faun had never looked dangerous before now, but he drew himself up to his full height and bared his teeth. "I'm much more interested in what your mother has to say. I don't know why she didn't come here herself. It's so weird of her to send a mouthpiece who's much more pleasant to look at than listen to."

Darlene looked at Syl, eyes wide. Wil gaped and so did the elf princess, looking a lot less haughty with her mouth open. The only person not shocked into complete silence was Timothy Twist, who howled with laughter and clapped enthusiastically.

"Fantastic, fantastic!" he crowed, kicking the air in his enthusiasm. "Well, you've got me halfway to convinced to give him a chance."

Arabella somehow flopped over more, resembling a cat pretending not to care. "I *am* very pleasant to look at, aren't I? Pity you don't even have that, you obnoxious, garbage-eating, farmyard reject."

"I don't know . . . , you found me pretty enough after a bottle of hob whiskey," Syl returned, but the fire was out of his eyes. Arabella smirked and then signaled acknowledgment and acceptance with a wave of her hand. Crisis averted.

"I must admit," said the princess, "I find this entire affair very boring, but Mother insisted. She is interested in seeing how much your people have developed culturally. Centuries of isolation and boredom, and maybe even humans could be a worthwhile distraction."

"There's nothing I'd love more than to trade music and food and stories," said Wil, desperately latching onto the topic. "There's a lot we can learn from each other if we're all willing to try to move forward. Calipan has wronged you, but Harper Valley is a good place with good people, and I believe we can figure out how to coexist."

The two fae leaders looked as though they were considering it, and Syl appeared pleased. A loud noise drew Wil's attention to one of the doors leading outside. *WOMF, WOMF* went the sound of an enormous and familiar being setting down on what was now obviously a landing pad. The stub of a broken nose horn peeked into the council chambers, followed by a triangular head. The storm dragon approached his throne and curled up inside of it, resting on the lower half of his body as he considered the two humans.

"You," Wil gasped, taking a step back. "It's you!"

Darlene looked between them, realization dawning on her. "Oh my gods, is that the dragon that flooded the valley?"

A bone-deep, thunderous rumble filled the air. It took Wil a second to realize it was laughter. The dragon bowed its head in greeting and acknowledgment.

"I am he," the dragon whispered, deep enough to echo off the far ends of the chamber. *"Greetings, Wilbur McKenzie. I cannot say I am pleased to see you again, but neither am I displeased. You are well?"*

Wil blinked. A dragon, *the* dragon, was trading pleasantries with him. "Uh, yes, I appreciate you asking. And how about you? Has there been any lingering effects from the curse?"

"No, I am recovering well. The human who cursed me was powerful and cunning. I came close to death before you intervened. I trust my payment for your services is acceptable?"

It took Wil a second to realize he meant the piece of horn. "You gave this to me as payment?" Wil ran a thumb across the runes carved into the wood. "It allowed me to make an excellent staff and display to the world that I had the honor of saving not only my town but also a venerable king, it turns out. I can't think of anything better."

Syl and Darlene looked impressed, but it was the truth. As nice as it was to have a new source of power to draw on for his spells, a dragon horn was also a trophy and would be a serious symbol of status among other wizards. It had been weird to walk with it constantly, but after a week, he now felt inseparable from it.

"An excellent answer," Skalet rumbled gently. He turned to Twist and Arabella. *"I, too, vouch for this human. For now. Enough that we may discuss the rift and how we may close it permanently, and end this problem once and for all."*

"You don't want to keep it open and have access back and forth?" Darlene asked in a halting voice.

Skalet turned to examine her with an eye almost as tall as her. *"Before I returned home, I was cursed by one of your wizards. He intended to enslave me and break my will. Wilbur's actions may have been true, but little good comes from interacting with your kind. It would only be a matter of time until all of Faerie is overrun. We must find a way to close the rift before that can happen."*

And with that, Skalet lowered his head on his tail and closed his eyes. It didn't seem he was trying to sleep so much as making a declarative statement that he was finished talking. Wil respected it.

He turned to the other two and let out a breath. "Well, we have a lot of ground to cover, but I'm sure we can find something that satisfies all of us. Shall we begin?"

"Aren't you forgetting something?" Darlene whispered to him. "Weren't there supposed to be five representatives?"

"Yes," a gravelly voice said from behind them. Wil turned to see a huge ogre clad in iridescent chitinous armor standing in front of the portal. He stood just a little taller than Syl but was twice as wide. Eyes filled with murder peeked out of a helmet resembling a beetle's head and horn. Slung across his back was a massive club, about as long as Darlene was tall.

"Gods, are all you ogres this sneaky?" Darlene muttered under her breath.

Grimnar must've heard her, because he let out a terrible growl and stomped forward, looming over the two of them. Wil instinctively put himself between Darlene and the ogre king. Grimnar smiled, showing huge, gapped, blocky teeth.

"It is good you are here now, Human," he said. "Now I can formally call for your immediate execution!"

CHAPTER 13

Obligation

The great ogre's threat echoed horribly throughout the throne room.

Arabella groaned from her reclined position on her throne. "Really? A new record for bloodthirst and threats. Well done, Grimnar."

The ogre growled at the elf. "That's *King* Grimnar to you, Princess. I will not tolerate any of your sass today."

Wil looked at Darlene, who looked just as lost as he felt. Maybe he should've been alarmed by one of the five leaders of Faerie demanding he be executed, but after nearly a week of travel that had included being attacked three times, he was just annoyed.

"And what is it I'm being executed for?" Wil asked incredulously.

"You are responsible for the destruction of the key leyline keeping our worlds separate," said the ogre king. "You have opened up our lands to war once more. If it were up to me, that alone would be worth your head."

"Then we're glad it's not up to you," said Darlene, more offended than Wil at the idea of his death.

"Furthermore," Grimnar continued as if uninterrupted, "all of the hostages we took for information and study are unharmed. Our scouts tell us you've murdered three of our own. As the representative of your town, it is on you to take the punishment for murder. That's three more reasons your head will belong to me."

Syl approached Grimnar and tried to whisper in his ear, but the ogre put a hand on Syl's head and casually threw him to the ground. Syl hit hard. If the threat to his own life hadn't done it, seeing his new friend hurt fired Wil up.

"I was promised safe passage to your capital, and I've been attacked three times on the road," he said, taking a step forward and pointing accusingly at Grimnar. "Twice by a wampus cat—"

"A wampus cat?" Timothy Twist whistled. "You're in trouble, Wizard. I do *not* envy you."

"And once by two ogres who said they were contracted for Wil's head," said Darlene. "They tried to kill all of us!"

Grimnar considered them for a long, silent moment before chuckling darkly. "My people are free to take contracts from anyone in the realm. It is understood that their actions reflect upon their employer, not on their people. It was the understanding we reached after my people covered our retreat into this world. We were the ones to sacrifice our lives to get the rest to safety."

Wil held back a sigh, looking fiercely at Grimnar. He didn't react well to bullies. Most of the time, his instinct was to duck away or try to reason with them. Even he knew it was one of his biggest flaws. But standing here, he knew he couldn't blink.

"The ogres who attacked us sacrificed their lives on behalf of an employer who wants us dead. This is after we were promised safe passage." Wil let a fraction of his power channel into his staff, runes glowing a pale purple. A symbol of his office and strength.

His voice hardened. "Now that the entire council is assembled, I demand an answer for this breach of oath."

An odd twinge of power made the collected groups shudder. Obligation, in Wil's favor. It manifested as a sort of strength, a metaphysical high ground over the others. In them, he could sense an itch, an uncomfortable compulsion to balance the scales. Even just recognizing it in the council, Wil had no desire to ever be on the receiving end of Obligation.

"But," said Wil, "I am willing to call it even, on one condition. After the rift between worlds was opened, you took some of our citizens, and we not only took captives but killed three of your people. Our history is bloody and our hands are not clean, but our people were defending their homes from perceived attack. Still, you have three lives lost.

"There were three attempts on my life by members of the fae." Wil looked around the room pointedly. "Three breaches of your promise. I say we call it even, and from this point forth, we try negotiating in good faith with a common goal of working together. What say you?"

Unsurprisingly, Syl was the first person to speak. "I believe that is a wise and honorable agreement and a way to move forward with purity of intent." Wil's feeling of power over Syl diminished, leaving only a trace. The faun genuinely looked impressed by Wil, and he wasn't alone.

Arabella sat up straight and didn't look quite so haughty anymore. The feigned boredom was nowhere to be seen and she looked at Wil with eyes so dark he felt he was being drawn in.

"I agree," said the princess. "A fresh start." The same sense of lightening as before made Wil shudder. Power was different here, more potent.

Timothy Twist shrugged, looking away. "Three lives for three attempted murders feels a little uneven to me. It's not exactly like they *succeeded*. But I suppose we should look forward."

Skalet remained where he was, curled up on his enormous throne. Wil didn't expect more, and he realized there was more Obligation there than there had been in the others, he just hadn't known what it was until now. The dragon didn't seem to be in any hurry to pay off any remaining debt.

Grimnar, to the surprise of no one, shook his head. "I do not agree to those terms. You will pay for their lives, one way or another." He drew his weapon, slapping the club down in an equally huge hand.

"Hold on now," Syl tried again, but Wil waved him off.

An idea was brewing. A dangerous idea none of his loved ones would approve of. Grimnar didn't just want Wil's head. If what Syl said was accurate, the ogre king wanted a fight. Long-lived beings like this could carry a grudge. If he executed Wil, it would certainly mean war. A war he definitely wanted.

"You want a chance to see me dead, King Grimnar?" Wil asked. "Fine. You've insulted and threatened me, and two of your people tried to kill me. I will not stand for it." Oh gods, he was really going to do this. "I challenge you to a duel!"

"*What?*" Darlene didn't hide her shock.

All around the room, the fae stirred. Syl remained frozen, while Arabella and Twist looked on with naked glee. Grimnar blinked but recovered the fastest. "What are your terms?"

Wil pointed at Grimnar with his staff. "My magic against your strength. We start at opposite ends of the room and fight until either I die or you submit or fall. If I win, you not only agree to my original terms, but you owe me a big favor."

Darlene gasped. "Are you nuts?" She grabbed him by the shoulder and whispered in his ear, "I thought that you were terrible at combat!"

"Yeah," said Wil belatedly, not bothering to whisper back. "I skirted every combat class I could and focused on growing crops and taking care of animals and the land. But I'm good at all the basics and I'm pretty strong. Trust me."

Grimnar took the bait. "I accept those terms! The arrogance of man never fails to amuse me. I remember how limited you wizards were the last time we fought. With your death, I'll get what I've always wanted: a rematch."

A shudder went through Wil as the agreement settled in the core of his being. If he tried to run away from the fight, it would mark him forever, possibly worse. If he ran, he died. If he didn't win a fight against a warrior king, he would die. A lot of people would die. Although he respected how risky his act was, he was unafraid.

Syl stepped forward again, looking miserable. "Witnessed and honored by the council, yes?"

Arabella clapped her hands enthusiastically. "Yes, honored, indeed! Either Grimnar is put in his place or we get to see the human splattered on the ground. No matter what, I win out on this."

"I thought your mother wanted trade. If I die, you get war instead," Wil said, taken aback.

"Yes, my *mother* wants that," Arabella said slowly, as if she were speaking to an idiot, "but I'm on the fence. Prove to me you're worth the fuss." She smirked at Wil, who tore his gaze away before he got caught up in it again.

Grimnar rolled his neck, popping it in several places. "Any requests before I kill you, Human?"

"Yes, actually," said Wil, lighting up. "Two. The first is I would like fifteen minutes to prepare myself. A man should go to his death open-eyed, yes?"

The ogre nodded approvingly. "Yes, you may have time to consider your imminent demise. And the other?"

Wil probably could've won without the second condition, but he decided to let the ogre's arrogance work in his favor. "Would you be willing to let me cast one free spell before you crush me?"

"Careful, Grimnar," Timothy Twist warned. "You don't know anything about this human. I'd put money on him playing you like a fiddle."

Grimnar laughed and slammed his meaty fist into his armored chest. "Human magic is weak, and my people are resistant. You may have your one spell. Make it count!" He stomped over to his throne and sat down, laying his club across his lap. He made a shooing motion with his hand.

Wil nodded and led Darlene over to the far side of the room. She was practically shaking with frustration and fear.

"What the hell are you doing, Wil? We both know you're not a fighter! Why are you doing this?" Tears shone in her eyes.

"You're right," said Wil, pulling her into a hug. "I'm not much of a fighter. Each of those times we were attacked together, I was on the defensive. I didn't have time to think then, or plan. This time will be different. I know what I'm doing, so trust me!"

Darlene looked unsure, but she knew she didn't have a choice at this point. "If you die, I'm going to be upset at you. You know you're risking Bram and little Pearl Patterson, right? If you lose, what do you think will happen to them?"

"I know, I know," Wil said, holding his hands up to stall any further arguments. "But I know something none of you do. Something I've felt a bit since I arrived, but noticed more when fighting for my life. I know this is hard, but trust me. And if I'm wrong and fall, I'm going to need you to take over negotiations and get the hostages home. Can you do that?"

After a second of glaring at him, she capitulated. "Yes, damn you, I can. But you'd better not die!"

CHAPTER 14

The Master Wizard

Although he'd asked for fifteen minutes, within only five, Wil knew exactly how he was going to win. The council chambers were extensive, and there was more than enough room on the floor for him to cut loose without worrying about hurting bystanders or being cornered. He didn't know exactly what Grimnar's strategy would be other than bludgeoning him with his club, but he wasn't worried.

"He's faster than he looks," Syl warned him, repeatedly looking back and forth between the two combatants. His idea of a pep talk was similar to Darlene's in that he berated Wil for a couple of minutes before giving whatever advice he could. "And if he gets close, you're dead. What's your plan for winning?"

"Yeah, Wil," said Darlene, "what's your plan for winning?" She was irritated with him for keeping her in the dark.

"Leave that to me," said Wil, as mysteriously as he could. Being a master wizard, it wasn't often he got to lean into the role and have some fun with it. "I've got this. Seriously. Just enjoy the show and be ready."

The faun pursed his lips in frustration before letting out an irritated bleat. He stomped to the final throne and sat, crossing his arms over his chest. Darlene sighed and kissed Wil—for either good luck or goodbye, he couldn't tell—and joined Syl at his side.

Wil stepped up to the edge of the center ring, channeling power through his staff. It was absurd how easy it was to do here in Faerie, magic everywhere at his fingertips, and his new implement made it easier still. For the first time in his life, Wil looked forward to a fight. He nodded at Grimnar, who took his place dozens of feet away.

The ogre king looked huge, even at a distance. His shimmering chitinous armor covered his chest, arms, and legs. His armpits, feet and shins, and eyes appeared to be his only vulnerable spots. He stretched and held his club firmly, staring Wil down. In any other circumstances, Wil might've been intimidated.

"You ready to die, Wizard?" Grimnar called out.

"Neither of us is dying today, Your Grace," Wil called back. "Does this mean I'm good to cast my first spell?"

"Sure. Do your worst!"

Oh, he had no idea. Wil pointed his staff at the ceiling and stirred it in slowly growing circles. Each circuit gathered more power, collecting moisture from the air. While all magic seemed easier with his staff, this was exactly the kind of spell it was made for. Clouds formed at the ceiling, gathering in thick clumps until it started raining. Slowly at first, then coming down harder and harder.

Skalet stirred on his throne, head only now lifting to watch the dispute with interest. Wil wondered if he disapproved, but it was too late to worry about it now.

"This is your big spell?" Grimnar yelled even louder to be heard over the sound of raindrops hitting the floor. "What do you hope to accomplish? Doesn't matter. I am ready!"

"Then I guess there's nothing else," Syl's brash voice easily carried over the rain. "You ready Wil? Okay. Begin!"

Syl had scarcely given the signal before Grimnar charged forward. Every powerful stomp sent water splashing up around him. It wasn't more than an inch deep in the recessed floor, but it was enough to slow him down. He raised his club and roared, totally trusting in his ability to resist magic.

Wil let him get almost halfway across the makeshift arena before he pointed his staff and sucked all the heat from that spot, taking the energy into his staff and holding it for later. The sudden shift in temperature made it easy to focus the energies. The rain-slicked floor froze in a fifteen-foot circle.

Grimnar's next step sent him slipping and falling flat on his face. His club went flying at Wil, who caught it midair with magic and sent it right back. The huge log of what Wil now saw was petrified wood flew straight into Grimnar's head with a resounding clunk. The helmet's beetle horn broke off entirely.

Up on the thrones, the assembled council members winced as one with the hit, except for Darlene, who cheered, and Skalet, who remained silent. Wil raised both hands into the air and roared with a magically enhanced voice.

"You think that means anything?" Grimnar shouted as he fought to climb to his feet. Every time he tried, he slipped and fell back down. "This is nothing!"

"How about this, then?" Wil shouted. He siphoned away more of the heat until his staff burned in his hand. The falling rain froze and peppered the ogre with shards of ice. His armor protected him from most of it, but Wil hadn't been counting on that to do any real damage. He'd just needed to make the air frigid enough for his next move.

Grimnar snarled and slammed his fist into the ground. The ice shattered, and a few more quick blows let him stand and collect his weapon. Slivers of ice jutted out of his cheeks and feet. He advanced again, slowly this time, but covering ground.

Wil's staff threatened to scald his hand, but it was time to let it out. Once more, he pointed the dragon horn at his opponent. This time, he unleashed a monstrous gout of flame that engulfed the ogre, rapidly heating the area. The fire itself didn't stop Grimnar, but Wil didn't mean for it to.

His real goal was simple science. Where his flame hit rain and ice, it turned to scalding steam, fogging up the arena. Wil casually circled, leaving an unmoving illusory image of himself. It wouldn't stand up to any real scrutiny, but it would do the trick. Gods, it felt good to channel this much power.

Grimnar may have been tough and resistant to magic, but Wil doubted he was resistant to the laws of thermodynamics. He poured more and more heat into the area until the steam was too hot to handle. The ogre made for a dark figure in the center of the arena, barely visible through the haze.

Maybe it was Wil's imagination, but Grimnar seemed even slower now. The ogre paused to look around, close enough that Wil dropped another copy of himself in place and continued circling the arena. Grimnar swayed, then dropped to his knees. Wil dispelled the fire, exhaling a held breath. He kept circling, dropping another copy.

This was more magic than he'd moved around in quite some time, but Wil found it came as easily as breathing. He'd noticed it when Isom had attacked, and then later in what little Wil remembered of the hobgoblin anniversary party, when he cast spell after spell to entertain the guests.

Faerie was saturated in magic, and Wil had taken it in day after day.

"YOU READY TO SUBMIT, GRIMNAR?" Wil's voice projected from the other side of the room. "I PROMISE YOU, I'M JUST GETTING STARTED."

Deep in the fog, the ogre king stood. He looked around slowly. Wil felt rather than heard the growl.

"Is this supposed to impress me, Wizard? You inconvenience me, but I assure you, I will not tire before I crush you!"

Wil suppressed laughter. Was it wrong to enjoy this? Academically, he understood that other wizards at the academy enjoyed the feeling of dominating in a duel. So many of them made it their entire personalities, but Wil never imagined he'd know what they were talking about when they called it the thrill of conquest.

He didn't want to hurt Grimnar. Not for the sake of causing pain, at least. The threat to Wil's life meant little after surviving the past week, and nobody would ever call him sadistic. It wasn't even the joy of demolishing a bully. Behind Wil, the council watched what they thought was a fight.

"ALRIGHT. JUST REMEMBER, YOU ASKED TO BE EMBARRASSED IN FRONT OF THE OTHER REPRESENTATIVES. I WANTED TO NEGOTIATE PEACEFULLY."

"Show your face then, Wizard! Stop hiding behind tricks and fight me," Grimnar bellowed.

Wil took a deep breath, and when he blew it out the rain slowed, and the fog split in two. It rolled out the open doors on either side of the council. Within seconds, it had stopped raining and Grimnar could see once more. The ogre froze and spun in place, looking at the ring of illusory doubles of Wil.

None of them were impressive at first, but they didn't have to be. In the last remnants of the fog, Wil got a chance to see his imperfect faces, each full of pieces of what he knew to be him. The more he looked around, the sharper the illusions became, until they were near perfect. All took a step forward as one.

"WHAT'S THE MATTER, GRIMNAR?" Wil's voice came from different angles around the room, each instance echoing over another. "YOU WANT TO CRUSH ME? TAKE YOUR PICK!"

"Excellent," Grimnar said, huffing and puffing for air. "More of you to hit!" He took a swing at the nearest Wil. His club passed through harmlessly. Wil closed his eyes and detonated the illusion. It exploded into a piercing white light.

Grimnar tried to shield his face, but it was too late, and he staggered backward. He blinked rapidly. He swung again before his vision could clear. That illusion turned into the sensation of biting insects all over his body, even under his armor. Grimnar cried out and shuddered violently.

Desperate now, he kept swinging around again and again. Not once did he ever come close to the real Wil, who stayed in one place while the illusions moved and distracted the ogre. Each one became a new sensation, from a gunshot near the ogre's ear to a horrible tickle in his throat, and finally, one illusion exploded into the overwhelming aroma of the old farm outhouse. That one broke him. The ogre dropped his weapon and clawed at his face. He ripped off his helmet and flung it to the ground, screaming.

Wil's heart pounded with the exertion now. It was thrilling, spinning so many complicated, layered illusions. It took focus, will, and a lot of power to keep so many going at once. Only now did he feel the strain of the performance. It felt good to let loose.

He took pity on his opponent and dispelled the illusions. All of them. Wil stood there, casually tapping his staff in inch-deep water. Grimnar looked up. With his helmet off, he had a squat, ugly face that looked like he was made of rocks. He stared at Wil with a mix of hatred and horror.

Wil motioned for him to come, and cast a spell to make himself lighter. Grimnar didn't pick up his weapon this time. Seeing Wil's staff light up again, he broke into a frenzied charge, arms reaching for his foe.

Wil let him get close before he used telekinesis to push as hard as he could against the ground. He launched himself into the air above the ogre king, coming close to the ceiling. Grimnar looked up in time to see his staff light up brighter than before.

It wasn't all of his power. Wil had no idea what that would look like here in Faerie, powered up to at least double his normal strength and who knew how much more endurance. It was just enough energy that he let the staff do what it did best. Lightning cracked around the base, spiraling along the wood until it burst downward through the horn, striking the ogre with the force of Skalet's storms.

Grimnar tried to shield himself with his arms and gave the bolt of lightning somewhere to go. It traveled down his arm and through his body, connecting with the pool of water below.

Wil wasn't worried about the lightning itself. As far as he knew, it being magical meant it wouldn't completely destroy the ogre. The pool of water, on the other hand, was the perfect thing to amplify his attack and make it count. He kept it up for just a couple of seconds before he let go and gently floated downward.

Grimnar swayed on his feet for a couple of seconds before crashing face-first onto the floor. He twitched violently a few times before settling. Wil waved his staff and flipped him over onto his back. Burned, bruised, battered, bleeding, but still breathing. Good enough. Wil put his foot on Grimnar's chest.

"Do you submit?"

All the ogre could do was groan in pain. He nodded, barely perceptible, but apparently it still counted. A weight lifted from Wil's shoulders as the conditions of their agreement snapped into place. Harper Valley's slate was clean now, as far as the fae went. And more than that, a huge surge of power flowed into Wil.

Grimnar owed him one major favor, to be called in at any time, that he could not refuse without severe penalties. More than that, Wil felt a sense of power over the ogre directly. He'd bested him and now stood above him. Obligation was everything here. Wil smiled and went up to the thrones.

Arabella and Syl burst into thrilled applause, while Timothy Twist looked like he was finally taking Wil seriously. Skalet rumbled something that might've been approval before lying back down.

And Darlene . . . Well, Wil had never seen anything like the expression she now wore on her face. His girlfriend looked shocked, amazed, and almost as though she didn't recognize him. He went up to her, grateful when she didn't flinch away from him.

"Hey," he said. "I told you I had it."

"You did," said Darlene quietly. "I stand corrected."

"I'm still me," he whispered. "I don't do things like this because I didn't want people scared of me. But now, I think we need people to be scared of me."

To the council, Wil said, quite clearly, "Now that we officially have a fresh start, let me introduce myself. I am Wil McKenzie, master wizard."

CHAPTER 15

A Gilded Cage

"What a display of power, Master Wizard," Arabella said, leaning forward in her seat. "Interesting. And you say you're not a fighter?"

"I'm not," said Wil, smiling apologetically at Darlene. She still looked disturbed by the display. "I was near the last in my class when it came to combat magic. Mostly because I didn't have any interest in it. But I am more than capable of defending myself and my home if I need to."

Syl was all grins and barely contained energy. "That was fantastic! King Grimnar may never live this down, but at least he'll live. I think I can speak for the council when I say that now would be a good time to stop for the day. We'll clean him up and make sure he's coherent, and we can start in earnest tomorrow. Any objections?"

There were none. Timothy Twist eyed Wil as he slid off his short throne. He laughed at a joke only he knew, shaking his head and looking away. A layer of darkness covered him, and a second later, where he stood was a raven. Twist flapped his wings and took off through one of the open doors.

Arabella gathered herself up with liquid grace. "Perhaps I'll send for you to join me for dinner."

"Perhaps you won't," Darlene said, grinning fiercely. The elf princess looked her up and down, sniffing disdainfully. She walked past them, even taller than Wil now that she wasn't draped over a chair, and went through the portal.

"Territorial, huh?" Wil joked.

"More like cautious," Darlene replied, crossing her arms over her chest. "You're powerful, obviously, but you kept staring at her and you had this lost look in your eyes. I remember you telling me the fae often have a hypnotic allure. I don't think you're immune."

Wil opened his mouth to argue but stopped himself. "You're probably right. I mean, yeah, she's pretty, but I have no interest in her. That'd be stupid and dangerous."

"And?" Darlene asked, amusement spilling into her voice.

"And because I have a wonderful girlfriend I'm fond of, who is leaps and bounds more attractive, smart, and interesting?" Wil played it up, still riding the high of his win. "She doesn't have freckles. That's a deal-breaker."

"Acceptable," said Darlene, leaning in to kiss him. It was a relief, after the fight and just the general stress of the trip, to have a moment that felt normal.

Syl made a grating noise of approval. "Yeah, that's it! Nothing like a good frolic after a life-or-death fight! Let's get you two somewhere more private and comfortable." He waved for them to follow and started toward the edge of the room.

Wil looked over at Grimnar. "What about him?"

"I will ensure he lives long enough for you to call in your favor," Skalet said without opening his eyes. *"You used the storm well. My power is in worthy hands."*

Wil shivered as a little more of that feeling of concrete influence increased. It wasn't just about scales to be balanced, he realized. Not just favors, but also being favored. Skalet didn't owe him anything further, his payment had been enough, but the dragon favored him and it was strong enough to feel like power. Wil bowed his head respectfully.

With a twist in his gut, he looked at his staff. The pale light had gone out of it, but there was still a lingering heat, a buzz that said it was asleep, but it had one eye open. Wil had taken the time to craft it, and the dragon's horn was powerful, but it was the favor that brought it to life. Possibly literally.

"C'mon," said Darlene, tugging on his arm. Wil shook off his daze and followed her and Syl to the edge of the room, where Syl coaxed a door into being in the wood. It opened up to the outer ring of the tree and a staircase going down in a counterclockwise spiral. Syl clopped down rapidly, and they followed.

They caught glimpses of other rooms as they passed. First a kitchen, with elves and pixies busy at work, flying around and depositing spices in a big stew. Wil didn't know if it was safe to have a stove in a tree, but the smell reminded him of how hungry he was. Then a waterfall room, a glowing crystal cave with two ogre guards standing in front, and a cozy little library. Wil's eyes lingered as Syl brought them lower.

Nearly a dozen floors down, the faun stopped in front of a blank plane of wood. He looked over his shoulder at the two humans, making a face.

"So, this is something we've kept our word about, and I figured you'd want to make this your next big priority. Whenever you want to leave, you'll need to knock so I can let you out."

Darlene understood immediately. "This is a jail cell, then."

"Bram and the others!" Wil motioned for him to open the door.

"I'll wait out here," said Syl. He waved a hand and the wood of the tree parted, sliding sideways to make an opening for them.

Darlene ran through, Wil hot on her heels. Inside were living quarters that were better than their homes back in Harper Valley. A large communal living area was ringed by what looked like shared bedrooms with bunks carved into the tree itself. An old man played cards with a young girl on a couch in the center of the room. They looked up and the little girl, Pearl Patterson, Wil presumed, squeaked.

"Mr. Wizard!" she called out, dropping her cards. She ran up to Wil, calling out, "The wizard's here, the wizard's here! We're going home!"

The other hostages he knew in passing, but Bram was their friend. With Pearl so excited to see him, Wil was hit by a wave of guilt that they'd felt so faceless until now. He leaned down and held out an arm. She hugged him, and he squeezed her gently.

"That's right, I'm going to get everyone home! How are you doing, Mr. Sully?"

The old man was slow to stand, pausing to stretch out his back. "Can't complain. I guess I could, but what'd be the point? Not like Nancy's still around to miss me. I bet that's why it took you so damned long to get here."

"There's a time difference," said Darlene.

"Excuses!"

Out of one of the bedrooms came a bearded Bram, followed by a small ogre. Well, small in comparison to the rest of his kind and the giant next to him. He had on leather armor and held a spear, and had a look of surprise on his face. Wil was briefly wondering what was going on there when Bram charged them, arms spread wide.

"Look out!" Wil pushed Pearl out of the way before Bram scooped up him and Darlene in either arm and hugged them to his chest. He twisted and spun in place, earning an undignified squeak from Darlene.

"Put us down!" she said through her laughter. "I'm glad to see you too! Since when were you capable of growing a beard?"

Bram set them down, flushing. "I'm not. One of the people who came in to entertain us made our hair and fingernails grow and shrink and change colors. He gave me a big beard and I asked him to keep it. Doesn't it look great?"

"Very 'lost at sea for months,'" said Wil, shaking his head in disbelief. "It suits you. People came in here to entertain you?"

"Yeah," chirped Pearl. "People come every day and play with us and put on shows!"

"Huh," said Darlene, "I guess Syl was telling the truth. They were well treated."

"Well fed, too," said Gilbert, cracking a smile for the first time since they'd arrived. "Kitchen service on demand. If we're gonna be imprisoned, there are worse jail cells. They let us out for excursions, even. The Benton kids are probably out in the stables, helping take care of the animals. Not sure those two will wanna go home."

"Huh," Wil repeated. "Then none of you were harmed or coerced in any way?"

Gilbert and Bram both made a face.

"Not as such," said Bram, scratching his beard. "They asked a lot of questions. Simple things, like people we knew, things we did together, what our average day was like. Innocent things, you know?"

"I got asked about my military service," said Gilbert with a nod. "Don't like to talk about that much, but they wore me down over a few drinks. Didn't tell them nothing sensitive, and they didn't ask. Just general questions. Still felt like I was betraying Calipan a bit, but they weren't hurting us or anything. Just asking questions while feeding us and laughing with us."

"Wow," said Darlene, "Sinclair dropped the ball. Here y'all are living like kings while Sheriff Frederick shot and killed a couple of them and keeps the others in a cage. I'm really glad your little stunt worked to clear that up, Wil."

"What stunt?" Bram asked, looking at Wil. He finally seemed to notice the staff Wil was holding. "When did you make that?"

Wil smiled. "You said day and night kitchen service, right?"

Their guard, a young ogre named Gallath, escorted them out of their prison and down to another level of the tree, out onto one of the many branches. Bram was careful to stay in the center of the path and not get close to the edge or the unfathomably long fall, tense the entire time. At the end of the branch was an outdoor seating area with a smattering of different fae eating together.

There, they had drinks and lunch brought out, and Wil tried to tell Bram what had happened. He'd managed to tell him about meeting Declan, and finding out that he'd altered a leyline and opened a rift, and he told him about crafting the staff, but the moment the stories involved Syl, the faun prince took over with enthusiasm.

Wil half expected Syl to make himself the star, but it was worse. Syl embellished the stories and played up Wil's abilities and contributions until Wil was squirming in his seat and Darlene was laughing at him. When Syl finished telling the story of Wil's triumph over Grimnar, he had to chime in.

"It's really not that big a deal," Wil complained. "Any other wizard could've probably achieved that if they were here in Faerie. This entire realm feels like a more stable and less hazardous leyline."

"Oh, knock it off," Darlene said, nudging him with her foot. "You've been holding out on us this entire time. I thought I was impressed when you made the earth swallow all those bandits. Are you going to try to tell me it was all just because we're in Faerie?"

"No," said Wil. "It's also thanks to my staff. Without it, I wouldn't have been able to make it rain or shoot lightning."

"Is that why you're glued to it?" asked Bram. He adjusted his glasses, looking at the staff with both admiration and amusement. "Even sitting down, you're keeping it close to you."

It was true: there was no danger. They had promises of safety that Wil trusted this time. He did not need the staff, yet there it was, leaned up against the table and within easy reach.

Syl grinned, wide and incorrigible. "Well," he said, "if I had a staff that magnificent, I'd feel awfully attached to it too. I might even want to show it off and always have a hand on it, just to remind myself it's there."

Darlene rolled her eyes and threw a hunk of bread at Syl's head. "Men," she scoffed. "But he's right, you've been attached to it since we've been here. Maybe it's time to let go a little. We're safe here, right, Syl?"

"Very. Unless you get too close to the edge and a stiff wind blows you over," said Syl, keeping a straight face as Bram whimpered. "Happens all the time."

"Fine, I get your point," said Wil. He grabbed a chair from the next table over and turned it around, then lay his staff across it. Even a few feet away, the power in it still felt connected to him. Good enough. "I probably won't need it for the rest of the trip, anyway. Tomorrow, we begin negotiations in earnest, and I'm honestly worried."

Bram raised his glass of fae barbenberry wine and said, "Well, then it's a good thing we're together again. We've got all day to think of how to get out of this. How hard could it be?"

Darlene joined him, lifting her cup. "I'm so glad we've got you back, Bram," she said. "With the three of us, we'll figure it out."

"Four of us," said Syl brightly.

"Uh, you're kind of one of the people we're negotiating with," said Wil. "Not sure you can count as being on our side here."

"That's where you're wrong, Wizard." Syl kicked back, drinking straight from a bottle of his wine. "Our interests align, and I have insight into what the others may want or need. I'd go so far as to say you need me."

Wil smiled. He had a point, and if he couldn't trust Syl by now, who could he trust? "Then I guess the only thing to do is begin."

CHAPTER 16

Diplomatic Ammunition

"So, obviously, the least desirable outcome is war," said Wil once they were back in their jail and Bram's bedroom. He and Darlene sat on Bram's plush bed while Bram sat on Gilbert's bed and Syl stood, arms crossed over his chest. Wil left his staff in the sitting room, if only to prove it didn't need to be near him at all times.

"The problem is, any number of hiccups or mistakes could lead us there. So I think it comes down to this: What do the fae want?"

Everyone looked at Syl.

"Well, that's complicated, isn't it?" he bleated. "We each want different things. Grimnar wants war, and barring that, a presence in your world to better monitor you."

"That doesn't sound so bad," said Bram.

"Which would mean taking land away from Harper Valley," Darlene said, catching on instantly.

"Which would lead to war," said Wil. "Calipan's still expanding; Cloverton wouldn't be happy about losing any land. Especially not a piece of the last refuge of stability before the southern front. They're fighting against Ilianto right now, but you'd best believe they'd turn around and take the valley back. What else do the fae want?"

Syl shrugged. "My father wants trade. He wants access to the scientific advances your people have made, and some of the engineering. We don't do much in the way of metalwork outside of making jewelry. We work with softer metals, while you do wonders of your own without magic. It'd require some safety since we can't abide iron, but there's a lot you've created over the past century that intrigues us.

"Hmm. Who else? You can trust what Arabella said about her mother. The Fair Folk are social creatures, constantly in need of novelty and passion. They also live a long time, and are fascinated with short human lives and how it affects the way you people are." Syl thought about it and laughed. "I don't know if they want to study you or play with you, but it's mostly harmless."

"Not sure I want to trust Arabella at all," said Darlene.

Bram lit up. "Ooh, did something happen?"

"After I kicked Grimnar's ass, she started making eyes at me," said Wil, unable to avoid smiling. Darlene opened her mouth to protest, so Wil hurriedly added,

"She thinks Arabella's trying to ensnare my mind, and she's probably right. I have to be careful." He winked at Darlene.

"Not a bad idea. These fae can be enchanting . . ." Bram trailed off, looking off into the distance thoughtfully.

Now it was Darlene's turn to tease. "Oh, really? Did you meet someone here, Bram? Are we in danger of losing you permanently, after we came all this way to see you?"

Bram flushed and squirmed. He adjusted his glasses and said, "No, no, no. Not like that. It wouldn't work out, probably, and of course I'm coming back with you two. It's just that this was such an interesting, magical thing to stumble into. I wish my mom could've seen this place."

Any teasing they had left in them died. He'd been mostly okay since Addie had passed on, but now and then he'd get a reminder that brought him to his knees. He seemed mostly fine here, just introspective.

Wil cleared his throat. "If we're able to get what we want and can come and go, we could always get some of her flowers and bring them here, so she can see for herself."

Bram's eyes watered and he nodded, not trusting himself to speak. Wil understood and smiled at his friend, trying to convey without speaking that it was okay, not to worry.

"Coming and going is the plan," said Syl, bringing them back on point. "But I'm not sure we'll have the votes. You can count on me and Arabella, of course, to vote along those lines, but Grimnar's a hard no and Skalet isn't likely to vote at all, or, if he does vote, it'll be a no."

"So that means it comes down to that Timothy Twist guy," said Darlene. "I don't get him. What's his deal, even? Other than being a short weasel who laughs at everything."

Syl shrugged. "That's a huge part of him. Unlike the Fair Folk and the Woodlands Association, Twist and his Wee Folk tend to be very . . . independent, let's say. They're big on living by their own rules and pranking or terrorizing anyone who crosses them. Most of it is harmless, but it's hard to get a read on them."

"Do they have any special reason to hate us more than others?" Wil asked, remembering the chaos when Harper Valley had come under attack for one night. "As we said to him, the attack on our home seemed mostly by Wee Folk, with a few Fair Folk as well. Do goblins count as Wee Folk or Ogre Federation?"

"Ehhh . . . ," Syl said, wiggling his hand. "Depends on where their allegiance lies at any given time. Some gobs and hobs join the Ogre Federation, usually the ones especially good at or driven by fire and destruction. Most of them stick with the Wee Folk, and others are Heartless. Julietta and Roberto were Heartless, out homesteading with their family."

"What was it you did for them, back in the day?" Darlene asked. "Now that you don't have to pretend to not be a prince."

The faun laughed and ran a hand through his short beard. "They were from rival families, One Hearthless, one Wee Folk family. I helped smooth over the differences and set them in that stretch of land off the main road. It gives the Hearthless some better roots without being tied down to one leader. Might've stopped a minor war, but you know, that's just the job."

"And what job is that, Syl?" Wil pressed, playfully. "Pampered prince?"

"My *official* title is Woodlands ambassador," said Syl, drawing himself up to his full height, until the tops of his horns scraped the ceiling and he jerked away. "It's my job to be social and find mutually beneficial solutions."

"So what's your solution for getting Twist on our side?" Darlene asked.

Syl opened his mouth and then paused. "Well, he's tricky, okay? He doesn't lead the Wee Folk so much as speak for them and occasionally rile them up enough to be vaguely on the same page. He doesn't seem to ever *want* anything much, other than a good meal and some laughs. If you can promise him that, you might be able to sway him."

Bram rumbled thoughtfully. "One of the things I've noticed here is that your people are a lot more indulgent than ours. That's not a bad thing," he added hastily, "I appreciate it about you. There *is* a lot of obligation and duty, but those seem more like compulsions than actual desires.

"Take Gallath, for example," Bram said, nodding toward the door where their guard stood on the other side, keeping an eye on the other humans. "He's honor bound to do his duty and guard us. I think he'd lose something important to him if he outright shirked his duties or tried to do something else. But when he's not working, he doesn't want to do anything big or important or vain. He just wants to enjoy himself with a couple of drinks and conversation.

"Now, you take someone from Harper Valley, and they're going to be looking for every last bit of work they can do before they let themself have a moment of peace. Look at your dad, Wil," Bram said, gesturing at him.

"My dad ends every day with a beer and a couple of pipefuls of staggerleaf," said Wil, chuckling. "Not sure that's the best example you could give."

"No, but that's my point," said Bram, "he'll indulge himself and he loves it, but only if *all* the work is done and he can't do anymore. Same with your mother. Meanwhile, I think the fae live for indulgence whenever they can get it."

"You're not wrong," said Syl, pulling out a silver flask from the pack perpetually at his side. He took a swig and offered it to the humans, who all waved him off.

"So how do we *use* that?" Darlene said. "Let's say Twist is an irresponsible, hedonistic, chaos monster, like you guys seem to think. What could we possibly offer him that would sway him at all?"

"Well, assuming you guys have been taking care of the brewery, we could always offer the council some of our brews," said Bram, stroking his new beard thoughtfully. Wil was certain it was half the reason he even wanted a beard. "Between that and your mom's cooking, Wil, we could convince anyone."

Wil blinked. "Are you suggesting that we get over centuries of conflict by inviting them over to Mom's house for dinner and drinks?"

"Well, when you put it like *that*," Bram muttered, looking down.

"I don't think it's a *bad* idea," said Darlene, elbowing Wil in the ribs, "but it might take more than that to get us started. If we can get them to even want to come to Harper Valley and try things out, that might be exactly what it takes to help convince them that the majority of us are just people."

"The majority of us," Wil echoed. "But not all. I want peace and for things to smooth over, but I'm not just here for myself or us. I have to represent the town and come to an arrangement that will make them, and by extension Cloverton, happy. Hell, Cloverton probably won't be happy I went off without messaging them, but it felt like an emergency."

"How much longer would your people have been stuck here waiting if you hadn't acted fast?" Syl asked. He then added, "Not that Bram here seems to mind. All you can eat and drink, and he even found love!"

"Shut up, Syl," said Bram, turning red again. He pointed at the faun, a playful grin taking over. "Just because you were right doesn't mean I'll ever forgive you for it."

Wil and Darlene traded confused looks. Seeing it, Syl shook his head and told them, "Long story, nothing you need to worry about right now. When Bram first got here, I was responsible for helping set up your people with a place to stay and making sure they were fine after being questioned. I gave a few pointers for getting along. Anyway. Seriously now, what do you think your people will want you to argue for?"

Rather than guess, Wil took a moment to think about it. He blew out a breath. "Other than getting their people back, at bare minimum I can see them wanting to make sure that everything underneath the forest is their territory, to be respected. If there is to be trade, they're probably going to want reassurances that fae products won't replace our own if the fae want to use Harper Valley to get to other parts of Calipan.

"Our best bet would be to try to ensure that trades are made directly with us, and we then sell or trade for a profit." Wil made a face. "You know me, I don't have a head for business or anything like that. This is the only thing I can think of. Ensure that Harper Valley will come out on top no matter what I decide, and maybe we can sell it to Sinclair and Cloverton."

They all took some time to think about it. Wil hated how ill-prepared he felt for this entire thing. The majority of his thoughts on the trip had been about Bram and the other prisoners, and getting them back home. That much was all but guaranteed, and now there was so much more at stake.

"We'll figure it out," Wil said after a brief silence. "But for now, why don't you show me around a bit more? We'll work more on this later, maybe at dinner. For now, my brain's fried and I could use some time to just clear my head. That okay with everyone?"

A chorus of agreement sounded.

Syl pushed away from the wall. "I could use some air as well. Would the rest of you mind if just Wil and I went out for a bit?"

No one minded.

The two made a stop in the common room to retrieve Wil's staff, and together they descended the spiral stairs on the edges of the tree and headed for the nearest portal. Wil wondered if Syl had something he wanted to talk about, but he was also content to just get out for a bit and think.

CHAPTER 17

King of the Rings

At no point did Oakheart Spiral ever become less magical to Wil. The fact that they were walking around the inside of a tree that housed a vertical city blew his mind. Every time Syl touched the wooden walls to open a way through was just as exciting as the first time. Wil resolved that when he returned home, he would make his house more magical and wondrous to anyone stopping by. Just about everything here inspired him.

The portals, on the other hand, he didn't care for.

"Is there any way to make that less horrifying?" Wil asked with a shudder as they arrived at the same guarded nook that had brought them to the council chambers. He didn't enjoy being snapped like a rubber band.

"Well, next time you could jump off a branch and float down," said Syl with a sly smile. "It might take a while, but it would give you plenty of time to think about what convenience is worth to you."

They went back up to the first floor and Wil couldn't help but gasp again at the wide, open space and the drizzle of rain over a bunch of market stalls a hundred yards away. An ogre taller than the stall he worked at threw a covering over the front before disappearing inside. The trio of elves were still dancing, but this time to a newer, more playful song. Their heads and hips bobbed about unnaturally as they moved. The lead elf wore only a wrap around his waist and was slimmer than any human Wil had ever seen, but for the elf, it seemed to work.

"So, where do you want to go?" asked Syl, gesturing around. "I'm happy to show you anything that isn't off-limits."

Wil thought about it for a moment. "You and the others talk up how community-minded you all are. I want to see it for myself. Show me a place where there's a sense of community and fellowship—that isn't a bar, tavern, or other place to get alcohol," he added as the faun's face lit up.

"Okay, that rules out three-quarters of our best options. Let's see . . ." Syl stroked his shaggy chin hair. "Not yet dinnertime and we ate a lot at lunch. After the past week, you probably don't want to see people training to fight. Ooh, I know. You want community, fun, and mutual respect and admiration? You got it." Syl tugged on Wil's sleeve and went off to the side.

Wil followed, gawking as they went. More than a few fae unabashedly stared directly at him. Few, if any, felt hostile, but there was some confusion and uneasiness. Wil tried to smile and wave and just generally present as nonthreatening, but there was only so much he could do without time to talk to anyone.

Syl led him through an "outdoor" school filled with everything from pixies to elves, and even an ogre child, sitting in a semi-circle around a woman with skin the color of ash and leaves in her hair. They were separated by a pool of sand with unfamiliar writing etched in it. The teacher waved a hand and the writing changed and some of the children nodded.

Wil wished he could've stayed and observed longer, but Syl was relentless and, as usual, inconsiderate of those with shorter legs. Wil jogged to keep up as they headed for what he assumed was the outer ring of the tree. The big, open center closed up again into hallways, looking more like a living area for families on multiple levels. The only constant was plenty of children.

"Where are we going?" Wil finally asked after fifteen minutes of going through the city. The tree's passage had turned into a tunnel gently sloping underground.

"To a place where children play and people watch and cheer," said Syl. The tunnel dipped one last time before coming back up, a staircase carved into the wood. Daylight shone from the top.

"Whoa," said Wil, stopping at the top and drinking it all in.

The wood spiraled around them as they climbed up and outside of the tree, to a large clearing nestled between three massive roots. Two of them wound around and came to a point together, shaped like a big egg. One root continued into the air and hung over the center of the clearing, about thirty feet up. A series of large wooden rings dangled at various heights, some at the very top and a few just ten feet off the ground. They swayed and spun in the breeze. The rings were colored either green or purple.

A ball flew through a green ring and it turned purple. The crowd, sitting on the two roots along the ground, went wild. The fae had either carved or shaped the tree into something not unlike bleachers, where hundreds of them sat and watched a dozen children play a game on the field in the center.

"What game are they playing?" Wil asked, watching as a hobgoblin threw a small fireball at the ball, launching it away from an elf who had been jumping for it.

A pixie caught it and flapped his little wings. With the weight of the ball, he couldn't fly, but he directed the ball at a lanky ogre boy, who caught them both. The ogre laughed and hurled the ball, pixie and all, up at one of the top rings. The pixie waited until the ball hung suspended in the air, about to drop, then flipped it through one of the highest rings. The ring turned purple.

"King of the Rings, or King's Rings. Rings, if you're fond of brevity." Syl clapped Wil's shoulder. "Exciting, isn't it?"

The pixie plummeted, laughing the entire time. His ogre buddy caught him and spun him around in a victory dance as the other team alternated cheering and good-natured boos and jeers.

"It sure is! What're the rules?" Wil and Syl walked down to one of the bleachers. A lovely, slightly transparent older woman scooched to the side to make room for them. She smiled warmly, though the air around her was cold. Wil smiled back and decided not to ask questions or stare, focusing instead on the game.

"Whoever throws the ball through one of the rings gets that ring for their team," said Syl, pointing as a dwarf chucked the ball through a low-hanging ring and turned it green. "Each level of rings has a certain number of points attached to it. It's easy to score the low-hanging ones, so they're worth fewer points. You get more points the higher you go, and can only score points if you change its color. And if a team manages to turn every ring their color, the round ends and the team who did it gets double points. Otherwise, it's four fifteen-minute rounds, adding up the points they end each quarter with."

"That sounds simple enough," said Wil. He winced as a faun leaped into the air and slammed his head into the ball. The ball bounced off to the side and fell between two people crashing together. A little elf girl lashed out with a vine, wrapping around the ball. She yanked it back and used the momentum to fling it up through a ring on the second level. The vine crumbled into nothing.

"Any other rules?" Wil asked. "It looks like anything goes to get the balls through the rings. Are they in any danger of hurting themselves?"

"Of course they are," Syl scoffed. "Any sport has some danger to it. That's why we always have professional healers on hand. Otherwise, they just try not to hurt each other. If someone acts out, the arbiter will determine whether they broke a rule or not. If they did, the wronged party gets a free throw. And if they make that shot, they get another, so penalties aren't encouraged."

Wil nodded, understanding well enough to appreciate it. "Plus, I imagine if someone did it too blatantly, the other team would gang up on them."

"True. And woe to the one who picks a fight they're unprepared to finish." Syl clapped enthusiastically as that same ogre and pixie combo as before scored another conversion. The field was more purple than green at this point.

"I'm surprised to see so many people out here," said Wil. "It's the middle of the day. So many are watching children play instead of working."

Several people sitting near them looked at him funny, including Syl. "Most of the people here have finished their work for the day. Or haven't started yet, but at this hour most of the people are done. Was Bram right? Do you people spend most of your day working? I thought you were more efficient than that."

Wil flushed. "Well, we're plenty efficient. We just tend to work for a good chunk of the day because there are plenty of things that need doing. We need the money to feed and house ourselves, and then we work longer and harder than that so we can move up in the world and have fun."

"When?" asked Syl. "If you're working all day, when do you have time to have fun? And you're saying food and shelter aren't guaranteed for all? My father used to tell me stories of how big you were and how fast you humans could spread and take over an area. Seemed like you were constantly branching out just to have more places for families to live, he said."

"Yes," said Wil, shrinking. "That's true. We stay with family until we have enough money to rent or buy our own place, and often that means moving somewhere else if there's not enough room, or if the homes are too expensive."

"Too expensive? What could be so expensive about it? It's a place to live. Everyone needs it. Wait a minute." Realization hit Syl. His tone turned incredulous. "Are you saying you'll move to a faraway place because a nearby empty house costs too much money?"

"Well, not me," said Wil. "I'm paid well and have my own house, thanks to being a wizard. But a bunch of friends of mine were bandits for a while because they couldn't afford to live anywhere. We're helping them out and finding them a place in Harper Valley."

An uncomfortable silence fell between the two of them. Wil tried to focus on the game and the children running across the field, passing the ball back and forth, or going for an impressive throw. It made for something to focus his eyes on while he tried to ignore Syl's inscrutable stare, boring right into him.

"I guess we really are different," said Syl, sighing. "We have trade and commerce, just the same as you. But no one goes hungry or cold unless they break the rules of hospitality. Everything about you humans seems so damned . . . competitive. Like you're all fighting to get as much as you can, everyone else be damned."

"And it isn't like that here?" Wil dared to ask. "I've never dealt with the fae before this whole mess, but my people had stories about how cruel and vengeful you could be, and how much some of your people treat backstabbing like a game."

Syl inclined his head in acknowledgment. "Yes, there's plenty about us that's not perfect. But no one starves, and we don't work all day unless we run our own business. And we keep our promises, good and bad."

After another short silence, Wil sighed and said, "I can't pretend my people aren't awful in a lot of ways. Not all of us think that way. I think we can find common ground, and maybe learn from each other. I like how you take care of each other, but I also like the competition and working hard. I agree no one should be without food or a home, though. That's a change I'd make if I could."

"Hmm. You at least seem capable of change, Wizard," said Syl, smiling once more. "But do you think the rest of your people are ready for it? What about your town, Harper Valley? Think they're ready for change?"

"I don't know," said Wil with complete honesty. "I'd like to think they could, but it all depends on how we present it. And I'm going to try my absolute hardest to be there to make it happen and see it through smoothly. And I'd like to do that together. I think we could be great friends, humans and fae."

"I hope so," said Syl. "I trust you. It's the rest of your people I'm worried about. But you make me want to give them a chance, at least."

It was enough for now. Tomorrow they'd face each other in the council chamber, and the discussions would begin in earnest. They'd be on the same page, but not on the same side. For today at least, they could just be a faun and a human, watching children play King's Rings. Wil cheered for them all, enjoying the rare moment when he could afford to root for everyone equally.

CHAPTER 18

Roundtable

The council met the next day in the late morning. As much as Wil would've preferred Darlene's and Bram's presence and advice, now that the talks were to begin, Wil had to go it alone. Syl, although now a friend, was still on the other side of the table, so to speak. The actual table they sat at was round and large enough to fit them all without any risk of bumping elbows. Syl sat on the other side of Arabella, to Wil's left. Timothy Twist and Grimnar were on his right.

Skalet was nowhere to be seen, and the grand council room felt all the emptier with his absence.

Coming down to the meeting with him, Syl had been nervous. There had been none of his cocky, easygoing attitude. He was a prince, representing his land on behalf of his father now. Wil wondered if that had something to do with it.

The air was different in the council room today, more charged and serious. When Wil had arrived, there had been polite greetings and they'd all sat in silence and waited for the last person, Timothy Twist, to arrive. Even when the leader of the Wee Folk showed up, there had been only a murmur. Wil wasn't willing to be the one to break the tension, so at first he just sat back and observed.

Looking around, he noticed Grimnar glaring at him, likely trying to intimidate him. Wil knew the ogre could probably destroy him if he was caught off guard, but not while Wil had Obligation on him. It was easy to write Grimnar off as nothing but a hiccup, a squeaky wheel he'd need to deal with eventually. But the ogre was inherently oppositional. That made him a known quantity.

Timothy Twist was drumming his fingers together, looking somewhere over Wil's shoulder with a thoughtful expression. Somehow, he managed to not look ridiculous despite being half the size of a man and dressed like a dandy.

Sitting sideways in her chair, Arabella was watching Wil with an intensity that matched Grimnar's, but with a decidedly different tone. He tried not to look directly at her, keeping Darlene's warnings in mind, but her presence was still distracting. Worse, he could smell a scent he imagined must be hers, inviting him to lean a little closer.

Wil found himself more annoyed that he had to work to fight off any attraction than he was about her trying to affect him. He could no more blame Arabella for what she was than he could a fox for entering a henhouse. Still, it gave him a chance to put his mind magic skills to use. He'd been worried about getting rusty.

It wasn't unlike wrapping himself in a wet towel to help shield against the smoke and flames of a house fire. Wil drew a line in his mind between himself and Arabella and closed the borders. The urgency faded but didn't disappear entirely, like music heard from the other side of a wall. Without it, Arabella was beautiful but not irresistible.

"If you were doing that on purpose," Wil whispered just loud enough for her to hear, "that was rude."

Arabella frowned. Rather than respond to him, she addressed the table. "I think at this point we can assume that Skalet has no interest in being here for today's talk. Let's move on without him. Are there any opposed?"

No one was.

"Wonderful. Then as today's lead, I bring this council meeting to order." Arabella didn't sound bored anymore. "Our first order of business is the broken leyline. What do you, Wilbur McKenzie, intend on doing about it?"

Wil blinked. He looked around, finding all eyes on him. Syl appeared curious about the answer. The faun shrugged, as if to say Wil was on his own.

"Well," Wil said, "what do you expect to be done about it?"

The elf leaned over the table until he had no choice but to look at her. Her sharp-featured face frowned, disappointed in him.

"Is that nothing, then? You rip open a tear between worlds and fundamentally alter the land itself, and you shrug and expect us to lead you in how to clean up your mess?"

"I thought we were going to discuss opening up trade and relations," said Wil, looking around. "You said you were up for it."

"It's a good question, Wizard," said Timothy Twist, drumming his fingers on the solid wood table. "Your actions have put us in a bind and entwined you in our destinies. If peace happens, it'll be because you made it happen. If war comes, then every single death that occurs will be your responsibility. What do you intend to do?"

They'd blindsided him. Even now he felt the weight of Obligation, mostly in his favor at the moment, about to shift. They had a point. Nothing especially bad had happened yet, but he was in their world and affecting their people, and so this mattered. And if he took responsibility for his actions, he could be crushed by it if the worst happened.

"Well," said Wil, wetting his lips, "I intend on using it to usher in a new era of peace and understanding. If that isn't possible, then I will do everything in my power to find a way to close the door for good." The weight of his declaration increased with every word. Wil stood poised on a precipice. "I don't know how. To my knowledge, this has never happened before. But if I found a way to break it, then perhaps I can find a way to fix it."

The trick was to talk big but commit to nothing. It went against everything he stood for, but promising too much would strangle him.

"Is that acceptable for now?" he asked, looking around the table.

Syl nodded. "It's acceptable," he said.

Grimnar shook his head. "No."

Timothy Twist considered him. "I reckon that's enough for now. Acceptable."

"Acceptable," Arabella echoed.

The weight eased, a shadow in the back of Wil's mind. Gone, but very much not forgotten.

"We may now proceed," said Arabella. "King Grimnar?"

The ogre leaned forward, looking like he wanted to leap over the table and grab Wil by the throat. Wil had left his staff behind, not wanting to bring what was now obviously a powerful weapon in his hands to a negotiation. Now, he wished he had it.

"If Faerie were to open up trade with the humans and allow for some level of open borders, what would Calipan's stance be on crime and punishment? *When* you humans break our laws and try to hurt us, how much resistance will there be to our sovereign justice?"

Wil swallowed. Maybe he wasn't as prepared for this as he'd hoped. Steepling his fingers, he took a long, deep breath. Mostly just to buy himself some time and not freeze as he worked his brain over for every last bit of history and politics he could remember.

"Standard Calipan protocol has always been to handle punishments ourselves," Wil recited, remembering the lesson. "Faerie justice was seen as too unpredictable and too personal to be something we've ever been comfortable with. Sleeping for a decade or two or being turned into a small animal is inhumane."

"And yet torture and slavery are good?" Grimnar retorted. "The human idea of punishment is to exploit the transgressor for labor or to cage them. Our punishments fit the crime."

"I'm not defending my country's criminal justice system," said Wil, who could probably go on for hours on the subject. "Just stating how it is. My opinions over whether the punishments are good or not are irrelevant. Harper Valley is likely where matters of justice would take place."

"And is it set up to handle conflicts of this nature?" Syl asked. He, at least, sounded like he genuinely wanted to know and wasn't ganging up on Wil.

"Generally, yes," said Wil, thinking of the Harper Valley courthouse and how they only had a couple of judges who handled everything from criminal cases to personal rivalries. "We have arbiters who handle disputes and who I believe would be up to the task of judging individuals for crimes against Faerie if they occur.

"And if the situations were reversed," Wil added, "if fae came around and terrorized my people again and were caught, we would turn them back over to you. We might compile a list of Faerie citizens not allowed in our world, under threat of imprisonment or death. We'd expect you to do the same with human citizens."

At least now it sounded like proper negotiations. Grimnar considered it with a grimace.

"We each take care of our own problems. Acceptable for now."

Timothy Twist stood up in his chair. It made him look almost like a child misbehaving. "My problem is how different we are. As we've seen recently, some of my people were a tad bit overzealous with their pranks, and your people responded in kind. Now, I know the scale's balanced, but the fear has yet to go away. What's to stop it from happening again the next time there's a problem?

"Talking about criminal justice is fine and dandy, but what about preventing that from even happening? And what about preventing unwanted incursions into our territory? We've scouted you out. We got our tat, and now your country will want its share of tit. Which some might say is fair, but I don't think King Grimnar would tolerate it. Not with your track record."

Wil nodded in understanding. "I can't speak on behalf of my military, only my town." And that was the problem, he realized. He should've waited for Cloverton, but leaving had seemed so pressing, and Wil still believed there was a good reason he left, other than just guilt. This was something he could do, if only to get it started and primed to go in the direction he wanted.

"However . . . ," he said slowly, feeling the answer come to him. He knew he should think it through more, maybe ask Darlene and Bram what they thought, but they weren't the town representatives. They weren't the people who could handle this. Wil could, and the only idea he had was as bold as it was tricky.

"I have a different solution," he said finally, looking around the table. "You have all expressed serious doubts as to Calipan's commitment to dealing fairly, and I can't fault you for any of it. I'd be just as skeptical as all of you. I can't undo centuries of bad blood, but I can try to help us all move forward. You need proof? I can give you proof.

"I'm not asking you to just open up trade and borders immediately. You want a firsthand look at the Calipan of this century? I'm inviting this council to send representatives of their own to come back with me to Harper Valley. Each of you can bring a small number of people representing your faction, and we'll show you our hospitality and let you judge for yourselves whether we've changed enough to be worth dealing with.

"In fact," Wil added, heart pounding in his head, "if the council isn't satisfied and wants to retreat into Faerie for good, I personally promise to find a way to heal the leyline and seal the rift."

All around the table, council members gasped as Wil's promise took root. Obligation the size of a mountain, an entire world, settled over him. It could drop and destroy him if he ever intentionally broke his oath. He settled back into his seat.

"Wil," said Syl, breaking the silence that took over. "Are you insane?"

"I might be," said Wil with a shrug. "But you're right. The rift is my fault, so I'll handle it. One way or another."

"Well," Syl said, looking around in a bit of a daze. "I find that prospect agreeable. How about the rest of you?"

Arabella stared at Wil. Dimly, he could still feel her allure and intention in the back of his mind, but it seemed less an effect and more earnest now.

"You know," she said, "I've always wanted to see the world we left behind. The Fair Folk find this agreeable."

Timothy Twist sat back down, clapping enthusiastically. "Now *that's* showing some commitment. How could I ever refuse such earnestness? The Wee Folk will send a group and see what you've got to show us."

To everyone's surprise, Grimnar laughed. "You would willingly give my scouts a chance to appraise your defenses? Agreed, foolish human."

Wil breathed out a sigh of relief. "Then I think now it's just discussing how to make it happen and who, right?"

He couldn't make the huge decisions on his own, but this would give him a chance to send the problem up to Cloverton finally and use what he'd learned here to help out someone who *could* negotiate on behalf of the country. Meanwhile, this was the best he could think of for Harper Valley. They needed a chance to see that the fae weren't the capricious monsters people thought they were.

Partially because of him. Wil winced. Well, if things went sour, he could just fulfill his side of the promise and close the rift. Do something impossible a second time. No problem.

CHAPTER 19

Are You Crazy?

The rest of the meeting lasted another couple of hours after that, but they were no longer squabbling over potential plans. They were squabbling over one specific plan and how to make it work for everyone involved. And for that, Wil mostly had to sit back and answer questions about the town and the temperament of the people involved.

Part of him worried he was giving more information than necessary or safe, but his gut told him this was an honest deal. As honest as any deal got, at least. They needed to see for themselves that humans were better than they had been, and it was up to Wil to make them believe that.

Just as it would be his job to make the people of Harper Valley believe that the fae weren't out to get them. That would be harder.

Finally, when the meeting ended, Syl stayed behind with Wil. As soon as he was sure no one else was around, he said, "That was some bold thinking to get them to go along with everything, but . . . *are you crazy?*"

Wil stood up and smiled, stretching out his back. "Thinking any of this will work is probably crazy, but if I didn't believe in it, then I couldn't do it, you know? That's kind of how magic is, too, for me."

Syl bleated in frustration. "I'm talking about making a promise to close the rift if things go wrong! How exactly do you plan on doing that?"

"Hopefully, I won't need to," said Wil, laughing at Syl's growing distress. "Let me worry about that, Your Highness. The main part of the plan is still showing you all Harper Valley and seeing what happens. We can go from there and renegotiate, if need be. And if all of that fails . . . I'll figure it out. If I changed the leyline once, I can do it again. Probably."

The faun shook his head. "You're unbelievable, Wizard. You've got some balls on you. I like it."

"Thanks, Syl," said Wil. "I'm glad you like my balls." They kept a straight face for only a few more seconds before the dumb joke cut through the strain of the day and unmade them. They left the council chambers still laughing.

Bram, Darlene, old Gilbert, and Joey Jackson sat around the table playing cards. Joey was one of the few people of Harper Valley who didn't have anywhere to stay. He'd been a lawyer once, before he cracked and gave up on his professional life. Here in Faerie, he'd been cleaned up and looked better than Wil could ever remember seeing him.

"Who's winning?" he asked, sitting down beside Darlene.

"Joey is," Bram grumbled, eyeing the middle-aged man with distaste. "Saw us playing and just came up and asked what the rules were. Then he hustled us."

"I sure did," said Joey. He smirked and plopped down a couple of raspberries on a plate in the center. "Raise." The rest of them threw their cards down on the table. Joey cackled and raked the pile of small fruits over onto his plate.

"Where did you even get cards?" Syl asked. "We have cards but they don't look anything like that."

"I always have a deck on me," said Joey. "Never leave home without them."

"But Joey," said old Gilbert with the smile of someone assisting with a joke, "you ain't got a home."

"Well, then, it's a good thing I've still got my cards, now, isn't it?"

"You have my staff?" Wil asked, looking around.

"Yes, we still have your staff," said Darlene with a roll of her eyes. "You're not getting insecure without it, are you?"

"No," Wil lied, "I just put a lot of effort into making it, and I just want to know it's safe."

Bram jerked a thumb at the apartment behind him, where Gallath stood and watched their game with his usual stoic grace. Out of all the ogres Wil had seen since coming to Faerie, he alone seemed to be quiet and still. Seeing Wil looking at him, Gallath nodded cordially at him, one hand kept on his spear as he stood at attention.

"Thanks," said Wil, standing up.

"Where's Syl?" Darlene asked, as she and Bram stood up, ending the game.

Wil bit back a smile. "He said something about needing a stiff drink after the session today and my insanity."

Darlene was serious in an instant. "Your insanity? What happened in today's talks?"

Wil shrugged and said, "If you want to find out, maybe you should join us for drinks. That won't be a problem, will it, Gallath? Just taking Bram. The rest of the prisoners will be here safe and sound under your guard."

The ogre considered it. "I really shouldn't," he said, in a deep and smooth voice that reminded Wil of the rumble of machinery. "My instructions are to keep the captives in here unless out with an escort."

"I'll escort him," said Wil. "And Syl might be there too. Surely that's gotta count for something."

Bram cleared his throat. "I promise you, I will not try to escape. And if I do, you can chase me down."

Gallath shrugged and leaned back against the wall. "Bring me back a prize."

It was almost funny how unsuitable Oakheart Spiral was for most humans. Syl had taught Wil how to open the walls of the tree where doors would go, a simple spell that just required the briefest touch of magic and intent to command. The fae were inherently magical, just like wizards. This meant the humans didn't need a guard, given that they couldn't leave their prison other than by jumping off the balcony.

"So how did the meeting go?" Bram asked as they descended the stairs. The nearest kitchen level was ten floors beneath them, and weeks of going up and down stairs had done the giant some good, slimming down his stomach and making his legs even bulkier. "Anything we should be worried about?"

"That . . . depends," said Wil, keeping a steady downward spiral going. "I think I managed it well, but Syl thought it was insane."

"Oh, no," Darlene groaned. "What did you do, Wil?"

He told them, and by the time they reached the kitchen level, they, too, needed a drink.

"Are you crazy?" Darlene asked as they left the stairs, panting slightly from the exertion. "You promised that if they don't want to deal with humans you'll close the door behind them? You said that ripping open that leyline was one of the most draining things you'd ever done."

"Yeah," Wil confirmed. "But a lot was going on at the time. I don't need to have a solution ready, just to work toward one in case the worst happens. I'll keep at it until I find one."

"And if the worst really happens and Cloverton decides it's best if we invade?" Bram challenged. "You think they're going to sit by and let you close the door on them?"

It wasn't as if Wil hadn't thought of that. "You know," he said, "there's a saying I heard once. Worrying means you suffer twice."

Darlene shot him a withering look and walked through the open arches, where the scent of smoky meats wafted out.

"What?" Wil asked.

Bram shook his head, chuckling. "You're getting bold and reckless in your old age, Wil. Ever since stopping the storm, you seem to keep throwing yourself into things that could get you killed. What's going on?"

"I don't know what you mean," said Wil. At Bram's raised eyebrow, he gave in. "Look, it's not like I'm intentionally trying to do dangerous things. I'm just trying to find the best possible way to solve my problems, even if it makes for bigger problems later. When I first came back to Harper Valley, I had just graduated and I went from being powerful and visible to being just Wilbur again.

"And because of it, I sort of held myself back. I didn't want to scare anyone or seem like the kind of jerk-ass wizard who acts like he owns whatever room he's in. Believe me, there's *so* many of them."

Wil took a breath, watching Darlene choose a table and hold up three fingers to the nymph who came by for her order. "And now I can't keep making myself fit into a box. Wizards aren't safe or cuddly, no matter how much I try to be both. We're dangerous, and our lives are dangerous. And being assigned to my hometown doesn't change that."

Bram thought about it for a long time. "I think you're wrong," he said finally. "You seem safe to me, and according to Darlene, you like cuddling more than she does. You look a little too boney to be good at it, but no accounting for taste."

Wil laughed and punched Bram in the shoulder. "At least we're not hiding who we're seeing, lover boy. Which of the fae ensnared your senses while you've been here? Maybe we can get her to come along with all of the envoys."

Every so often Bram tried to shrink or skulk like he was a normal-sized person, and every time, it made Wil want to burst out laughing. With the way his head sank below two massive shoulders, Bram resembled nothing so much as a giant, now bearded, turtle.

"I don't know if that's possible, but we'll see," he said. "Let's go before Darlene gets annoyed."

Darlene had drinks and fried potato slices on a plate waiting for them at a table in the corner. She eyed Wil, not breaking her gaze even when she took a long chug of her drink.

"So, what happens if you're unable to fix the leyline and close the rift?" she asked.

As tired as he was, Wil almost responded with some lighthearted snark but thought better of it. Darlene didn't like being helpless, and that's what she was, having to wait behind for him like this.

"Then all the bad things we've been talking about as a possibility could happen," Wil said. "With the addition of me dying horribly, or losing my magic, or becoming a slave to the fae. Based on how badly my oath is broken, that is." He took a sip of his drink and nearly made a face. The fae loved their drinks too sweet.

"You know that's not preferable, right?" Bram drained half his glass in one go. "We kind of count on you and don't want anything bad to happen to you."

"Then it behooves you both to help me make sure we pull this off," Wil said, setting his drink back down. "I can't do this alone, and we're going to need all of us to make this work. The details are light so far, but what we do have is, they're going to spend a month or two in Harper Valley, possibly until spring."

Darlene sighed and rubbed her eyes. "How do you plan on selling this to Sinclair and the rest of town? Before we left, they were really not happy with the fae. And now you plan on bringing dozens of high-ranking fae home, among a bunch of angry farmers who feel threatened? What about Cloverton? What's going to convince *them* to play nice and not just go in, guns blazing?"

Syl and Arabella had come upon that answer. "Faricite," said Wil. "It's a crystal made of concentrated magic, incredibly useful for enchanting and powering enchanted objects. It can be created by wizards, but it takes a lot of effort and time. Here, it grows naturally anywhere a lot of magic happens. Such as, you know, the capital."

"And what's going to stop Cloverton from getting greedy and taking as much of it as they can?" Darlene didn't sound accusatory or smug, just tired. Wil could relate.

"Because if they tried, the fae have the means to destroy them en masse and make any victory for Cloverton a hollow one." Wil ate a potato slice, making an appreciative sound. "This doesn't seem like fae food," he said.

"It's not," Bram chirped. "I got them to start making it, along with a few other dishes. They've been showing me their goods, and I've been showing them mine."

"Oh my." Darlene couldn't stop herself. Bram's face darkened immediately.

"Not like that! I mean—" he sputtered.

Wil shook his head fondly. Talks would resume the next day, but he figured he'd bought himself some time with friends. Getting this plan to work would be difficult, and there were still a million things left to do to make it work, but they were together again, and it could wait. Tomorrow.

CHAPTER 20

Party Animal

Although talks had gone better than Wil had expected, a party in their honor (sort of), surprised him. A couple hundred fae, about half of them important, milled around with drinks and snacks as a few bands played on opposite ends of the giant ballroom.

As Wil discovered, one level of Oakheart Spiral was dedicated almost entirely to parties, celebrations, festivals, and the closest the fae got to religious rituals, depending on their race. The colossal room they were in now was illuminated by more of that glowing moss along the walls, as well as hundreds of glowing wisps in the air, constantly moving and making the shadows and colors shift as they went.

"So why should I go and risk my life among the humans?" a gnome with a particularly curly black mustache asked Wil, sipping on wine. His name was Frahnk, a pronunciation that was just different enough to throw the wizard off.

"You wouldn't be risking your life," said Wil, more or less truthfully. "Once we bring your captives home and we free ours, it'll be like a clean slate."

"Feh!" the gnome laughed derisively.

"I mean it!" said Wil, putting on his best friendly smile. "Besides, Prince Sylano told me you were the gnome to speak to when it came to business. He said there's no one here more adept at sniffing out gold and silver than you, and that you'd be open to a good proposition."

"Hrm." Frahnk stroked his short beard. "He spoke correctly. What do you have for me, Wizard?"

Wil took a sip of wine and made a face. Too sweet, much too sweet. "Well, word is, your family are the best miners and metalworkers in Faerie. Especially good with jewelry, but you've got access to some good mines. We humans have tools now that can make mining easier and safer."

"Human machines," said Frahnk, making a face. "Bah."

"Human machines have come a long way," said Wil seriously. "They aren't the rinky-dink things that barely worked the last time our people were in contact. They could make your life easier. And even if you didn't want that, your gold and jewelry would go far in Calipan."

All around the party, Bram, Darlene, Syl, and Arabella were having similar conversations with prominent fae, ones whose support could make or break formal treaties and relationships with the humans. People who would, they hoped, also be the ones most likely to be charmed by a trip to a foreign world and dealing with humans.

"I'm not a greedy gnome," said Frahnk, with the air of someone who wasn't lying so much as very much mistaken. "I don't want or need that much. I love my work and get to share it with people who appreciate it. That's enough for me." He started to turn away, but Wil leaped on his chance.

"Then why not share that work with an entire large country? Princess Arabella showed me a necklace you made. I promise you that my people have never seen such craftwork and would trip over themselves to be the first to have some of their own."

Frahnk paused, and Wil knew he had him. "Think about it," he pressed. "Frahnk and Sons' jewelry will be synonymous with quality Faerie goods. A lot of people are scoffing at the trip, but you know they're secretly making plans. Everyone wants to be the first one to benefit from it."

"You know," the gnome said, "I think you might be onto something. My boy could use some broadening of his horizons. And if it ends up benefiting both of us, well, that's just dandy, now isn't it? You're on, Wizard. I'll let him know right now."

"Excellent. I'm glad to have spoken with you, Frahnk," said Wil. It had been so hard to talk to people and shake hands all night without thanking them for their time. He'd almost done it once when they were practicing what to say, and Syl had clapped his hand over Wil's mouth before he could fall under Obligation.

"Likewise, Wizard." Frahnk bowed his head respectfully and stepped away.

Wil breathed a sigh of relief. He'd been at this for about an hour, and he was getting tired. It wasn't enough to just say that they'd bring a party to Harper Valley and show them around. They needed volunteers—normal, if influential, fae. Frahnk had to have been the twelfth person Wil had spoken to, and he was ready for a break.

He wasn't alone. Across the room he spotted Darlene. She had just finished talking to a distinguished-looking elf about the same height as her. The elf raised her hand to his lips and kissed the back of it. Darlene pretended to laugh, and then they parted. She met Wil's eyes and motioned with her head toward the balcony.

Wil met her there, stepping outside the chatter and overlapping music, where it was mercifully quiet. A few other people were on the balcony, staring up into a sea of stars or just enjoying the evening. They went over to the side and leaned up against a polished wooden railing.

"Any luck?" Wil asked.

"Tons," said Darlene. "Or at least tons of fae who want to flirt with me. Whatever works, right?"

"Should I be jealous?" Wil asked playfully.

"I don't know," Darlene retorted, "should you? You seem to be pretty comfortable with that bratty princess. Should I be worried?"

"Absolutely not," said Wil, wrapping an arm around Darlene and pulling her in close. "I have room in my heart for both of you."

Darlene laughed and pretended to struggle to get away before she settled in and rested her head on his shoulder. The tips of her spiky hair tickled his neck. "You're lucky I like you."

"Very."

They stood in silence for a while, just enjoying each other's company and the break from working. It may have been a party, but fun was off the table for them, save for what time they could get together.

"Did you see Syl working earlier?" Wil asked after a few minutes. "He's probably doing more than either of us can, but I think us being there helps."

"He's really good at switching from being a flaky clown to sharp and convincing," Darlene agreed. "You guys have done a really good job making it all happen. I'm still a bit worried about Mayor Sinclair and the rest of Harper Valley, but if we can manage this in Faerie, surely we can do it at home too."

"I think we can," said Wil honestly. "It's just a question of finding problems ahead of time and smoothing them over. The fact that we'll have a couple of days to prepare people and get them used to the idea, and that we have the captives to bring home, will help. Them saying how good they had it should smooth things over. Especially with the gifts they'll be bringing along."

That had been Arabella's idea, funnily enough, to help convince the humans that it was a misunderstanding by loading up Pearl and old Gilbert and the Benton kids with gold and little magical baubles and toys. Just enough to be an apology nobody could deny.

"The only things that worry me still are the ogre assassins," said Darlene, breaking away from him. "We never found out who hired them. What if they try to ruin things?"

That had been bothering Wil a little, too, but with things being so busy, it was hard to spare a second thought toward the failed assassination attempt.

"If they try again, I'll deal with them," he said with a shrug. "After Grimnar, I'm not really worried about much of anything. I'm strong enough on my own, and with my staff I'm a force of nature. Literally."

"But you don't have your staff now," said Darlene. "And we're out in the open, away from safety."

A rough, growling voice from above them said, "That's just what I was thinking."

Wil looked up to see a familiar six-legged wildcat clinging to the side of the tree. Isom's snaggletoothed grin was triumphant, and Wil had just time to register that he was about to be attacked, again, before the wampus cat pounced.

Wil barely had time to push Darlene to the side and raise a shining silver shield before Isom crashed into him and sent him to the ground hard. He hit his head and the world wavered for a second. The cat probably weighed as much as Bram, but it was all lean muscle and killing power.

The nearest bystander let out a scream. "Wampus cat!" They took off running back inside to the party. Isom snapped his jaws, trying to get over the lip of the shield to get at Wil's face. His teeth caught on the magical energy blocking them, and Wil did his best to keep pouring power into it.

"Wil!" Darlene cried. He didn't have his staff, and she didn't have her iron bar. They were caught off guard, right where it was supposed to be safe.

Rather than being afraid, Wil becoming angry. "Knock . . . it . . . *off*!"

Even without his staff, the magic in the air came to him now as if it had been waiting. The land itself had resisted him when he first came into Faerie, and now it answered and delivered when he asked. It took almost no effort at all to throw force at the wampus cat, sending him crashing against the side of the tree.

Wil took that opportunity to scramble to his feet while Isom did the same. Darlene stood between them, frozen as Isom's one vivid green eye darted between the two of them and he let out an unsettling purr.

"Just you and me, Isom," said Wil. "Let's settle this."

The wampus cat looked at the door leading back to the party. Armed ogre and troll guards came charging in. Wil held up a hand and pushed with a bit of force, just enough to slow them to a stop. They kept their hands on their weapons and waited.

"That is agreeable, Wizard," Isom purred. "Keep them away and your woman is safe."

"Agreed. Darlene, get out of here."

"But—"

"I'll be fine, trust me." Wil shot her a pleading look. Finally, Darlene nodded and ran between the two combatants, over to where the guards were. The balcony was now clear, and a decently large arena for them to fight in.

Once it was just the two of them, Wil and Isom circled, neither one willing to crack and make the first move.

"You know, I'd nearly forgotten about you," said Wil. "I figured you'd be too cowardly to try anything here in Oakheart Spiral."

Isom laughed, a rough, grinding sound like a yowl. "You hid well for a while, spent time in places where I could not go, and you call *me* a coward? You will be the sweetest meal I've ever eaten."

"Eat this," said Wil. The power he'd been gathering coalesced into a greenish ball of energy, flickering wildly in intensity. He flung it at the floor in front of Isom, where it detonated wildly, throwing the cat back. It hadn't worked against the Nullbear, but the wampus cat had no such protections.

Wil didn't wait to give Isom a chance to recover. He threw another, and another, ball of energy. Each time, he threw it close enough only to fling Isom away from it without actually hurting him much. Without his staff, the effort dragged on Wil's strength. It was not a spell he had occasion to use often.

Darlene cheered and the guards joined her, apparently not too stoic to enjoy a free show.

Isom was flung from spot to spot, yowling in pain. When Wil paused, another green exploding ball of energy in his hand, Isom charged him. Wil flung it right at his face, but Isom blinked out of existence. Wil felt, more than heard, the cat land behind him, and he threw himself to the side just as Isom went for his legs.

Wil rolled once and came back to his feet with a gentle magical push against the floor. Isom's razor-sharp claws were extended, buried into the wood as he turned his head around. Wil threw raw force at the cat, slamming him up against the railing and over. Isom scrambled to keep from plummeting to the ground below.

"Why do you keep coming after me?" Wil demanded, staying at the ready. "You have to know you can't beat me."

"You can't survive every time," Isom purred, seemingly unbothered by his predicament. "I only need to get lucky once, and then you're dinner."

Wil groaned. "Seriously, this is getting old."

Isom pulled himself over and sat down on the ground. Despite how ready he was for it, no attack came. The wampus cat cocked his head to the side. "You're trickier than the others. They weren't as strong as you. Human magic was supposed to be weak."

"It was. In the past. We've had plenty of time to refine our art and get stronger," said Wil. He didn't mention that Faerie made him stronger too. "I don't know how long ago it was you ate those other wizards, but you won't find us easy prey anymore. So now I'm asking you to leave and stop bothering me. I'm leaving tomorrow anyway, and then you can go back to eating whatever you can catch around here."

"You're leaving?" Isom almost sounded hurt. "But what about our great rivalry? The big battles, the eventual meal?"

"Not happening," said Wil. "Now, if you promise to go in peace, I'll let you live."

"Very thoughtful of you, Wizard," said the wampus cat. "I decline." He opened his mouth and Wil readied himself for another pounce, but it didn't come. Isom breathed, and a green gas came out of his mouth and enveloped Wil.

It stank to high heaven and make his eyes water. Immediately, Wil began coughing up a storm and backed up. Isom sauntered forward, seemingly immune to his poisoned breath. The edges of Wil's vision grew fuzzy. He blew outward, coughing and choking, but he focused.

A second later, Isom stopped, gagged, and looked tortured. He might not have had to breathe or smell in what he'd created, but he wasn't immune to illusions. Wil flooded the cat's sense of smell with every foul scent and taste he could think of. Outhouse, week-old fish, and the academy locker room after combat class.

Isom turned and jumped over the side of the tree. Wil moved forward, covering his mouth and nose and still he coughed. The wampus cat clung to the side of the tree. He gave Wil one last look before he ran down the trunk. His voice came from behind Wil a second later.

"There's nowhere you can run that I won't follow. You *will* be mine." And then he was gone.

"Are you okay?" Darlene asked, hesitant to step forward. The edges of the gas floated in her direction and she waved it off, coughing.

"Yeah." Wil's voice was hoarse. "That must've been the other spell he devoured. Blinks, some kind of obfuscation glamor, aural illusions, and noxious breath. Gods, who knows what he'd get if he was capable of beating me. Shall we go inside?"

Darlene shook her head at him but hugged him tight. "You're really not afraid of him?"

Wil shook his head. "Honestly, at this point I think he's kind of funny. A bit one-note, but not like we'll have to deal with him after tomorrow."

"Oh, I don't know about that," said Darlene in mock seriousness. "He said he'd follow."

No, Wil couldn't say he was too worried about the wampus cat. Not when he had the power he did, and the creature needed to announce himself. At this point, he recognized that Faerie was as beautiful as it was dangerous, and he didn't take it personally.

"C'mon," said Wil with a chuckle. "Let's go back inside. We have more people we need to schmooze with."

INTERLUDE

Twisted Words

After days of preparation, the fae were finally ready to get moving, and Timothy Twist couldn't have been more excited.

It was like one grand party, seeing everyone off. Of course, Twist and the other fae wouldn't leave until tomorrow, but the party mindset was infectious. All around the edges of Oakheart Spiral they gathered, the four factions of Faerie. Skalet and the Hearthless, of course, didn't give a crap about the excursion and were nowhere to be seen.

Well, that suited Twist just fine. Without the dragon there, there was no one to notice or question his actions. None of the other representatives had any special love or trust for him, but they accepted him as the creature he was. That was the good thing about Faerie, and the bad. After centuries of isolation, they were so . . . predictable.

All four factions mingled freely, but they held separate camps where the representatives and their retinues rested right before they'd leave for Harper Valley. A total of sixty people would be going, a number higher than Twist thought wise for peace. With that many people showing up to town with only a few days' notice, it would probably look like an invasion. If he was lucky.

"What a lovely dress you're wearing, Arabella!" Timothy Twist chirped as he came up to the Fair Folk's enclave. They were all graceful, beautiful, well dressed, and somehow made even wagons of supplies look elegant and refined and not at all like they were simple travelers. They'd *so* fit in a farming town.

"It is lovely, isn't it?" Arabella pretended to barely notice him, but she primped and preened over the compliment. The dress in question was a rich green, like a forest just after dark, and ended fairly high up above her knees. She was nearly twice Twist's height, and it always gave him a pleasant perspective.

"It is, made better by being on you," he said, giving a bow and peeking up through his eyebrows at the bottom of the dress. "But it might be even better *off* you. I think, in the name of experimentation and fashion, we give that a try."

Arabella's lip curled. "You are a disgusting little pig, Twist. Do you want something, or must I shoo you away like the pest you are?"

"Oh, it's nothing much. Just a little concern I thought I'd share with you," he said, doing his best imitation of contrition. "Assuming you want to keep your head, of course. It *is* a pretty head."

The elf's scowl deepened. "Speak," she said, crossing her arms under her chest. Her allure didn't work on Twist the same as it did on others, but it still worked a little. It made it fun and distracting to look at her, and she'd come to expect it and write him off. So predictable.

"Well, some of my people got shot at when they scouted out Harper Valley that first time," he said, wetting his lips.

"You mean when your people tried to burn down the town and cause as much mischief as possible before being harshly rebuked?" Arabella countered.

Twist shrugged. "If you like," he said. "You know my people. We aren't half as sophisticated or civilized as you and yours. Is that a crime?"

"Yes," said Arabella. "I believe the wizard mentioned arson, and a lot of it."

"*Anyway*," said Timothy Twist, hiding his laugh behind a cough, "they overheard some things. The humans are particularly susceptible to the charms of elves and nymphs and . . . , well, anything, really. They're not known for their restraint or discipline."

Arabella raised an eyebrow at him.

Twist shrugged again, giving an innocent smile. "Point is, you might want to turn it down. Maybe not flaunt so much."

The princess's fine-featured face became razor sharp. "I will flaunt as I please, you obnoxious little worm. If the humans cannot resist my innate beauty and grace, then that is their problem. Maybe I'll even take on a couple of them as pets to study and play with."

Timothy Twist let out a long-suffering sigh and shrugged, throwing his arms up in the air. "You'll do what you want, Princess. I just thought somebody ought to look out for this enterprise. Could be I'm overestimating your allure too, so maybe you're right and there's nothing to be nervous about."

Arabella stared daggers at him and pointed away from the tent. Timothy Twist bowed his head graciously and made himself scarce, not bothering to hide his laughter. That was one task down, another few to go.

Next, he made a stop at the Woodlands Association's enclave. Their wagons would be pulled by big, muscled beasts that looked like especially grumpy boars. They grunted and squealed as he got close. Twist held his hands up to calm them, whispering a little charm under his breath. They calmed.

A faun and a dryad looked his way but quickly looked away when he winked at them. They'd been warned about him. He ignored them and went to the wagon in the back, where the gifts to Harper Valley were kept. With a force this large on an actual diplomatic mission, instead of the petty council squabbling, gifts were a necessity.

Timothy Twist had no idea whether the humans would reciprocate or whether they'd just take and take and take, like they always did. He leaned toward taking but was always happy to be surprised. But just the same . . .

He pulled a bottle of the satyr king's finest vintage, a gift to the mayor of the town. Whispering another quick charm to muffle the sound, Twist opened the bottle. Goodness, it smelled fantastic. It was almost a shame to spoil it, but there was always a cost when it came to a good prank. Giggling to himself, he poured a pouch of purple powder into the wine.

Looking around to make sure no one was watching him, tucked away in the back as he was, Twist gently swirled the wine around until the powder dissolved. He'd no more stuck the pouch back into his pocket when the prince of the Woodlands stepped around the corner of the wagon.

Normally, Twist didn't care that much for people more than twice his height, but Syl was alright for the most part. A bit of a fool, but that foolishness led to shenanigans, so how could he not appreciate his company sometimes? No one threw a party like the Woodlands Association.

"Timothy Twist," Sylano said, making him freeze, bottle still in hand. "What do you think you're doing?"

It was true the fae couldn't tell a direct lie, even if they wanted to. They could be wrong, they could be deceptive, but they couldn't lie. Timothy Twist was just fine with that. He smiled, licking his lips.

"Well, Syl, to be honest, I was a bit worried that the wine wouldn't have enough of an impact on our esteemed hosts. So I came over to inspect it personally, if you take my meaning, and make sure it has the effect I'm hoping for. Say, don't you think this vintage is wasted on the humans? Why don't we share this bottle and replace it with something from the kitchens? They'll never know the difference!"

Sylano snatched the bottle out of Twist's hands. "Absolutely not! The purpose of this is to be honorable and give our best, even if the humans are too thick to appreciate it. It's the gesture that matters." The faun lifted the bottle to his face. "Doesn't look like you drank much of it."

Perfect. "You caught me before I could take a drink," said Timothy Twist. "C'mon, brother, let me have just one taste. Don't I deserve it for helping make all of this happen?"

The faun snorted and held out his hand. Twist dropped the cork in it. Syl stuffed it back into the bottle and put it back in the wagon. Looking over his shoulder, he said, "Do I need to make you promise me you won't try to drink it again?"

Timothy Twist rolled his eyes good-naturedly. "Of course not, Syl. I just got a bit bored and wanted to cause a tiny bit of trouble. Nothing catastrophic." Well, not specifically catastrophic. He'd have been perfectly happy with it being a minor disaster, but he couldn't really say, now, could he?

"Does that mean you're finished preparing?" Syl asked, sounding annoyingly responsible for a change. He was even wearing a nice leather vest and some jewelry, like a proper prince and not a vagrant hooligan. Was he growing up? Pity.

"More or less," said Timothy Twist, kicking a rock away. "Just a few last things to settle and then I'll be good for tomorrow's departure."

The faun paused. "And are you causing problems?"

Timothy Twist grinned, showing perfectly straight, white teeth. "Always."

Sylano sighed and waved him off. Timothy Twist bowed and practically danced away, cackling. He'd put a pot of gold on Sylano not suspecting a thing. Not anything worse than his usual antics, at least. That made for two. Only one more planned stop for the day.

Grimnar, unlike the others, was waiting for him. The Ogre Federation had the fewest representatives going to Harper Valley, but that was probably for the better. No one expected the ogre king to ever budge on his desire for war. He was, in fact, the one person Timothy Twist wanted to be predictable.

"Report in!" Grimnar barked at him from inside his tent. The ogre king had a big tankard of ale in front of him and a few guards who were smaller and less imposing than he was. Timothy Twist pretended not to be annoyed by the fool's bad habit of addressing him as an inferior. It was all part of the game.

"Operation Sabotage is a go," said Timothy Twist in a whisper. "I've been at work all morning and half the afternoon. My people have their innocent instructions and don't know what they'll be contributing to. Arabella's easy to play with, and the package was delivered. You've got a handle on the time?"

The agreement had been to change the passage of time while the mission was on. First, a day in Faerie would flow slower, giving the humans a couple of days to prepare. Then it would even out, and pass at the same time, more or less. That was what the rest thought, at least.

"Of course I do," Grimnar grunted. "My men are in place. With Skalet leaving the capital, there'll be nothing to stop us from raising the men and preparing for war."

"Let's not get ahead of ourselves," said Timothy Twist, grabbing the tankard off the table with both hands. He had to struggle to raise it to his mouth to drain half of it in one go. Slamming it back down on the table, Twist let out a belch several times bigger than he was. "Maybe humans have changed."

Grimnar scowled at him. "A person can't change their nature. I'd sooner believe you are more capable of honor than them. My fool of a nephew has his instructions and will be ready to do his part when the time is right. We'll get our chance for revenge."

"And against the wizard himself?" Timothy Twist pressed. "You after a bit of personal satisfaction after he humiliated you in front of everyone?" Oh, what a joy to live dangerously.

The ogre growled. "He won through dirty tricks. I'll not underestimate him again."

"Or give him time to cast spells first, thereby controlling the entire fight?"

"GET OUT!"

Timothy Twist ran out of the tent, ducking the tankard Grimnar had hurled his way. He laughed all the way back to the center of the preparation grounds.

That's where he literally bumped into the man of the hour, crashing into the wizard's knees. He bounced back and landed hard on his back.

"You alright?" Wil said from a mile above him.

Timothy Twist groaned and sat straight up, swaying in place dramatically. "You're not as big as that friend of yours, but ouch."

"Sor— An unfortunate accident," said Wil, catching himself before he apologized.

Damn, it would be good to gain some Obligation and favor over the wizard. Twist took Wil's outstretched hand, and pulled himself to his feet.

"My own fault for running around with everything this busy. How does the day find you, Wizard? Nervous? Hopeful? Pants-on-head terrified?"

"All three," Wil admitted, chuckling. He looked at the dozens of people who had been running around but were now starting to settle as everything came into place. "I was hoping I'd find you, actually. I had a question."

"Oh?" Timothy Twist cocked his head.

"Do you know anything about the ogres sent to kill me?"

The human just blurted it out, with no grace or preamble. It was enough to make the puck shudder in irritation.

"Why would I know about that?" Twist evaded. "You might consider asking Grimnar again. Possibly even using that favor you hold on him to get the name of the employer. He acts like it's out of his hands, but he's a control freak and always knows."

The wizard considered him, his long and kind of horselike face serious for one so young. His short mustache and beard helped, but the boy had yet to grow into them and looked like a young man pretending to be more than he was.

"I don't get you," Wil said, with that same damn lack of elegance.

Timothy Twist grimaced, then hid it behind one of his big grins. "What's there to get? I'm just me. I'm sure others could tell you stories about me, but I wouldn't dream of talking myself up too much in front of such an esteemed guest."

The wizard laughed in derision. "You don't strike me as the humble type. Everyone's stories are to not trust you as far as you could throw me, but you weren't too bad at the council meetings. My gut, however, is telling me a different story. What can you tell me about the attempts on my life?"

"Well, I can't say much for the wampus cat," said Timothy Twist, honest for a change. "They come and go and hunt who they please. The younger ones are full of bloodthirst and will go after anything, but the older, more powerful ones are patient and pick their targets well. You must have a lot to offer!"

Wil shook his head. "I'm not worried about Isom. Tell me what you know about the ogre attack."

Timothy Twist tapped his lip thoughtfully. "And what would such information be worth to you, if I should happen upon it? I could always make some inquiries and see what I can dig up on the attack, if you've got something to offer."

"What if . . . I owe you a medium favor if you tell me something that can help me out?"

Oh, this was too perfect. It had never been so hard to hold back his laughter, but something told Twist that if he laughed, there would be no deal. The wizard already looked unsure of his offer. So Timothy Twist just stuck his hand out. Wil took it and pumped it once, and the magic locked their deal in.

"After I learn more about the attack, I'll come to you with what I know," said Timothy Twist, bowing his head graciously. "Until then, I wish you the best of luck in your upcoming endeavors. You've made it clear it won't be easy to convince your mayor."

Wil grimaced and nodded. "I'll figure it out. I suppose I'll see you in a few days, then. It was nice talking to you, Timothy Twist."

"And to you as well, Wilbur McKenzie!" Twist was completely honest. What a joy it was to find a nice, earnest boy he could lead around by the nose. And then, because he couldn't help himself, he added, "May your mayor get a taste of his own medicine someday."

The smile he got in return was unsure, but then the wizard bowed and turned to where his girlfriend and the giant with the ridiculous beard waited. His friends, near and dear to each other. They'd all see what would happen when one of them died. When the time was right.

Timothy Twist laughed merrily to himself and went back to his enclave for a drink.

CHAPTER 21

Safe Passage

The way back to Harper Valley was a lot shorter. With an agreement reached, Skalet created a doorway from just outside the fae capital to the top of the mountain where Wil had once saved his life.

It was a much more pleasant experience than portals, Wil decided. Going through the rift between worlds the first time had created an odd tingle and an upside-down feeling, followed by flipping around right side up. This time, it was more like walking through a door with a strong gust of wind pressing down from all sides. It lasted just a second, and then they were back in Harper Valley, up in Skalet Peak.

"We're home . . . , right?" Pearl stepped forward, looking at the changed clearing at the top of the mountain. It looked more as if it belonged to Faerie, and maybe it did. The grass was blue, and Calipan didn't grow as many mushrooms, let alone ones the size of trees.

"Yeah, things have gotten a bit weird since you were taken," said Darlene, keeping her tone bright and cheerful. "I kind of like it, don't you?"

Pearl nodded hesitantly.

"This is fascinating. Do you think things will continue like this until the worlds are permanently merged, or do you think it will stabilize soon?" Bram was, naturally, instantly interested.

A chill went down Wil's spine. "I don't know," he said. "That's something that we'll need to find out with time. I think that if it's an ongoing thing, I can probably stop it. Given enough time."

Old Gilbert snorted derisively. "Watch, you've brought us home only for the whole valley to get eaten by the rift." He moved forward in his slow, limping gait, not waiting for the rest of the party to get going.

"Can we go home now, Mr. Wizard?" Reina, one of the Benton twins asked. Her brother, Reino, was a quiet kid, content to observe. She often spoke for them both.

"Almost," said Wil. "Gotta send the signal."

Beside him, Bram rubbed his hands together. They'd discussed Wil's increase in magical power and whether it would be different once they got back. Closing his eyes, Wil extended his senses to the land around him, both intimately familiar and new, alien. There was more magic in the air than before, but not as much as there was in Faerie itself.

Wil drew in the magic of the land and let it channel through him and into his staff. The power was electrifying but gentle, completely in his control. Bigger, stronger, and a little wilder, but it was still his. He took a deep breath and let the illusion craft itself from an image in his mind's eye.

A gargantuan white dove shimmered into existence above them, flapping its wings as it flew straight into the air. It was bigger than Skalet and glowed so it would be visible, even in the middle of the winter day. Once it was high enough, it let out an inescapable musical trill, making the hairs on the back of Wil's neck rise.

The song continued for a minute, with the colossal white dove flying in circles around the mountain. It was the agreed-upon sign that they had returned, safe and sound and with no problems. A symbol of peace and serenity. Even old Gilbert stopped his trek across the clearing to look up and watch.

"There," said Wil, exhaling gently. "They know we're home."

"And you two's little experiment? Was it easier?" Darlene asked. Bram nodded enthusiastically, motioning for Wil to speak.

"I'm stronger now," said Wil. He waved off the illusion. It took about the same strain as his demon illusion used to, despite being larger and aural with a huge range. Something in him had changed, possibly because of spending time in Faerie. "C'mon, let's go home."

Wil, Bram, Darlene, and the rescued captives made their way down the mountain slowly, catching up to Old Gilbert's pace and sticking with him after he ignored their offers of aid. By the time they reached the bottom, where forest met the Patterson farm's farthest field, a welcoming party awaited them.

Half the town had showed up, and Wil suspected more were coming. The parents of the three stolen children charged forward. Wil held back and motioned for the kids to join their parents. They met in a crash of hugs and tears and loud cheers from the sea of people behind them.

"You know," said Darlene, leaning against Wil's shoulder, "the whole trip was worth it, just to be a part of this."

Old Gilbert limped forward, and people Wil thought were his neighbors joined him, helping him along in the light snow. With Joey Jackson having stayed behind in Faerie, the children and Old Gilbert were all that most of the town cared about. Bram looked no worse for wear now that they were back in Harper Valley, though he, too, had thought about staying longer.

"You doing okay, Bram?" Wil asked.

Bram looked back up the mountain, then nodded. "Yeah. Honestly, good for Joey for staying, but I didn't think I could. I have too much to do here to move to an alternate world of magic. Besides, you guys need my reassurances that the fae were compassionate jailers."

Darlene left Wil and hugged Bram. After a second, the giant hugged her back. Then all three of them joined the growing celebration.

"Mr. Wizard!" Patty Patterson cried out, charging him for what was probably going to be an enthusiastic hug. Wil quickly tossed his staff to Bram and caught her, patting her on the back. "Thank you *so* much for bringing my daughter home!"

"It was my pleasure to be of service," said Wil. He gently held her away from him, smiling serenely. "I want you to know, your daughter was never really in danger. She was well treated, well fed, and entertained the entire time she was there."

Patty's face, so full of gratitude and joy, fell. "Then why did they take her?" she asked. "What did they do to her?"

"Nothing," Wil insisted. He raised his voice to get the attention of the crowd. "That's what I need everyone here to know. All of the prisoners were treated kindly and are home safely, except for Joey Jackson, who liked it so much that he chose to stay. The fae don't have to be our enemies. They've asked me to talk to all of you and tell you this: we can be good friends and neighbors."

A hush fell over the crowd. Any goodwill he'd bought by bringing the children back froze with his statement. Mayor Sinclair arrived, pushing his way through the crowd until he stumbled out ahead. He caught himself and adjusted his tie. "What are you saying, Wizard?" he called out.

Wil caught Bram's and Darlene's eyes. They nodded at him, lending a bit of their strength. He injected some power into his voice, enhancing it and broadcasting louder so the entire crowd could hear.

"The last time we encountered the fae, our people fought and drove them off into their own world. Now, they took a few people for questioning and to learn about us. A young child, two preteens, and a couple of older men. And my friend Bram. They used this opportunity to learn about who we've become over the last hundred years. To see whether or not there's a chance for peace."

Wil paused for effect before continuing, gesturing up at the mountain. "The Skalet Range is now the source of a rift between our world and that of the fae, a doorway that anyone can pass through to either world. And after hours of discussion and compromise, the fae agreed to give us a chance, if we as a town are willing to give them a chance.

"So in three days, a large party from Faerie will be crossing over to tour Harper Valley and get to know us. This is our chance to make history and establish peace and trade."

Again, silence. Sinclair stepped forward, a look of pure hate on his face. Wil hadn't expected his decision to be embraced with open arms by everyone, but Sinclair was livid. Then his face changed, with a smug, knowing smile. He nodded to himself.

"How large a party are we talking about, Mr. McKenzie? Where are they going to stay?"

"About fifty of the fae," Wil said, pressing on before people could protest, "and they will stay in camps we set up on my parents' property."

"Did Bob and Sharon agree to that?" Sinclair asked, almost laughing.

Wil shrugged. "They will. They'll understand how big an undertaking this is and will be happy to help. The fae will be staying until spring, talking to us and trying to learn from us. And at the end of the season, they'll make a decision. Either they'll leave the rift open and we can see about trade and traveling, or we close the rift for good and leave each other in peace. War is the last thing they want."

"Then they shouldn't have taken our children!" a voice called from the back, followed by a chorus of agreement.

"They're all back, safe and sound, and our fae neighbors will come with a gift for those families affected. An apology and a promise of a favor in the future. Favors are very big with the fae, and should be considered something of an honor." Wil summoned his staff magically and stepped forward.

"You have my word as your town wizard that I've worked hard to bring you a good deal, and good company, to Harper Valley. This is a tremendous chance for our town to grow and change into something big, something never before seen in all of Calipan!"

"Well, I don't know about that," said Sinclair, with a laugh that goaded some of the others into joining him. "I like Harper Valley just the way it is, with the people in it. You did your job as town representative, but I think it'll be up to the people to decide whether or not they accept any deals." Utterances of agreement came from behind him.

Darlene jumped in. "Absolutely. We just negotiated for the chance to present the case for friendship. Bram here was one of the people taken, and he'd be glad to share his experiences in Faerie over a round of drinks. Our treat!"

And with that, she stole Sinclair's thunder entirely. The crowd cheered and Bram stepped forward, waving enthusiastically, though he had a growing blush.

"It was great, honestly," he said. "We played games and I ate good food, and we got to sample all their different brews. It was amazing, and I . . ."

As he spoke, he disappeared into the crowd, which parted and closed behind him as he headed toward town. Only the Pattersons and Mayor Sinclair remained.

Sinclair nodded and Perry Patterson stepped forward and offered his hand to Wil. Wil took and it gave it a hearty shake.

"We owe you so much for bringing our Pearl back," he said, tears coming to his eyes. "If there's anything we can do, anything at all, name it and it's yours."

Wil inclined his head respectfully. "All I ask is that you keep an open mind regarding the fae, and maybe help me out with something a little later in the season."

"Absolutely," said Patty, hugging Pearl from behind. "Thank you, Mr. Wizard."

With one last nod, they turned to walk across the fields home, Pearl chattering happily about her stay in Faerie.

Finally, it was just Sinclair, wearing that smug, satisfied smile from before.

"That's a mighty big decision you've made for all of us," he said.

"That's Wil's choice to make," Darlene retorted.

"Sure," said Sinclair. "You made that abundantly clear the last time we spoke. And now you brought our people home. Good job, Wilbur. Good job, indeed. But it's out of both of our hands now."

Wil didn't like his tone. "What do you mean?"

Sinclair shrugged, spreading his hands wide. "I sent a telegram to Cloverton. They're sending a mage to represent the government. You did your part, but now you'll be sidelined, just like me. You've got a matter of days before they arrive and take over. So enjoy it while you can, boy." He turned and left as well.

"What an asshole," Darlene muttered.

"Yep. Want to go see my parents and grab lunch?" Wil asked. Her face lit up, and together they headed for his family's farm.

CHAPTER 22

McKenzie Hospitality

More often than not, Wil appreciated how well his family knew each other. Not once had he expected his parents to show up with the rest of the town to greet him. They waited for him to come home, knowing it would be one of his first stops, and they were there to greet him with arms wide open.

"You did it!" Sharon said from the porch, getting out of the chair and running up to hug him. "I was so worried!"

"Aw, Ma," said Wil, hugging her tight. "It was only, like, two days for you!"

"And two weeks for you, right? Damned time difference. What about Bram?" She backed up, as if only just now noticing that he and Darlene were alone.

"He's with the rest of the town," said Darlene, stepping up for a big hug of her own. "He's telling stories of what it was like in Faerie and how well treated he was. He has this goofy beard now."

"You're kidding! He can't pull off a beard."

"Try telling him that," said Wil with a big smile. He joined his father on the porch, taking the newly empty seat next to him. "Hey, Dad. Everything go alright while I was gone?"

"Yup. As it turns out, I've got years of experience sitting around and enjoying myself in winter and didn't need your help to manage that. Smoke?" Bob offered his pipe.

Wil waved it off. "Thanks, but I think I want to keep a clear head for the next while. There's . . . It's a lot."

"Did you get everything done that needed doing?" Bob asked, rocking gently in his chair.

"Sort of," said Wil as he got comfortable. "There's a lot left to do, and I'm afraid I made some big decisions for the family without asking anyone. You're free to say no, but I'm kind of banking on this."

Bob considered him for a moment. "This is bigger than any of us. Whatever you need from us, you'll get it. Just tell me what it is."

Sharon and Darlene came up to the porch. "Is anybody hungry?" Sharon asked.

It was, naturally, a trick question. Even if they weren't hungry, it was time for Mom to make lunch so they could discuss it at the table like a family. Wil wasn't about to complain. Sharon whipped together sandwiches she swore were simple, but no one else could make them half as well. They wolfed them down with hot chocolate on the side, while Bob and Sharon alternated telling them about their neighbors' reactions and general mindsets on the whole fae fiasco. The short of it was that the people of Harper Valley were irritated and scared.

"I'm not surprised," said Wil, sipping at his drink. Only a couple bites of ham sandwich remained, but he was content. "It was not a good start to new relations, and I'm not especially happy with the fae about it, either. But if we want to move on and have a good future, it's something we'll need to put behind us. They'll be putting behind plenty of bad blood of their own."

"If you're hoping both sides will be the bigger man, I'm worried you're in for disappointment," said Bob. "We'll do what we can to help it along. Now, we've done a whole lot of talking, and now it's your turn. What the hell happened in Faerie?"

"Well," said Darlene. "We got there, got lost in the woods, were attacked by a wampus cat, met a princely goatman who became our travel guide, spent a few days partying with hobgoblins, got attacked by ogre assassins, and then Wil beat the king of the ogres in a duel to the death to make the fae listen to us."

Bob and Sharon stared at them in alarm. Darlene burst out laughing, and then went into the actual story, with details this time. Wil took over when it came time to talk about the meetings with the fae, and what their plans were. In that time, he pushed himself to finish the remnants of his sandwich and drink and was about ready for a nap when he got to the point.

"So, the fae are coming to Harper Valley for the winter to observe, interact with us, and see if they'd rather have the door closed behind them or not. But I don't think they'd do well at the inn, or bunking with random people around town. So I offered to use some of our land to build some temporary dwellings for them. It's winter and we're not using it, and whatever damage is done you know I can fix it, and—"

"Relax," said Bob, raising a hand to cut off Wil, just as he realized he was starting to ramble. "We've already been hosting some of the Appleton crew, why not host the fae as well? At this rate, we might as well convert the farm to an inn!" He chortled, but Wil still felt bad.

"Do they have any eating restrictions?" Sharon asked immediately.

"Ma, you don't have to cook for all of them for every meal," said Wil.

"Besides," Darlene interjected, "there's going to be fifty of them. They'll be taking care of their own meals or eating at local places. We'll need to go around and make sure there's no exposed iron that might hurt them, but that should be fine. The harder part will be convincing the rest of the town to be considerate. Some people might cling to any iron they have as a defense."

Bob grunted in the affirmative. "You can count on that. Sharon and I'll do what we can, but . . ." He cleared his throat and sat up straight. "If we're still serious about me running against Sinclair, it's about time to announce my candidacy."

"I thought you were going to announce it at the Midwinter Feast," said Darlene.

"I am," Bob replied. "That's not the issue. With Wil bringing these people to tour Harper Valley, that's gonna be contentious. We might be able to convince people to be open-minded and give it a try, but we're not gonna be able to convince everyone. If there are enough people against the idea, we'd just be handing Sinclair the victory as soon as he stands against it."

Wil nodded thoughtfully. "Yeah, that's something I've been thinking about. In some ways, we're lucky. The fae will be here for the feast, and that's something good we can share with them. If we can convince people to at least try to connect, maybe the feast would be an even better time to announce it than before."

"That's a pretty big if, sweetie," said Sharon. "You can't force people to get along by just shoving them together in one place and telling them to make nice. We used to try that with you kids and it never ended well. It usually ended with Jeb stealing your toys and running away with them."

Darlene cleared her throat for attention. "That's another thing we were hoping to get your help on. We're not just planning on throwing people together and hoping for the best. We were hoping we could have people volunteer to show them around, and you'd be perfect for it, Sharon. Your entire family would."

Bob made a face. "Even Jeb?"

Wil sighed. "Yeah, I figured he could be in charge of showing some of the Wee Folk around. They like pranks and aren't serious. Mostly. We'll figure it out. There's one more thing. Sinclair sent out a telegram, and Cloverton is sending a mage to represent Calipan."

The table fell silent, until Sharon asked, "What does that mean for you and everything you've done? Are you worried about this mage?"

Wil shrugged. "There's no telling what it means for me. There's a good chance I could get in trouble for jumping into Faerie to save our people, but that's also more or less what they trained us to do. This is supposed to be my area of expertise, and I think I did the best job I could have, but there's always a chance I'll get chewed out over this. As for the mage . . . , it's hard to say. Mages are about on par with master wizards, except they hold rank in the military as well. Whoever it is will be ready and willing to fight if they have to. They're not likely to be as fond of compromise as I am."

"Do you know who it will be?" Darlene asked, putting her hand on his. "I know you've said the magical world is a small one. Is there any chance it could be a friend of yours?"

"I mean, I suppose it's possible," said Wil, blowing out a long breath. He took her hand and squeezed it. "Chances are this is big enough that they'll send someone well-known enough to be an authority, but they're not sending an archmage, so it won't be one of our absolute best. I'd say that whoever it is, we probably know each other in passing."

He tried to think of who could be sent down there. Most mages were already engaged on one of their multiple fronts, either in the south or along the east coast. There were a few Wil knew who floated between tasks without a permanent assignment. Rosen wouldn't be so bad if he could be convinced to not be comedically offensive. Chinis wouldn't pick fights, but he wouldn't take any crap, either. Hugo would be a nightmare, as would George or Sherman. It was a coin flip, really, over getting someone reasonable.

"Whoever they send," said Darlene, "we'll handle it. Between me, Bram, and your family, there'll be more than enough people to help guide the groups. And we've got plans for events and things to do to help steer people in the right direction. We've got this!"

Bob eyed the front door longingly, where he no doubt wanted to get back to a busy day of rocking and enjoying the lovely winter day.

"Whatever you need, Wil, we'll do it," he said. "Just tell us what and when. We trust you, and we're proud of you for doing this much for not just Harper Valley but the fae too. Regardless of what that mage brings, you're the right man for the job."

Wil tried not to look too pleased. "Thanks, Dad."

They still had a few more days to prepare, but Wil was confident. Things would go wrong, of course, but he'd deal with them as best as he could. At this point, he was beginning to believe he could handle anything the world could throw at him.

CHAPTER 23

Man to Man

Wil walked into the evening, grateful for the first chance in two weeks to catch a breath of fresh air alone. Darlene had stayed behind with Sharon to coordinate activities and presentations they could make for both groups. As much as Wil loved to help and come up with ideas, the nitty-gritty had never been his strength. Darlene had all but pushed him out the door with a quick kiss and an order to relax for a bit.

The problem was, he couldn't remember the last time he'd let himself relax. The past month had been a busy time with everything involving the fae, and before that, there'd been the storm, and before that . . .

Ever since Wil had got home from school, things had been go, go, go, with only the occasional breather hanging out with Bram and Darlene. He worked long hours happily and always needed something to strive toward. Wilbur McKenzie was not a man made for rest. Truth be told, the time spent in Faerie between busy meetings had been the closest thing to a rest he'd had in months. Thinking about it showed him exactly what he wanted to do with his night. Something he hadn't gotten to do since before winter.

Wil went for a casual walk, leaving his staff and worries at his house, and just enjoyed seeing Harper Valley under a light layer of snow. He drank in the sights, the smells, and the general feel of the air. It was his first winter back in six years. By the time he hit the main road going to town, Wil's feet were moving on their own and he abandoned himself to the joy of a simple walk with nowhere to go. Extending his senses around him, Wil reached out for the land as he went.

Warmth, even in winter, radiated from the land. This was a loved place, sleepy now but enduring and powerful. But there was a slight difference to it he couldn't quite put his finger on. Something familiar enough that it didn't feel wrong, but alien enough to not be natural. A look up at the top of the mountain gave him his answer.

The broken leyline was leaking magic into the valley, breaking the smooth river of power coursing through the area behind the scenes. Off in the distance, on top of the peak, the tree mirrored Oakheart Spiral in Faerie. If he had to close the rift, would things go back to normal, or were they forever changed?

Wil didn't know, and for a change, not knowing didn't bother him. That was a problem for future him. Tonight, it was enough to just enjoy the walk and being back in Harper Valley.

He passed people on the street, waving and occasionally stopping to chat for a few minutes. Never anything big or important. Mostly, word had spread of the incoming fae party, and people wanted reassurances. It cost nothing to ease their minds, and as Wil found himself doing it again and again, he had a destination in mind.

The sun was down by the time Wil arrived at Bram's farm. The lights were off in the house, but an orange glow came from the barn, as did the sound of laughter. It got louder and more raucous the closer Wil got, until he was near enough to hear Bram's voice.

"Now the thing you gotta know about ogres," said Bram, "is that they're all built like me, only stronger. This particular ogre is known to be a runt, and oh boy, he hates being reminded of that. He was our guard, in fact. Can you imagine being hired to be an intimidating guard and you have to look up to talk to your prisoner? He hated it."

Wil walked through the open barn doors to find Bram sitting at the head of a battered old dinner table, joined by Jeb and some of his friends. This was where he did all of his brewing, and equipment and crates of bottles lined the shelves. It made the barn look cramped. As soon as they had the money for it, they were going to build a proper brewery with a place for people to eat.

Bram grinned and waved at him, making his ridiculous beard wobble. "Gallath's his name. Well, one of the times he was 'guarding' me, we went out for drinks. We could go pretty much anywhere we wanted, so long as he was with us. Well, this one time, I was missing home and getting frustrated by how long it was taking Wil to get there."

Jeb turned to see Wil in the door, and he scoffed. "Yeah, what's wrong with you, Wizard? Your best friend was waiting for you and drinking himself silly." He brought a bottle of their wheat beer up to his lips, winking.

"Yeah, Wizard, what took so long?" Jeb's friend Billy-Ray chortled. He and Wil had never particularly gotten along, but it was hard to take the farmer seriously now. Billy-Ray was the spitting image of his father, so Wil knew what he'd look like in twenty years. All the bullying in the world didn't matter when Billy-Ray's future was that sad.

"Just wasn't important enough, I guess," said Wil, fighting the growing smile. "Besides, every day I was gone was another day Bram had to find love."

The entire table turned to Bram, who turned bright red.

"Is that so?" a blond, lean man named Elmer asked. "Wouldn't have figured anyone would go for your ugly ass. Especially not with that goofy beard."

There was more laughter, but Bram wasn't among them. Wil summoned a gust of wind and knocked Elmer's beer into his lap.

"Oops," he said, with a smile that didn't reach his eyes. "You should probably get home and change. Especially in this chill."

The laughter died. Jeb was the first one to stand up, eyeing Wil not with anger but understanding.

"C'mon, boys, we've bugged Bram long enough. He and my brother probably got potions to make or whatever the hell it is these two do."

Billy-Ray and Elmer got up, eyeing Wil with a mixture of irritation and fear. If anyone in town was going to be too scared to make any moves, Wil was glad it was them. He remembered too many years of them teasing him or hiding his books, and dunking his head underwater for too long in the river until he had a panic attack, and then never apologizing for it. For example.

"Bye." Wil got out of the way as they passed. Jeb trailed behind, shaking his head in amusement. Finally, it was just Wil and Bram and a bunch of empty bottles on the table.

"So what was the rest of the story?" Wil asked, taking Jeb's spot and magically pulling a bottle of barley wine from a crate. It sailed through the air lazily until he snatched it and opened it with another little spell.

"Show-off," said Bram with a chuckle. He finished his beer. "I was telling them about the time I got in a drinking contest with Gallath. He boasted that ogres were tougher than humans, even if I was bigger than him."

Wil nodded along. He took a sip of the dark, rich ale and sighed. "So, who won?"

"Good question," said Bram. "I crapped out first since I could barely see straight, and there was just enough of 'responsible Bram' left to decide to call it before I blacked out entirely or got sick. Gallath laughed and stood up and looked like he was about to go on a rant about how he defeated me. Then he fell over. We decided to call it a draw."

"I'm impressed," said Wil. "I've got firsthand experience with how tough ogres are, but to match you drink for drink? The only person I can think of who could beat you would be Skalet, but somehow I doubt he's a drinker."

Bram bowed his head in acknowledgment. "Feels like I was made to make and drink beer. We're starting to get low, and there's still another week before the next batch is ready. I was hoping we'd have more for the fae when they get here. A guaranteed way to spread goodwill, you know? The next batch is a big one, but I'm pretty sure we're just going to give it all away."

"Probably," Wil agreed, "but it's going to a good cause. We made sure to check on your brews before we left to come get you. I trust everything was in order."

"Yeah," said Bram with a nod. "Everything was pretty much exactly as I left it. Which is a shame, because my house was a mess."

"I already helped clean your house once," Wil joked. "From now on it's on you."

A comfortable silence settled between them. For a couple of minutes, they didn't talk, just drank and relaxed in the quiet. Wil had a million questions running through his head, but he pushed them to the side. This was a time to relax, not fret—until curiosity got the better of him, and he had to ask.

"You ever going to tell us who you met in Faerie?"

Bram froze with the bottle halfway to his lips. "Eventually," he said, putting the bottle down. He stood and gathered a bunch of the empties, and deposited them in one of the other crates. "It's not that simple. I mean, we're from two different worlds, right? There's no telling if it could last."

"Is that enough to stop you?" Wil knew better than to try to help with the cleanup. The place wasn't that messy, Bram just needed something to distract himself. That didn't mean he could dodge Wil's questions.

"It might be. What's the point of going for it if we might be at war if things go wrong?" Bram pushed the other chairs back under the table.

"You know," said Wil, "that's a good point. What's the point of living if you know you're going to eventually die?"

"Oh, shut up," Bram groaned. He collapsed into his chair again. "I know what you're saying, but it's really not that simple. I don't have to just worry about people here judging us, I also have to worry about other species with their own strange rules judging us."

"Are you so worried about being judged?" Wil asked.

"I am for this," Bram whispered. "You know how it is in a town like Harper Valley. People won't be mean to me, but they'll whisper behind my back, and laugh at me, and maybe that gets ugly and someone tries to hurt me."

"Doubt it," said Wil. It was hard to find the right way to be supportive without being dismissive. "If they tried, they'd have to get through me. And while I can't do anything as creative as turning them into a rat, I could do a lot to mess with them. I've got your back, no matter who it is."

Bram smiled but said nothing.

"Let me just ask this," said Wil. "Is this person part of the expedition to Harper Valley?"

"Yes." Bram looked away.

"Well, then, that's perfect, isn't it? It might blow up in your face. All of this might blow up in all our faces. But can you really not try to find happiness if it's right in front of you? You deserve it after how many years you spent boxed up, afraid of your dad and afraid for your mom. You deserve to come out of that box and live a little."

Bram took a couple of deep, halting breaths, and Wil realized he was trying not to cry. He did the thing a respectful friend would do and looked away, instead focusing on his drink while his best friend took his words in and calmed down.

"Yeah," Bram's voice was hoarse. He cleared it, and most of the pent-up emotion left. "Yeah, that's . . . I'll give it a try. But forget about that for now. We've got much bigger problems. Are preparations looking good?"

This was the perfect time for a change in subject. Wil laughed, shrugging wildly.

"You'd have to ask Darlene. She and Ma got into one of their back-and-forths where I would've just gotten in the way. That's why I came here. Figured you were done talking to all the good citizens about your luxury vacation in Faerie. How did that go?"

Bram's eyes lit up again. He took off his glasses and cleaned them on his shirt. "About as well as it could go. Everyone was curious, and a few people thought maybe I'd been bewitched, but I think I was able to convince them. Candy asked me *so* many questions about it. I think she wished she was one of the ones kidnapped. And then . . ."

Wil smiled. An hour or two of not working was about as much rest as he could take. He settled into his chair and listened as Bram talked about his day. Worrying could come in the next few days, as they prepared for the arrival of the fae. For now, though, it was enough to spend some time with his best friend.

CHAPTER 24

Welcoming Committee

Two days later, the fae arrived at the top of Skalet Peak. Wil and company were already there, waiting for them, dressed for the occasion in their best clothes. Wil held his staff firmly in hand.

First came the lower-ranked fae: merchants or artists who came along for the experience and to spread word of their findings. One second the ring of mushrooms in front of the great tree was empty, the next a parade of elves came through, followed by a wagon packed with supplies.

"Welcome, everybody!" Bram called out, waving enthusiastically. "Keep it coming, there's plenty of room up here since the storm leveled everything."

He and Darlene accompanied Wil as planned. The three of them would lead the fae down the mountain and make sure the first meeting went well. The rest of Harper Valley had been informed, and while Wil was wary, he wasn't that worried about trouble. If anyone tried to start something . . . well, he wasn't sure he could count on Sheriff Frederick, but he could handle it.

"It smells funny here," one of the elves in front said, wrinkling up an angular, delicate face. "And it feels a bit thinner."

"That'd be the lessened magic," said Wil in understanding. "Took me a bit to get used to Faerie's air too. Give it an hour and it should be mostly normal after."

"If you say so," said the elf, helping guide his beast of burden farther away from the Faerie Circle. They continued past the trio, stopping once they got to where the clearing ended and the slope down the mountain began.

Next came a small wagon with pixies and leprechauns hanging all over it, singing together raucously in an unfamiliar language. They were pulled by a pair of silver mules, who brayed along with the music. A portly leprechaun in a fashionable suit tipped his hat to them as they passed.

The Woodlands wagon was next, with most of the occupants walking instead of riding. There was an unfamiliar faun, a brawny centaur with a bow slung over his back, and a lovely dryad woman with vivid green and yellow hair. They were followed by a big carriage for the Ogre Federation.

Maybe it was personal bias, but Wil found they always looked angry and suspicious. He supposed he couldn't blame them, but he also had no idea how to reach out to them and be friendly. A seven-foot-tall troll with curved tusks looked at

Wil as he passed, giving him the Nod of Respect and Acknowledgment with what could've been an agreeable grunt.

"We're finally here!" Syl was the next to pop out of the ring of mushrooms, followed by Arabella, Timothy Twist, and Gallath, who turned out to be Grimnar's nephew. Wil never would have guessed, but no one was sad to see that Grimnar had stayed behind and sent his much more reasonable kin in his place.

Syl stepped forward, sniffing the air. "It smells weird here."

"So we've heard," said Darlene. "You have a good trip? Get lost on the way?"

Syl and Timothy Twist laughed, and even Gallath smiled, but Arabella rolled her eyes.

"Yes, yes, very droll. Bring us to your leader so that we can get ourselves set up."

"As you wish, Princess," said Wil, bowing deep enough to make it clear he was teasing. "We'll head up the caravan."

"I'll stay behind," Bram blurted out. "Gallath needed my help with something."

The ogre cleared his throat and nodded. He was armed and armored, but unlike his uncle and the assassins, he looked more like a tall, noble knight from a different time than a savage warrior.

"While I am representing my people, I'm also in charge of security and wished to pick Bram's brain on a few things."

Wil shrugged. "Sure. Darlene?" He offered her his arm.

"Wil," she returned, taking it. They nodded to the representatives of Faerie and headed to the front. "You nervous?" she asked.

"A little," Wil replied, "but there's no real need to worry. At this point, it'll go either well or poorly. I'll figure it out as we go."

"Look at you," Darlene said with a laugh. "Picking and winning fights and not fretting yourself to death. Who are you and what did you do with my boyfriend?"

Wil smiled. "I let him out of the box I kept him in."

The fae procession headed down the mountain, taking the largest path. At a few places where the route was too narrow or a tree got in the way, Wil gently reshaped the land, giving them room if the wagons drove single file. This time, Wil kept his senses extended and felt for the leyline, still flowing powerfully, spurts of magic releasing into the air and earth every second.

It was better, in some ways, that the top of the mountain now resembled Faerie more than Calipan. It gave the fae something familiar as they wound their way through the forest down to Harper Valley. Wil led them farther south, skirting around the farms at the edge and stopping at the train tracks. They had to cover the tracks with thick canvas to cross, and then it was on to the fairgrounds, where a crowd awaited them.

As soon as the people of Harper Valley came into view, Syl powered his long, gangling legs to get to the front of the procession, with a bottle of wine cradled against his chest. The faun prince was dressed to impress with his nicest vest, golden rings on his fingers, and lovely blue and pink flowers in his hair and beard.

"Anything I should know before we meet up?" he asked hesitantly.

"Sinclair is a snake but he's all smiles face-to-face," said Darlene. She patted his arm reassuringly. "Just be your normal charming self and maybe don't talk about how awful humans are at first. If you can resist that, you're golden."

"I can resist that, no problem."

"Can you, though?" Wil muttered. It earned a snicker from Darlene and an aggrieved glare from Syl. Then came the last stretch down, where the town waited.

Wil cast a lightening spell on himself and then magically pushed against the ground. He flew through the air in an arc, slowly floating down and landing in front of Sinclair and the townspeople. Sheriff Frederick stood right by Sinclair, as did cranky Mr. Carrey.

"PEOPLE OF HARPER VALLEY," Will boomed, his magically enhanced voice loud enough to be heard in the back. "ALLOW ME THE PLEASURE OF INTRODUCING THE LEAD REPRESENTATIVE FOR HIS PEOPLE, AND A NEW FRIEND: PRINCE SYLANO OF THE WOODLANDS ASSOCIATION OF FAERIE."

He gestured back at Syl with his staff, drawing colorful lines in the air, spelling out Sylano's name in glowing colors. It was just in time for the faun to stand underneath the words, ten feet away from the mayor. He and Wil grinned at each other and then at the mayor.

Sinclair was unimpressed with the introduction and Wil's theatrics, but the crowd ate it up. There was more applause than Wil had expected, and he hoped at least some of it was enthusiasm for their guests.

Syl bowed gracefully. Even bent over, he was taller than Sinclair. "It is my pleasure to make your acquaintance, Mr. Mayor. And on behalf of all of us from Faerie, I present a gift for you." He held the bottle out with both hands like he was cradling something precious. "A fine vintage from my father's private collection. A gift worthy of kings."

To his credit, Mayor Sinclair looked properly moved. He took the bottle from Syl, checking it for a label. Remembering himself, he cleared his throat.

"Thank you, Prince Sylano. I'm Mayor Bartholomew Sinclair, but you can call me Bart or just Sinclair. The circumstances of our meeting aren't ideal, but on behalf of the town, be welcome to Harper Valley."

This got some more polite applause, from the town and from the fae. It was enough to give Wil hope. Now that the caravan was all down, Arabella and the other representatives stepped forward, each with a gift in hand.

"PRINCESS ARABELLA OF THE FAIR FOLK, DAUGHTER OF QUEEN ARIA."

Arabella handed over a rolled-up piece of canvas. "A gift from my mother, queen of the elves," she proudly proclaimed.

Sinclair rolled it out, and then quickly bundled it closed again. His face was bright red. "That's . . . that's a nude painting," said Sinclair.

"Yes," Arabella said in a tone that implied he was slow. "Of my mother. We don't know how well your people have progressed, socially, and thought you could use some art and beauty from Faerie to remind you of what you've been missing." There were snickers all around them.

"Th-thank you, Princess Arabella," said Sinclair, recovering more smoothly than Wil would have expected. "A gift of beauty is always welcome, in a world so often ugly." He handed the painting and the bottle over to his harried assistant. Some of the townspeople craned their heads to get a better look at it.

"TIMOTHY TWIST OF THE WEE FOLK," Wil announced next.

Timothy Twist swaggered up to Mayor Sinclair, looking right up at him. He held out a closed hand. Sinclair tentatively opened his hand and held it out. Twist dropped something in it and took a step back.

"These are . . . beans?"

"Aye, beans." Timothy Twist nodded seriously. "Magic beans. Plant these and you'll never go hungry again." There was an extra twinkle in his eye. Wil wasn't sure if he was serious or not, but he couldn't tell a direct lie.

"Um. Thank you, Timothy Twist. Welcome." Little to no applause for him, but he looked pleased just the same.

"AND FINALLY, GALLATH OF THE OGRE FEDERATION."

Gallath drew a gleaming silver sword. Sheriff Frederick put his hand on his gun, glaring at the ogre, but Gallath strode forward confidently and offered the sword hilt-first to the mayor.

"A weapon forged by my father, best of the ogre smiths, made of our purest silver. This weapon represents our bloody history and the possibility of working together toward a common goal. And barring that, a promise that we are capable of defending ourselves."

It was the most Wil had ever heard the ogre speak at one time. He had a deep, smooth voice that was calming and serene and so unlike his rough and boisterous uncle. Beside him, Bram clapped enthusiastically, but he was one of the few that did. No one wanted a reminder that war was still possible.

"Thank . . . you?" Even Sinclair couldn't hide the unease. He raised the sword up and did his best approximation of a salute with it, still holding the beans in his other hand. "May words prevail so we never need swords."

"Maybe we should've had Syl go last," Darlene whispered in Wil's ear.

Wil cleared his throat and projected his voice one last time. "FOR THE NEXT SEASON, THE FAE WILL BE LIVING AMONG US AND OBSERVING. THEY WILL NOT HURT YOU IF YOU DO NOT HURT THEM. THEY WILL NOT INSULT YOU UNLESS YOU INSULT THEM. FIRST, WE'LL BE SETTING THEM UP WITH A PLACE TO STAY, AND THEN WE'LL SHOW THEM AROUND TOWN. I HOPE YOU'LL ALL HELP ME IN SHOWING WHAT A WONDERFUL PLACE HARPER VALLEY IS!"

Maybe it was the reminder to take pride in where they lived, but that got the greatest reaction of all, complete with cheers and whistles.

"We'll be here, and we'll give you our complete hospitality," Mayor Sinclair said. But his mask slipped, and Wil saw a smugness there he didn't like.

"See you guys around when we give out tours!" Wil called with a wave. He led his party around the assembled crowd, where they would wind their way along the main road and to his parents' place in the southeast.

"Well," said Syl, falling in step beside his human friends, "that went well, right?"

"Could've been worse," Wil admitted, "but there's a long way to go. Let's get you guys set up with a temporary home."

CHAPTER 25

Home Away From Home

While the bulk of interested people had been present to greet the fae, the way through town brought many more curious eyes. The caravan went largely unbothered, and Wil, Syl, and the others waved to people as they passed, doing their absolute best to present as nonthreatening and friendly. For the most part, it worked, with only a couple of people turning and walking the other way.

Just as he'd requested, Wil's family and the Appleton crew were there at the farm waiting for them. The Appleton crew weren't strictly necessary, but Wil figured it'd be good to have twenty friendly faces about. They were people who knew the value of a second chance and trusted Wil. Maybe a bit of chatting with them would do their new guests some good.

"This is where you grew up?" Syl asked him as they walked down the lane.

"Yep. Probably nothing compared to what you grew up in, *Prince*, but it was nice." Wil elbowed Syl in the hip. "Taught me the value of hard work and sticking together with family."

"I like it," said Syl, flashing him a lopsided grin. "Not what I would've expected out of someone who can move the heavens and earth and change leylines, but that just makes it more impressive. I can't wait to try some of your mom's food!"

"Trust me, she'll love your enthusiasm." Wil laughed, recalling the detailed interrogation Sharon had put him through when she found out just how many guests they'd be hosting. Even knowing she wouldn't be the primary caregiver for them, she insisted on being a good hostess.

His family waited for him on the porch, with Jeb and Sarah out front and their parents in front of the doors. The caravan stopped twenty feet away, and the representatives stepped up to the McKenzie house.

Bob and Sharon came down from the porch and joined their children. Wil stood between the two groups. It might've seemed silly to his family to make such a big deal about it, but that's how they did it in Faerie. Syl had flat-out called it necessary for them to be able to rest easy on the land.

"Greetings, McKenzies," said the faun. He bowed low. "Prince Sylano of the Woodlands Association, at your service. Might we impose ourselves on your hospitality? We can pay for our stay."

Bob stroked his beard, looking hesitant. "And would you pay for a place in my home with coin or baubles?" He managed to make the line sound natural.

"We could," said Syl. He rose from his bow. "But we offer you something better. We offer our friendship, our favor, and our service to match. An oath that we'd be honorable guests, and should we dishonor ourselves, we pay ye in both coin and service further. And a promise that when we move on, we leave the land a better place than we found it." He held out his hand.

Bob smiled warmly. He didn't have to fake his enthusiasm as he took Syl's hand and pumped it. "Then we gladly agree, and vow to be honorable hosts, and do you no harm, and watch out for you as if you were our own. For the duration of the stay, you are under our protection and care."

Everyone, fae or human, felt the tingle of a binding magical contract. Jeb and Sarah looked as if they'd been slapped and were shaken. Sharon gasped but recovered and nodded. Bob braced himself and his smile deepened. There was a tear in his eye as he released Syl's hand.

"What the hell was that?" Sarah demanded.

"The power of Obligation and promise," said Wil. "I tried to warn you about it, but it's strange and you really feel tied to it. Damned uncomfortable to be on the wrong side of it."

Syl chuckled and bowed again to Sarah. "My apologies, Miss McKenzie. But it's all a fancy way of promising to not hurt or betray each other and to act fairly. It's a safety thing for our people."

"Does it require you to talk like you got a stick up your ass?"

"Sarah!" Sharon gasped. Before she could reprimand her or apologize, Syl threw his head back and bleated out obnoxious laughter.

"It does sound like that, doesn't it? It's all old and stuffy and inescapable. It's a nightmare sometimes, but it's necessary. Perhaps I could explain better later?" Syl winked.

Wil bristled. "Syl?" he said.

The faun turned to him. Wil shook his head once. The smile faded from Syl's face. He looked back at Sarah, who just rolled her eyes at him. The last thing they needed was an entanglement like that.

"Well, welcome," said Bob. His smile had turned into a fatherly scowl. Syl shrugged sheepishly.

After that, introductions were made all around. Arabella bowed so low and deep that Jeb craned his head to get a better look. Wil smacked his arm before anyone else noticed. Timothy Twist did a little dance before introducing himself, and Sarah openly laughed at him, to his delight. Gallath acquitted himself well, with his stoic grace and a promise to help protect the home.

Now that the oaths had been made, the fae emptied their wagons, bringing out supplies, tools, and musical instruments. A band made up of a centaur guitarist, an elf singer, an ogre drummer, and a pixie flautist played an upbeat tune.

Their enthusiasm was infectious, and it charged the air with an undeniable sense of optimism.

First, the field was cleared of snow by a team of pixies and hobgoblins who blew the snow into piles and then melted them under a ball of fire. Another faun brought a pickaxe down into the earth, piercing the barely frozen ground. He stepped to the side about twenty feet and did it again, and then once more.

Syl beckoned Wil forward as he and the other representatives joined with a dryad man with reddish leaves for hair. The dryad had in his hands three seeds. Wil made a face and then spat into his hand. Syl followed, then Arabella, Twist, and Gallath. None of them hesitated, and the dryad didn't seem as disgusted as he should've been.

He closed his hands over the seeds and whispered a spell into them. A twinge in the back of Wil's mind stirred him. He reached for the earth and felt it. Though it was winter, the land was awake and something big and deep and old had an awareness of the people assembled. Wil swallowed and tried to pull away, but he was stuck. The land he looked into looked right back into him.

The dryad deposited a seed in each spot the faun had created with the pickaxe. Wil felt the moment the seed hit the dirt. The land sought each new visitor eagerly, curious in its vast, impersonal way. It wasn't a rejection, at least. The seeds were full of life, vastly eclipsing their meager vessels.

The leaders of Faerie formed a semicircle around the seeds. Wil took his place without thinking about it. With his wizarding senses pried wide open, their mutual achievement was just sweeter.

Life bloomed in those seeds, taking root in the welcoming earth. All those assembled poured some of themselves into the holes, and the three seeds grew into increasingly massive trees. The first grew sideways, stretching out across the frozen farmland, the bent trunk rose ten feet before sprawling out sideways for another hundred.

The others grew tall and straight, maturing from humble seeds to massive sky-scraping growths in just a couple of minutes. Behind them, Wil's family gasped and watched them work. It was uncanny, being a part of something and feeling his partner's connections with magic. It was unlike his own personal connection with magic, but no less intimate or special. Working with one goal in mind, he didn't have to direct anything. He just joined in with the fae, who knew what they were doing.

Finally the trees stopped growing and instead groaned as the insides hollowed. Windows and doors split open the wood, shaping themselves from the tree itself. There were a good fifty fae who had come to Harper Valley, and the trees they were raising would be enough to hold all of them and then some.

One by one, the fae leaders released their grasp on the project. Wil held out until it was just him and Syl and the dryad attendant. And then he, too, let go and allowed the mundane world to come crashing back down on him. Panting for air, he leaned hard on his staff. A satisfying weariness set in, but there was still plenty of work left in the day.

"Is this how you always set up temporary housing?" Bob asked in hushed awe.

Syl wiped sweat from his brow. "Only if we're looking to stay for a while. Otherwise, we might've just made a small mushroom village or something cozy like that. They've still got some work to do, making sure all the rooms are equipped to handle us, but we're done. What now, Wil?"

Every eye turned his way. Wil took a deep breath and tried to will away the fatigue. "From here, we split up into groups and we start to show you around town. We'll keep it light today and then try to show you something new every day. Bram's volunteered to take the Ogre Federation around, is that right?"

Gallath nodded. "We are well acquainted and he promised us his homemade beer. I intend on keeping him to that promise." A ghost of a smile crossed his features.

Wil shook his head. "Of course. Fantastic. Darlene's going to show the Woodlands Association around today. You'll be in great hands with her."

Syl sidled up to Darlene and put an arm around her shoulder. It was awkward with the height difference, but Darlene just rolled her eyes and put her arm around his waist. Not once did Wil think to be jealous, though maybe he needed to talk to Syl about avoiding Sarah.

"That just leaves Jeb with the Wee Folk, and me with the Fair Folk."

"Wait a minute," said Jeb, stepping up. "Why can't I show the Fair Folk around?" He eyed Arabella with all the subtlety of a charging bull. She didn't seem to mind the attention.

"Because we want you to avoid getting in trouble," said Wil pointedly.

"What about what we want?" Arabella demanded. "I've gotten to know *you*, Wizard. We've already established you're a cut above the rest of humanity. Let me see what this common country bumpkin can show me."

Jeb's eyes darkened. Wil headed that off as best he could. "That common country bumpkin is my brother," he said.

"I know," said Arabella, sniffing. "That's what makes this such a delicious contrast. I can't wait to see how different he is, and whether or not all the family talent went to you." She turned a wicked grin Jeb's way.

"I've got plenty Wil doesn't," said Jeb, crossing his arms over his chest. Wil didn't know if he was angry or intrigued or both. "Be more'n happy to show you, Princess."

Wil rolled his eyes and sighed. "Fine," he said, "anything to move on and not have to witness whatever's going on there. Timothy Twist? You and yours are with me."

Timothy Twist spun his hat around in his hand. "A pleasure, Wizard. I can't wait for you to show us this land you love so much, that we must've taken for granted all those years ago."

Wil looked around, from Bram and Gallath standing close together, to Darlene and Syl being good friends. Jeb was a bit of a concern, but so was Timothy Twist. Wil didn't know what the Wee Folk liked or wanted as opposed to the other factions, but maybe this was an opportunity to get to know them better.

"Alright," Wil said. "Meet you back here for drinks after!"

CHAPTER 26

Faerie Crossing

At the end of the day, Wil trudged his way back to the farm, exhausted. The sun was poised to set over the mountains in the west. The moment they passed through the gates, the group of Wee Folk flooded past him and rushed to the new tree house. Wil stood there and watched them run, chatting and cheering and otherwise having the time of their lives, heedless of his fatigue.

"Well, I'd say that went okay, wouldn't you?" asked Timothy Twist, coming up to stand beside Wil and watch his people head for the shelter. "About as well as I could've expected . . . you know, minus the guns being pointed in our faces. You humans really don't change, do you?"

Wil sighed. "We do, but not fast enough. I thought your people remained unchanged for hundreds of years at a go. Do you really have any room to criticize us there?"

Twist shrugged. He took off his hat and tossed it into the air, where it spun in place for an unnaturally long time. It fell and he caught it again.

"I suppose not. You can't blame a beast for their nature, can you? It's in your peoples' nature to be greedy and angry, just as it's in mine to poke at sensitive areas."

"You keep at it, I might not be able to stop you from getting shot," Wil warned. "And that would ruin my plans, so please keep your damned mouth shut if someone has a gun on you."

"Duly noted! See you tomorrow, Wizard." Twist threw his hat high into the air. It lingered just long enough for the small man to look up at Wil and wink before it landed perfectly on his head. He sauntered over to the trio of trees with the rest.

Taking a deep breath, Wil headed for his parents' house. Everyone else was already there waiting for him, with drinks and dinner. Wil collapsed into his chair and groaned.

"It went that well, huh?" Bob joked, pushing his mostly empty plate away from himself.

"It wasn't the worst it could go, but it wasn't easy either," said Wil. "I'd say it's like herding cats, except I'm reasonably sure I could do that with no problem. Did any of the rest of you have much trouble?"

Bram shook his head, smiling. "No, we had a good time."

"I . . . Well, it turned out mostly good?" Darlene said, making a face.

Jeb, on the other hand, looked pleased with himself. "I happened to have a great day today. You bringing these fae home was one of the best decisions you've ever made." Everyone looked at him strangely. Jeb just shrugged with a cheeky smile.

Sharon rose and ladled stew into a bowl for Wil. "All the people who stayed behind were great to talk to and a lot of help," she said. "They listened to our rules, and I think they'll make fine guests."

"Plenty of new things for me to draw," said Sarah. She wore a wicked smile. "Any chance Cloverton will pay for some in-depth studies of our new friends?"

"Probably," said Wil, slurping up the delicious beef stew. "Start drawing up a storm and see what you can get. Though I think they'll be far more interested in photographs. We didn't have cameras the last time they were around."

He scarfed down his food as fast as he could while still being able to taste it. He reached for the cold beer provided for him, and asked, "So, who should go first?"

"You," said Bram with a chuckle.

"You," said Darlene.

"Me." Jeb grinned.

"C'mon, now, Wil," said Bob. "You've been working hard to make this all happen. Tell us how it went, Mr. Ambassador."

With everyone staring at him, Wil shrugged. "Alright. It wasn't *that* bad. I hope."

It had begun so simply and easily that Wil had honestly not expected any trouble. Timothy Twist had already assembled a group of half of the Wee Folk. That included a mischievous-looking goblin, a portly man about Twist's height who jiggled with each step, a red-headed pixie woman wearing a tight blue outfit who flew at about Wil's eye level, and a young gnome with only the start of a beard but amazingly bushy eyebrows.

The other half would stay and make their rooms in the tree livable and prepare for the season ahead in Harper Valley. In the next few days, they would rotate who went on tours. Not just them, but every faction, until Wil and the others were confident they could get by without constant supervision. He didn't know how long it would be before they could unleash the fae on their own, but he didn't fear that happening yet.

After today, that fear had grown exponentially.

They began with a simple stroll across the farmland in their area of the valley and talked about the community.

"That's where Gabe and his kin live," said Wil. "They mostly tend to sheep and goats, and their cheese is to die for."

"Can we try some?" asked the goblin in a voice that sounded seconds away from giggling.

"Yeah," agreed the pixie, "I want cheese!"

"Cheese! Cheese! Cheese!" the assembled Wee Folk demanded.

Wil was unsure what to do. So he just shrugged and said, "Okay, okay, let's get some cheese, then."

He led the procession right up to Gabriel Gandor's place and knocked on the door. Gabriel's wife, Jenny, opened it, freezing when she saw who was there.

"Cheese! Cheese! Cheese!" the fae demanded, stomping their feet and laughing uproariously. To their credit, they didn't sound angry or threatening, just louder than a small group their relative size should've been. "Cheese! Cheese! Cheese!"

Wil forced a smile. "Hi, Mrs. Gandor. Could I buy some cheese off you?"

Jenny blinked. "How much?"

After buying everyone at least two different wedges of cheese to try, they faced another problem.

"How the hell are we supposed to enjoy cheese without bread and beer?" the thick-browed gnome demanded, though the point was undercut when he took a bite into some mellow aged goat cheese and hummed with pleasure.

"Yeah," said Twist, elbowing Wil in the hip. "Cheese is a good start, but who just walks around eating cheese as they go around viewing the land? Odd choice, Mr. Wizard."

"I didn't choose this!" Wil protested, but it fell on deaf ears as a new chant was taken up.

"Bread and beer! Bread and beer! Bread and beer!"

Wil had intended to introduce them to the neighbors and get them all in with the idea that they were simple people of the land, the same as most of the Wee Folk. A little connection before he took them out for lunch and asked them all to share stories of where they were from with people in town.

Instead, he bought them cheese, and then they stopped at a baker, and then later Old Brown's brewery. While Wil wasn't hurting for money, he hadn't quite expected to treat a group to some of the best Harper Valley had to offer. Well, if it made them happy, it made him happy.

Now laden with beer, bread, and cheese, the tour group resumed their initial trek between farmlands. They were just passing between two of the biggest farms when Wil tried again.

"Now, these two farms belong to Mr. Carrey and Madame DuBois, some of the first families to settle here, about a hundred and fifty years ago." Wil raised a hand in greeting to one of the farmhands off in the distance.

"Oh, I remember this place," said Timothy Twist. He looked up into the sky and inhaled deeply. "We used to have gatherings here to celebrate the passing of seasons and the days when the sun and moon would become one. And it's just used to grow crops to sell now?"

"Uh, yeah," said Wil. "Mr. Carrey's farm is probably the largest and most prosperous of all in town. He's got the best land for it, so he's influential."

Timothy Twist grinned. "Perfect place for a picnic, then. Alrighty, lads and lasses, this is where we'll be enjoying ourselves!" A cheer went up through the Wee

Folk before they crossed the border and ran into the wintery field. But where they ran, the snow melted and the land warmed and blossomed.

Wil didn't need to extend his senses to feel the fae gently tug on the leyline as if anyone could do it and create a patch of spring. Once it was done, they sat down and passed around baskets of bread, bottles of beer, and cheese with bites taken out of them.

Wil stood there with no clue what had happened or how to gain back control. On the one hand, they weren't doing anything harmful. At this point, Wil understood just how much they cared for the health of the land, any land, and they wouldn't do anything to jeopardize it. And chances were they couldn't harm the leyline running through the land. Wil might if he tried, but the idea of the rift tearing wider or growing more unstable terrified him.

"C'mon, Wizard, join us! This is indeed good cheese and good drink, so enjoy some good company!" Timothy Twist patted a spot of grass next to him.

Well, if you can't beat 'em, join 'em. Wil took the spot and sat cross-legged in a ring with the other fae. The pixie woman held up a beer as large as she was and guzzled it as if her life depended on it. Meanwhile, the goblin conjured balls of fire to melt the cheese onto the bread and toast it before eating it. Wil hesitantly took some spread cheese on toast and a beer.

"Such a fine, fine place," said the gnome, practically falling backward to roll around in the grass. He let out a booze-powered belch that made the assembled fae bust up laughing. "Why'd we go and let you guys take this from us?"

"I'd love to share it," said Wil, taking a drink. "I believe everyone should be able to enjoy the fruits of the land. This should be for everyone."

"But this is Mr. Carrey's, no?" Twist smirked. "Hardly belongs to everyone if it's his land. Looks like we're not especially welcome!"

Wil followed his gaze to see Mr. Carrey and his farmhands coming their way. With a groan, Wil stood up and met him about thirty feet away from the gathering.

"Mr. Carrey! Good to see you, sir. As you can see—"

"What the hell's all this?" Mr. Carrey demanded, pointing a gnarled finger at a waving Timothy Twist. "What are they doing on my land?"

"As you can see," Wil continued as if he hadn't been interrupted, "we're having a picnic. If you care to join us, I can make you a chair. We're sharing beer, bread, and cheese." The goblin held up a hunk of bread sodden with melted cheese and wiggled it helpfully.

Mr. Carrey's leathery, tanned face stretched taut. "I want these things off my land!"

Wil's eye twitched. "These *people* are just passing through and reminiscing about their shared past," he said. "This area used to be relevant to their religious ceremonies."

"I don't give a damn, Mr. Wizard! I don't want them to do anything weird to my land like what happened up in the mountains. Am I gonna have to call the sheriff? Or start shooting?"

Wil had known there would be pushback on his efforts, and Mr. Carrey being one of them to provide it wasn't a surprise. What was a surprise was how strongly Wil wanted to just . . . push him down. Smooth things over and force him to get off his back, at least for one day. The temptation came bubbling up strong like bile after encountering an awful smell, but Wil choked it back down.

"No, there's no need for any of that, Mr. Carrey," said Wil. "We'll leave peacefully. But I do hope you give our guests a proper chance in the coming days. They're good people."

The old man's scowl deepened. "That's why they tried to burn my house down last time they were here, then? Do good people do that?"

"I take responsibility for that one," Timothy Twist shouted helpfully. Either the little imp of a man had better hearing than Wil thought or Mr. Carrey was loud enough for them all to hear. The latter seemed more likely. "But Wil and the rest of us squared this away, so that grudge is over. But if you're still sore, I offer you a gift, Mr. Carrey!"

Timothy Twist hopped to his feet and cleared his throat. He began singing in an oddly deep voice, in a language Wil was not familiar with. All around the ring, the other Wee Folk joined in, their voices both high and low, mingling with Twist's and coming together like a magical symphony.

It was magic that came to them as naturally as breathing, like when they grew the trees on Wil's parents' farm. It would've taken Wil and a group of like-minded wizards tons of planning and agreements and test casts before they could attempt what these fae were doing as a matter of course. All around them, the snow melted and plants bloomed again.

The magic spread along the ground like a wave as the land came to life and greedily sucked in the sunlight. The temperature rose, like the glow of a fire too far away to be more than lukewarm. When their song finished, a quarter of Mr. Carrey's farm was in a pocket of spring. Birds sang, and a breeze blew through wildflowers that had taken over the well-loved land.

"Uh . . ." Wil took a deep breath and crossed his fingers behind his back. "This is a very generous gift, Mr. Carrey. What do you say?"

"So, what did he say?" Bram asked, rapt with attention. The table had been mostly packed away as Wil spoke.

Wil screwed up his face into something pointed and miserable looking, and croaked, "'The hell did you freaks do to my land? Turn it back right now or I'll have every one of you shot!' And then he had his workers point rifles at us."

"Wow," said Darlene, "that's a bit much, even for Mr. Carrey. How did you calm him down?"

"I didn't," Wil admitted. "After that, I grabbed everyone and we ran and had our picnic elsewhere. The more they ate and drank, the more they wanted to play games. That part was fun, but Mr. Carrey is old, cranky, rich, and loud. The last thing we need is an incident with him. In a few days, I'll see about reversing it. What about you, Darlene? Did your group get into any fights?"

Darlene laughed. "Not quite, but we got into a bit of trouble of our own."

"Ooh, I gotta hear this," said Bram.

Jeb snorted. "My story's better, I guarantee it."

"Oh, shush," said Bob. "Let's hear it, Darlene."

CHAPTER 27

Shopping Shenanigans

Out of all of the groups going, Darlene had truly believed she got the easiest bunch. She didn't envy Wil. Dealing with Timothy Twist seemed like a terrible headache. Bram's hardest part would be keeping his cool while dealing with his ogres, and she doubted the rest of them cared about Bram's secret. Jeb was . . . Jeb. He'd probably say or do something to mess it up, but they'd fix it later.

Darlene, though, was lucky enough to get to hang out with Syl and his people. As far as the fae went, they were easygoing, friendly, and curious. Unlike Wil and Jeb, she could at least claim to be friends with the leader of the group. That made things so much easier.

"Stick close, everyone," said Syl as they approached the rest of the town. Darlene led the group, with Syl just a step behind. "Best behavior, yeah? Show them how friendly the Woodlands are."

The day's group consisted of Syl the faun prince, Alexis the dewdrop pixie, Raxis the centaur, bringing up the rear, and Medes the owl, resting on a perch on Raxis's shoulder. Darlene hadn't known how to react when introduced to Medes. Talking owls shouldn't have been a surprise at this point—the Woodlands were full of awakened animals. It made sense to bring at least a few along for Harper Valley to get used to.

"What are you showing us first?" Alexis's voice was tiny but carried well.

"The most human thing of all, and something we pride ourselves on in Calipan," said Darlene as the dirt road curved and became an actual street. Tightly packed buildings lined either side of the street, branching out in something of a circle around city hall at the center. The nearest building advertised winter clothing. "Shopping!"

She didn't expect a round of cheers, but she got one anyway. Syl led it, clapping and whooping, and the others joined in, with Alexis putting two fingers in her mouth and blowing the shrillest whistle Darlene had ever heard. Only Raxis was less than enthused.

"But we can purchase things at home," the centaur said with an airy, wispy voice. His blond mane and beard were wild, and he had a frowny, somber sort of face. "Do they have anything we might need for our stay here?"

Darlene shook her head. "No, no, no, that's not the point of human shopping.

You get to go around exploring and searching for treasure. It's not about need, it's about *want*. What do you want, Raxis? Whatever it is, we'll find it."

"Peace," said Raxis with a serene smile on his face.

"Well," Syl said, "of course. But I'm not sure we can or want to buy peace. So why don't we focus on trinkets and little things that might be pleasing?" He nodded at Darlene, as if to say he had her back.

"Did anyone bring something to carry things in?" Alexis chimed in. "I forgot my bag back at the farm."

"I'm not sure there are any worldly possessions that interest me," Medes said as he flapped his snow-white wings.

Okay, those were all good points, but Darlene wasn't about to let that stop her. They just needed to hear it in a way they could relate to. She could do that. Smiling, she gestured to the buildings.

"The thing about shopping is, it isn't always about getting something. Sometimes it's just about looking. Go around and see what people and this world have to offer. Look at their wares, talk to them, and think about what you could possibly want. Markets sell you clothes and trinkets, but they also sell you dreams and possibilities."

Darlene took a deep breath, looking around. The fae looked at her curiously.

Syl, of course, looked pleased by her little speech. "Well, you don't have to tell me, twice!" he cried out.

With a bleating laugh, he trotted carefully over the icy street. A couple coming out of Hank's Furniture stopped and gaped. Syl bowed graciously to them as he passed. He turned into a clothing store and let the door swing shut behind him.

That was all it took. Raxis shrugged, and Medes flew off his shoulder and circled the area. Alexis fluttered over to Darlene. The dewdrop pixie was just over a foot tall and one of the most adorable people Darlene had ever seen.

"Can you show me something good, miss?" Alexis asked sweetly.

"Of course, just stick with me!" Darlene motioned for her to follow. Maybe it was racist of her, but after spending two weeks in Faerie, a candy store seemed like a good idea. As soon as they were in the door, Alexis went nuts, flying from shelf to shelf and narrowly avoiding colliding with a young girl's head as she went from saltwater taffy to colorful hard candies.

A shout from behind made Darlene turn around. Raxis stood halfway inside of a leatherworking shop. His horse half stuck out into the street, stamping impatiently. The proprietor had come out from behind the counter and tried to shoo the centaur out of his shop like an animal.

"Go . . . go away, go on! We don't allow animals in this store!" The middle-aged man waved his hands around to ward him off.

"But I'm a person," Raxis said, looking honestly hurt. "And I can be careful. I don't want any trouble, I just want to see what you have."

"I can't have a horse stomping around the store!"

Darlene jumped in. "Hello . . . , Mr. Rodney, right?"

He huffed. "Yes, I'm Rodney. I'm not sure I'm comfortable opening my store to their kind."

She turned on all of her charm, pitching her voice up and smiling wide. "You're among the first people in town to get to meet our new neighbors. He's interested in . . ."

Raxis pointed a finger at a leather jacket hanging off a hook on the wall. "That looks good. I would like to have this."

Rodney considered it. "Can he pay?" he asked Darlene, deliberately ignoring the centaur. She supposed most people would be a bit wary of having a large horseman in a small, enclosed space, but in the end, it came down to money.

"How much?"

"Five hundred zynce." He had a smug smile Darlene wanted to wipe off. It was technically a fair price for that kind of thing, but on the high end. She was about to haggle with him when the centaur fully entered the store, carefully maneuvering between racks and shelves.

"I can pay," said Raxis. He pulled out a large handful of silver coins and offered them to the leatherworker. "Is this enough?"

Rodney took the coins, his hand drooping when he felt how heavy they were. His face lit up. "You know, I think this will probably do. Good doing business with you, Mr. Horseman."

Just as Darlene was about to snap at him for calling him that, another cry sounded, this time from the candy store. She took off running, pushing her way through a crowd of children. One of the shelves had been cleared off and scattered on the floor. Alexis lay on the floor, stomach distended past what should've been possible. Chocolate covered her face.

"Oooh," she groaned, rolling to her side. "Too much . . . So good . . ."

"Who is going to pay for this?" Mrs. Pataki demanded.

Sighing, Darlene pulled out some bills from her purse. After paying nearly double what the candy probably cost, she scooped the pixie up and left. The crowd in front of the store had turned around to look at Raxis, who looked incredible in his new leather jacket. It was a bit tight in the arms, but open in the front, showing off his muscular chest. Not being entirely naked did wonders for his appearance.

"This was an excellent choice," said Raxis. "Thank you for encouraging us."

Looking down at a still groaning Alexis, Darlene said, "Glad to hear it. That's two for two for now. Where did Medes go?"

Alexis pointed a finger past Darlene. She turned and saw the owl perched up on the roof of one of the buildings. One taloned foot held on to the wood, and the other held a bloody rabbit in place while the owl enthusiastically dug in.

"Look, Mommy, that bird's ripping that bunny apart!" little Suzie Camren called out in awe. "There's *so* much blood!"

"Three for three, I guess," Darlene muttered to herself. It wasn't shopping, but at least he had found something to enjoy. "That just leaves Syl."

She looked up, expecting a scream or the sound of broken glass—anything. Aside from the people getting close and chatting quietly with an animated Raxis and a few people watching Medes eat, things seemed peaceful. Darlene didn't trust it.

"Here, watch her for a bit," she said, depositing Alexis into Raxis's waiting arms.

MacDougal's Finery wasn't a disaster, a wreck, or a travesty. Crowded, but with Syl involved, Darlene tentatively took that as a good sign. She pushed her way past the crowd of mostly older women and came to a stop. Sighing, she said, "Really, Syl?"

The faun stood in front of three mirrors that only went up to his chin, but he still primped, preened, and twisted to check himself from every angle. Darlene didn't know if human fashion was likely to catch on among the fae, but between Raxis and now Syl, they were off to a good start.

The faun wore a ridiculously fluffy and opulent white fur coat that was oversized on his slim frame. But that wasn't all. A tiny, stylish striped hat sat on his head between the curls of his horns. A new necklace dangled on his chest, bright gold with a red gem in the center. And finally, he had a bright green scarf around his neck. Everything clashed horribly, and somehow he still managed to make it work.

"What?" Syl asked, shrugging with an innocent grin. "Is it a crime to look this good? It should be." He turned his back to the crowd and posed for himself in the mirror.

"So other than making a spectacle of yourself, nothing is wrong?"

"Nothing at all," said an older woman, her eyes firmly locked on Syl's backside and the stubby tail that wagged. Darlene stared at her before covering her face with her hand. Was everyone but her going to be into the fae?

"There *is* the matter of payment," said the well-dressed shop owner, Mr. Tosk.

"No problem," said Syl. He reached into the pack still around his side, only now under the coat. Deeper and deeper he sank, until he was up to his shoulder. He pulled out an entire gold ingot and handed it over. "This should be good, right?"

Mr. Tosk sputtered. Raxis had given what was probably a fair deal, but Darlene knew damned well the faun was being generous rather than ignorant.

Syl winked at her and put his arm around her shoulder. "Who's ready for lunch?"

"That doesn't sound so bad," said Bram brightly.

Darlene shook her head. "No, but that started something. Syl went around spending and made himself pretty popular, at least. It got a lot of people asking questions, and trying to touch his new fur coat. I hate that he looks good in it. It's stupid."

"Sounds kind of boring," said Jeb. He grinned at them all. "Now me, I got a fun story to tell."

"No." Wil shook his head. "You want it too much. You can wait. Bram, you're up!"

"Me?" Bram sat up straight. Then he got up. "Why don't we move to the porch for this? I could use a smoke."

There were no disagreements there. They relocated, packed some pipes, and Bram began.

CHAPTER 28

Frigid Firefight

Out of all the groups, Bram was pretty sure the ogres were the least sought after to show around. And why not? They were large, intimidating, and more often than not soldiers or mercenaries. They were the ones who had fought, killed, and died for Faerie. Centuries of bad blood couldn't be washed away overnight, but Bram wasn't worried.

Mostly, he was excited and grateful. It would've been nice to hang with Syl a bit more, but he had no interest in Arabella, and Timothy Twist scared him. It was a thought that amused him: the six-foot-six behemoth couldn't stand to be around the three-foot-tall fae in a gentleman's suit. Worst of all, Twist knew it and would likely have messed with him the entire time.

Gallath wasn't like that. Gallath wasn't like anyone Bram had ever known. He was kind, especially for an ogre. Patient, quiet, and above all else, subtle. The ogre didn't let most things show and seemingly kept to himself, but to Bram he was all but an open book and incredibly expressive. No one else had seen the little upturning of his lips when Bram volunteered to guide them. He'd been pleased, and also unsurprised.

"Where are we going, then?" a cyclops named Borbos demanded. At just over seven feet, he was the only one taller than Bram, with one big yellow eye and a horn on his bald head. "Who are we going to fight?"

"We're not fighting anyone," said Gallath in his smooth baritone. "We're going to be playing nice and seeing what the non-military side of mankind is like. So long as I'm in charge, there will be no battling or assaults on anything. If you are attacked for any reason, retreat to the farm and I'll handle things. Is this understood?"

The members of the Ogre Federation grunted their begrudging agreements. Borbos didn't seem too bothered, but the troll Thunt grumbled, punching the ground. Trolls were mostly bipedal and looked a bit like green, tusked apes with a worse temperament. The other ogre of their group, Shak, wore an inscrutable scowl. It occurred to Bram that maybe he had the toughest job of all the tour guides.

"Well, if you'll follow me, I'll show you some of the natural beauty in Harper Valley!" Bram chirped, motioning for them to follow.

It was right about then Bram wished he had put more thought into where he could take them. Darlene and Jeb seemed to know what they were doing, and Wil was good at improvising. Bram could plan, but he'd been a bit . . . distracted, lately.

He took them to the northeast side of town, where Harper Valley met up with their neighboring town of Gallard Springs. While Harper Valley was mostly farmland, Gallard Springs was filled with people who worked the farms in Harper Valley and those who were excessively spiritual. It made it an interesting place to visit, and the fuzzy border between the two towns livelier.

They came up to one of the bigger parks in the area, where children were playing. Higher up than the farm had been, the snow here was thicker than the light dusting on the ground elsewhere, and the jungle gym and swings were covered in fresh powder. About ten kids were playing there, and they stopped to stare.

"So, uh . . ." Bram realized he should probably be talking and giving a tour. "This is right on the border of two towns, and because of that, we put a park here. It helps promote inter-town friendships and is just a good place for children to play."

"Ahh," said Gallath with a barely hidden smirk. "This is where you train your young in warfare."

"What? No!" Bram's face turned red, which had no doubt been Gallath's point.

Thunt pointed a gnarled finger in the direction of the kids. "Squad?" he asked in a thick voice. "Enemies?"

"Not enemies, no!" Bram's eyes darted among the group.

Shak grunted and said, loud enough for the kids to hear, "Definitely not enemies. These puny children are no match for the Ogre Federation!" He pounded his fist into his open palm. The others joined him, grunting and laughing.

Just twenty feet away, the children looked at each other. One of them, a dark, messy-haired boy of about twelve, tentatively came up, hands behind his back.

"Hi," he said, in a small voice. "Are you guys new here?"

Bram was amazed by how calm the kid sounded. While he looked amazed to see a bunch of burly fae there, he didn't look or sound scared at all.

"Yes," said Gallath, giving the kid a little bow of his head. "Visiting."

"Well," the kid said, a wild grin growing on his face. "Welcome to Gallard Springs, butt-breath!"

The next thing the fae knew, the kid revealed the snowball he'd been hiding behind his back and chucked it at Borbos's face. It hit the cyclops right in the eye, which made him fall hard on his ass.

"Ow!" Borbos cried, clutching at his face. His one big eye blinked rapidly, filling with tears. "That really hurt!"

"Enemies!" Thunt cried, pounding the ground. "Enemy squad!"

"No, he's just a kid," said Bram, putting himself between the suicidal boy and the fae. "Please do not make this worse. He didn't mean it."

"Yeah I did!" the kid said brightly.

Shak crouched and scooped up some snow. In one massive hand, he packed it in together. The boy saw it and took off running.

"Heh. Nice try," Shak said, hurling the snow.

Bram watched helplessly as a snowball the size of the kid's head arced in the air. The ogres, Gallath had told him, had never been especially good with bows or similar, but their ability to throw things was a point of pride. The kid made it most of the way back to his friends before the ball came crashing down on his head, sending him tumbling face-first into the snow.

"Oh gods," Bram groaned, wondering just how much worse it could get. The fae cheered at Shak's impeccable aim, patting and jostling him.

"You know, I think I'll allow this. This is going to be fun," said Gallath.

He turned out to be right.

The children helped their friend up, and then as one turned to glare at the fae. It was then Bram knew the kids weren't scared of these massive warriors. A second later, they were all hard at work, scooping and balling up. Most of them were done at the same time and raised as one.

"Incoming," Gallath called out, stepping to the side behind Bram. A dozen snowballs sailed through the air, peppering the fae and Bram. The shock of wet cold hitting him in the face made Bram sputter. He scooped the snow out of his beard.

Borbos covered his face and got another snowball to the back of his hands. Thunt got hit with three missiles, two in his massive forearms and another in his face. Shak got most of the rest, calling out as a good five missiles pelted him. Gallath alone hadn't been hit. He stuck to the back, watching the rest with obvious amusement.

"Bastards!" Shak cried out before dropping to his knees. The other members of the Federation joined him. They didn't immediately grab more snowballs to throw. Instead, they started stacking and packing the snow up to form walls they knelt behind. All the while, the children below threw snowball after snowball.

Another one hit Bram, and this time he laughed, though he had to take his glasses off and clean them. Gallath chuckled and stepped in front of him, shielding him from the next snowball. Though the ogre was short and slender for his kind, he was still six-three and muscular. Bram ducked behind him.

In that time, the others had managed to make a decent wall that protected them from the worst of the children's onslaught. Borbos packed the biggest snowball yet, building up his weapon until it overflowed from his hands. He rose and spotted the kid who'd got him in the eye.

Smiling, Borbos flung the snow. The kid had plenty of time to dodge, but he didn't. He stared, eyes increasingly wide as it came for him. When it connected, it hit him everywhere and sent him flying backward into the snow.

The other kids looked at the boy, who didn't get up immediately.

"Victory or death!" Borbos cried.

"Victory or death!" Shak repeated.

"Death!" Thunt cried out.

And then all three of them charged the kids, hands full of snow boulders. Thunt waddled more than ran, as his massive arms were too full to knuckle-walk as he normally did. Shak carried his ammunition in his left arm and pelted the kids as he ran.

Bram watched helplessly, wondering if he was about to witness the murders of several children by overenthusiastic fae. He needn't have worried. The fae stopped short and pelted the children with their snowballs until they were out, laughing obnoxiously the entire time. The children had lost and were laughing as well, now half buried from the onslaught.

"Huh. I guess no one's really that upset after all. This could've been way worse, right, Gall—"

Bram turned to his friend just in time to get a face full of snow. He sputtered, wiping his face clean again. Gallath's barely existent smirk made him want to tackle him to the ground. He leaped.

The two collapsed and rolled in the snow until Bram pinned the ogre to the ground. "Surrender!" he demanded.

"Mm. I think not," said Gallath, still struggling beneath him. "This ends with one of us submitting."

"So be it." Bram raised just enough to scoop snow all over Gallath's face and head. The stoic ogre laughed and sputtered. For a moment, the others didn't matter. It was just the two of them having fun, and Bram wouldn't have traded the moment for anything.

"So then I buried his head in the snow until his friends came and pulled me off," said Bram, finishing up.

He had gotten a bit bereft of details by the end of his story, staring off into the distance and losing the momentum he'd built up. Wil didn't know what was going on there, but he wasn't going to ask. Not with everyone else around.

"So that's it?" asked Jeb. "You and the most dangerous, badass fae got into a snowball fight with children? I guess that could be expected of you, cream puff." He blew staggerleaf smoke in Bram's direction. Now that he'd been drinking and smoking for a bit, he was an insufferably obnoxious goofball.

"I suppose this means we have to hear Jeb's story," said Darlene, rocking in her chair. She alone had declined to smoke, instead just enjoying the story and the chilly evening.

"If we have to," said Wil with a sigh.

"Screw all of you. I got the best story of all. You think you had fun? Nobody had more fun than me!" Jeb set his pipe down on a nearby table and leaned forward, eyes alight with excitement.

"Now, me and the Fair Folk . . ."

CHAPTER 29

The Princess and Jeb

The princess of the Fair Folk was the most beautiful woman Jeb had ever seen, and also one of the least likable, from the way she stood to the way her impossibly dark eyes narrowed in judgment at his every move. She looked right through him and judged him as beneath her. Somehow, that made her even more beautiful.

"Well, Bumpkin, why don't we get on with this?" Arabella clapped her hands as if he were a dog. She wore a white fur stole that stood out against her vibrant reddish skin.

Jeb closed his eyes and counted to ten. "My name is Jeb, Princess. I don't know what your idea of being a guest is in Faerie, but you're making your people look awful right now. When I agreed to help in my brother's venture, it's because I love this town and my brother, and I want things to work out for everyone. You will treat me with respect."

The elf princess was stunned. She lowered her head. "You are right, human. I have given thee grave offense, and must repay mine host!"

"Arabella doesn't talk like that," said Wil, crossing his arms over his chest.

"Sure she does," Jeb said, shrugging while not quite meeting his eye. "She talks in that weird hoity-toity, 'I'm better than you' way."

"Uh-huh," Darlene said, smirking. "Are we to translate this from Jeb Story to real events, then?"

Jeb puffed hard on his pipe and blew smoke right at her. "I'll have you know that everything I'm saying is true. I don't need to make things up with the day I had."

"No," said Jeb, "you owe me nothing but manners. Someone as beautiful as you shouldn't be so rude."

Arabella sniffed, her sharp, lovely features drawn up in irritation, but most of all respect. "Of course. Jeb. I am Arabella, daughter of Queen Aria of the Fair Folk, and I would be honored if you would show me around your quant, charming town. And so would my almost-as-attractive friends!"

From behind Arabella, two gorgeous fae women popped out. One was tall and slender, with milky skin and golden hair that made her green eyes pop vibrantly. The other was shorter, more delicate-looking but curvier, with reddish leaves for hair. She looked shy but excited to be there. And finally, there was a tall, stodgy-looking elf man who was unamused by the attention the others were getting.

"I'd be happy to show you all around," said Jeb. "And since you are guests, it's my duty to bring you to the finest socialization points around town, and to make sure you have good company and good fun. Follow me!"

Jeb started off, and the four Fair Folk followed him down the road.

The first stop, naturally, was to get his best friends. If he was going to have some fun, they'd want to be involved, and they could help him show these damned elves how Harper Valley had fun.

"Ladies," said Jeb, throwing an arm around his buddies, "this is Billy-Ray and Elmer. They're the smartest, most dangerous men in Harper Valley, and the three of us will be running this town one day."

Billy-Ray sucked in his gut and leered at them. Elmer winked at the redhead. The Fair Folk were floored, of course.

"If this is what humanity looks like, we've been fools," Arabella said.

"Could you at least try to make this believable?" Darlene complained.

Jeb scowled. "This is more or less what happened! Sort of. I mean, she may have made a comment about more country bumpkins, but her friends took to my boys pretty fast. They were here, bored, and we showed 'em a good time."

Wil had a bad feeling he knew where this was going, and was glad his parents went to bed. "Just . . . try not to embellish," he said.

"Fine. Where was I? Right, we had beers and babes, and we took them to Haley's Hollow up by the waterfall."

Haley's Hollow had been just about the only thing Jeb could think of doing. He knew the others would probably be proper tour guides, doing touristy crap to try to show off their little town. Jeb knew better. He'd show them a good time and let them relax. If they were going to be allies and friends instead of enemies, that meant acting like normal people.

They had an almost perfect number of people to interact with one-on-one. They walked in a line of two, with Jeb and Arabella in the front, Billy-Ray and Eliza in the middle, and Elmer and Vitalya in the rear. Oh, and the lone elf whose name Jeb didn't bother to get brought up the rear, quietly seething.

"So this is your idea of showing us your world?" Arabella scoffed as they walked along the river. The men had cases of beer under their arms. "Go out to a random point in the woods and get drunk?"

"Pretty much," said Jeb, flashing her an incorrigible and handsome smile. "I could tell you what history of the town I know, but what do you care? Same with local gossip. Doubt you'd care that Creepy Dan got arrested for stalking Mrs. Denna, or that Sheila's now dating Anderson. I can show you a nice place and get to know you some."

She was a good foot shorter than him but had no issues keeping up. "What makes you so special that I'd want to know you? I'm a princess. In a few hundred years, when my mother steps down, I'll rule over my people and a fifth of Faerie. What do you think you can offer me?"

"Well, for one, I ain't gonna kiss your ass, Princess." It was tempting to grab a beer from the case and drink one on the way, if only to help punctuate just how unimpressed he was with her ego. "I'll treat you fairly, but I'm not my brother. I'm not just going to politely smile at you while you treat me like shit."

"And this is a good thing . . . how?"

Jeb snickered. "Well, it means you know I'm gonna be honest, and I know how much your kind hates my kind for being able to lie. A lot of my people lie to be polite. I'll tell you exactly what I think of you."

Arabella looked up at him, mirth in her eyes. "Why don't you do just that, Bumpkin?"

"Well, okay. You're kind of a stuck-up asshole. If I have to put up with you, at least you're nice to look at."

Part of him expected that to set her off, or make her attack him back. It's what he would've done. Instead, she chuckled. It was a low, throaty sound, and the first real thing out of her since they'd met.

"I suppose that's mutual, then. You're an arrogant little shit, but you do have a sort of charm to you. It's nice to see an example of a man who isn't quite so . . . symmetrical."

Jeb didn't know what to make of it, so he took it as a compliment.

The river coursed beside them, providing a nice white noise in the background as they followed it away from the road and to the side of the mountains separating them from Orangeville to the north. The waterfall was soon visible, though they had to squeeze through an outcropping of rock to get closer.

"This is what you had to show us?" Arabella sniffed. "Not bad. You do realize we have waterfalls back in Faerie, right? This is not new."

"Oh, hush," Jeb said, leading them over to where there were several stashed chairs and tables all along a clearing before the waterfall. Jeb set the beer down on a table and brushed the chair clear of snow and leaves. He gestured for Arabella to sit. She did, as did the other pairs, all slightly apart with their partners.

Billy-Ray and Elmer looked ecstatic and were busy in conversation with the two other fae. Perfect, that let Jeb focus on the princess. The tall, lanky elf in the back glared at him and took a seat alone, but he wasn't Jeb's problem. Turning back to Arabella, he cracked open a couple of beers and handed one to her.

Arabella sniffed it and made a face. She took a drink and made an even worse face. "The wizard's friend swore the drinks they made were excellent, but what is this swill?"

"Cheap, easy, and guaranteed to get you drunk," said Jeb cheerfully, taking a long drink. Afterward, he let out a belch: his people's mating call.

"You're disgusting," said Arabella as she rolled her eyes and took a longer drink. Then she let out an even larger belch and the two laughed.

"See, isn't that much better?" Jeb said. "Just have fun, enjoy the sights, a nice winter day, and a good drink."

"Good is not the word I'd use for this swill," she said, but she took another drink anyway.

"That makes it perfect for a game." Jeb sat down and moved the beer so they could have a clear view of each other. It was chilly out, but they were dressed just warm enough for the weather.

Well, *he* was. Arabella wore a fur coat, it was open in the middle and showed off a lot of her skin, so much darker than his, but it wasn't a tan. After a few seconds, Jeb realized he'd been caught looking. Rather than apologize or blush, he just leaned back and smirked at her.

"You seem to have a high opinion of yourself, Jeb," said Arabella. Her dark eyes bore into him, and he couldn't look away. "It's genuinely amusing."

"I could say the same to you. It's always great when a spoiled brat makes an ass of herself and acts like she's better than everyone." He took another drink.

"What's this game you spoke of?" Arabella asked. She swung one leg over the other to get comfortable, taking her time and watching Jeb's eyes dart over.

"It's called 'never have I ever.' What we do is we take turns saying what we've supposedly never done. And if we've done it, we have to take a drink. Then it's the other person's turn."

The elf thought about it. "Sounds like an excuse to brag and get drunk. I'm in. You may start, Bumpkin."

"Much obliged, Princess." Jeb took a moment to consider it. Did he want to just go for it immediately, or draw it out? He swirled his half-drunk beer around as the waterfall raged not too far off. The sound always helped him think.

"Never have I ever gotten so drunk I've puked on myself."

Arabella looked at him, rolled her eyes, and took a drink. So did Jeb. It was a nice start at least, but the elf was determined to play dirty.

"Never have I ever made love to three people at the same time." Smirking, she took a drink, while he did not.

"Oh, so that's how you want to play it, huh? Never have I ever . . . won a fistfight." He took a drink, but she did not.

So it went, back and forth, with each of them just trying to one-up the other with boasts of what they'd done in the past. From dances and parties to increasingly darker and lewder things, they both got drunker, until they were a few beers in and lounging in their wooden chairs.

"This wasn't such a bad idea after all," said Arabella airily. "Amusing and a way to pass the time. You *are* more debauched than I had imagined from a small town of prudish human settlers. I'm not impressed, but nor do I think you quite as pathetic."

"No? High praise. You've, uh, been around a bit, huh?" Jeb eyed her appraisingly.

"Centuries more experience than even your oldest and most hedonistic human," was her reply. She stretched out in her chair, spreading her legs and sending a knowing grin his way. "I'm pretty sure I've got more to show you than you do me."

Jeb licked his lips. "Wanna test that theory?"

"Oh gods, Jeb, please tell me you didn't," Wil groaned. He covered his face with his hands and tried to forget the past few minutes.

"Tell you I didn't what?" Jeb challenged. "Show the princess a good time? Prove that I had plenty to surprise her with?"

"You have to be careful," said Darlene. "Getting . . . entangled with the representatives could threaten our mission here."

Bram shifted uncomfortably. "Not sure it's the kind of thing you should be bragging about," he said.

Jeb looked around at them as if betrayed. "Well, screw all of you. I had fun, and I promise you she did too. Better than having a damned picnic with midgets or a snowball fight with kids." He got up and stormed off.

Wil sighed. "And that's my cue to go home, I think. Want me to walk you home?"

"Actually," said Darlene, "I thought I'd go home with you."

Bram stood up. "Then I won't wait up. Great work, guys. We just gotta keep it up and . . . and keep it in our pants, I guess." He gave Wil and Darlene a hug and trudged off east.

Wil and Darlene linked their arms and headed home together. That was one day down, and the rest of the season to go. Jeb's antics notwithstanding, Wil believed they had a chance now. They could make it work, humans and fae. It would just take time.

CHAPTER 30

Whispers in the Woods

The next day, Wil didn't want to have to get up. After the business of the last month or so, it felt good to just lie in his ridiculously plush bed with Darlene curled up next to him. For the longest time, he just let himself float between sleep and wakefulness, until his bladder demanded he get up and take care of things. Darlene remained asleep, limbs splayed out chaotically under the blanket.

Smiling, Wil got dressed, then went downstairs and started breakfast. The good thing about having a three-story home with a tower was being able to wake Darlene with the smell of cooking bacon. He didn't keep much in the house, preferring to eat out and spread his ridiculous paycheck around, but he did keep a few easy-to-throw-together things. He added sausage patties and eggs.

Just as the food was ready, Darlene staggered downstairs, dressed but still unkempt. Her spiky hair stuck up all over wildly, and sleep remained in her groggy eyes. She collapsed at the kitchen table just in time for Wil to set down her plate and coffee.

"Bless you," she moaned, immediately putting a bit of sugar and milk in her coffee and taking a rapturous sip.

Wil joined her at the table with his food. He nibbled on a piece of toast and observed her. "Going to enjoy a lazy day today?" he asked her.

"Gods, I hope so," she said. "I don't think it's likely, but I feel like we've earned a small break, don't you? Your parents can handle our visitors for a few hours, even if some neighbors do show up."

They'd already made those plans, but Wil knew Darlene felt as guilty as he did about taking any time away from their big project. They had put so much time, energy, and effort into things that just sitting and relaxing was . . . Well, how could anyone justify that?

"I'll probably still pop by," said Wil, biting off a crispy chunk of bacon. "Not do anything, just watch and be there in case they need me. That's not too much, right?"

"Right," said Darlene. "That should be doable. And I know Bram's going to take stock of his inventory and see what we need to continue with Wiseman Brewing even after all of this. Maybe I'll help him with that."

They ate in companionable silence, nothing but the scrape of forks against plates and chewing. By the time they were finished and just had their coffee left,

Wil was good and anxious at the idea of doing nothing. So when a knock at the door jolted him from his thoughts, he jumped out of his seat.

"Hello, Sheriff," said Wil, opening the door. His gut dropped at the ornery expression on Frederick's face. The man's thin lips were pursed, exaggerating his mustache. He clearly wasn't happy.

"What happened?" asked Wil warily.

"Mr. Carrey called me about an hour ago over one of his cows being killed," he said. "Mutilated beyond recognition. Think any of your fae friends knows something 'bout that?"

"I doubt it," said Wil, surprised. The shock roused him, and though it was a problem, he found himself eager to have something to solve. "But I can finish getting dressed and go out there right now and check it out."

Sheriff Frederick nodded slowly. "You do that, then, Mr. Wizard. Seems I got a whole bunch more people to keep an eye on now, so any help you can give is . . . appreciated."

"Absolutely, Sheriff." Wil shut the door on him. All of their fae visitors had been drilled extensively on what to do and what not to do. He doubted it was them.

Sometimes this happened in winter—a wolf or a bear whose hibernation was disturbed would venture close to one of the farms up against the forest and take a cow or sheep. It wasn't much of a problem, but it was one he could ward against easily.

"What was that?" Darlene asked when Wil returned to the kitchen.

"The sheriff. Cattle was found mutilated. I'm going to go check that out real quick, then go to my parents' farm. You think you'll spend today helping out Bram?"

Darlene nodded, a smile spreading. "That and talk to him about his new lover."

Wil paused. "He told you who it is?"

"More like I figured it out. It wasn't exactly hard. Don't worry about it, he'll tell you when he's good and ready."

He probably would. Wil put it out of his mind and leaned down for a quick kiss. "Then I'll see you for dinner tonight." he said.

It was such a beautiful morning, Wil didn't even mind dealing with Mr. Carrey's temper and bluster. As soon as he arrived, the old man started shouting and pointing and spitting and talking about how he knew it was those damned fae, and Wil still hadn't taken care of what they did to his land, and *blah, blah, blah*.

"I'll be happy to take a look, sir," Wil said, interrupting the gnarled old man's tirade. "Where's the body?"

Mr. Carrey scowled. "Southwest part of my land, right before the forest."

"So it was probably a wolf," said Wil. "Especially this time of year."

"I know what wolf attacks look like, dammit!" Mr. Carrey's dark eyes were alight with renewed fury. "They don't rip cows to shreds, they just eat!"

"Okay, okay. I'll check it out now." Wil held his hands up and smiled. It only made Mr. Carrey angrier, but it gave the wizard time to slip away.

The mutilated cow wasn't hard to find. The rest of the cattle stayed far away, as if afraid the same would happen to them. For a second, Wil thought about questioning them before he got to the corpse, but cows weren't very good conversationalists, especially when afraid. So he continued on.

Even before he managed to get close to the body, Wil had to agree with Mr. Carrey: this hadn't been a wolf attack. Entire limbs had been ripped off, and the rips were torn open. Most of the best meat had been eaten, but this was no simple quick kill and feast of opportunity. Whatever had done this had enjoyed it. A trail of blood led directly to the trees.

Looking at the corpse dispassionately, Wil briefly considered trying to relive the cow's last moments, then decided he wasn't interested in any light, mid-morning trauma. He headed to the forest, sharply aware of how possible it was that whatever had done this was still relatively close.

And whatever had done this hadn't tried to hide any of it. Footprints lead down to a hidden clearing around a hill. Before Wil got close, he heard the sound of a child sobbing.

He held his breath, listening harder. The sound got louder, followed by weak cries for help. Wil took off running and was nearly there before realization hit him, and he slowed to a stop.

"ALRIGHT, ISOM," Wil boomed. "NICE TRY. COME ON OUT."

Silence, then the echoing sounds of harsh, growling laughter came from all around him.

"How did you know it was me?" the wampus cat asked, though he didn't reveal himself.

"You left me an obvious trail and then tried to lure me in. You're not subtle, my friend." Wil realized he was smiling and dropped it. "You shouldn't have come to my world, Isom. You realize I now have to take you seriously and do something about you, right? I can't risk you hurting any of my people."

Wil had just enough warning to look up and jerk away before Isom dropped to the forest floor just a few feet away. He landed in the snow, all six legs holding up his bloated form. He'd definitely been the one to eat the cow, and from the looks of it, he'd eaten well. The big cat grinned at him.

"That *is* a problem, isn't it?" Isom sauntered forward.

Wil thought about blasting him or keeping him away, but there was a casualness, a fluidity to the wampus cat's movements that was different from before. Isom strode up to him and violently headbutted his hand. Wil responded instantly, scratching behind Isom's ears and earning a purr.

"It is," said Wil. "If you kill any of my people, I will put you down." He couldn't believe he was saying that as he pet his . . . enemy. Frenemy?

"It's a shame," Isom said with a sigh. He circled Wil, purring up a storm and demanding more pats. "Eating humans makes me smarter. And the smarter you get, the smarter you want to be. I could do some damage, eating my way through your town."

"And then I'd incinerate you," said Wil, petting along Isom's side. The big cat paused and leaned hard against him.

"What do you get from eating cows?" Wil asked.

Isom paused, then flopped over on his side. Wil wasn't stupid enough to try petting his stomach. Not when the cat had that extra pair of legs, which meant even more claws that would rend the flesh from his bones for daring to touch a tummy. Wil leaned against a tree and crossed his arms over his chest, waiting.

"Did you know that cows are kind of dumb, but are among the kindest and most compassionate creatures in existence?" Isom said. "And you people just cage them and fatten them up for food."

"Not my choice," said Wil, face heating up. He'd heard similar arguments before from people who were against keeping animals for food. "And I'm not sure I see a point to—"

"Easy, relax," said Isom, rolling around on his back. "It's a compliment. You gotta taste it, right? The friendliness, the kindness, the softness. Even you tasteless humans have to notice. That's what I get out of it. For a little while, I get to feel what it is to not be a solitary predator."

Wil was surprised, but he supposed not too much. "So you went after a cow so you could feel kinder and softer for a little while?"

"No, of course not," Isom scoffed, laughing. He turned his one good eye on Wil. "I ate it because it was big and made of meat, and *so* delicious. The fact that it makes me like this is dangerous. It'd be real easy to put me out of my misery, wouldn't it?" He batted at Wil's feet playfully. "I'm counting on you being too softhearted and cowardly to kill me right now."

"Uh-huh," said Wil, nudging the big murder mittens with his boot. "Well, it's a good gamble. For some reason, I find you more endearing than alarming. I don't want to hurt you."

Isom rolled around again and then looked up at Wil upside down. "What if I made a vow to harm no humans of Harper Valley?" he asked. "I keep my hunt exclusively to you. And the occasional delicious farm animal, of course."

Wil was taken aback. "You'd do that?"

The cat purred louder.

"You want the chance to hunt me *that* badly?" Wil laughed and covered his face with his hands. This was absurd. "Then make your vow and we'll keep our little conflict to the two of us. You may eat sheep, cows, and pigs, but never hit the same place twice. Understand?" He'd pay for the fallen animals until their little game was settled.

Isom nodded. "I, Isom the incredibly powerful, talented, and dangerous wampus cat, do vow to do no harm to the humans of Harper Valley, with the exception of self-defense and any wizards I may wish to devour."

Like all promises made by a fae, Wil felt it. It was good enough for him. He crouched down and gave in to the impulse to rub Isom's exposed tummy. Isom playfully swatted at his face, missing by inches. Wil really wasn't afraid right then. There was an unspoken truce. They'd try to kill each other for real later.

"So, what do you hope to get out of me, when you do manage to kill me and eat my heart? Or whatever it is you have planned."

"Mmm. Invisibility would be nice. As would being able to make copies of myself. Oh, that would make the hunt *so* much more fun." Isom's eyes drifted closed as he thought of it, whiskers twitching in anticipation. "More confusion, more fear, more drawing out the kill. Great fun!"

Wil counted off Isom's abilities on his fingers. "Blinks, ventriloquism, poison breath. And then illusions of some kind. Don't you want to hunt any war mages or something like that for a more dangerous, direct spell?"

Isom's eyes snapped open. He slapped Wil's hand in disgust. "Absolutely not. That'd take all the fun out of things, wouldn't it? The hunt is important. Far more important than being able to succeed at it instantly. Hmph."

Well, that was good to know. Genuinely. Wil appreciated learning a more about Isom. It made it harder to hate the cat or hold his single-minded determination against him. Wil was about to say so when his stomach twitched. He looked up and did a double take.

Through the bare branches of the forest's trees, Wil could see a ship flying in the sky. He stood in a hurry, jolting Isom into seriousness as well. The cat was on all six feet, looking upward with a growl.

"What's that?" Isom asked.

As the twisting in his stomach grew, Wil said, "I think that's the mage from Cloverton."

"Another wizard to eat?" Isom sounded hopeful.

Wil shook his head. "Not if you want to keep your head."

INTERLUDE

Hugo and the *Flying Calamity*

The *Flying Calamity* was one of only a dozen flying ships in Calipan's armada. Eight were used for the military, bringing elite troops to any corner of their empire in a matter of weeks instead of months, and four were used for the highest-level diplomats, including the president during his travels.

Mage Hugo Jefferson liked to think both diplomat and military commander applied to him, even if he wasn't in charge of any particular squads at the moment. He had been before and he would be again, when the time was right and this current mission was taken care of. High-end diplomat . . . well, he must've been one if they trusted him to handle dealing with the fae after all these years.

He smiled as he stood near the helm of the *Flying Calamity*, watching the mountains open up into some of the most picturesque farmland he'd ever seen. It was something out of a storybook, complete with a quaint little town where everyone undoubtedly knew each other and got along. The poor bastards didn't realize just how much danger they were in.

"Captain?" Hugo called out in a high, somewhat nasally, self-assured voice. "How long until we land?"

"Fifteen, twenty minutes or so. Sir." Captain Nesbitt stood nearby, always at attention. He didn't like Hugo, and that suited the mage just fine so long as the captain had a healthy fear of him. In his experience, dislike mixed with fear made for the most efficient workers, so long as their fear outweighed their hate.

An imp dropped out of the sky and onto Hugo's shoulder. It was only about a foot tall, with large leathery wings and a snaky tail that ended in a spike. It looked like a mockery of a human, almost like a monkey, twisted and hateful. Its face was blank, eyes empty, just like the rest of Hugo's retinue. The mage had felt him through their mental link before the imp had gotten close.

"Report," he whispered.

The imp didn't move, but it did open up its mind to him. Hugo saw glimpses of memories go rushing by at the speed of thought before he mentally dove in and picked one. The imp, especially with its mind properly broken and obedient, was an excellent scout. These particular memories covered a conversation between the paper pushers sent along with Hugo.

They didn't want to be there, and they were terrified of him. That much tracked—and was fine. It made Hugo smile even wider, thinking of how much it must've galled them to be working under someone with a reputation like his. But as the memory of two men talking in the ship's depths continued, one thing stood out to him: they didn't want war.

Hugo dismissed the memory, just as it was getting good and they discussed what to do to sabotage the mission if need be.

"Good boy," he said mockingly, reaching up and scratching the imp's bald scalp. Somewhere, buried very deeply, what was left of the imp's mind recoiled.

Out of all of his slaves, Hugo loved his imp the most. It had been the first mind he broke thoroughly, the first one he reshaped and reprogrammed according to his wishes. It had no loyalty, because it was not capable of that, but it was still the mark of when Hugo had first truly grown into his specialty. The other imps, demons, devils, elementals, and fae he'd broken over the years had never been quite as sweet.

They were all over the ship, watching the crew for him. Captain Nesbitt feared Hugo's slave squad, but there wasn't anything he could do about it. They went with Hugo everywhere he went, his eyes and ears and weapons. They were how he'd earned the title of mage, and how he'd eventually become an archmage. Thanks to the return of the fae, that time was now.

Harper Valley rolled beneath them, beautiful even under a foot of snow. He had no clue why some insignificant farm town in a pretty but unimportant basin bottleneck was where the fae had decided to leave the world, but it would give him a chance to see how his old student was doing. The fact that Wilbur McKenzie of all wizards was involved was more amusing than he could ever rightly say.

"Landing, sir," the captain informed him.

The ship slowed down and lowered in altitude, making Hugo's stomach flip pleasantly. This was the slowest, worst part of using a flying ship. Docking and disembarking were strange when you added a third dimension to it.

"I'll be using the *Calamity* as quarters, so no need to get my things. Have some of my creatures brought down to scout out the land. Understood?" Without waiting for an answer, Hugo muttered a spell under his breath. He took a running start and leaped over the side.

Downward he sank, faster than a feather but slower than a rock. Hundreds of feet beneath him was a large gathering area, and just about the only place the ship could safely dock. There were already people there, including, presumably, the mayor. Hugo angled through the air until he was directly over where he wanted to land and let gravity do the rest.

The crowd watched him come down, his expensive jacket and hat fluttering in the wind. Hugo was a pale man with vivid orange hair, expensive clothes, and more power than any of these pissants would ever know about, let alone wield. And he loved that their first impression was of him jumping and floating down. He landed next to a nervous, balding man in a bad suit in front of a podium.

"Are you the mayor?" Hugo demanded.

The poorly dressed man nodded and opened his mouth to speak. "Yes, I'm—"

"Fantastic," Hugo interjected. "I'm here to take over. You and your office can support me by doing what I say and staying out of my way." He reached over to give the mayor's arm a sardonic pat. "You're in good hands now, Mr. Mayor. Cloverton has your back."

The mayor looked at him, then tried again. "I'm Bartholomew Sinclair, and—"

"Do you have logs of all of the disappearances and times when your resident wizard made his major moves?" Hugo pressed.

"Well, yes, of course."

"Get me everything you have. I want a paper trail I can follow before I start interviewing people and interrogating the fae. This has already been handled poorly, and that ends now. Cloverton will not tolerate any threats to our sovereignty or power, and that . . . Wilbur!"

Wilbur McKenzie, his former pupil, ran as fast as his lanky legs could take him. He cleared a path through the mayor's people and the handful of others who had come around when they saw a flying ship come in. Holding him back was a fine looking staff that positively crackled with power Hugo could feel, even at this distance.

"Wilbur McKenzie, you beautiful bastard, come up here!" Hugo called out, applauding so that others around him would as well.

Wil hesitated, and the look of fear and uncertainty on his face filled Hugo with joy. Well, that was just a taste of what he deserved for embarrassing Hugo the way he had. The mage motioned for Wil to join him on the stage.

Wil looked behind him, where an enormous man and a pretty enough townie girl followed, huffing and puffing. Then he looked back at a grinning Hugo, grimaced, and did as he was bid. He climbed the stairs to the stage, standing a healthy distance away from the mage. His friends stayed nearby. Good, at least they knew this was a time for wizards to speak.

"You will not *believe* my surprise when it turned out you were the one behind all this!" Hugo said with an uninhibited laugh. "*Wilbur McKenzie*, in the middle of a multidimensional diplomatic nightmare? After going back to his little farm town? For someone who flat-out rejected a position that would make use of his extensive talents? And yet here we are, and it's up to me to bail your ass out. Funny little world, isn't it?"

Grimacing, Wil said, "Hello, Hugo. I wondered if they would send you. As it turns out, I'm actually doing a really good job of handling this as is, but—"

"If you were doing such a great job, you would've alerted Cloverton first and awaited orders," said Hugo. There was a special delight that came in interrupting people when they were wasting his time. The look of surprise, rage, and helplessness came together and tickled the cockles of his heart. "This is bigger than a simple master wizard."

Wil's normally stoic, passive, kind of bony face twitched. "Last I recall, we were basically the same rank," said Wil. "Since you didn't make archmage, what makes you more qualified?"

Hugo grinned. He looked around at the gathering crowd. They were inconsequential to him, but Wil had to live with them. It looked like McKenzie needed some humbling.

"You are such a *joker*, ha! But I don't think anyone else is in on the joke. Shall we clue them in?" Hugo pretended to look around and settled on Wil's friends. "Wil used to be my mentee. I was about to make archmage, conditional upon mentoring this young man right here, who almost became a mage himself. What happened, Wil?"

Wil's friends looked at him strangely. Oh boy, they didn't know! The master wizard himself shifted uncomfortably under the weight of their gazes.

"It doesn't matter," Wil muttered.

"Oh, I think it does! You mention me not making archmage. I should be angry at you for that," he said, wagging a finger in Wil's direction. "But I'm angrier about the waste of talent. You were one of the best mind mages the academy has ever produced, and you focused on *illusions* instead? Sad."

Whispers went through the crowd. While most people didn't know their ass from a hole in the ground when it came to magic, certain kinds had a reputation. Judging from the expressions of the townspeople, Wil's true specialty was a surprise. Hugo's day just kept getting better and better!

"Listen, Mr. . . . ?" The mayor tried once more to get involved.

"Oh, right, how silly of me. I'm Mage Hugo Jefferson, and as of now, I expect full cooperation from the entire town. To aid me is to aid Cloverton, and that will be rewarded. To get in my way is to impede Cloverton, and we have no tolerance for that. This is a once-in-a-lifetime potential crisis we are taking very seriously. Any information you have on the situation can be given to one of my assistants, which will be passed on to me.

"As for our master wizard here . . ." Hugo winked at Wil. "I'm sure you've been very busy and hard at work, holding down the fort for me. I'm going to give you until tomorrow to talk things over with the fae and apprise them of the situation. Debriefing at nine a.m. Over breakfast! We've got *so* much catching up to do."

Hugo didn't wait for an answer or a reaction. He pushed past the mayor and left the area entirely. The thing they needed to understand was, they now operated under his pleasure and he was in charge. Assuming Wil hadn't changed much in the year and a half since they'd spent time together, he was likely still a doormat, crying about ethics. And there was a place for that, of course. Just not among people with a knack for the craft.

This was a wizard's world, and the rest of them would learn to live in it.

CHAPTER 31

The Reluctant Mind Mage

Although there weren't many people at the fairgrounds, Wil was mortified. How many people had heard Hugo just shout out his greatest shame? Darlene and Bram for sure—they both looked at him with curiosity and concern. Sinclair glared at him, but that wasn't really any different from the usual. Wil looked around wildly, counting off each person focusing on him.

Including his friends, it was maybe five. Far fewer than it could've been, and a little more than he wanted to deal with. He channeled power through his staff and cast a different sort of spell. It wasn't an illusion to make himself invisible. Ironically, it was a form of mind magic: an aura he generated that encouraged people to ignore him. Nothing invasive, just a permanent distraction, of sorts.

And then he slipped away, trying to ignore the hammering in his chest. Wil didn't know where he was going until he was there, making his way through the fairgrounds to an upraised area with park benches. He sank into one and stared out at the southernmost point in town, where the road led to Appleton, and let himself just think.

Of all the people Cloverton could've sent, Hugo was . . . well, if not the worst, then really high up there. Wil didn't think it was on purpose, but someone back east must've had a real chuckle at sending Hugo to clean up Wil's mess after Wil had all but destroyed the man's career.

Wil tried to think of how Hugo might have handled going to Faerie, how he might have dealt with the rift opening . . . everything. Not a single thought went anywhere good. As much as Wil was aware of his own weaknesses and soft heart, the alternative was certainly worse. With Hugo in control of Calipan's response . . . Gods, what could Wil even do to prevent any of it, let alone the very worst an egotistical monster like Hugo could and would do?

"Wil?" He looked up. Darlene and Bram stood nearby. Darlene nibbled her lip. "Can we join you, or would you rather be alone?"

He motioned for them to sit, turning around and facing the table where his staff lay. They weren't in any danger, but it felt good to have it nearby when he felt like this. Darlene sat beside him, and Bram across. Probably for the best, as even Wil and Darlene together didn't equal his weight and their seat rose a couple of inches.

"Are you okay?" Bram asked. He mercifully didn't pry too far into Wil's past, though that was inevitable. That secret was out, and now he'd have to face it.

"Not really," said Wil, laughing. "All of our hard work is about to go into the crapper. If Cloverton wanted peace and commerce, they would've sent Rosen or Glover. Instead, they sent someone used for war and espionage. Someone who keeps mind-broken slaves."

They both winced. "Seriously?" Darlene looked as disgusted as Wil felt. "I thought slavery was made illegal fifty years ago."

"For humans, yes," said Wil with another bitter laugh. "Hugo Jefferson skates past that by enslaving demons and elementals and fae. He summons otherworldly beings, breaks their will, and keeps them as pets, scouts, and bodyguards. There has to have been a reason they chose *him* to lead these talks."

Bram decided to be the brave one. "And your former teacher, huh? Are you seriously a mind mage? I thought you were an illusionist, with a side focus on earth magic."

Wil took a deep breath. "I am. But that's not . . ." He set his jaw. "There are a few different reasons I stayed longer at school. Part of it was because I was afraid I'd never go back if I visited, and part of it was because I switched focus late into my education. At first, I was double majoring in illusions and mind magic. Turns out I've got a knack for the latter, which makes the former easier.

"Natural mind mages are fairly rare, and they're highly sought after. I was given an offer for a full ride if I enrolled in the military for a specialist position. And Hugo was the person they got to tutor and try to shape me into the type of wizard who would be good at infiltration, information extraction, and hurting others."

"So, in other words," said Darlene, "someone else entirely. I'm guessing it didn't go well."

"No," said Wil. "It really didn't."

"What all can mind mages do?" Bram asked, doing his best to not look or sound nervous. He almost succeeded. "What can *you* do?"

Wil sighed. "Do I have your permission to demonstrate? I won't hurt you."

Bram shrugged. "Sure. Just so long as it won't hurt."

"Alright. Look me in the eyes."

As soon as Bram turned his warm brown eyes to Wil, the wizard let himself sink into Bram's mind. It didn't require eye contact, but it helped. It was the awareness that did it, that moment of personal connection between two people who perceived and were focused on each other. Wil may have been rusty from disuse, but it took almost no effort to dive right in.

He kept it surface-level. There was no need to delve through Bram's memories or explore his mindscape, as tempting as it was. There was nothing to stop Wil from grabbing hold of him and taking control. Bram got up from the table and started dancing in place.

"I am the most graceful swan in the lake," said Bram with a pirouette he never would've been able to do on his own. "My beard looks silly and I should shave it off. I'm in love with a member of the fae and won't talk to anyone but Darlene about it." Then Bram leaped forward, legs stretching before and behind him before he landed gracefully.

Wil released him, swallowing hard. It had drained him, but not by much. Bram himself didn't look very pleased. A full-body shudder went through him, and he pulled at his beard. Not hard enough to rip it out, but it looked like it hurt.

"What the hell was that?" Bram demanded, sounding appropriately violated.

"A small taste of what I can do if I try," said Wil, his voice hardening. "Now pair that with invisibility and the ability to silence all sound in an area. What do you get?"

"An assassin," Darlene answered instantly. "And possibly one of the most valuable agents they could've had. But it couldn't ever have been you."

"Do you believe that?" Wil whispered.

Darlene grabbed his hand. "Of course I do! We all know what kind of person you are, Wil. You're the absolute least qualified person to be an assassin."

Bram shivered. "I really didn't like that just now, but it could've been so much worse. Was it really that easy? What else can you do? Can you hear thoughts?"

Wil debated how honest to be. Darlene was right in that he didn't like lying, but there was plenty he didn't tell others. Maybe now was the time to open up. If he couldn't trust them, he couldn't trust anyone. He squeezed Darlene's hand reassuringly.

"You'd have no defense against me if I were to try. I could probably hear thoughts if I tried. It would just take a spell to make me process it like that. I tend to have to go all the way in. It's not hard, but I have to choose to do it.

"As for what else I can do." Wil took a deep breath. "I can go through your memories and experience them. I can make *you* experience them. Again and again. I can put a nightmare in you so deep that you'd never sleep right, ever again. I can blend illusions and mind magic together. That was going to be my big final project. Mind magic and illusions combined to create *real* illusions. Things that can actually affect your body. You want to know what I could do?"

The first tears trailed down his face as the memories hit him. Wil swallowed a lump in his throat that wouldn't go away. "It takes a lot of effort, but I can make an illusion of a man, planted straight into your brain. Only you can see him. And I can make him choke you. To the rest of the world, you'll just be standing there alone, gasping for air while you asphyxiate from an illusion you can't reject. It was difficult before, but that was before crafting my staff and going to Faerie. Who knows how easy it would be now?"

Darlene pulled him into a fierce hug, and Bram joined in, enveloping them both. They comforted him and gave him time to gather his composure. Darlene stroked his hair gently.

"Is that what they tried to make you do?" she asked. "Did they tell you to kill someone and you refused? Is that why you dropped out of the program?"

Wil lost it again, crying harder while his friends silently lent him their strength. It hit him like an avalanche, slow at first and then building up to a crescendo that buried him. It took a good ten minutes before he calmed down enough to pull away and wipe away tears and snot on his sleeve. He laughed and slumped.

"You know the funniest part, Darlene? You just hit me with what I could inflict on anyone at a moment's notice. And I didn't like it. I won't use it if I can avoid it." Guilt hit him again. "But I . . . have used it. Remember when Jerry attacked us on the road to Appleton?"

"Hard to forget," said Darlene with a chuckle. "I remember you hissing something and he ran away screaming. That was mind magic?"

Wil nodded.

"Is Hugo a mind mage too?" Bram asked. "He was your mentor, right? He's the one who tried to make you . . ."

"Yes. That's why he isn't an archmage. I refused, failed out of the program, and it tanked his chances for a promotion. He's obviously not fond of me." Wil stood. "And now more people in town know I'm a mind mage. This means no matter how much I hold myself back, people will be afraid of me. Even other wizards are usually uneasy around mind mages."

"I still trust you," said Bram. He grinned, adding, "So long as you never do that to me again."

The relief Wil felt nearly knocked him over. "Thanks, Bram, I needed to hear that."

"And Hugo, can he do everything you can?" Darlene asked, suddenly looking about, appropriately horrified.

"No," said Wil, breathing a sigh of relief. "I'm good at connecting with a person directly, which gives me a lot more precise control. More control than I have with any other form of magic. Hugo is more powerful but far less delicate. He's good at overpowering people, but it doesn't leave them in a good state afterward. Never allow yourself to be alone with him."

"Gods," Bram whispered. "Don't worry, I won't be. But what are we going to do? How can we handle this and come out ahead?"

That was the worst part. Wil collected his staff and leaned on it. It made him powerful, but he wasn't sure power was going to save the day this time. No amount of raw magical strength and good intention would stand up against Hugo's cruel, demanding nature. Not on its own.

"I'm not sure there's anything I can do about him," Wil admitted. "But I can warn the fae, at least. Let's go. They need to be able to defend themselves against him."

CHAPTER 32

Party Pooper

Wil, Darlene, and Bram arrived at the McKenzie farm to find a party in full swing. It wasn't yet noon but over a hundred people, fae and human, were mingling without a care in the world. The entire farm was a temperate island in the winter wonderland, complete with Sharon's flowers blooming larger than ever. The three of them slowed to a stop at the mailbox, gawking at the sight.

"Did you know about this?" Bram asked Wil. "I thought there weren't any real plans today. We were just going to sit back and relax for a day while your family introduced the fae to a few neighbors."

Darlene burst out laughing. "Sharon and I talked about this as a plan, but it was going to be smaller than this!"

Wil continued toward his family's house, waving and forcing a smile when passing by people he recognized. Which was damned near everybody. All of their closest neighbors within a couple of miles and their entire families were there. Bob and Henry Hagger had some ribs turning over a flame on a camping grill. In the thawed section of the nearest field, a group of human and fae musicians had set up and were playing together in a strange cacophony of familiar songs.

Wil had to stop to let the Lane children run past him, chasing after a couple of pixies flying just out of reach. He nodded and greeted Patty Patterson but didn't stop until he reached his father.

"What is all this?" Wil gestured wildly. "This wasn't part of the plan!"

"That'd be my fault," Mr. Hagger chortled. He was a very large, strong man, one of the few in town who didn't look small compared to Bram or Bob. "After you left to get our people back, Bob and I had a terrible argument. When you came back, I did what any man would do and apologized and admitted I was wrong. He told me to think about giving them a try, even though some of those damned things tried to burn my house down. So I got a few of the others and we decided we'd make a day of it."

"So you didn't plan this party?" Wil asked his father.

Bob shrugged with false modesty. "Of course we did. Just not to this extent. That was all our neighbors. Besides, it's winter. Even with the feast coming up, it's any excuse to get together and eat until we burst. Just so happens to be a good time to share that love with our new friends, right, Henry?"

Mr. Hagger laughed again. "Truly, I'm surprised. It was that nice goatman fellow, Syl, I think, who made me rethink things. That boy's a charmer!"

He didn't know the half of it. "Where is Syl now?" Wil asked. "Something big happened, and he and the others need a heads-up."

"That flying ship?" Bob nodded. "Yeah, we figured that meant the mage is here, right? But at that point we were already starting the party. He'll be welcome if he comes and . . . Oh, he's not welcome?" Bob's tone changed in a hurry upon seeing the look on Wil's face.

"I think this is my cue to be elsewhere. Nice seeing you, Mr. Wizard!" Mr. Hagger slapped Wil's back, then took his beer and left.

"He's a former teacher of mine," said Wil, thinking of what to say. There was no way he would tell his father that the mage sent to Harper Valley had once tried to force him to kill a man in cold blood.

"One I didn't get along with too well. Honestly, he's a bastard, and the fae need to be warned that things are going to get harder. They might need to cut and run."

Bob grimaced. "It's that bad? Damn. Look, son, even if it could get worse, it's not there yet. There's still time, right?"

"Yeah, I guess," said Wil, feeling a bit better at the thought. "There's no guarantee things will be a complete disaster. We still have a lot to do, but it still might crash and burn."

"That's the spirit! I'll keep working on our neighbors. This turnout, though?" Bob nodded toward the group of people dancing. There, Wil found Syl, dancing with Sarah, of all people, who had a manic grin on her face. "I think it's a sign things aren't hopeless. We just gotta keep working hard and make sure we win, no matter what."

Wil grabbed his dad in a one-armed hug, which was returned with a hearty slap on his back. What was with older men slapping each other on the back? Chuckling, Wil pulled away.

"Thanks, Dad. You're right. The mage, Hugo Jefferson, doesn't want to meet until tomorrow, so that does give us time to prepare. Are those ribs ready, by any chance?"

"Another half hour, minimum," Bob said.

"Damn. Well, I'll go grab Syl and the others and . . . Oh, they beat me to it."

Darlene and Bram were already there, talking to Syl. They looked his way and then pointed to the barn. Wil nodded and followed after them. As he did, he passed the fae's housing and marveled at how it had felt to be a part of raising the trees and shaping them into something habitable. That, too, gave him hope that maybe cooperation wasn't out of the question.

He passed by Princess Arabella, who sat in a chair pretending to look bored while her foot jiggled in time to the music. Jeb sat next to her and pointed at a group of people, saying something Wil couldn't quite make out. He wasn't sure he wanted to, come to think of it.

The barn was noticeably colder than the rest of the farm, which amused Wil, as usually it was a bastion of warmth in winter. It was still good enough for the sheep and cows they kept for personal use, and it had the familiar smell of beast and crap that Wil found oddly comforting. Bram and Darlene were filling in Syl and (to Wil's surprise) Gallath.

"So Wil says that we're going to need to be careful, you guys especially," Darlene finished. She nodded at Wil, and everyone's gazes followed hers.

"Is it true?" Gallath asked, sounding angry for the first time since Wil had met him. "Did your government send a man who has enslaved fae to negotiate with us?"

Wil winced. "Yes, it's true. The mage is known for mentally breaking creatures and keeping them. I don't know how many fae he has. When I knew him, it was just a few, and—"

"Just a few? *Just a few?*" Gallath wasn't much taller than Wil, and he was slim for an ogre, but in that moment Wil understood that he could be as dangerous as any of his kin. Gallath stalked forward until he was nose to nose with Wil. "How many of my people as slaves would be an unacceptable number for you, then?"

"Gal, it's not like that," Bram said, coming up behind him and putting a hand on the ogre's shoulder. "Wil's not happy about it either."

Gallath sneered, not turning around. "And what do you plan on doing about it, Wizard?"

Syl spoke up. "What do you expect him to do about it? You want him to fight him off? Tell his government to send someone else? Come on, Gallath. You know as well as I do that we don't get to choose who is sent as a representative. You and I didn't exactly volunteer. Though I would have," he added quickly, "if my father hadn't already told me to go."

Wil held up his hands in surrender. "It's out of my hands, but I'll do everything I can to help stop this from getting worse. If I had to guess, I'd say that Cloverton is trying to use this as a power move. A reminder that we . . ." Gods, did he really have to say it?

"That we *what*, Human?" Gallath spat.

"That we won the last war and are stronger than you," Wil finished, swallowing down his distaste. "It's stupid and petty and the kind of thing my people feel necessary to do, so they can get whatever it is they want. I love Harper Valley, but Calipan . . . Honestly, we're bullies a lot of the time."

Gallath growled but relented. He sat down on stacked hay and crossed his arms over his chest. "So what do you propose to do, then?"

Everyone turned to look at Wil. Not for the first time, he was reminded that whether he liked it or not, he was the leader and responsible for things. Even if all he wanted to do was run away and let someone else deal with Hugo.

"I don't have a plan *yet*," said Wil. "But I'm going to work on it. For now, I just needed to warn you that he'll likely try to goad you all into a fight, and he might make big demands. Tell Timothy Twist and Arabella that, and to never be alone with him. I'm going to do what I can to find out more from him, and we'll go from there. As long as I'm around, I won't let him hurt you guys or start anything big."

"Even if that means killing him?" Gallath demanded.

Wil grimaced. "I hope it doesn't come to that. If he dies, chances are that could start a war immediately. But if he tries anything, I will stop him. If he pushes for war, I will stop him, somehow. I will not let Faerie be threatened by him if there's anything I can do to stop him. You have my word."

Obligation hit him again, another big promise made to the fae that he wasn't sure he'd be able to keep. Still, the feeling of connection, power, and possibility was now established between him and Gallath. It was enough for the ogre, who stood up.

"Fine. I'll let the others know." With one last glance at Bram, Gallath stormed out of the barn.

"Think I should go after him?" Bram asked.

"No," said Darlene, putting her hand on his arm. "Not just yet. Let him be mad for a little while. It'll be easier to soothe the anger once it burns itself out a bit. Probably."

Syl let out a sigh and tugged on his goatee thoughtfully. "Well, this news is a real mood killer. Did you really have to tell us *during* the party?" It sounded like it he was joking. Probably. The faun went to the barn doors and peered out. "You said he has enslaved fae by breaking them. How obvious is it?"

Wil shuddered, thinking of the dead looks in their eyes and the way Hugo's thralls went about their duties with no life or enthusiasm to them. He'd peered into them, once. They weren't gone entirely. Their personalities and will had just been crammed down to the darkest crevices of their mind, too deep to do anything against Hugo's commands.

"Obvious. If he does anything to any of you, I'll know about it. Depending on the extent, I might be able to reverse it."

Syl pursed his lips. "Well, I trust you well enough to protect us or heal us from whatever happens. There's not much we can do today, so why not just enjoy ourselves? If he's intent on being a bully, I'm just going to make it that much harder for it to work. We'll worry about this tomorrow." He stepped out of the barn and went back to the party.

Then it was just Wil, Bram, and Darlene.

"Are you okay, Wil?" Bram asked.

"Do you need anything from us?" Darlene added.

Wil thought about it. "I need . . . a plate of ribs, a beer, and maybe a lot of staggerleaf."

They laughed, and each threw an arm around his shoulders, leading him out of the barn and back toward the party.

CHAPTER 33

Empire

The next day, Wil set off for the *Flying Calamity*, dread settling in his stomach like a lead weight. He'd enjoyed the party as best as he could, while Gallath and Syl took care of informing the other fae that the new player in the game would likely be hostile.

Wil had seen flying ships only a few times in his life, and they filled him with a sense of awe and wonder. Having made a working flying carpet, he knew an entire ship like the *Flying Calamity* would be roughly a thousand times more difficult and the work of dozens of wizards cooperating. It was a beautiful, modern warship, though it lacked masts for sails, propelled instead by magic as well as aerodynamics.

At the fairgrounds, a full crew was already working on the anchored ship even at half past eight. Men scrubbed the deck and did general maintenance. Two men worked an elevator to deliver supplies down to more of the crew below. A few were guards, with their guns out and bored looks on their faces, until Wil showed up.

And beside them was one of Hugo's slaves. An eight-foot-tall earthen form, with crude features and green flames for eyes. It looked almost like a golem, but Wil recognized it as an earth elemental. It turned its head to him, and Hugo's voice came out of its mouth.

"You're early, Wilbur. I said nine. However, I remember your obnoxious habit of always arriving long before you're welcome. I'll be down in a few minutes."

"Okay," Wil said. As far as he knew, Hugo possessed a sliver of awareness and senses from each of his slaves but could only reasonably focus on one or two at a time. Wil waited patiently as the minutes ticked by.

Closer to nine than not, Hugo appeared at the railing. He wore a wolfskin mantle he often bragged he got from mentally dominating a wolf pack and then killing them for their pelts. With a wave, he floated down to Wil, hitting the ground and immediately closing the distance between them.

"Did you need to bring a staff with you?" Hugo asked, rolling his eyes at him.

"Are you saying your sleeves aren't filled with wands?" Wil scoffed. As much as he did fear Hugo and what he could do to their plans, pent-up anger and resentment were easier to focus on. It felt better to be angry than scared.

"You have a point," Hugo allowed, a playful smile spreading across his face. "I have a reason to be cautious. Here I am in your backwater little town, where our enemies have managed to not only hide from us but also launch an attack and take our citizens prisoner. Not only that, but I have a faithless, cowardly apprentice to worry about betraying me. Again. Can you blame me for being cautious?"

Wil's eyes dropped, lingering on Hugo's impressively shiny boots. "I didn't betray you. Not on purpose. I just realized I didn't want to be a killer. I can and have killed to save myself and others, but I could never do it in cold blood."

"You killed someone?" Hugo's tone changed immediately. "Who? When? I'm proud of you!"

"There's nothing to be proud of!" Wil snapped. "In Faerie, there were a pair of assassins. I let them think they killed me, then had them eaten by giant carnivorous plants." He didn't think of the moment often, but sometimes it came back to him and lingered. It had been necessary, but he took no joy in any of it, other than the fact that he and his friends were still alive.

"Well, well, well. Maybe there's hope for you after all," Hugo said with a nasal chuckle. "You won't have to stay in this sleepy town forever if you can grow the hell up and serve your country like a man. Now, I'm famished. Take me someplace. Show me what you locals like to eat."

Wil grunted but otherwise didn't bother to respond. Hugo wouldn't listen anyway. He motioned with his head to follow and set off north, casually using his staff to heat the snow around them and carve a path for them to walk through.

It was quiet at first, but before long Hugo started in again, just as they crested a hill and saw the town sprawled out before them.

"Why did you want to come back here?" the mage asked, not bothering to hide his disdain. "You may be soft-hearted, but you're a good wizard. Why stay in the middle of better cities?"

"It's home," Wil replied simply. The cold air was a pleasant balm on his increasingly hot cheeks. "It might not look like much to you, but I know the potential this place has. I want to help see it grow."

"Potential?" Hugo scoffed, eyeing a passing farmhand Wil knew by sight but not name. "If it wasn't for the rift opening, no one would give half a crap about Harper Valley. It's a pit stop between real cities. What do you have here that nowhere else does?"

"My family and friends, for a start. You know what friends are like, right, Hugo?" Wil turned a nasty grin his way. "Or do you only have slaves?"

"I have friends," Hugo said loftily. "Other wizards. No one else is worth my time. No, don't even *think* about touching my things!" he suddenly shouted, eyes clouding over. "If I catch you in my quarters again, I'll add you to my collection of thralls and there's nothing your captain will be able to do to stop me."

Wil stared, before realizing Hugo wasn't addressing him, but one of the *Flying Calamity*'s crew, he presumed. The mage's eyes focused again and he turned to Wil with a smirk.

"There's *always* someone who thinks they can rob me. It's always some ignorant neg who is jealous of his betters. How soon until food?"

"We're almost there," Wil muttered, ignoring the mage's derogatory term for non-wizard humans. He resumed walking.

He almost took Hugo to Mack's Shack, then decided he liked Mack and Candy too much to do that to them. Instead, they went to a small place open only for breakfast. If the mage wanted to disparage the entire town for being a bunch of farmers, Wil would give him the experience to match it.

The place was crowded, as usual. A bar wrapped around the wall and across the front counter, with stools scattered about. Most of the people in there were men, though Wil recognized Sarah's best friend Jane's mother at the front counter, scarfing down a hearty breakfast of home fries and sausage.

"My gods," said Hugo, loud enough to be heard over the sound of conversations and cooking, "do we eat out of a trough in here?"

Plenty of people turned to shoot him dirty looks. Most paused when they saw he was with Wil and realized who he was. Wil just made his way to the corner where two stools were free. Setting his staff against the wall, he sat down and scooted forward. After a moment's hesitation, Hugo joined him.

"I don't like having my back to people," Hugo said.

"You don't think you're in any danger from a bunch of 'negs,' do you?" Wil wasn't in the habit of using the rude term, but it did the trick. Hugo scowled and got comfortable.

"You're different, Wilbur. It's almost like you have a spine and some teeth now. It's as if you're no longer afraid of me. Is that so?" His blue eyes twinkled mischievously. "Are you no longer the scared little illusionist?"

Wil wanted to laugh. He was terrified of Hugo, no matter how hard he mouthed off to him. A year and a half hadn't been nearly enough time to fully recover from what he'd been through. Spite though, was a wonderful motivator. To people like Hugo, you didn't show anything but strength if you knew what was good for you.

"Morning. Can I take your orders?" a less-than-enthused waitress asked. She had a pad of paper and a pen ready and wasn't quite able to hide her frown.

"Two coffees and two Growing Boys," Wil answered, before Hugo could harass the poor woman.

"You got it, Mr. Wizard," she said, disappearing into the back.

Hugo burst out laughing. "Look at you, 'Mr. Wizard.' Are we on a date? Ordering for me is sooo assertive. I'm all flustered." His eyes went out of focus again for a few seconds, but he didn't bark orders or threats this time. When they cleared, he was serious again.

"I know about the storm and the dragon you defeated. My mentor tried to bind a dragon recently. It didn't end well for him, and the dragon escaped and headed west." He smirked. "I assume that's where you got the horn for that staff. Master Krine's dragon came here, and you killed it or contained the damage while it died, I assume. Either way, it is an impressive tool."

Wil felt as if a bucket of cold water had been dumped on him. The clamor of the diner faded into the background and all he could focus on was Hugo and the sudden spike of cold fury that stabbed him in the heart.

"The dragon's name is Skalet," said Wil. "He's fine now. He gave me his horn as a gift for curing him of the curse that was killing him. A curse your master placed on him, I'm assuming. That means your master is responsible for countless deaths across Calipan and the near destruction of Harper Valley. And thus responsible for the rift opening too."

It was odd to find another connection. Realizing that the storm that had nearly wiped away his town had been caused by the mentor of the man who had nearly broken Wil would be funny if it wasn't infuriating. Wil had ripped open the leyline, but all of it had turned out to be just cleaning up someone else's mess.

"Yes, I've been meaning to ask about that rift, since you didn't include it in your report back to Cloverton." Hugo turned around in his stool to give Wil his undivided attention. There was an unpleasant gleam there Wil didn't care for. It was as though everything he said slid right off the mage.

"There wasn't time," Wil hedged. "I only found out about it after the fae had already crossed over and took a few people back home for questioning."

"Children," said Hugo, though Wil doubted the man truly cared. "An act of war."

The waitress came by with their coffees and a carafe of milk. She set them down, muttering that their food would be ready shortly, then disappeared. Wil took the opportunity to pour in a splash of milk and swirled the mug around. He took a sip, then added a heap of sugar. The coffee here was as terrible as the food was plentiful.

"An act of desperation, considering what we've done to them in the past," Wil countered. "They gave them back, safe and sound."

"Doesn't matter, they still took our people. Tell me about the rift, then. How in the hell did it suddenly just open up?"

Wil had given a lot of thought about how he'd answer that. He decided to mostly go for the truth. "I tapped into the leyline up on the mountain as I diverted a flood. I pulled too hard and it tore open. Turns out the fae had anchored the doorway to their pocket world in Harper Valley's leyline system. When the leyline ripped, it bled its magic all around and the fabric between worlds softened.

"Then they came and scouted out, and I went and got our people back and negotiated for a possible peace treaty. When I said I had it under hand, that's what I meant." Wil's voice hardened. "They like and trust me, and I managed to smooth over multiple crises already. I can deliver us peace and trade negotiations that will get Calipan more food, tourism, and a steady source of faricite."

Hugo mulled it all over silently. He took a sip of coffee, grimaced, and poured in twice as much sugar as Wil.

"That's a lot you've accomplished Wilbur," the mage said, with none of his usual smugness. "You have a lot to be proud of. Maybe there's something to be said for letting a soft-hearted, second-rate wizard negotiate with a lesser people."

"They're not lesser," said Wil.

"Whatever," Hugo said, waving it off. "The problem is, if they do have access to enough faricite for our needs, why not just go there and take it? We've consistently beaten them, driven them away, and taken their land. It's what has allowed us to expand the way we have, improve our magic, and get even stronger. Why would we let them dictate the terms when we're in charge? They should feel lucky we didn't wipe them out entirely the first time."

Wil stared at him. "Are you insane? Why would we even need to hurt them if we can get what we need without bloodshed? It would be easier and painless to just deal with them as . . . well, if not equals, then at least taking them seriously as a nation. Instead of, what, finishing the job and wiping them out?"

Hugo shrugged and took another sip of the awful brew. "We're not in the habit of showing charity to others. When we broke away from Albetosia, we made an enemy for life and they *still* want to take us back and take control of our lands. Ilianto, too, wants this continent, and we're fighting daily to keep them from coming north and threatening us.

"We're at a critical point in our growth, Wilbur. We're the fastest-growing empire out there, and if we keep on at this pace, we can rule over half the world with little effort. No one has our land, our logistics, and our staggering number of wizards. We're in a position of power, and we can either use it to build ourselves up to be the best we can . . . or we don't, and someone else gets there first.

"So, yes, Calipan has very little interest in playing nice and doing things on some backward magical peoples' terms. They'll give us what we want, or we'll take it from them. And you're going to help me do it, Wilbur."

Wil's blood ran cold. "Am I?"

"You are," said Hugo with a pleased smile. "See, this is your perfect chance to make up for screwing me over. If you won't serve your country as an agent, you can help ensure we get what we want. And if you are really so concerned about the fae, you can convince them to give in and save themselves."

The waitress came by with two heaping platters of eggs, sausages, bacon, potatoes, and toast, with country gravy on the side. She came between them, setting each meal down with an audible grunt.

"Here you are. If you need more coffee, just give me a shout." As if to demonstrate her point, someone called for her, and she left.

"Is all your food so greasy?" Hugo asked, spearing a sausage and eyeing it. He took a bite and chewed it loudly, eyes fluttering closed. "Mmm. I suppose if you're going to willingly remain here, at least the food isn't awful. After breakfast, we'll go meet the fae and I'll introduce myself and make Calipan's stance clear. Understood?"

Wil swallowed. Yes, he understood perfectly. He was going to have to either seal the rift or find a way to stop Hugo from bringing the full might of the Calipan military into Faerie.

CHAPTER 34

Gunboat Diplomacy

Going to the meeting with the fae didn't help Wil's nerves. Before they headed to city hall where the meeting would take place, they made a stop at the *Flying Calamity* to pick up more people. As it turned out, Wil and the fae liked to handle their negotiations by speaking at length and then coming to a decision after.

Meanwhile, Calipan's representative needed an entourage of ledger men and pencil pushers to log everything and report back. Wil understood, even if it made him impatient and irritable. Two of the team sent to Harper Valley came with them, a secretary and a policy advisor.

Worse than that, Hugo decided to also bring along a couple of his thralls: a lifeless ogre in just a loincloth and a pixie who didn't fly so much as float along lazily. Neither could be mistaken for anything other than broken shells of what they used to be.

"Bringing your slaves along is a good way to piss them off," Wil had said, nose wrinkling in distaste.

Hugo just shrugged him off and said, "And? Unlike you, I'm not out to make friends with my enemies." And that was that.

Hugo's entourage arrived at the meeting late. Mayor Sinclair sat at the head of the long oak table, effectively in the middle. The four representatives of Faerie waited on the other side. Their happy faces upon seeing Wil dropped when they saw the thralls. He winced as a maelstrom of shock, realization, and anger dropped the temperature of the room by ten degrees.

"Greetings, people of Faerie," Hugo introduced himself, soaking in the hateful stares coming his way. "I am Hugo Jefferson, and I'll be taking over negotiations on behalf of Calipan. I'm allowing Wil to remain here as we transition to proper negotiations instead of . . . well, whatever he was doing."

Silence. Hugo didn't care and just took his seat. Wil followed at his side, flashing an apologetic smile at people he'd largely come to think of as friends, in their own way. The rest of the entourage fell into the seats on the other side of the table. The secretary of the group was already taking notes.

The fae sat back down, but they didn't stay quiet for long.

"I must object," said Arabella. "Wil may be a naive, idealistic child . . ."

"Thanks," Wil said, sighing.

"But he's been with us from the start and has treated us fairly," the fae princess continued. "I do not approve of a change in main negotiator."

Hugo smiled. "Your objection is noted. Maxwell?"

The secretary jotted it down. "Objection . . . noted."

"Fantastic," said Hugo. "Unfortunately for everyone here, Wil acted without instruction and has likely set us back by giving a wrong impression about our country's intentions. Are there any other objections before we begin?"

"Yes," said Gallath. He pointed at the broken ogre with a trembling finger. "What do you call that?" Knowing about it ahead of time had done little to soften the blow.

Hugo looked over his shoulder. "That? A good servant, and someone who shouldn't have tried to hurt me. Don't worry, there's not much left of him deep down, so I doubt he's suffering. Probably."

Everyone began talking at once. Arabella and Gallath got to their feet and shouted in roughly equal amounts of fury. Syl stared at the pixie with distinct sadness and said something Wil couldn't make out. Only he and Timothy Twist were quiet, though Twist didn't seem to share Wil's helplessness. The little man watched with distinct interest and even amusement.

"How *dare* you bring that . . . that *thing* into a meeting with us!" Arabella hissed.

"Should have your head for that alone," Gallath said. "Do you think we'll tolerate such an insult?"

Hugo smiled and sat back, hands folded across his chest. The angrier they grew, the happier he was. The noise rose to a crescendo, too big for the small conference room. Wil got fed up and blanketed the area with silence, save for himself.

"Please, *please*, none of this," he said as the others settled down a little. Every eye was on him, most of them with some level of irritation. Even if he wasn't the main negotiator anymore, he could still be a mediator. "Nothing will be solved with violence," he continued. "We're here to talk, so let's talk." He released the spell.

"Well, that remains to be seen, doesn't it?" Hugo said. "Violence did the trick a hundred-something years ago. I just thought it might serve as a reminder that Calipan is strong and we do not have to tolerate disrespect of any kind. Especially not something like stealing our children."

"Wil already took care of that," said Timothy Twist, taking a sip of water. "When he went to Oakheart Spiral, we already had that issue squared away."

"For you, maybe." Hugo smirked, and Wil wanted very badly to punch him. "Once again, he spoke without our authority, and any deal he made with you is subject to serious scrutiny. Consider this a fresh start."

Syl cleared his throat and spoke up. "If you do that, that also brings into question the fae killed during the brief altercation between our people. Your people were all returned home, safe and sound. Three of our own were not. If you are now the person to talk to, what do you intend to do about that?"

"Nothing. They were killed in an attack on my country. They deserve nothing but our contempt for their actions."

Wil groaned as the arguing started back up. Hugo positively glowed from the reactions he was getting. Not for the first time, Wil wondered why the hell they had sent the worst possible person to negotiate. Hugo was an excellent operative and leader in war, but like many wizards, he was in love with his own sense of power and cared little for others.

It took a few minutes, but voices finally quieted, though the rage had clearly not diminished. Gallath silently seethed so intensely that Wil could practically see smoke rise off the ogre. Arabella breathed hard, so angry that none of her indifferent, playful masks could be seen. Twist appeared excited by the conflict. Syl alone tried to keep things going.

"So putting that aside for the moment, it comes down to this, I suppose. What do we want that you have, and what do you have to offer?"

Hugo's policy advisor whispered something in his ear. "I hear talk of faricite and good land. Start by providing us with a healthy tribute of faricite and other goods, and Calipan can consider that a good beginning. You know, because you've been here on our land, and now are expanding to one of our towns."

"Tribute?" Gallath's skin was already orangish, but he was looking closer and closer to red. "That's your offer to us? We give you our belongings and you'll leave us in peace?"

"No, not at all," Hugo said. "That's a *start*. The way we see it, you never fully vacated the world when we drove you off. This is a gesture to pay for all of the damage you did to our armies and settlements on the way out. After that, we can talk about real deals."

Wil wanted to strangle Hugo. He couldn't recall ever having so much loathing for one person in his life. Knowing that the bastard was the mouthpiece for his country filled Wil with such shame he wanted to just leave.

"You can't seriously be allowing this," Arabella said, directing her attention to Wil. "You may be a naive bumpkin, but at least you're not a bastard. Do we have to deal with this buffoon?"

If anything could wipe the smile from Hugo's face, that was it. He leaned forward, voice dropping dangerously. "Wil is not here to allow or disallow anything. He is a mid-ranked wizard with no experience dealing with international relations, or the realities of the world. He is here at my sufferance and can be removed at any time. Insult me again, Princess, I dare you."

As if to demonstrate his point, the broken ogre in the back stepped forward, leaning his meaty knuckles on the table until it creaked dangerously. The pixie flew up beside Hugo and glowed a malevolent red.

For the first time since the meeting had started, Wil looked at Sinclair. The mayor looked about as delighted as Twist did, if not more so. He smiled at Wilbur, taking a personal pleasure in the wizard being shunted to the side, just as he had promised. The dumb jerk didn't seem to realize that if war happened, it would be on his doorstep.

"Well, all of this is leading to some hot tempers, isn't it?" said Timothy Twist, unconcerned. "If you continue to growl at us and bare your teeth, we might as well just leave. And if we have to leave, we'll just have Wil close the door behind us, permanently, as he promised, and also fix the leyline."

Oh, crap. Hugo turned to face Wil, confusion plain on his face. "What's he talking about?"

Before Wil could answer, Twist decided to be helpful once more. "Nothing much! Just that if things went sour with you or whatever other bastard they sent to beat their chest and rattle their sabers, we'd just leave and Wil would fulfill his oath to us and make sure you can't follow."

"Is this true?" Hugo demanded.

Of all the questions Wil didn't want to answer, this was one he couldn't dodge. Closing his eyes, he just nodded.

"This meeting is adjourned," announced Hugo as he stood. "We'll continue tomorrow morning at the same time. I for one consider this a good start to negotiations. I've made our position clear, and now you and your kind need time to adjust. I get it. Perhaps tomorrow you'll be more understanding of the position you're in. McKenzie, come with me."

Hugo left, as did his entourage. With one last look at his fae friends, Wil turned to follow.

CHAPTER 35

A Rock and a Hard Place

"Why the hell did you not say anything about this promise?"

The moment they were out of the conference room and in the mayor's office, Hugo pounced. He grabbed Wil by the front of his shirt and shoved him against a wall, while his secretary and policy advisor hovered nearby. Mayor Sinclair watched passively from behind his desk.

"I didn't think I needed to," Wil started. Panic struck him. The previous few times he'd been in any danger, he could do something about it. But Hugo was more powerful and had the weight of Cloverton behind him. Just defending himself could get Wil in trouble.

"You didn't think you needed to!?" Hugo barked out harsh laughter. There was madness in his eyes, a brief spark of anger so personal and all-encompassing that Wil instinctively gathered power and readied it.

"You made a binding verbal contract with the fae, promising to do the impossible, and you didn't think you needed to tell me?"

As fast as the rage came on, it was gone. Hugo laughed uproariously and pounded Wil's shoulders. He released him, wiping a damp eye.

"How stupid are you, McKenzie? Do you have a death wish? What was going through your head?"

What *had* been going through his head? It had been an act of desperation, but in his heart, Wil had known he could probably do what he'd promised. If he told Hugo that, there'd be no end to the questions, and he might even be forced to prove it.

"I think," said Wil, wetting his lips, "that I made an impossible promise I had no intention of keeping because I thought that Cloverton would send a diplomat, not some murderous lunatic determined to start a war just so he can get a damned promotion!"

The secretary and policy advisor gasped and backed away slowly. The mage's incredulous smile disappeared, but Wil continued while he had the momentum.

"I promised them that if things got ugly, I'd cover their retreat and close the door. It was a last-ditch effort to get them to cooperate. It worked. Until now."

"How very disappointing," said Mayor Sinclair from his desk. He had a glass of whiskey poured and looked exhausted but smug. "I didn't think someone so pure and incorruptible would lie to anyone."

Hugo turned his way. "The adults are talking, Ben."

"It's Bart," the mayor said flatly.

"It's irrelevant!" Hugo snapped. He waved a hand and barked out, "*Riov!*" The magical backlash of a spell made Wil extend his senses, but it was simply quiet.

Mayor Sinclair opened his mouth and nothing came out, of course. His face turned red, and he glared at Wil as though he'd been the one to silence him this time. Sulking and sighing, he returned to his whiskey.

Hugo jabbed a finger in Wil's chest. "You need to get it through your head that not everything can be solved with good ol' country friendliness. Sometimes, you need to be a bastard and defeat your enemy preemptively so you can move on with the finer details after."

"Maybe," Wil admitted, thinking of the fight with Grimnar, "but only an asshole would resort to that first and not even consider other options."

The clearing of a throat made them both turn their heads toward Hugo's secretary, Maxwell, who looked terrified.

"Actually, Mr. Jefferson," said the secretary, "he's right. Our military is stretched thin right now, and I'm not sure we can—"

"*Riov!*" The man's mouth continued to move without sound. Hugo released Wil and went up dangerously close to the man, who froze. "You are here to make sure everything I decide is recorded and handled properly, Maxwell. That's it. I will never care about your opinion, and you would do well to stay silent and out of my way. Especially considering I overheard your treasonous little chat. Tread carefully."

Maxwell blinked, then nodded rapidly. He took a step back, as did his partner. With that out of the way, Hugo smiled and turned back to Wil.

"All of that said . . . , I think there could be some merit in your foolish promise. You are uniquely suited to playing good wizard, bad wizard."

Wil straightened his clothes, thinking. He hated how fast Hugo's mood could change, but sometimes it worked out in his favor. The mage was a stubborn, conceited bastard, but if you hammered a point home enough, sometimes he'd crack.

"How do you mean?" Wil asked.

Hugo swept his arm out, gesturing to the door. "You've already laid the groundwork to get what we want from them peacefully. I showed them how rough we're willing to play. The more they hate me, the more they'll be inclined to go with whatever deal I suggest through you. They won't cut and run if we can thread the needle right, and you're in a perfect position to help me do just that."

It was hard to look past his hatred and distrust of Hugo to see the merits in it, but Wil did. It would mean lying, which he wasn't good at, and improvising, which . . . , well, he was getting better. More importantly, it kept him at the table instead of giving the mage a reason to sideline him. Wil didn't have to think about it too hard.

"If that's the plan, then you're going to need to fill me in on what our actual goals are," he said. "Tell me, and I'll do what I can to make sure we can avoid a war. Because that's what my goal is. I will *not* help you start a fight. Is that clear?"

Hugo's smile twitched as if he was avoiding laughter. "Crystal. Our goal will be as much faricite as we can get as well as a permanent military presence in both Harper Valley and Faerie. We want access to their world and are willing to give limited access back to Calipan. If that means defanging them and taming them, so be it."

Wil grimaced. "They're already weakened and in much smaller numbers. There's no need to defang them. Let them keep their autonomy and maybe don't remind them every ten minutes that we can destroy them. That would go a long way to keeping them happy. They actively want open relations. All we have to do is not spit in their face. That's not hard, is it?"

The two men with him nodded along to Wil's words. Hugo didn't notice. He stroked his chin thoughtfully before he capitulated. "No, that sounds like a good plan. We'll see how tomorrow goes and come up with a more concrete plan. Maybe you're not going to be a hindrance after all. C'mon, boys, we've got an uncomfortable conversation ahead of us."

Snapping his fingers, Hugo walked through the door. His two men scrambled after him, while the broken ogre trailed behind, closing the door after they left. Now it was just Wil and Sinclair.

Sinclair waved at him and pointed to his throat. Nodding, Wil countered the spell. The mayor then said, "He might be a bastard, but he's right. You're much too weak to be leading negotiations. As long as people like him are around, peace is never going to be an option. You know that, right?"

Wil turned on him, frustration building until he couldn't help but draw in magic and seethe it out. Sinclair's smile faded as Wil's presence grew spiky and imposing.

"If that maniac brings war upon us, Harper Valley will be the battleground," Wil said between his teeth. "You know that, right?"

"Maybe," Sinclair allowed, trying hard to hide his unease and not quite succeeding. "But hey, it's hard to unseat a leader during wartime. I imagine that if war happens because of you, you'll be removed, and frankly—"

Wil silenced him with a wave of his hand. After a second thought, he reinforced it, making sure Sinclair wouldn't be able to make a sound for at least the rest of the day. Smiling at the rage on the mayor's face, he, too, left the office.

Although the winter morning air was brisk and refreshing, Wil felt nothing but frustration and an unrelenting anger. He wasn't the type to be angry for long, or to want to hurt anyone. Wanting to hurt Hugo, or even Sinclair, made him sick to his stomach, but there was no escaping it.

Wil knew he should probably meet up with the fae, Darlene and Bram, or maybe even his parents to ask them for advice. He did none of those things and instead went to the home he rarely spent much time in, grabbed a book from the shelf, and did his best to lose himself in it.

At first, it didn't work. His thoughts kept going back to the way Hugo had grabbed him and looked ready to throw down, right then and there. The fact that Wil didn't know if he would've been able to defend himself scared him, and that fear cut so much deeper than anger. So he let himself be angry.

After spending fifteen minutes on the same page, Wil swapped books for one of his favorite adventure stories when he was a kid. He flipped to one of the big action scenes, in which the heroic sorcerer fought off a demon horde that threatened an orphanage. Surprisingly, it helped.

Channeling all his anger, Wil pretended that each demon that was swatted down was Hugo or one of his slaves. Soon, the hero stood victorious over his enemies, but Wil was no closer to being calm. Now he actively wanted a fight. He let out a garbled growl and dropped the book on the floor.

"It's that kind of day, isn't it?"

Wil looked up to see Darlene in the doorway. She looked about as tired and frazzled as he felt.

"I guess so," he said, smiling weakly. "Something happen to you too?"

"Not quite. Syl's been arrested."

Wil blinked, and that urge to fight and lash out spiked hard. "What? Seriously? Why?"

Darlene sighed. "I'll explain on the way?"

Letting out a series of the worst swears he could think of, Wil grabbed his staff and followed Darlene out the door.

CHAPTER 36

Reckless Influence

"So, what happened?" Wil asked as they made their way down the street. City hall and the jail weren't very far from his house, but the less time Syl spent locked up, the better. He smiled pleasantly at a passing older woman and her grandchildren.

"He hit on Candy," said Darlene.

"So?"

"In front of Mack."

Wil stopped in his tracks, eyes fluttering shut. "Oh no." He covered his face with a hand and took a long, deep breath. "We should've warned him."

"How would that work?" Darlene scoffed. "Warn him against flirting with every single person in town? Should we have sent out a pamphlet saying 'Beware of horny goatman'? I'm just grateful he told me he doesn't touch anyone who's married."

"Thank the gods for that," Wil muttered, continuing down the road. "So that's it? He hit on Candy and Mack beat the crap out of him?"

"Not quite. To hear Mack tell it, he overheard Syl talking to Candy and being . . . well, Syl. Mack came out and warned him, Syl just doubled down with a grin, and before they knew it, they were trading blows. From what I saw, they beat the crap out of each other pretty well."

Wil thought he could fill in the blanks. "So what, Sheriff Frederick shows up and arrests Syl because he's fae?" The dirt road turned into a stone path as they got closer. City hall was in sight.

Darlene made a frustrated sound. "More or less. The funny thing is, Mack didn't even want to press charges. When the sheriff got there, they were sitting outside and sharing a cigarette and laughing about it. Candy had brought them both a beer when Frederick arrived. They told him the story, and he arrested Syl on the spot."

That tracked. Wil put on an extra burst of speed. He didn't have to try hard to be angry enough to summon the power, will, and intent to do what came next. Once they were close, Wil channeled raw force through his staff and blew down the door. Darlene looked at him, startled, but he kept going.

Sheriff Frederick was on his feet instantly, with his gun out, pointed at the floor. Syl sat on the cot in one of the cells, scrunched up to avoid touching the iron bars. He was much too tall and lanky to be comfortable. Mack stood in front of the cell, arms crossed over his broad chest. Though he was in his late fifties, the tall, dark-skinned man looked like he could and would fight anyone.

"What in the hell do you think you're doing?" Sheriff Frederick demanded. He relaxed a little but kept his gun out.

"I could ask the same of you." Wil stepped over the fallen door. "What is the meaning of arresting one of the *lead representatives* of Faerie?"

Sheriff Frederick scowled at him. "Arresting a troublemaker. He caused a brawl and property destruction and has been harassing women."

"That's a load of shit!" Mack protested. "I threw the first punch, and then things got out of hand. That counter needed replacing anyway. Under no circumstances do I want to press charges against him!"

That, more than anything, caught Wil's attention. He pointed at Mack. "Why not?"

"Well, it was just a misunderstanding, right?" Mack ran a hand through his short, silvery beard. "He's a cheeky lad. A few rounds later, we settled it. He's a good kid."

"I'm older than you, Mack!" Syl called out.

"Shut up," Frederick snapped. "You mean to tell me you started the fight and then felt bad about it afterward? I don't buy it. I bet this creature got to you. The wizard said they're tricky. And even past that, this is my town and I'm not going to accept *any* trouble from these things. A night in a cell should cool you off."

Wil thought of Gallath, and how angry the previously cool and friendly ogre had been earlier. Syl being stuck in jail was a good way to spook them all and cash in Wil's promise to close the door behind them. No, he had to deal with this. Darlene was of a similar mind.

"Look, Sheriff," she said, stepping forward with her hands raised. "I understand where you're coming from, but we had an agreement on how things would be handled if there was trouble. You don't get to arrest and hold the fae just because you're angry he's flirting with local girls."

"And some boys," Syl added.

Darlene sighed. "Please stop trying to help, Syl," she said. The faun nodded and kept his mouth shut. She turned back to the sheriff. "The point is, if you have complaints, then you can log them, but the worst that can happen right now is that Syl gets confined to the McKenzie farm for a few days. That's equivalent to a night in a cell, I think."

The sheriff sneered at her. "I didn't agree to none of that. This is *my* town and I'll be damned if I let some headstrong pup assert his own rules over the law. The creature stays in the cell, and the rest of you are going to leave before I lose my temper and lock you up for obstructing me. Do I make myself clear?"

Mack looked like he wanted to strangle the sheriff, but he was a law-abiding citizen. He smiled apologetically at Syl and left the jail.

"And now, the rest of you," Frederick barked. He motioned with his gun for them to leave.

That, more than anything, set Wil off. The sheriff used a weapon so casually, threatening them, ignoring all of Wil's hard work and the delicate international agreement just so he could beat his chest and feel powerful and in control. In that moment, Wil despised the sheriff and saw him as little more than a pathetic, small-minded bump in the road.

"Put the gun away, Sheriff." Wil's voice was soft, cold, and dreamlike. He hardly recognized it.

"I don't think so, boy," Frederick said, raising the gun a little higher. "Gettin' real sick of your crap. Unlike the mayor, I'm not gonna be bullied by some boy I used to see pick his nose and eat it."

"Sheriff, please," Darlene started.

"LEAVE!" Sheriff Frederick bellowed.

Wil saw red. Light filled the markings on his staff. All the power of the dragon, all that power absorbed from his time in Faerie, flowed through him. The spell practically crafted itself.

"Sheriff . . . ," Wil said, power lacing his voice. "Look at me. *Look at me.*"

Frederick's head jerked his way. They met eyes, and Wil latched onto the connection. With Bram, it had been easy to fall in and play around. They had a solid, good connection. They were friends. Frederick was his enemy. No other word could sum up their relationship nearly as well. The sheriff was his enemy, and he wasn't invited. Wil pushed past all of that and dove into the man's mind.

At first, not much changed. They were still in the jail, only it was bigger, cleaner, and floating in a giant black void among the stars. The cells along the wall were plentiful, full of dark shapes that whimpered and cried into the night. The sheriff sat at his desk, legs crossed and feet kicked up.

Everyone's mind was different, and those with no magical or psychic power tended to have reflections of themself, with very little control or intentional design to it. They were what the people were, good and bad. Wil's mindscape was much more refined, but he'd had plenty of time to work on it. They were all different, but Wil had some experience in navigating hostile minds.

"Excuse me, I was wondering if you could help me," he said to the man behind the desk. The sheriff looked younger, and almost in shape. His mustache wasn't quite so ridiculous, and the years hadn't made him into a suspicious, hateful old man.

"Perhaps I can. What're you here for?" Frederick asked, uncrossing and then recrossing his legs. He made it clear he had no intention of getting up or doing anything if he didn't have to.

"I'm looking for a friendly warning and some understanding," said Wil. "I'm pretty sure it'll do you some good. Help me, help you?"

The mental construct sucked on his teeth. "Wish I could help you, but my hands are tied. If the sheriff locked someone up, I'm sure they deserved it. We don't lock up innocent people, right?"

Changing someone's mind wasn't hard, per se, but it had to be done carefully. Wil could've stomped his way through and forced Frederick to do his bidding, but he wasn't Hugo. He cared about the damage he could inflict and would minimize it. Sometimes that meant taking the roundabout way of doing things.

"Can I see your personnel files?" Wil asked.

Frederick pointed over at a filing cabinet near the wall.

"Thanks, this will only take a minute." Wil went to the files and, on a whim, went for thirty years in the past. He focused on the jail, on Frederick himself, and the idea of youth, and let himself be sucked into a memory. So many mind mages fell into the temptation of just going through memories like they were books to be read. The second Wil got what he needed, he gently pulled away.

Then he crafted an illusion in Frederick's mind. One second it was just Wil and the shadow of the man himself, and then suddenly a short, bald man with a much more powerful mustache appeared. He wore the same uniform, and had an antique gun at his hip and an incredibly powerful voice.

"Dammit, Fred, what do I hear about you locking people up for petty, personal reasons?" the short man bellowed.

Frederick was on his feet in a second, color draining from his face. "Sheriff LaMellie? I thought you were dead."

"Never mind that," LaMellie barked. "I know I taught you better than this. If a man breaks a law, then he's to be dealt with. If no crime was committed or no charges are pressed, you let them off with a *warning* and then you *let them go*. Do I make myself clear?"

"Y-yes sir!" Frederick said, looking genuinely terrified.

LaMellie shook his head in disgust. "I thought you were smarter than this, Fred. Do something like this again and you're out on your ass, and I don't care what I promised your parents! Let that poor boy go, apologize, and don't trouble him anymore."

"Yes, sir," Frederick repeated, hanging his head.

That was Wil's cue to leave. He let himself float up and out and back into his own body. If any time had passed, it might've been a handful of seconds. When in someone's head, you move at the speed of thought.

Sheriff Frederick had a faraway look in his eyes. A few seconds later, he turned his dazed expression over to Syl. "Sorry about the misunderstanding," he said. "The boss man says I should let you go and apologize. So I guess I'm sorry, but you watch your ass. He won't always be around to protect you."

"Oh. Huh." Syl looked at Wil, puzzled, before he understood what had happened. His eyes lit up with excitement. "That's alright, Sheriff. You're just doing your job, and I definitely learned my lesson."

The sheriff got his keys out and unlocked the cell. Syl carefully stepped out and went over to Wil and Darlene. Wil nodded and said to the sheriff, "Sorry about the door. Take it out of my wages." And then they left.

Once the jail was safely behind them, Darlene said, "Wil, what did you do?"

Her question was innocent enough, and it was enough to make him stop and lean against his staff.

"Gods, what *have* I done?"

CHAPTER 37

Guilt and Acceptance

By the time they got back to Wil's house, he had fallen into despair. All that anger, frustration, everything, had made it so easy to give in and do the one thing he said he wouldn't do. It took so little effort to invade and take over. It didn't matter that Wil had been gentle and left no real trace. No matter how he justified it, he had subverted another being's free will.

All of that bounced around in his head, repeating every time he came close to thinking of something else. Wil hadn't noticed when Darlene and Syl directed him into his favorite chair and got him a stiff drink. His hands shook as he took a sip and let the burn of the liquor bring tears to his eyes.

"Wil?" Darlene was right in front of him, but her voice came from a million miles away. "Are you okay? Talk to us." She and Syl stood only a foot away, too close by far. Syl's face was lumpy and bruised, one eye swollen most of the way shut.

Wil shook his head and took another drink before setting it down. When he opened his mouth to speak, he just croaked.

Syl put his hand on Wil's knee and patted him. "It's going to be okay, Wil. I think I understand. You did something to help me out. To help out all of Faerie. And now you're beating yourself up about it. Why? That's the part I'm having trouble with. What's the big deal?"

He had never looked less human to Wil, who could only blink.

Darlene answered for him, tactfully choosing her words. "The kind of magic Wil did is frowned upon and is considered rude and easy to abuse. It's something he doesn't like using." Her eyes darted back to Wil, full of pain and sympathy.

"What, mesmer magic? That's something most fae can do. Everyone influences everyone, right?" Syl laughed. "The better you are, the more powerful it is. Especially when Obligation is involved. The sheriff was in your way, so you dealt with him. Not like you hurt him or anything. Judging by the look on his face, he'll be out of it for a bit and then be back to normal, no muss or fuss."

Wil swallowed hard. His fingers dug into the arms of his chair and his heart pounded. He must've made a sound, because Darlene grasped his hand in hers and squeezed.

"Syl?" she said.

"Yeah?" The faun smiled.

"Shut up for a bit."

Wil would've kissed her, if he could move. The worst part of this, the worst part of all, was how much he had enjoyed the experience. That had always been the problem. The professors had theorized that Wil's friendly nature and inclination toward mind magic together made it easier to connect with others, and the more he did, the more effortless it became to rummage through their minds.

There was a serious part of him that had enjoyed going through Frederick's memories. He had kept it only to the sheriff's memories as a youth, his first summer as a deputy. Seeing the sheriff as a man Wil's age, full of promise and hope for the world, had been eye-opening. He didn't let himself linger, but he found the man's role model and used that against him.

It wasn't as bad as killing someone, as the academy had wanted, but it still reeked of misuse of power. Was it weird that it bothered him way more than ending the ogre assassins' lives? They'd been trying to kill him, but Frederick had pointed his gun at Darlene. Just the thought of it fired him up again, but at least it cut through the pain.

"It's the kind of thing Hugo would do," Wil said. "Violating others because it's convenient and they're in his way. He'd do it and wouldn't think twice about it."

"Which means you're nothing like him," said Darlene, a small smile blooming. "You're thinking about this a lot more than twice. You wouldn't do this just because you can. That's not you at all. And for what it's worth, I think it was the right move to make. He was starting to scare me."

That helped. Wil took his hand back and finished his drink, wincing a little. "I just want you both to know, I don't do that casually. I don't want to do it again if I don't have to."

Syl raised his hand. Wil chuckled and motioned for him to speak.

"This magic, it's a part of you, right? Why be afraid of it like this?"

"Because it would be too tempting to use all the time. No one should have that kind of power over another person." Wil ran his hands through his hair, resisting the urge to just pull until it hurt. "I wouldn't change who or what I am for anything, but it's a lot, being more powerful than everyone around you. Doesn't it bother *you*?"

The faun bleated in amusement. "Why should it? I am what I am. I was born a prince and raised to love life and still be responsible for my people. There is nothing about who I am that I fear or hide from. Can you really deny a part of yourself like that?"

"Syl," Darlene warned.

"No," said Wil, "he's . . . he might be right."

"I know I'm right," said Syl brightly. "And I can prove it! I want you to use your magic on me. I give you full permission."

Darlene looked like she wanted to protest again, but checked Wil's reaction first. Permission did make a difference. He wasn't sure he wanted the chance to go through a friend's mind, even to prove a point. Then he thought about it and realized the alternative was being miserable.

"Okay," said Wil, stomach still fluttering from fear. "I'll . . . Is there anything specific you want me to do or look for?"

"Nope! Just go for a peek and see what you find. Show me what you can do." Syl pulled his chair closer and folded his hands in his lap. Despite the manic grin on his face, he mostly looked serene and pleased with his suggestion.

"Don't be afraid to back out if it gets uncomfortable," Darlene reassured Wil. "I'll be right here."

Wil nodded and swallowed the lump that wouldn't go down. "It won't take long. Look me in the eyes, Syl. Just like that."

At first, Wil didn't know if he was going to be able to enter Syl's mindscape. He'd never looked inside the mind of a fae and had no idea how different it might be. There was the sensation of falling, and darkness, and then all of a sudden a great many bright lights.

Wil blinked and shielded his face from possible attack, but aside from ever-changing colors lighting up the night, the only thing that assaulted him was a heavy beat from massive drums. The inside of Syl's mind was, unsurprisingly, a massive party. Beautiful fae of all shapes and sizes danced together, very close. Wil even recognized some of them.

Grimnar shuffled in place, looking sullen. Arabella was . . . not naked so much as only wearing paint. It was a bold look that suited her well, and she was comfortable that way. Of course the faun would remember her like this. Syl himself wove in and out of the crowd, spinning and striking poses the entire time.

"Hey, Syl," said Wil. "Is this really what makes you, you?"

The faun grinned, purple and orange lights alternating across his face. "Heya, Wil. This is definitely me. Who else could it be? The one! The only!" He pointed up at the sky, where the moon was full. "SYLANOOO!" His face appeared on the moon, winking at the cheering partygoers.

"Got anything specific you want to show me?" Wil asked, genuinely a little afraid to look too closely without more permission.

"Hmm. Yes, I know exactly what to show you. Go dance with my father!" he pointed to a big throne at the end of the party, where a massive satyr lounged sideways. "He'll show you something good."

Well, there was only one thing to do. Wil carefully made his way across the meadow, blinking every so often to try to get the lights out of his eyes. When he finally made it, he was already a bit tired. Syl's greatest defense was his excess enthusiasm.

"Um, excuse me? King Martinus?" Wil waved at him.

The satyr king sat up straight. His big belly looked hard as a rock, and he had a ring in each nipple. Martinus's left horn had a crack in it, and his big, bushy beard made Wil think about a wilder version of his father.

"You must be the wizard! How can I help you, son?"

"I, uh . . . Want to dance?" It sounded stupider than he thought it would, but there wasn't anyone around to judge him.

Making the noise all big, older guys make when they get up, the king rose and stepped onto the grass with Wil. He held out his hand.

Wil tentatively took it, and the next thing he knew, the party was gone and instead they were in a gazebo in the middle of a grand garden under a hot sun. Syl was just a child and playing with some flowers while a younger Martinus watched from afar.

"Father, Father, I made it grow!" Syl called out, stomping his little hooves in place.

"Did you?" Martinus called back, full of boisterous bluster. "I didn't see it. I bet you can't grow anything!"

Little Syl puffed up as big as he could, face red. "I can too! *Watch*." He turned back to the flower, which Wil saw was red with black spots all around it. Syl bowed his head and muttered under his breath. Up the flower went, getting taller and wider until it was bigger than Syl himself.

He dropped the magic, panting and puffing. "You see? I did it!"

"I suppose you did," Martinus allowed, failing to hide a proud grin. "Well done."

Just as the warmth threatened to overwhelm Wil, they were back at the party, where a lone voice was singing a haunting song at odds with the frenetic instruments. Wil looked around again, and it dawned on him that everyone at the party was someone Syl had memories with. He wasn't hiding them, and they didn't show up as mirrors of ordinary life. He carried them with him openly, never truly alone. Wil thanked Martinus and went through the people milling about, careful not to touch anything. He approached Arabella, keeping his eyes level with hers.

"Dance?" he asked.

She rolled her eyes but held out her hand. Wil was prepared this time, and a few seconds of dancing transitioned into a scene on the beach. Syl lay on the sand, legs splayed open comically. Arabella herself stood a few feet away, behind an easel. She was painting the faun, and doing an excellent job of it.

"Are we done yet?" Syl groaned. "I'm bored. You're taking too long."

"I've barely started!" Arabella snapped at him. Pursing her lips, she added a few more dabs of paint, carefully creating his pointy beard. "If you want this to be something we hang up in the halls, then you need to be patient. I swear, art is wasted on the likes of you. What would you rather be doing?"

Syl waggled his eyebrows. Arabella visibly thought about it, and Wil took that as his cue to leave. Back at the party, Arabella smirked at him. He thanked her and let himself go back to the real world.

Both he and Syl took a deep breath. There was a tear in the faun's eye, but also supreme amusement in his expression. Wil shook his head, laughing and feeling good for the first time all day.

"Gods, Syl, do you think about *anything* else?"

Darlene looked confused for a second, then got it and rolled her eyes. Syl just laughed and shrugged.

"I'm in the prime of my life and don't need to take a queen yet. Why not have some fun?"

"Well, for one, it might get the crap kicked out of you," Darlene said, shoving Syl playfully.

He nodded thoughtfully. "Very true, but it was worth it. Those were good memories I got to relive. Thank you, Wil. It doesn't have to be a bad thing. Think of the good you could do with it."

Wil shuddered. "Thanks, Syl. I . . . I think I need to lie down."

"Of course," said Darlene. She leaned forward and kissed his forehead. "But I'm staying here in case you need me."

Syl got up and stretched, making a very similar sound to the one his father had made in his memory. "Then I'll see you tomorrow, for round two of negotiations."

Gods, that sounded miserable. But a nap wouldn't hurt. As he rose and went up to the top of the tower to his bedroom, Wil thought about what Syl had said. He lay on his bed and tried to think of the good he could do with his mind magic ability. Before long, he fell asleep.

CHAPTER 38

Elf-Centered

The next day of negotiations went slightly better than the first. They didn't come to any agreement on where to start, but they did decide on *how*. It was better than nothing, and after a few hours of it, Wil was able to relax some.

Hugo managed to mostly behave. He was still as insufferable and aggressive as before, but he toned down the threats of violence and even pretended to listen while Wil kept things under control.

Wil had never expected to be the moderator for the talks, but there was no one better suited for it. Discussions back and forth on resources, tariffs, security, and borders grew monotonous when they couldn't seem to agree on anything. Worst of all, this was not the kind of thing Wil had a good head for. However, neither did Hugo. He finally let his two babysitters, Freddie, Hugo's policy advisor, and the secretary Maxwell, deal with the numbers and details.

Cloverton asked for a lot. More than Faerie was willing to give. Syl managed to keep a good head on his shoulders, and nothing ever seemed to phase Timothy Twist. He could argue and make things worse forever. Gallath and Arabella were visibly getting irritated by the lack of progress.

At the end of the third day of negotiations, the assembled representatives all split and went in different directions. Hugo had been particularly annoyed and left muttering under his breath as he headed back to the *Flying Calamity*. Gallath went to Bram's house, as he often did these days. Syl and Twist went to grab lunch together, which left just Arabella and Wil. He decided to try to chat with her a bit.

"Other than Hugo being a bastard, have you been settling in okay?" Wil asked outside of city hall, leaning against the wall.

Arabella hmph'd noncommittally. "It's passable. This resembles some of the farming communities on the outskirts of my lands, where we meet with the Woodlands Association and Wee Folks' borders. It's ... quaint. The people are largely small and uninteresting, but passionate. I can respect passion. I will much prefer it when these talks are over and I can move on to a real city, full of brighter, more worldly people."

At this point, Wil wasn't taking her casual insults too seriously. He was half convinced she did it on purpose just to project an image. "You seem ... satisfied enough, with some of the people here," he said. It was as close as he could come to acknowledging her and Jeb.

Arabella rolled her eyes. "For now. One of the great things about being me is I get to reinvent myself every couple of decades and try something new. Who cares if I spend a season or two slumming it with a foreign peasant or three? It's all part of the journey. Some fun, sometimes disastrous memories to carry with me for the next thousand years."

"So it's not serious, then?"

"Definitely not serious. Your brother can sometimes be tolerably charming, always defiant, and he's fit enough. Mostly though, he's wonderfully *tall*. Much taller than elf men."

Wil laughed. He wasn't sure how much more he wanted to know, but if being tall was the number one prized feature . . . well, Jeb was pretty tall. "Bram is even taller than Jeb," Wil pointed out.

"You have as much chance of me touching iron as you do of Bram giving me a second look," she said with a crystalline laugh. "Be well, Wizard. Your brother intends to treat me today, and I won't be late for it."

Wil watched her go, mulling over her words. Bram would tell him who he was seeing in his own time, but there were only a few people it could be, and Wil wasn't sure any of them lined up right. Oh, well, no use worrying about it. What was more important was he had an open day with no responsibilities or worries.

The fae were getting more comfortable being out and about on their own, and were often seen paying visits to the neighboring farms or shopping. Plenty of them got food out for every meal, any chance to be out and enjoy hearty human cooking. Other than Syl's hiccup, the only real issues had been a few fights and heated situations that had been defused.

All in all, Wil was pleased with how things were going. Hugo could ruin it, but every day proved Wil was right about it being time to come out and try friendship.

Wil had no clear direction in which to go, so he went to the family farm as well. Rather than catch up to Arabella, he took his time, letting his mind wander. When he arrived, he resolved to make more of the self-propelling sleds in his off time, and maybe some specially heated scarves.

The McKenzie farm had never fully recovered from the party they'd thrown. That wasn't to say it was messy or in disarray, just that it looked less and less like a farm with all the people there. Wil passed by and waved to Jerry and Danielle from the Appleton crew on his way to the house. He popped inside, but it was mostly empty. The only person to be found was his sister, Sarah, sitting at the kitchen table.

"Hey," he said, sitting down across from her. "It feels like forever since we've had a chance to talk or do anything."

"Mmm." Sarah didn't look up from her drawing. It was a large study of Syl. Most of the foundation looked done and now she was shading it, filling in dark spots for his hairy goat legs. "Been busy?" she asked.

"Incredibly. I can't believe how hard it's—"

"Just kidding, I don't care." Sarah paused her shading to look up and give him a catty smile. Wil laughed and felt a surge of affection for his little sister. She'd never be impressed by him, and he loved her for it. "But it would be great if you'd hold off on any other major upheavals for at least a year after this."

"You know, if this goes well, I think I can manage a year of peace and calm," said Wil. He had no clue if he could, but it sounded like a good goal. "Seriously, though, how've you been doing the past while? I feel bad I haven't checked in."

Sarah put down the charcoal and sipped some hot chocolate. "I'm fine. Mostly. They're loud, but it's not like I expect fifty people living on my farm to be quiet. But they're like, *always* active. Mom and Dad are having some sleeping issues as well, but they like the guests and have been having a good time."

"What about you? Are you having a good time?"

Sarah grinned. "Making some good money, if nothing else. Everyone, fae or human, wants my pictures. No one knows if things are going to last, so they're getting reminders. Even that snooty princess wanted a portrait of Jeb." She planted her hands on the table and gagged melodramatically.

Wil shook his head, grinning. "Yeah, not sure I'm happy about him going for Arabella when we warned him not to, but what can we do? It's Jeb."

"He's been *so* obnoxious about it," Sarah said. All traces of her feigned disinterest were gone, replaced with the kind of enthusiasm that came only from talking trash about one's siblings. "Everything now is about his time hanging out with the elves. It's all about the things they showed him and how much better elf fashion and wine are."

"*Really?*" It had been just under a week since they'd taken the fae out to introduce them to the town. There hadn't been nearly enough time for Jeb to go native, had there? Wil struggled to keep the mirth off his face. "He's giving his all, isn't he?"

Sarah shuddered. "You should've seen him today. He was cooking up a storm, trying to impress Arabella. She's got him on a short leash. Not literally, thankfully."

"Arabella did say he was treating her. But Jeb, cooking? This I gotta see."

Sarah tilted her head thoughtfully before turning to her drawing. "You'd be surprised. Over the last few years, he's gotten pretty good at it. Mom insisted he learn, in case he never managed to find a wife who'd take care of his dumb ass."

"Huh. Still not going to pass this up." Wil stood. "Catch you later, Sarah!"

She waved him off without looking up.

Despite having helped raise the trees, Wil hadn't gone inside them and seen what the temporary homes were like. Time to change that. He started with the two upright trees, climbing the stone steps to the first opening. It reminded him a lot of Oakheart Spiral, on a much smaller scale. A winding staircase climbed the inside of the hollowed tree, leading to four small rooms on every level.

It was the first clue that something was off, since the trees weren't *that* big. Blinking, Wil stood in the doorway, looking inside and out until he realized that it was, in fact, bigger on the inside.

"Mr. Wizard!" A voice from the second story caught his attention. Wil looked up to see the gnome Declan standing at the railing. "It's been a bit! How are you doing?"

Wil hadn't seen him since the prisoner exchange and felt guilty for it. "Pretty well!" he said. "I'm surprised you didn't head back to Faerie after experiencing our mayor's hospitality. You doing okay?"

"Oh, just fine," Declan said, chuckling and hooking his thumbs behind his suspenders. "That was a good time for introspection, and now I just find I want to stay for the duration. You know, see it through to the end."

"I respect it," said Wil. "Do you happen to know where Jeb and Arabella are?"

Declan pointed out the door he came in from. "Last I saw, they were in the eatery, probably toward the end. Arabella likes to hold court in there."

Wil smiled and saluted with a tap to his forehead and went back around. The horizontal tree sprawled across a wide swathe of land. He followed it, stopping to greet and chat with some of the fae hanging around outside. Chairs and tables littered the lawn. Honestly, Wil loved the little slice of Faerie, even if it was in his father's favorite field.

He slipped inside the last door on the end and marveled once more at the spatial distortion spell. It was something he couldn't quite pull off, and he appreciated how different the fae's magic was from his. The space was dimly lit by gently glowing bulbs hanging from the ceiling. It looked a lot like a series of restaurants set side by side with small common areas.

Arabella sat in a chair that obviously had been designed for her and resembled her mother's throne in Oakheart Spiral. The regular entourage of familiar elfin faces crowded around her, but so did Jeb. Wil had to keep from laughing.

Jeb wore poorly fitted elven clothing, which couldn't be comfortable given how tight it was. Elven clothes were designed for warmer weather, so it was also a lot more revealing than anything Jeb had ever worn in public in his life. The rich, earthy colors suited him well, but half his chest and back were revealed, as well as most of his legs.

"What're you doing here, Mr. Wizard?" Jeb asked, eyes darting around at his present company. As if he were embarrassed by Wil and not his ridiculous clothing. On the table between him and the elves was one of their mom's casserole dishes, filled with a familiar meal.

"I could ask the same of you, but it looks like you're about to eat. I wouldn't want to interrupt," said Wil, eager to see what happened.

"Good. Maybe find yourself elsewhere? I'm just about to show my friends my famous cottage pie." Jeb beamed.

"Famous, huh?" Wil pulled up a chair and forced himself between a reddish dryad and an elf man who looked like he didn't want to be there. "I'd love to see how you all like it. I know human food is something special to you folks."

Arabella pursed her lips. "Jeb's been telling us all about it for days now, so we'll give it a chance. Life's an adventure, no?"

Jeb took a knife and spatula and slopped a plate with the food. Minced beef, peas, and gravy bled all over, and Wil didn't miss the way Arabella winced. She took the plate and silver fork and speared a dripping bite. She took a slow bite and pulled away the cleared fork, chewing thoughtfully.

"What do you think?" Jeb asked, though her mouth was still quite full. "I tried using some of the mushrooms you had in your pack, to give you a familiar home flavor on top of our good beef and seasonings."

The elf princess swallowed and set the plate down. "Those weren't ordinary mushrooms," she said breathily. "It's . . . very rich. I'm not sure I can have more than a few bites, nor would it be safe. Well, what are you all waiting for? Try a bite. Tonight will be fun!" She let out a laugh and the other elves echoed like the good followers they were.

The cottage pie was divided up, leaving half. Everyone tucked in. Arabella turned to Wil, eyes alight with mischief. "And what of you, Wizard? Are you going to join in the festivities?"

Wil watched Jeb tear into his cottage pie eagerly. He had a bigger portion than the others and didn't seem like he'd eat any less, even knowing about the mushrooms.

"You know," said Wil, "I think I should probably refrain. But I'd *love* to check on you all in a few hours."

They waved him off, and Wil went outside and leaned against the tree. Maybe Jeb wouldn't ruin things after all. Everyone in his family seemed to be doing well with the fae as guests. A weight lifted from Wil's shoulders and he let himself enjoy the moment of peace. If tomorrow was anything like today, it would be a battle to be heard through the arguments.

But that was for tomorrow. Tonight? Tonight he'd watch Jeb slowly freak out and learn a valuable lesson about knowing his ingredients.

CHAPTER 39

A Widening Rift

After another fruitless meeting, Hugo stopped Wil before he left city hall. "I need to inspect the rift and the leyline, and you're coming with me."

As drained as Wil tended to be after negotiations, he perked up immediately. "Right this second?"

"Why?" Hugo scoffed. "You got somewhere better to be? Does a local need help milking his goats or chasing pests away?" He found the descriptions of some of Wil's earliest tasks to be beneath wizards, and hadn't given Wil peace since.

"No," said Wil, fighting the rising heat in his cheeks. "I'm just surprised you haven't gone up there yet. I figured it would be one of the first things you did."

Hugo motioned with his head to follow and Wil did. They wound south out of downtown. "I wanted to, but I needed to see the fae's temperament first, and learn how dangerous coming close to a portal to their capital would be."

"It's not a portal," said Wil. "It works almost like one, but the entrances and exits I've gone through tend to be rings where the fabric between worlds is thinnest and easier to cross."

"And all of this is possible due to the broken leyline?"

Every time the subject came up, Wil tensed. It didn't matter that he and Hugo had found a way to work through their dislike of each other and represent Calipan together. If Cloverton found out he'd discovered a way to change leylines, he'd never have a moment of peace. Part of him wondered if he owed it to his country to share the knowledge, but . . . not until he knew for certain, and not until he knew what the potential consequences could be if they went around changing leylines without a care in the world. Someone like Hugo would do just that and not lose a wink of sleep if it meant more power and influence.

"As far as I know, yes," Wil hedged as the road became rougher and they turned west toward the mountain. "It was a taxing night, and I didn't really know about the extent of the damage until a couple months later. Once the leyline broke, the area slowly started to change, and the rifts opened." He kept his eyes forward, trying not to sound too nervous.

Hugo grunted his acknowledgment and they fell into a silence Wil both hated and needed. It lasted until they arrived at the canyon where Harper Forest's newest river emptied. The easiest, gentlest slope up the mountain followed the river most of the way up.

"Did you seriously create this river yourself?" Hugo asked, almost impressed. "You?"

"It was mostly from using the leyline," Wil said, shrugging. "I passed out immediately after and nearly drowned. When I woke up, the leyline was different, and I had bigger problems to worry about. C'mon, this is the best way up, and there will be plenty to see along the way. The woods are weird now, and it's quite the sight."

It didn't take long for the weird animals to show up. They walked over some fallen branches, and the snap flushed a brown bunny out of hiding. It ran in a zigzag. A shadow passed overhead and was followed by the shriek of a hawk. The bunny vanished from sight, though it left new tracks as it ran over the snow to safety.

"Well, that's interesting," said Hugo, his face lighting up. "Has this happened to many of the local wildlife?"

Wil nodded and they continued. "I've seen blue deer and purple birds with six wings. I think it's safe to say that it's affecting nature pretty strongly. The changes line up with what I experienced during my trip to Faerie."

Hugo took a long, deep breath. "Does that include how the air feels? It tingles and is reinvigorating."

"Yes," said Wil, answering without thinking. "It's like that in Faerie too. The place is saturated in magic."

"Oh, really?" Hugo's eyes lit up greedily. A chill that had nothing to do with the winter evening went down Wil's spine. "What was it like in there?" asked the mage. "How exactly did it affect you?"

Two questions Wil didn't want to answer. If he lied, Hugo would probably be able to tell. If he told the truth, he'd be borderline betraying his friends. And if he didn't answer soon, Hugo was going to get suspicious.

"It's like . . . ," Wil started, buying some time. He held out his arm and felt for the ambient magic in the air. A tingle told him Hugo was doing the same. With that in mind, maybe he wouldn't notice an illusion of a calm face overlaid on Wil's face, projecting the confident expression Wil wished he had.

"It's like drowning in booze, in some ways," said Wil. It was close enough to the truth. "It's intoxicating, but not necessarily in a good way. It warps your senses and feels good, but it wears on you. It's too much, and honestly, I think it might present a health hazard. I feel changed from my time there."

Even he knew that the best lies were hidden among the truth. He felt pretty clever about it until Hugo burst out laughing.

"You almost got me, McKenzie. I can feel the magic in the air, and it's changing me, but it feels *good*. I feel energized and on top of the world from here alone. What's it like at the peak?" Hugo craned his head, looking up the remaining distance.

"It's a lot, Hugo, and—"

"Meet me up there," Hugo said. The magic in the air thrummed and drew in around the mage. Wil's stomach did a flip as the strange, primal language Hugo used brought the spell to life. *"D'ka!"*

Hugo rose into the air, slowly at first, but then he picked up speed as he skipped the path entirely and went straight for the peak. Wil stared at him in shock for several seconds before his senses caught up to him and he gave chase.

Unlike the mage, Wil couldn't fly without his carpet, but he could do the next best thing. He lightened himself and flung raw force against the ground behind him. Going uphill, he had to jump again and again but he soon fell into a rhythm of throwing himself up the mountain. It became easier the closer he got to the peak.

The great tree greeted him like an old friend, and being back at the gates of Faerie filled Wil with a sense of longing and relief. Harper Valley had its own life, its own magic, but the leyline was *his*. The thought shocked him before it felt more and more appropriate with time.

Wil bounded through the air one last time before landing next to an excited Hugo. They were not alone. Several kinds of fae were around and had made a camp of sorts. It was something they'd discussed, keeping an eye out and communication open. And it was also where they had guards to hold the line if Calipan suddenly decided on war.

"These creatures are telling me to leave," Hugo said in disbelief. "As if they're not living off of our land, drinking in *our* leyline."

"Hugo, you need to stand down," said Wil. "We had an agreement that no wizards would be allowed into or out of Faerie for the duration. Not until we understand what it does to us." He motioned for some of the fae to back off.

A goblin and an ogre relaxed, but the two trolls and one hob kept their hands on their weapons. As agreed, they were some of Faerie's finest fighters, equipped with masterwork, magical weapons. It was not a fight Hugo would win on his own. The two of them combined could pull it off. Worse yet, Wil would be expected to back the mage's actions.

"That was before I got a feel for what we're dealing with, and what your foolish, idealist ass would just give away!" Hugo slashed the air with his hand, and one of the ogres reacted, jerking forward. *"W'kul!"*

The ground beneath their feet lost all its traction. The ogre's feet slid out from under her and she landed on her back hard. The trolls let out a roar of anger as they, too, slipped and slid around helplessly. Two elves came through a ring of mushrooms, carrying twin daggers. They looked more than ready to fight.

Wil threw himself between the two sides. "STOP!" he boomed. "STAND DOWN NOW OR I WILL TAKE *EVERYONE* DOWN." Even with his voice elevated and echoing from every direction, Wil didn't make for a particularly intimidating figure. The fae, however, kept their distance. He'd take it.

"Stand down, Hugo," Wil said, softening his voice. "We had an agreement, and it doesn't matter if you're not happy about it. I will not stand by and let you break that agreement, even if I have to stop you myself."

"As if you could," Hugo scoffed, circling Wil slowly. The fae tightened their grip on their weapons as he got close, but all of his attention was on Wil. "I know what you're capable of, McKenzie. Fighting me is not one of them."

"You think you know me, Jefferson, but I am not the student you kicked around anymore. I will *not* have you mess up my project with your hunger for power." Wil relaxed his stance and made it clear this was not a fight unless he pushed it. "We are negotiating an approval process for visiting wizards, remember? Once this deal is done, you can be fast-tracked. You could be one of the first few into Faerie in over a hundred years."

Wil could see then that he'd got him. The paperwork that would make Hugo Jefferson a pioneer in, a way to give him a leg up over even Wil and take the glory. All of Wil's criticisms could be ignored so long as the mage got what he wanted.

"You know what? You're right. I'll be one of the first ones in. There's no need to cause a fuss now. You might even have a point about there being something about the air." Hugo laughed, pretending to relax as well, though there remained an obvious threat in his eyes. "Just as well. I'd hate to see what my pets could do to your friends."

From the sky, a large demon crashed into the ground near them both. When it stood, it was easily as big as their largest foes. It had a sharp, cruel face and wicked horns, great wings, and a bladed tail. Its dead eyes stared holes into space. One of Hugo's own ogres flanked him.

The mage smirked, holding up his hands. A screech later, an imp dropped out of the sky and perched on top of a giant mushroom. "You think you could take me, Wilbur?" it challenged.

Wil didn't break a sweat. "If I had to. Part of me almost wants the chance."

It was the wrong thing to say.

CHAPTER 40

Grudge Match

The rules were simple. A duel to incapacitation or submission aboard the *Flying Calamity*. Just personal magic, no tools or weapons, and no slaves. By the time it was arranged, he wasn't as keen about fighting Hugo, but at least it had shifted the mage's focus away from the entrance to Faerie. Wil considered that a win, even if he was probably about to get his ass kicked.

If nothing else, Wil was excited about finally getting to board the flying ship. They'd toured one being repaired in Manifee City during his academy days, and that had been one of the highlights of his second year. Wil and the other students had spent an afternoon exploring every inch of the vessel, which could hold hundreds of crew as well as haul ridiculous amounts of cargo, and that had been an older model.

The *Flying Calamity* was newer, built more for outright war than moving troops and supplies. It was three hundred feet long with forty cannons along its sides. It smothered the fairgrounds, and its placement meant the Midwinter Feast would have to take place somewhere else. Wil and Hugo got on the elevator, and the crew pulled them up.

"Captain, have the deck cleared immediately!" Hugo barked at a lean, steely-looking man wearing a very nice hat. "We have a duel to conduct and I don't want any of your boys to get in the way. We will, however, need a medic and cleanup crew on standby."

The captain looked like he wanted to strangle the man. "Aye, sir." He went to a mouthpiece near the helm and made the announcement over speakers around the ship. "ALL HANDS, CEASE YOUR WORK AND CLEAR THE MAIN DECK. OUR MAGE IS DUELING THE LOCAL WIZARD. ALL NONESSENTIAL PERSONNEL ARE FREE TO COME SPECTATE."

The nearest crew cheered loudly and picked up their cleaning supplies. One of them met Wil's eye and winked at him, mimicking a strangling motion and pointing at Hugo while the mage's back was turned.

Wil understood immediately. No one liked Hugo, and it would do them all a world of good to see him fall. Well, he'd try his best. Now that they were there and Hugo had decided to make a show of it, some of his confidence had vanished.

"I want to make something clear, Mage Jefferson," the captain said as he came down the stairs. "I will tolerate no damage to my ship. Whatever you two decide to do, if it can't be repaired by tomorrow I'll—"

"You'll *what*, Captain Nesbitt?" Hugo scowled at him. "You and your crew are here at my pleasure. You'd do well to remember that."

Captain Nesbitt's jaw clenched, and Wil saw his hands twitch near his sidearm. This was worse than Wil thought, but maybe that wasn't a bad thing.

"Don't worry, Captain," he said, respectfully inclining his head, "I'll not do anything damaging. The *Flying Calamity* is a work of art, and I would never risk it."

Hugo rolled his eyes. "More like you can't do anything destructive anyway, can you, Mr. Illusions? Take what time you need to get ready." He headed off to the far side, where a humanoid figure made of swirling dust and leaves stood at the ready.

When the mage was gone, Wil said, "I'm sorry you have to deal with him, Captain. I'm doing everything I can to try to make things go smoothly so you can be free of him."

Captain Nesbitt's eyes darted over to where Hugo was stretching and drawing in magic. "It's not your fault, Master McKenzie," he said. "And if this duel gets out of control and something happens to him, I'm sure we'll both have stories to corroborate that it was an accident."

Wil was so caught off guard that he burst out laughing. Nesbitt's lips twitched, but he otherwise didn't move.

"If the worst happens, I'm sure Cloverton will understand," Wil said. With one last nod, he moved opposite Hugo and did some stretches of his own.

It was less a physical thing and more just mentally preparing and opening himself up to the magic around him. Hugo didn't have as big a reservoir of power as Wil did, but he was more adept at drawing it in from around him, and he wore several gems and crystals that he could borrow power from. All in all, they were probably evenly matched.

The biggest difference was that Hugo was a proud killer, and Wil wasn't. Even in a nonlethal duel, Hugo had the advantage. Luckily, Wil had no intention of making this a fair fight. He may be a goody two shoes in Hugo's eyes, but he had something to prove.

By the time he and Hugo got into position, Wil had already cast two illusions. Hugo was none the wiser and stared Wil down with that infuriating grin on his face. Like he had already won and this was just a formality.

"You ready to be embarrassed, McKenzie?" Hugo called out.

"No," said Wil. "Are you?" It was hardly the cleverest thing he could've said, but it still made the crew cheer for him. They had assembled in a square around the massive hatch above the cargo hold, over a hundred of them. Wil guessed the majority of them wanted to see Hugo humbled.

Hugo cast a simple spell. A ball of red light he tossed up into the air. It hung motionless for a second before bursting in a flash of light. Wil ducked to the side immediately, invisible while his illusionary double dodged in the other direction. A red bolt of magical energy came screaming through where his head had been.

The mage kept moving, launching bolt after bolt after Wil's illusion. It was both easy and fun to make for near misses, his double sprawling out and rolling back up to his feet with a dexterity Wil himself could never match. He crept closer, keeping the show going as Hugo expended needless energy chasing the wrong target.

Just as Wil was ten feet away and considering his next move, Hugo raised his hand and blasted him with that red energy. It hit him like a colossal punch and knocked him out of his invisibility.

Wil rolled to his feet and deflected the next one with a silvery shield. "How?" he demanded.

Hugo just winked at him and leaped into the air. Wil got out of the way before the mage landed where he'd been standing, a burst of red light making his skin tingle and burn. Wil lashed out with raw force, but Hugo met it with some of his own, anchoring his feet and pushing back harder until Wil went sprawling.

"You really thought you could beat me?" Hugo threw his head back and laughed. "Pathetic!"

Wil got to his feet, heart pounding in his head. He flung an orb of unstable green energy at Hugo. When the mage brought up a shield of his own, it exploded and knocked him off his stance. The next three Wil sent in quick succession arced and swerved around Hugo.

The mage whirled around but couldn't shield against them all. Wil detonated them all at once. Hugo let out a cry in shock more than pain as two different spots on his clothes ripped open. He looked down at his ruined shirt and bruised skin. "You . . ."

His next attack came slowly, telegraphed well in advance, but there was nowhere for Wil to go. Hugo's index and pinky fingers extended and lightning arced between them, building up in intensity as he opened his mouth to say the word that would fry Wil.

Wil launched himself straight upright as the mage jerked his hand forward to unleash lightning. The lighting went through the space Wil had just been in and continued until it hit a crew member in the chest.

The crew member convulsed violently before dropping to her knees and hitting the deck. A cry went up from among the crew, but Hugo looked straight up at Wil with the same blind rage. He motioned with his fingers again, but Wil struck first.

He gathered his power and pushed directly against Hugo. The force at that angle shoved and pinned the mage directly against the deck. Wil kept it up as he floated down, pushing Hugo along the ground and him farther from him, until he landed next to the fallen crew member and friends.

"Is she okay?" Wil asked, keeping one eye on his enemy and the other on the shallow breathing of the girl.

"She's out," a bearded sailor seethed. "That bastard, that absolute—"

Hugo was back on his feet in a flash. Magically, he grabbed Wil's clothes and yanked him back down to the hatch. "I'm not finished with you, McKenzie!"

"Are you crazy? You hurt one of your crew!" Wil deflected another red bolt on his shield of light. His arm throbbed from the power Hugo threw.

"You burned my clothes!" Hugo roared. He pointed to the ground at Wil's feet. "*W'kul!*"

Wil was prepared for it and countered it with a slash of his hand, dissipating the magic before the spell could lubricate the floor. He leaped forward and tackled Hugo to the ground. Grabbing him by the shoulders, he stared deep into the mage's mad eyes.

And he dove in.

CHAPTER 41

The Depths of Hate

Wil hadn't planned on entering Hugo's mind. He'd been there enough times during his education that it was a place he preferred to avoid. But with the crew in danger and Hugo looking out of control, it was the only thing Wil could think of doing that had a chance of actually affecting the mage.

Hugo fought him the entire time. It wasn't a smooth drop into a mindscape—Wil had to push and fight his way inward, but the element of surprise was on his side. Pushing past the last of the resistance felt like crashing from orbit, but Wil had done it too many times to worry about imaginary damage to his projection.

He landed in Saint Balthazar's Academy of Magic, just as he remembered it. The wide, open halls and gorgeous marble crowning depicting various famous wizards were just as impressive in memory as they were in person. Classroom doors were open, and the sounds of learning spilled out. There were students here and there, but they were locked in their own little worlds, moving about the school like ants in a colony.

Wil didn't pay them any attention. He had to move fast before Hugo could catch up with him and boot him. With a giddy laugh, Wil darted between students, moving faster than he would ever be capable of in the real world. In the mind, everything was mutable.

He blew past several classrooms, ones he'd attended himself at various points during his education. The sound of Professor Figgis's animated rant tempted him. He peeked his head inside the classroom, and suddenly he was in an active memory.

"Too many of you damned fools ignore the order of operations!" the professor bellowed in a voice too deep for a small man like him. He wore the thickest glasses Wil had ever seen and looked ready to crumble to dust. He had no hair on his head, save for the wispy beard, but he could shout and rant better than anyone.

"When enchanting an object, you don't just slap on a mess of what you want a thing to do and hope it works. You *layer* it, for gods' sakes. The way you order them and power them on the first time leads to a priority. If you want your wands to just explode, then you— Yes, Jefferson?"

A younger Hugo sat at a desk, hand raised. "Sorry to interrupt, Mr. Figgis, but there's an intruder." He turned to Wil, grinning. "Think I wouldn't find you?"

"No, I knew you would," said Wil. "Hey, guess what."

"What?" Hugo tilted his head.

"You stink!" Wil focused everything he had on the most noxious illusion he could think of, and he flooded the room before bolting.

The world around him shivered and squirmed, but Wil kept moving. He'd just done the psychic equivalent of jabbing Hugo in the nostril with feces. The hallways Wil ran through sloped and curved dangerously, warping around him. As he passed another classroom, he flung an illusion into it.

A hair-raising scream flattened the floor again, and Wil crashed into the statue of an earth elemental. His mind expanded and he saw out of its eyes. Not into the mindscape, but aboard the *Flying Calamity*, watching a still picture of himself on top of Hugo and staring deeply into the mage's eyes. One of the crew was held back by the others and a frustrated Captain Nesbitt.

Hugo's thrall, Wil realized. He could see out its eyes, feel the remnants of the mind there, and measure the connection between them. Wil sent the elemental a single command. *Restrain.*

He was ripped away from the statue and found himself back at the academy, Hugo's projection furious with him. He grabbed Wil by the front of his jacket and lifted him with the strength that came from being in one's own mind. "What the hell do you think you're doing?"

"Keeping you from hurting the crew," Wil said. "Did you not notice you hurt and might have killed someone working under you?"

"It was your fault for dodging," Hugo snarled. "You would've survived it."

"Great logic there, Hugo," Wil spat. "How dare I piss you off enough to disregard others. Guess what."

Before Hugo could stop himself, he answered again, "What?"

Wil gathered all of his power and thrust both feet into the mage's chest, putting all his mental strength into it.

Hugo went flying through the hallway, crashing through a pillar. Wil floated back to the ground calmly. "I'm better at this than you." He disappeared from the hallway entirely.

Any wizard with an introduction to mind magic could conceivably build and shape their mindscape. Experts like Hugo and Wil could do more with it. The rules that governed each were loose, and a strong enough mind could alter those rules. One second Wil was in the figure eight of classrooms on the first floor, the next he was in the dueling arena outside the school.

Most people's mindscapes were a reflection of who the person was. Even those who could craft their own tended to follow intuitive conventions, and Wil knew how Hugo worked. He favored brute force and grand self-tribute. As evidenced by the crowd sitting in the bleachers, all cheering for him.

"Hugo! Hugo! Hugo!" they screamed as an exaggerated and heroic version of the mage stood in the center, going through various forms with twin wands. A shadowy opponent lost to him, again and again.

Wil waved off the shadowy figure and took his place in the arena. Just for good measure, he summoned the idea of his staff and it appeared in his hands, glowing a comforting purple. He pointed it skyward and spun it in lazy circles. Clouds gathered, turning bright day into artificial night. Rain poured down, and Wil drank it in.

Hugo turned to him, then looked around. "What is it you're trying to accomplish? You've already annoyed me, but you aren't going to be able to beat me like this. I am stronger than you, and we're in *my* mind. Do you forget that?"

"Not at all," said Wil. He motioned for the mage to come to him. It didn't matter how things went now. Wil had gotten what he wanted, and now he just had to see it through. "Finish me off, if you can!"

Lightning flashed, and Wil turned the bottom of the arena into mud. Hugo sank to his waist, fighting to avoid going under farther. A burst of hot flames hardened and cracked the mud and he flew out, crashing right into Wil.

There was no style or grace as Hugo grabbed Wil by the front of his shirt and punched him in the mind again and again. They sailed through the air, into the crowd, and crashed into a memory.

"Who do you think will win?" Emily asked a younger Hugo. A first-year, if Wil had to guess. It was hard thinking with the growing spike of pain in his head.

"Rosen is the best at what he does," Hugo said, nodding toward the dark-skinned sixth-year student. "When he's done, there'll be nothing left."

"Do you think you'll ever be as good as him?" Emily pressed. She was a distant friend of Wil's and one of Hugo's first victims.

"Absolutely," said Hugo. "Better, even!"

"And how did that work out for you?" Wil asked after they passed through and out into the outskirts of the campus, where the world warped and became a massive house Wil didn't recognize. "Oh, right, Rosen is an archmage . . . and you're *not*."

"Shut up!" Hugo screamed as he slammed Wil into the ground and discharged all his mental energy.

Wil came back to himself with a gasp and a splitting headache. He let out a pained cry, silenced when Hugo punched him in the real world. The two flipped over and Hugo punched him again, screaming. Tears poured down his face and blood leaked from his nose.

No doubt Wil looked just as rough, but it didn't matter. A couple seconds later, he was saved from Hugo by a pair of powerful earthen arms.

"Get off me! Get off!" Hugo shouted, but the earth elemental held him tight and squeezed. The mage's face paled. "What did you do to my slave?"

Wil stood, wiping away blood from his nose and mouth. "Nothing. Maybe your control isn't as good as you think it is."

The other thralls surrounded them, and Wil suddenly realized he wasn't out of the woods yet. The fear and loathing in Hugo's eyes scared him then. Wil had learned an interesting thing about Hugo, but it wouldn't do him any good if the mage lost control and killed him. He swallowed hard and held up his hands in surrender.

"You win, Hugo. Good match."

Hugo breathed hard, teeth clenched so hard Wil was sure they would crack. The mage's eyes fluttered closed, and the arms around him relaxed. He regained control of his thrall and took a minute to himself. "You're annoying, McKenzie. You can't beat me, but you can make me try, at least. That's better than I expected of you." He held out his hand.

Wil looked at it, then took it. Hugo pulled him in then, and hissed, "If you ever do anything like that again, I *will* kill you. Understand?" He pulled away, all smiles.

"Perfectly," said Wil. The next time it happened, Wil would need to finish it.

"Well, I'm tired and have a headache, thanks to you, so excuse me. I'll see you Monday for more attempts to negotiate." With his thralls covering his retreat, Hugo disappeared into the ship's cabins.

Captain Nesbitt surprised Wil by clamping a hand down on his shoulder. "Are you okay?" he asked, his voice hard.

Wil nodded. "How is your sailor?" He looked back at where several people surrounded her. At least she was awake now, and carefully drinking water with shaky hands.

"Unsure," the captain said. "But if her condition changes . . . well, I'm sure you'll know if it happens." There was a hardness in his voice that couldn't be restrained. Wil understood.

"I'm sorry for my part in it, Captain. I never meant for anyone to get hurt. Or for there to even be a fight. My friend is adept at potions and might have something to heal her. I can check for you."

"That would be excellent, thank you." Captain Nesbitt bowed his head respectfully. Wil nodded back, and with one last look at the injured sailor, he jumped over the side of the *Flying Calamity* and floated harmlessly to the ground.

Things could have gotten worse, but Wil knew now that he could beat Hugo if it came down to it. It would be narrow, but letting him win today would go a long way if it had to happen again. Wil just hoped that it wasn't *when*.

INTERLUDE

A Friendly Warning

Syl didn't let the unproductive meetings get to him. As soon as Wil told him about Hugo's arrival and the first meeting, he knew they were in for an uphill battle that could take them all season. Of course, the meetings were incredibly boring, and alternated between tense arguments during which either the mage or Timothy Twist made things worse, and then Syl and Wil did their best to cool things down again.

Arabella often proved to be the voice of reason, and as usual, it made Syl flip-flop between loving her and finding her utterly loathsome when she went back to being childish and vain. Still, she constantly worked with him to try to move things forward, and table things when the heat grew to be too much.

Gallath had been the biggest surprise. He'd been nominally for the peace treaties early on, but the more Hugo Jefferson pushed, the more Gallath dug in his heels. The cool-headed ogre was starting to resemble his uncle with teeth bared and fists clenched, but he kept his head on for the most part.

They met three or four days a week, depending on how aggravated they were at day's end. Today had been a lighter day, and seeing Wil and Hugo talking after, Syl decided to not bother the wizards and instead venture out into the town, as he had become accustomed to doing.

And why not? Syl knew how charming and approachable he was, and loved it. Every time he went out, he had a nice conversation or two and lifted someone's spirits. That was magic all its own—to be an influence for kindness in the world. It didn't hurt that many of the residents of Harper Valley were keen on him.

"Hello, Mrs. Mildred," Syl crooned as he passed a middle-aged widow, sitting out on her porch. He winked at her, and she waved him off with a blush.

"Beautiful day, right, Arnold?" Syl pointed at a kid and his friends as he sauntered down Main Street without a care in the world. He wore his fluffy white fur coat and hat, and that combined with his height made him incredibly easy to notice. Sometimes that meant trouble found him.

He was stopping by a coffee shop for a drink and a chat with the owner, Libby, when a sharp shove against his shoulder got his attention. A heavyset man in his late fifties with a small beard not unlike his own scowled at him.

"Hi, there," said Syl. "Something I can do for you?"

"Yeah," said the man, adjusting the cap he wore. "You can leave."

Syl stared at him for a second before laughing. "Leave? I just got here. Ohhh, you have a thing for Libby, huh? Can't say I blame you. She's got the *best* laugh, and when she snorts, it's like you want to laugh with her. Cute too, and— Are you okay?"

Every single word that left his lips seemed to enrage the man. It started with a set jaw, and then his face went through multiple shades of red before settling on purple. He planted a hand on Syl's chest and shoved him against the shop wall, next to the door. Nearby people turned to watch but said nothing as the man shouted.

"Leave this town. Leave Harper Valley!"

That's when Syl understood. There had been a few times when fights broke out among . . . well, usually men like this and some of the more masculine fae. It turned out that humans felt threatened when someone as good-looking as Syl was around and could charm the pants off anyone. Syl offered a friendly smile and held his hands up placatingly.

"I understand how weird this must all be, but we're here to be your friends, mister. What's your name?" Syl didn't have to think about it to add a bit of real Charm to the mix. It was something he always had on, but he strengthened it and did his best to look safe. Just a harmless faun.

The man pressed Syl harder into the wall. "There ain't any being friends with your kind. We were right to wipe you out a hundred years ago. You're already trying to take back the land we took from you. And that's not mentioning the women you got under your unnatural charms."

Sometimes, Syl's mouth ran away from him. He liked to think he was good at talking. Too good. Some things just needed to be said, no matter how much worse they would make a situation. Before Syl could register why it was a bad idea, he grinned impishly and said, "Actually, that's just bathing. You should try it."

He'd fully earned the punch the cranky bastard sent his way, but Syl was prepared for it. He dropped his head and took the punch dead on his left horn. He barely felt it, but the man howled in pain and pulled back. He turned to run.

Syl let him get far enough away to crouch down and use his incredibly powerful legs to spring forward and drive those horns right into the man's ass. The man cried out again and went tumbling ass over ears while Syl caught himself against the ground.

A few people in the crowd, like Arnold, laughed at the sight of the man scrambling to get away. After picking himself up off the ground and brushing snow off his fine fur coat, Syl flashed a grin. "Sorry about that, folks. He started it."

"Sure looked that way to me. But maybe you goat people inspire fights. Been in a few, haven't you?" A crusty old man stared balefully at him.

"Ah, well, I tend to live loud and free." Syl didn't have to fake his happy grin. "It suits me, and I suppose some might take offense to that. I do regret the commotion in public, though." He bowed and continued, skipping coffee for the day. He didn't want to be there in case that jackass wanted a round two with a gun.

That was the good thing about Faerie. He never had to worry about some random person taking offense and killing him. Ever since Sheriff Frederick had started waving his gun around, Sil had been increasingly terrified of being shot. It didn't seem right that it should be so easy for any lunatic with a gun to just kill indiscriminately. Easily the worst part of Calipan, in his opinion.

Sure, Syl had magic, but almost none of it was geared toward hurting others. He had a few tricks in his bag, but the humans didn't know what. They feared the unknown instead of being intrigued by it. Even he sometimes felt a bit sad about it; there were always good examples around town.

Mr. Hagger had forgiven the fae for their arson attempts and welcomed them with open arms and shared food and drink. What better way to make friends?

Mrs. Patterson adored the gifts the fae had brought them, and Pearl often fought to spend time at the McKenzie farm. Syl wondered if the mayor had tried the wine yet.

And hell, Mack, the last person he'd fought, well, they were friends after the first few punches. Sometimes Syl had a mouth on him and a good hit coming. Mack got a good punch in, and then Syl had given one back for good measure. Sure, the fight broke a counter and a couple of chairs, but he'd paid for it and they were friends now.

With that thought, Syl went to the diner to check in on Mack and see how he was doing. "Mack, you silver-haired devil, what's cookin'? Hi, Candy!" Syl spread his arms, all but demanding a hug.

Mack came through where the counter used to be and mimed punching him in the ribs a few times before they half hugged. "A little bit of everything and the kitchen sink too. You hungry?"

"After another day hearing that jackass threaten us? I want one of those . . . What did you call them? Borgors?" Syl plopped himself down on the nearest stool at the bar. "And that one coffee with whiskey in it."

"Cheeseburger and an Albetosian coffee, coming right up." Mack slapped his shoulder again and went to work, humming along to the muffled radio in the back.

Candy walked up to him, trailing her hand along his shoulders, and sat sideways on the stool next to his. The pretty redhead looked about as happy to see him as he was her.

"Have you given it much thought?" Syl asked.

"I have! You sure I'll be welcome?" Candy bit her lip.

Syl set his hand on hers. "Absolutely. You shouldn't hold yourself back the way you do. You've got real talent, and you'll have so much fun singing with my friends. Please, please, *please* come to the McKenzie farm for the Midwinter Feast."

Candy groaned. "I want to, it's just . . . I'm so used to going to the Carrey place for the feast, with family. They're old-fashioned and won't want to come to the McKenzie farm with me."

"How many people would you say are old-fashioned around here?" Syl asked, thinking of his brief scuffle. "I got attacked again earlier today. It'd be nice to know that the stubborn ones are outnumbered by those who are curious about us."

Candy chewed her lip thoughtfully. "I think so. I've overheard a lot of people talking, and a few times they've asked me what I thought. I've been open about liking you guys. Those Wee Folk are hilarious!"

Syl grinned and opened his mouth to speak. He was promptly slammed against the counter by a big man. A second later, pure agony latched onto his wrists. Syl jerked, and that just made it worse. He fell to the ground and writhed against the irons now binding him.

"Got you again, Goat." Sheriff Frederick stood over him, a satisfied look on his face. "You just can't help yourself, can you? You have to keep starting fights and causing trouble."

"I didn't start it," Syl cried out. "Please take these off! I surrender!"

Mack stormed out. "What are you doing? Get them off of him!" He jabbed a greasy spatula at the sheriff.

"Stay out of this, Mack. You interfere and you'll come along too." From behind the sheriff came a couple of men wearing silver badges. They were armed and looking for a fight.

Syl whimpered. The all-encompassing inferno clamped around his wrists and wouldn't let go. There was no escape from it, no hiding—just a crystal clear focus on the touch of faebane.

Sheriff Frederick crouched, getting too close to Syl. "I don't know what you did to me to get out of jail, but I'm never going to forget it. I know I didn't just give you a warning and send you on your way."

"I didn't . . . I didn't do anything t-to you." Syl started and stopped multiple times. The sheriff grabbed his irons, holding them away from his sizzling flesh. It took some effort to breathe through the pain, but he had no clue how long Frederick would give him.

"You must have listened to some part inside of you that thought it was kind," Syl tried. "I'm a fae, I can't lie!"

"Naw, that ain't it. See, I think you did some of that fae magic on me. Enchanted me, or whatever you call it. And you made me let you go."

"Sheriff, please," Candy tried. "He's a good guy, he wouldn't do that!"

"I mean, yeah, I would," said Syl, "but I didn't. I'll make you a deal, Sheriff. We fae never break deals."

Sheriff Frederick's mustache wiggled as he thought about it. "Go on."

Syl went for the classic fae sham deal. "I promise you that if you let me go, I'll tell you what I learn about what happened to your head. I could use my magic to investigate what happened. I swear that you will know more about it when I know more about it. If you let me go."

"Hmm." Sheriff Frederick sucked his teeth. "I don't trust you, but the wizard said you can't lie. Alright, I accept your terms." He dropped the irons again. Syl jerked away and cried out again as Sheriff Frederick fished for the right key. He took his time releasing him.

"Alright. Then I guess this time you do get a warning. A real one. But let me make this clear, Goat: one more slipup and there'll be no getting out of it. You do anything to disrupt the Midwinter Feast, you'll regret it." The sheriff and his deputies left.

Candy went to Syl's side and helped him sit up. Syl tenderly touched the burns on his wrists.

"Are you okay?" she asked.

"I *really* don't like iron," he said with a shudder. "It's not even just the touch, it's being *bound. Enclosed* in iron. I have something for this, though."

Very carefully he reached into his magic bag and summoned a jar with a dark green paste inside. With shaking hands, he opened it and dipped his finger in. "Just a little bit of this and— Ugh, this stings."

Syl whimpered, and then the pain was over as the paste was absorbed. It would still take time to heal properly. The faun took several deep breaths, mindful of all the people watching him. He smiled. "Wow, that does not feel good!" he said. "But I'm okay. I wish you didn't have to see that."

"See that? What the hell is Frederick's problem?" Mack seethed openly, grabbing a handful of his long hair and pulling on it. "He's not normally like this."

"Ah, well, I tend to live loud and free," said Syl. "He took offense to that, I guess. Don't worry, I'll be okay in a few minutes. But I could really, really use a borgor right now."

CHAPTER 42

Beans

It came as no surprise that Wil had a throbbing headache when he woke. After spending a year and a half avoiding mind magic, he'd now used it several times over the last few days. Worse than that, he'd let himself get knocked around. The fact that it had been strategic didn't make the pain any less persistent.

He stumbled out of bed and stood lifelessly in the shower for twice as long as usual. He barely remembered drying off and putting on clothes before he came downstairs and brewed a pot of coffee and got his secret weapon. There were potions for just about anything you could think of if you had the ingredients and the recipe.

This particular headache potion had been brewed by Bram. It came from a large batch they had on hand for fun weekends. Well, things had been too busy to drink much or play cards, but he appreciated having it now.

With his coffee ready, Wil shot down the potion. He had to swallow several times to get the viscous substance down, and it left a weird residue in his mouth. A sip of coffee helped wash that out, and almost immediately, he felt a little better. Not perfect, but the pain went from the slow steady beat of a war drum to the *tink, tink* of a faraway hammer.

Wil sat down and had cold cereal for breakfast. He ate haltingly, wishing for something better without having the drive to cook or be out in public. He had nearly finished when a sharp bang at the door made him wish for death.

The banging continued until Wil lumbered his way to the front door and opened it. Mr. Carrey stood there in his usual cap and leathery scowl. "Dammit, Wizard, these fae have got to go!"

After silently counting to five, Wil took a deep breath and said, "Good morning, Mr. Carrey. What did the fae do this time?"

Mr. Carrey pointed. "They destroyed my damned farm! Look!"

Wil followed Mr. Carrey's finger and did a double take. Even from this distance, he could see the massive plants engulfing the entirety of the property. Big green shoots went skyward before falling and growing in spirals, splitting up and seeking new purchase in the ground. And worst of all, they seemed to be slowly moving.

"Huh. Could you give me five minutes to get ready, and then I'll be with you?"

Wil closed the door without waiting for an answer. He buried his face in his hands and let out a muffled scream. That done, he finished his coffee, got shoes and his staff, and went back out the front door. He couldn't say he was ready, but they couldn't afford to wait until he was.

Up close, the plants looked much more impressive, and Wil was able to see what they were. Straight out of a storybook, the Carrey farm was smothered by an abundance of beanstalks. The farmhands largely stood and stared, unable to do anything. The stalks took up all the space and even blocked the drive up to the house in several places.

There were holes in the stalks that had been cut through, presumably so Mr. Carrey and his wife could get out safely. Each stalk had beans the size of people dangling and ready for harvest. Some of the workers had taken some down, and two men were actively eating one of them.

Wil had never seen Mr. Carrey so livid.

"This is what they did to my precious property! How am I supposed to deal with this? I'm ruined, and it's all their fault!" The old man choked back a sob, and as much as Wil didn't care for him, he felt a twinge of sympathy.

"I need more information," said Wil, rubbing his temples. The cool air helped his head, but the yelling did not. "How did this start? Why is it the fae's fault?"

Mr. Carrey gestured wildly. "Look what they did to my land! They said it was so I could grow more plants, as a thank-you, but it was a nasty trick! I planted those beans of theirs, and I—"

"Wait, what beans?" Wil asked, turning around. "They changed the land, but they didn't give you anything, did they?"

The old farmer's scowl vanished, replaced by a look Wil knew well: guilt.

"They didn't give *me* any beans, per se," Mr. Carrey started. He didn't say anything else until Wil's penetrating stare made him scowl again. "They gave them to the mayor, and then I bought them. Yesterday we planted them. Since you didn't come around and put my land back to order and all."

"And you planted all of them," said Wil. "The beans that . . . Twist promised would feed you forever. Dammit." This was just like the Wee Folk. A gift that was also a prank, but only if you approached it with the wrong frame of mind.

"I need to talk with the representative of the Wee Folk about this. In the meantime, be careful, and try not to get too close to them." Wil turned to leave, but Mr. Carrey's hand shot out and gripped his arm like a vice.

"You're not leaving without doing anything, are you? C'mon, Mr. Wizard, fix this!"

Wil sighed. "I'm pretty sure I can't, but I'll try." He pulled his arm back and aimed his staff at a wide section of horizontal beanstalk. Flames erupted out the end of the staff in a fifteen-foot cone, engulfing the plant. He kept it up for a few seconds and then smothered the flames. The plant was fine. Charred around the edges and withered, but within seconds it regrew what little had burned away.

Well, fine. When Wil tried again, he froze the plant and then blasted it with force. This worked to split a beanstalk in half. And then both halves regrew wildly, planting themselves in a fresh spot of ground and anchoring to the earth.

"Why isn't this working?" Mr. Carrey demanded.

"Because you're hovering," said Wil, impatience creeping into his voice. "No one gets work done when you hover and interrupt them every five minutes. I'm doing my best, but why don't you go somewhere else while I do this?"

"No, I ain't moving," Mr. Carrey said. "This needs to be fixed and I'm not gonna be waved away! With the fairgrounds taken up by that damned ship and the damned fae cursing my land to be warmer, we were going to hold the town Midwinter Feast here. What am I supposed to do now?"

"I don't know," said Wil. "Let's find out."

He tried one last thing, something he was suited for. Wil closed his eyes and tapped into the leyline. At once he "saw" the problem. The beanstalks were firmly attached to the leyline, greedily drinking in its magic and growing so well, they were all but indestructible. He still tried reaching out for the beanstalks themselves and gently whispering for them to let go. *Let go and shrink, no need to grow too big.*

The leyline made it easy to add his magic to the raging river of power and guide it. Opening his eyes, he watched as all the plants on the property started to shrink and wither. It always felt weird, encouraging plants to speed up their lives and die, but it was different this time. It felt like falling a tremendous distance and never hitting the bottom. The stalks browned and wilted, then paused.

The shrinkage stopped, and the farm-devouring growth turned green and swelled again. Wil let go as the beanstalks came back to life with an explosive vengeance. More massive beans developed instantly and fell from the stalks.

"You made it worse!" Mr. Carrey didn't sound angry so much as shocked. He took off his hat and clutched it to his chest.

"Well, there's good news and bad news, Mr. Carrey," said Wil with a helpless, sheepish smile. "You're going to have to find somewhere to stay for a bit and you can't host the Midwinter Feast this year. But on the bright side, you'll never go hungry again. I hope you like beans."

The next stop, obviously, was the McKenzie farm. The walk wasn't that long, but it still gave Wil plenty of time to get a head full of steam. He stopped at the end of the drive, where a jolly little gnome boy and a goblin girl were juggling balls together.

"Do either of you know where I can find Timothy Twist?" Wil asked, keeping a pleasant expression up for the children.

The goblin girl pointed at his parents' house, missing the rubber ball that hit her in the face. Rather than get upset, she and the gnome burst out laughing, and Wil waved and moved on.

The idea of Timothy Twist in his family's house bothered Wil, though he couldn't quite put his finger on why. Maybe it was the idea that Twist would just prank them. His ma didn't deserve that, even if his dad would probably get a kick out of it, after he was done being angry.

Wil burst in the front door, probably looking alarming with his staff and grimace. Sharon peeked her head out of the kitchen. "Oh, hi there, hon! Why the long face?" She came out, wearing a floury apron.

"Yeah, why the long face, Wil?" Timothy Twist followed, wearing an apron five sizes too big for him.

"You!" Wil pointed at Twist. "Mr. Carrey's farm got overgrown with the beans you gave the town. How do we get rid of the beanstalks?"

Timothy Twist pointed at himself, confused and aggrieved. "Me? I didn't give Mr. Carrey nothing. I gave the mayor some of our very finest, to be given out and used among the population."

Wil sighed. "He sold them to Mr. Carrey, who planted all of them."

"*All of them?*" Twist's eyes lit up. He burst out laughing, going so far as to roll around on the floor. "Every single one? Ohohohoho!"

Wil wasn't amused. "All of them."

"Well, that's just greedy, now, isn't it? I promised that one of them would feed a person forever. How was I supposed to know this would happen?"

Sharon stepped in. "What happened to his farm? Is he okay?"

Wil sighed and sat down at the kitchen table, burying his face in his hands. "He's fine, but he's cut off from his house. The farming half of his property is eaten by giant beanstalks. He's still got the land for his animals, but who knows if the plants will keep growing? They latched onto the leyline there and I can't destroy them."

Twist sat up, wiping away a tear. He put his fallen hat back on and straightened it. "Well then, that's unfortunate. See, normally they last for a full season, and then produce a single small bean to plant, you know? It's self-sustaining, and we give them out to hungry and needy families. One bean and you got all the hearty protein you need.

"But attached to a leyline? Hoo boy, that might be there for at least a year. Guess Mr. Carrey got what he paid for!" Twist's grin grew malicious. "Can't say I'm unhappy to see it. Bet he really wants to point his guns at us now, huh?"

Wil's eye twitched, but Sharon was always the practical one in the family. "So he's got giant beanstalks that grow back when they're cut down and produce endless beans? What's the problem? He could make a killing off that! The plant fibers alone . . ." She took off her apron and put it on a hook on the thin wall separating the kitchen from the entryway.

"Excuse me, I'm going to go have a little talk with Mr. Carrey and straighten things away." Sharon kissed Wil on his cheek as she passed, leaving him alone with Timothy Twist.

Wil stared at him, and the puck stared back. Wil didn't say anything at first, instead taking his time to get the words right. "I don't understand you, Twist. You seem happiest when other people are miserable."

"That's not true at all," Twist protested. "It's not when people are miserable. It's when they're *surprised*. It's when they're forced to deal with change. Too many people, if they get comfortable, they get stagnant. I happen to provide a valuable public service: keeping people from getting stuck in a rut."

Wil stood up. "Thanks to you, I have a lot more messes to clean up. I'm not mad about that, I'm mad about the fact that you don't seem to care whether your shenanigans endanger the talks here."

Timothy Twist just shrugged with a devilish smirk. "I am what I am. A cat can't change its spots. Besides, that's what we've got you for, Wizard! You're quite good at jumping from thing to thing, keeping everything from devolving into pure chaos. You're the only person preventing us from being at war."

It rang with truth, but Wil didn't know how to respond to it. Instead, he just shook his head. "Please try to be on your best behavior from now on. I don't want to give Hugo or Mr. Carrey or the sheriff any more reasons to want a fight." He walked out the front door.

It was bad enough that Frederick had got to Syl and hurt him. Wil had nearly had words with the man before Syl had begged for him to let it go. As good as things were on the farm, the rest of the town was still mixed. But maybe there was a way to use that to their advantage.

Wil did as he always did when things were hard. He went to his father for advice.

CHAPTER 43

Heart of the Community

Until now, there had never been a time in Wil's life when he had difficulty finding his father on the farm.

Not that Wil minded. It was genuinely a joy to see so many people living comfortably where he grew up. Not all of the fae kept to their tree houses, and dozens had worked together to dig an artificial lake where one of the fields had been. They promised to reverse it by the time they left and to pay Bob for the trouble, but he'd just laughed it off and said he'd always wanted a hot spring in the winter.

Their family had four growing fields and two grazing fields for their animals. It was slightly larger than average for their area, nothing special save for being right in the middle of a community of middle-class farmers, instead of the rich, expansive land to the south. Now it no longer resembled a farm, but something much closer to the area around the academy.

There was housing, a lake to swim in, and always music playing or stories being told. There were various places to get a bite to eat. Each time Wil visited, he had to stop and stare and try to focus on the pride he felt, rather than the guilt over the cost. Especially with his next request.

"Have you seen my father?" Wil asked Raxis. The centaur had opened up a small archery range away from the rest of the commotion. He spent his days teaching human children how to shoot a bow and hit targets, and loved every second of it.

"Wilbur!" Raxis's smiles always looked like he was somewhere else, or possibly drunk. "I've seen your father plenty of times. Today, even!"

"Okay, where?" Wil asked, chuckling.

The centaur looked around. He pointed over at the lake. "I saw him take a dip after breakfast, with Bosh and Kehn. Not sure how long ago that was. I can never tell human time." He shook his head thoughtfully.

Wil patted Raxis's flank. "Appreciated!"

Bosh the gnome was still there, lounging in the winter sun in little more than a loincloth and his beard. He didn't even open his eyes when Wil drew near, just rested with his hands cushioning his head on a towel.

"Howdy, Wizard! That's what you people say, right? Howdy?"

"Sure," said Wil. "Howdy. Have you seen my dad anywhere? I need to talk to him about something important."

"Ahh, your dad," Bosh sighed. "What a great feller. He should've been a gnome himself. Fun, friendly, hardworking, tough. It suits him better than human, I think. No offense, of course."

"I'm getting used to it."

"We were just talking about what he wants to do when he's done farming. Did you know he's running for mayor?" Bosh opened his eyes and gaped at Wil. "Wouldn't that be something? I'd vote for him."

"Do you know where he is right now?" Maybe the gnome had been day drinking. The fae didn't have quite the stigma attached to it that humans did.

"The barn, I think. One of the cows is giving birth."

Wil perked up. "Delilah's giving birth! Appreciated, Bosh." He ran toward the barn, excitement wearing out the last of his headache. It was hard to be frustrated when their favorite cow was about to have another kid. He hopped the stone wall and cut through the field, slowing as he approached the open side door.

He didn't see his father, but Sarah and a few of the fae had crowded around the birthing pen. Wil walked up to his sister, brushing past an elf and a goblin who watched eagerly. Neither said anything at first, just watching his father work.

"Easy now, Delilah," Bob crooned, gently patting her side. She stood for the moment, and slimy hooves hung out of her. "You're doing so well. It's almost over."

Delilah mooed her distress. Wil stepped forward, setting his staff against the gate. "I can talk to her," he said to his father. "Tell her what you said."

Bob beamed up at him. He wore some of his worst clothes and thick gloves. The miracle of childbirth was rarely clean. "Aww, that'd be nice. Pretty sure she knows, though. Ain't your first rodeo, is it, sweetie?"

Wil hadn't used the spell for a while, but with a second of concentration, Delilah's pained groans became words.

"This is the last time, I swear. I am *not* doing this ever again, and I don't care what you say!" Delilah stamped her feet, and her entire swollen middle swayed with the motion.

"I'll tell him," said Wil. "Dad, Delilah's done having kids after this, okay?"

Bob patted her side and leaned over to kiss her head. "Don't worry, girl, you'll have a nice retirement."

After that, things got very wet, very fast. A few hard pushes later and the calf's head was poking out. The denizens of Faerie weren't strangers to animals giving birth, but the elf among them just shrugged and said there was beauty in it. Wet, slimy, goopy, bloody beauty. Wil was on hand to cast a quick shield to avoid the splash when the calf dropped the rest of the way out. Delilah groaned in relief.

Wil helped clean up and get the calf and mother situated, then waited patiently until the fae left the McKenzies alone. Sarah sat on the ground, drawing like always.

"You ever get tired of drawing?" Wil asked.

"You ever get tired of magic?" she shot back. "Of course you don't. And neither do I. I've been drawing more than ever since our home got turned into a hotel." She looked up from her drawing. "It's fantastic. What do you need with Dad?"

Wil winced. His father was on the far side of the barn, taking off his clothes and washing up at the pump. "A favor. A pretty big one too."

"You ask for a lot of favors, don't you?" Sarah asked. A mischievous, catlike smile spread. "That's why I'm his favorite, you know. I don't ask for much. You and Jeb? Hoo boy."

"Yeah, well," said Wil, grinning back at her. "You were adopted."

"Which means they wanted me," Sarah countered, having heard the line a million times before. "See? Favorite."

Bob walked up, rubbing his hands together. He'd changed his shirt as well, but his pants were stained with various fluids. "What's up, Wil?"

"Well, Mr. Carey's farm had a . . . hiccup."

Wil filled his family in on what happened. Bob was shocked, while Sarah found the whole thing immensely funny. Especially Timothy Twist's non-reaction. That tracked. She and the puck probably got along well, come to think of it. Bob, on the other hand, saw the problem before Wil even brought it up.

"The Midwinter Feast," said Bob. "It can't be at the fairgrounds because of the ship, and Mr. Carey's place is now . . . well, it's not gone, but it might as well be gone." Bob nodded thoughtfully. "You want to have it here. The entire town."

Wil's shoulders slumped. "I know it's a big ask," he started.

"Huge. Tremendous," Sarah supplied as she shaded her picture with quick, light pencil strokes.

Bob held up a hand. "It's important to the mission, which is important to the future of Harper Valley and Calipan. Especially since there's been a little bit of friction lately. Things were fine at first, but there are a few people who don't want to give the fae a chance. I can't blame some of them, but they could be trouble. If we have it here, plenty won't show up. You know that, right?"

Wil nodded and crossed his arms over his chest. "I know. It's not about getting everyone, it's about making a space where everyone is welcome, and we can make a good showing. For the first time, we can see about making the Midwinter Feast not just about family and our local community, but about welcoming new people in and building bridges. If we can show acceptance and friendship to those different from us and have the whole town be part of it, then maybe everything will be alright after all."

Sarah broke the short silence. "How do you always manage to be so damned sappy?"

Bob waved her off. "None of that. It's one of Wil's best qualities. You're right, but I'm gonna be honest with you. I am not sure there's the money to do it. I've got plenty in savings, but I was planning on using a lot of that for the race. No way I'm going to be able to get any of Sinclair's donors from him."

"What do we need?" It wasn't a no, which meant Bob was thinking about it.

It's what he always appreciated about his father. Bob had always heard Wil out when he was a kid and asked for something.

Bob counted things down on his fingers. "We're gonna need a lot more places for sitting and eating. That's the number one thing. Places for people to do their business, which will mean digging and setting up outhouses. We'll need plenty of people to spread the word and talk for us, and they deserve pay for their time. We'll need people to keep the peace, just in case, and a whole lotta food."

Wil nodded along to the list, relaxing more and more until he was confident he had this in the bag. "Those are all easy. I'll help pay for things, and so will Syl and Arabella, more than likely. They both love a good party and excess, and are the ones most interested in our customs and holidays. More than that, this is a perfect chance for the fae to prepare a lot of their own food. That'll cut costs down and help our cause. And then, when all this is over, we can turn the farm back to normal." As much as Wil loved what the farm had become, it was still weird seeing what had happened to his childhood home.

Bob paused. "Sarah? Would you mind leaving us for a little bit?"

"If I have to." She got up and made a dramatic show of trudging away at half speed. It lasted until Bob sighed, and she laughed and trotted off.

"What's wrong, Dad?" Wil's gut told him this would be something huge.

"Well, it's all about how successful we end up being," Bob started. He leaned against the pen behind him, mirroring Wil's posture. "What happens if the two of us succeed in our goals, Wil?"

"What do you mean? If we both succeed, then you'll be mayor and there will be a peace and trade treaty with the fae." Wil shrugged. It sounded good to him.

"That's exactly it. If I'm mayor and the fae are going to need a permanent presence in our world, in our town . . . This place has kind of become an unofficial embassy. I think that by this time next year, it will be an official one. I'll be mayor, and won't have time to run a farm. And let's be real here: Jeb never wanted to take over."

Wil was shocked. Logically, he knew that his father couldn't be a mayor and farmer at the same time, but he'd always pictured things continuing as usual, just with Jeb in charge. "What'll he do, then?"

Bob laughed. "Judging from the way he's been behaving, he'll go have an adventure in Faerie. Maybe get his heart broken in the process, but he needs a chance to get out of Harper Valley and find himself. Sarah won't mind the place no longer being a farm. She's doing well with her pictures now, and we've got someone from Manifee City talking about putting them in a book."

"Wow, really?" The shock hit Wil with a sense of dizziness. What else had he missed when dealing with putting out so many fires? "When did this happen?"

"Recently, but don't say anything around her. She's keeping it quiet for now." Bob tapped his lips.

"So, if we both succeed, you'll just sell the farm?" The thought hurt more than Wil could ever expect.

After looking back and forth as if to check they were alone, Bob's voice dropped. "If we're both successful, Harper Valley's going to be a *major* destination. This land's only going to go up in price. I won't sell it, but I'll make a comfy retirement fund by renting it out."

Then only one thing remained, as far as Wil was concerned. "And you're okay with all of this? Everything's going to change. You've been doing this my entire life, and you're willing to upend it all just because of me?"

Pushing away from the pen, Bob grabbed Wil and pulled him in for a tight hug. "Son, life *is* change. And seeing you at work, you've never been more alive. And the same goes for us. We didn't ask for it, but you led us into it doing good work. We're making a real difference. I've never been prouder of you."

Wil hugged back tightly.

CHAPTER 44

Steak Break

The work went on and never stopped. It took some doing, but the combined efforts of Sharon and Wil calmed Mr. Carrey down. Sharon pointed out all the ways he could make money, no longer having to maintain fields. Wil couldn't destroy the beanstalks, but tapping into the leyline allowed him to fuel and shape the growth.

After an hour of work, he built an arch for the colossal plant to grow around, giving Mr. Carrey a way to his home. The house, a mansion by Harper Valley standards, sat in the middle of dozens of beanstalks like a treasure guarded by a greedy dragon. It was, at least, undamaged.

Then Wil had to run around town and use his influence as a heroic wizard to try to convince people that feasting with the fae would be a fun and novel experience. At least half the families would stay at home or visit neighboring towns to see relatives, but that still left plenty of people to invite. Including people he didn't want to deal with.

"You're kidding me," said Mayor Sinclair. "Why the hell would I want to go feast with your family? You and I hate each other." At this point, his office put Wil in mind of a moody teenager's room, where he hid away from the world and drank.

Wil sighed and bit back the half dozen sharp responses he'd cooked up on the way there. "That's part of the point, though," he said gently. "The Midwinter Feast is all about being mindful of what you have and being willing to share it with people in need. We've been at odds and everyone knows it, so you showing up would make us both look good."

It was sad Wil knew that exact line would get Sinclair's attention. The mayor's sullen glower turned thoughtful, and he sat up straighter. "You're not wrong," he said. "It would be a good show of unity when things have been tense. But that's the other problem, Wilbur. It would come across as a tacit endorsement of the fae, and I'm not sure I want to do that."

Ever since Sheriff Frederick had hassled Syl and burned him with iron, he and his new deputies had been everywhere in public, keeping an eye out for trouble. At least, that's what they claimed to be doing. In reality, they shielded the more conservative-minded people when *they* tried to pick fights.

"Almost all of the problems have been people from here," Wil pointed out.

"Yes," said Sinclair. "My voters. Especially if I take an anti-fae stance myself. And I just might, considering everything going on. Your desire for trade and open borders threatens some of my donors. Why should I show up and alienate them?"

Wil shrugged. "Maybe you shouldn't. You have plenty of reasons not to. But it's going to be the biggest event of the season. You not being there . . . , well, I'm not saying you'll look weak or out of touch or cowardly, but I'm not *not* saying it."

It couldn't have gone better if Wil had used mind magic on him. If looks could kill, Wil would've at least been wounded.

"Do you think I'm some dumb kid you can goad?" Sinclair asked.

"Maybe." Wil smiled pleasantly. "Mostly, I think that if you're thinking about running again, you don't want to be nowhere to be seen. Especially when someone else shows town pride, community, and leadership. The people might start looking to that person to guide them in the future."

Wil had the mayor there, and Sinclair knew it. He wasn't happy about it. Blowing out a held breath, he said, "Fine, I'll be there. Maybe I'll even break out that wine your goat friend gave me."

"His name is Sylano," said Wil. "And he wields considerably more power than you do. We'll see you there." Without waiting for a response, Wil left with a gust of wind through the door that opened for him. That was one great thing about being a wizard. He could make almost any entrance or exit dramatic.

Dealing with Sinclair was always a headache, and it marked the end of a particularly long day. With the sun already setting, Wil stopped by the butcher's and brought dinner home. Darlene was already waiting for him in the kitchen, half splayed out across the kitchen table.

"You too, huh?" Wil asked as he set the bag of meat in the icebox for later. He sat across from her.

"Buuuh," Darlene groaned against the table. She looked up at him with bleary eyes. "You know what's annoying? Being really good at the tedious parts of planning. No offense, but you're useless outside coming up with plans and being a pretty face."

"Aww, you think I have a pretty face?" Wil winked. Darlene snorted and he took that opportunity to lean forward and kiss her forehead. "I have nothing but respect and admiration for your ability to take my ideas and make them happen. Bram and I would be helpless without you."

His girlfriend's bright blue eyes lit up with joy and affection. "You know, you're getting better at saying the right thing. I've trained you well."

"Sure did! Tell me about your day," said Wil as he took one of her hands in his.

Darlene took a deep breath. "I managed to coordinate with Arabella about what dishes they should bring to complement and contrast our usual feast meals. Nearly got into a fight with her over it, which I think she wanted. She treated me a lot better after I snapped at her."

"That sounds like her," said Wil. "She shares that with Twist, I think. Liking or respecting you better when you bare your teeth at them."

"That'd make sense. She's going to take care of that. Then I went around and got volunteer work and donations for setting up and working the land. People who are sympathetic to us and who are going to be interested in your dad running for mayor. I made sure we had the right permits, and also measured how many outhouses we'd need to dig holes for. To be fair, your dad helped with that and said you could do a lot of the digging."

"And I will, happily," said Wil. At this point, it would take very little effort for him to shape the earth and save others from hours of hard work.

"And . . . I saw my dad today," Darlene said, eyes dropping. "Got into an argument."

Suddenly her low energy made a lot more sense. "What did he say or do this time?"

"Oh, just the usual," she said, chuckling bitterly. "Only now he's blaming me for helping get the fae into town and showing them around. Says that it's not enough that I abandoned the family business, now I'm trying to ruin him as well. Didn't say *how* it would ruin him, but I don't think it matters."

There was only so much Wil could do about Darlene's father. It was a sore subject they avoided, if only because Darlene knew there was no resolution incoming, no way to get through to him and get her old dad back.

An idea hit Wil, though he didn't think it was necessarily a good one. "What if I had something that might make him happy and help patch things up?"

Darlene cocked her head to the side. She said nothing, but he had her attention at least.

"When this treaty goes through, the fae are going to need inroads into markets here to succeed. What if we offer your father one of the earliest contracts?" Wil stood. "That way he'll get a piece of whatever comes through Faerie."

She smiled, though she looked sad. "Not sure he deserves it. If I want to have him in my life, I have to put up with knowing he'll never get better. I still miss him, so . . . maybe. It's a good idea, Wil."

"No, no, this is your idea," said Wil, as he rummaged through the cabinets for a skillet and some seasonings. "I'm just going to make it happen. We've already been talking about similar things, it's just a matter of getting him in on it. And given he's got the biggest store in town, it's a no-brainer. Are you hungry? I got steaks."

"I'll never say no to a good steak," Darlene said with a chuckle. She waited at the table as Wil started up their dinner, washing potatoes and dicing them with magic before putting them on to boil.

The way he saw it, she had plenty to think about and could use the quiet. He didn't even turn on the radio as he fixed dinner. When he got close to being done, Darlene cleaned off and set the table, and even mashed the potatoes while he finished up the sweet corn.

They were halfway through eating when Darlene suddenly said, "Do you think we could invite him to the feast? I know he's a jerk, and he'll probably be obnoxious but . . . I miss him. I know he'll never make things right, and I shouldn't have to, but I kind of miss Mom and want . . ."

She dropped her fork and covered her face with her hands. "I want him to be proud of me. Is that stupid? He's been a jerk my entire life and nothing's ever been good enough, and I just want, for *once*, for him to acknowledge the good job I'm doing."

Wil finished the bite he was chewing and washed it down with some beer. "It's not stupid at all. I think we all want that. I know how good it feels when my dad says it to me. I wish you had that too. So if I could maybe help make that happen, I want to. Besides, I know he'll come to the feast. I convinced Sinclair to come and he'll bring his donors."

Darlene's watery eyes lit up. "Oh, that's perfect. Doing it at your parents' house will look strong when Bob announces his candidacy. If we can time it just right— What, why are you laughing?"

Wil shook his head, covering his mouth and trying not to be too obvious in his mirth. "We always do this. We go to relax and then we end up talking about plans and schemes and how to get things done and . . . I'm not mad or anything. I love that about you. About us. We never stop."

Darlene smiled and raised her beer in a toast. "Of course we don't. We're unstoppable. But is that a sign I should drop it for now and enjoy dinner?"

"Well, I wouldn't say no to that," said Wil, raising his bottle. "Here's to us enjoying each other's company, and talking about plans in the morning, maybe."

"I'll drink to that," said Darlene. They clinked their bottles.

CHAPTER 45

Good Chemistry

The good thing about being so busy was that Wil got to postpone a few of the mid-morning meetings. Hugo wasn't pleased about being sidelined as Wil and the others prepared for the holiday, but the mage had been distant and less aggressive since their duel. Even in negotiations, he took a back seat and let Freddie and Maxwell talk details.

Wil knew Hugo was dwelling on the fight, because he was too. Did the mage suspect that Wil had let him win? Did he take his thrall restraining him to be just a hiccup? A coincidence? Whatever haunted Hugo, he didn't bring it up to Wil and didn't even taunt or aggravate him as much. He spent the negotiations with a distant, distracted look in his eyes.

Wil used the breathing room to get things done. With food and work done to prepare the farm for a few thousand people, the remaining week melted away fast. They were two days out from the Midwinter Feast, and everyone pushed themselves to their limits.

So when Wil finished a few normal winter work orders, he had time before he collapsed in bed. He'd gotten to spend plenty of time with his family and Darlene, and realized he hadn't been around much for Bram. Guilt and eagerness brought him to the Stevenson farm.

To his surprise, there was a crowd lined up in front of the barn. Wil stood at the end of the drive, head tilted to the side. A troll and a goblin stood in front of the barn and let people in one or two at a time. He was surprised by how animatedly old Mrs. Spencer was when speaking to the troll, who nodded along. Soon she was let in, and the troll bowed respectfully to her before the next person came up.

"What's everyone waiting for?" Wil asked the person in back.

Lonnie MacDougal was a handful of years older than Wil and worked for one of the local animal doctors. "New medicines and special mixes from Faerie," he said. "Oh, hey, Mr. Wizard! Bram's got the best connections and is getting them for us to try. He's making sure it's safe and not . . . you know."

"No," said Wil, "I don't. What?"

"Well, poisoned or something. Didn't the fae have a thing where they'd put people in enchanted sleeps that lasted a lifetime?" Lonnie craned his head to see the front of the line. "Like, smart fae. Not the knuckle-dragging guys up there. I think they just kill us."

"Not as much as we killed them," said Wil. He tried to keep the irritation out of his voice, knowing to pick his battles carefully. Instead of going off, he praised Lonnie. "That's a good idea, coming to Bram. He's very thorough with his mixes. I taught him some, and then he picked up more on his own."

Lonnie lit up. "I love the beer he—well, you guys, make. And his hangover cures and energy potions have been keeping me going this winter."

Wil leaned in to whisper conspiratorially, "We're giving out free beer at the Midwinter Feast my parents are hosting. But keep it hush, we don't want to run out."

"You got it. Thanks, Wil!"

Wil patted him on the shoulder and walked along the line. Every so often someone would greet him and he'd mirror it, but he made a clear beeline for the barn itself. The fae didn't try to stop him, waving him at him instead as he entered.

Bram was nowhere to be found. Instead, the ogre Shak sat in Bram's extra-durable chair behind the table they drank at. He had an older hobgoblin helping him fill out orders. "Here you are, Mrs. Spencer," said Shak as the hob handed her a small box with vials inside. "That'll be two hundred and fifty zynce."

"Oh," Mrs. Spencer's face dropped.

"But," Shak continued with a smile that did wonders for his brutish appearance, "Bram told us about you and said to knock fifty off. Does that work?"

"Yes, yes, tha—"

"Ah-ah-ah," Shak interrupted. The hob tapped a sign hanging above the table that said "Do not say Thank You, please and thank you." "I'm happy to help."

After paying, Mrs. Spencer took her box and went out the barn door, nodding at Wil. No one else came in just yet.

"What can we do for you, Wizard?" Shak asked, folding his hands together over his belly.

"Well, I was hoping to talk to Bram," said Wil, looking around. "When did you two start working for him?"

"Ahh, he needed a break," said the hob as he rearranged a series of small boxes. "So he's in the house right now, and we're manning the front. If you see him, can you tell him we're running low on the little blue stamina potions?"

"Sure," said Wil, looking back out the door at the line. "And there's been no issues, no one complaining about you two working?"

"Naw, I'm a charmer and Gerald is too invisible to hate," Shak said with a grin. The hobgoblin made a rude gesture.

Wil chuckled and left them behind. The house was unlocked, as he expected. It was also occupied, but not as he expected. When he turned around the corner into the living room, he saw that Bram wasn't alone, and he was quite busy.

Wil's friend and Gallath were lying on a couch, and the two were kissing furiously. Wil stood there, gaping, knowing he should probably make a sound or get the hell out . . . or *something*. Anything other than just watching in shock.

Eventually, he must've made a sound. Gallath's eyes fluttered open and he froze. Bram kept kissing him for another few seconds before he, too, looked up. Seeing Wil standing there, he fell off Gallath with a muffled thump and fought to get to his feet.

"Oh gods, Wil, I—it's—we . . . uhhh . . ." Bram's head dropped and his entire body trembled. "I was going to tell you," he said. "I swear I was, but . . . , well, can you blame me?"

Gallath sat up and wiped his mouth. Even through his orangish skin, Wil thought he could see bruises around his neck.

"Didn't know I was anything to be ashamed of," the ogre said, standing. "I'll let you two talk. Maybe you can give a rational explanation that'll make you feel better."

Wil got out of the way, still too stunned for words. Gallath let the door slam behind him, and then it was just Wil, his best friend, and a whole lot of awkward silence.

"I . . . wow, Bram. I didn't see this coming," Wil finally said. "Though maybe I should've. You've been spending all your time with either me and Darlene, or Gallath. Wow." Wil ran a nervous hand through his hair, trying very hard not to say the wrong thing.

Bram swallowed hard. A tear trailed down his reddening face, and then another. When he spoke, his voice broke. "Do you hate me?"

It was like a slap to the face. "What? No! Of course I don't hate you," said Wil. "I'm just a bit surprised. There's nothing wrong with being gay! I just . . . didn't expect it."

It was something of an odd topic around those parts. In Menifee City and at the academy itself, Wil had known a few different queer students, and it was treated as fairly normal, if something of a phase children went through. But in places like Harper Valley where tradition was huge to at least half of the citizenry? People talked in small towns, and Bram already had a few reasons for being somewhat of an outcast.

"I swear I didn't mean to keep this from you," Bram said, wobbling in place. Wil rushed up to help him sit back down on the couch before he fell. "I didn't know how to say it."

"It's okay, Bram." Wil patted his knee reassuringly. "I don't think any differently of you. And now a lot of things make sense in hindsight. Like, when Darlene didn't want to move in with me, but she felt safe moving in with you. Even though you— Didn't you hit on her when we were teens?"

Bram shook with silent laughter, wiping away tears as fast as they fell. "Yeah. I spent a lot of time trying to be things I'm not. I don't want to do that anymore."

"Then don't," said Wil. "Be out, be open, and be free. If anyone gives you any crap for it, they'll have to deal with me. Or, hell, you're good enough at potions now that you could probably think up something creative and petty enough to make them regret testing you."

With a deep, shuddering breath, Bram said, "Gods, what if no one wants to buy beer or potions from me anymore?"

At that, Wil burst out laughing. He jerked a finger at the door and said, "Have you seen the line out there? People are waiting to get beer and potions, and they don't seem to mind ogres being the ones to sell to them. If things keep on like this, I think you'll be fine. And if not? Well, then it'd be smart for all of us to get the hell out of here.

"The point is, people like and respect you. And you make good beer that's only going to get better and better with each batch. On that note, will there be enough to go around for the feast?" Wil hated changing the subject, but it had been one of the reasons he stopped by.

"Oh, yeah, of course." Bram took off his glasses and cleaned them with a handkerchief. "I'll be completely out after, but I'll just focus more on potions while the next batch brews. Hey, do you think Gallath is mad at me? He hasn't been happy about having to keep it a secret."

Gods, Wil had no clue what Gallath thought. The ogre was an enigma to him, often cool and sardonic for the most part, and then increasingly irritable during meetings. Not that Wil could blame him, but maybe that rising anger wasn't all Hugo's fault. "There's an easy way to fix that, you know."

Bram made a face and put his glasses back on. "But I'm a coward. Do you think you could maybe make me braver for ten minutes? Like, in my head?"

Wil shook his head and stood up. He motioned for Bram to follow him and went to the door. "Nope, only one way to handle that. You gotta tell or show him you're sorry yourself."

The giant paled, but he nodded and strode out the door. Wil followed him to the front of the barn, where Gallath had joined the other guys keeping the crowd manageable.

Gallath looked up to see them, but his expression was unreadable. Not for long. Bram took a deep breath and left Wil behind, practically running up to the ogre and scooping him up for a big kiss. It only took a second before the ogre wrapped his arms around Bram and kissed him back.

The line was dead silent. Wil didn't expect them to clap or anything, but the reaction was startled silence. Gallath noticed it too, and said something when Bram finally put him down. "What? Keep staring and we'll really put on a show."

That got a laugh. Then a loud "woooooo" and whistles, and soon the entire line had joined in, heckling Bram with the perfect acceptance that came from opportunistic teasing.

Wil watched with a smile. If nothing else, that had made the entire day worth it. Unlike Jeb, he trusted Bram and Gallath to not make things weird if something went wrong.

Bram and Gallath went in the barn, hand in hand.

CHAPTER 46

Open Invitation

"And with the matter of permanent residencies for citizens of both nations now discussed, does anyone have any objections?" Freddie the policy advisor asked, looking up from a thick stack of papers he and Maxwell had spent who knows how long preparing. "Anyone?"

Gallath and Arabella stared off into the distance, thoroughly exhausted from going in circles for so long. Timothy Twist looked around, surprised by the ongoing silence, and seemingly conflicted. Syl's eyes lit up when he realized that, for once, there wasn't anyone immediately shooting it down.

They all turned to Hugo, who was also staring off into the distance. When he realized they were watching him, he just waved a dismissive hand. "So long as I get my *supervised* trip into Faerie when this is all done, then I have no further objections," he said.

"Then . . . then we're agreed," said Freddie in disbelief. "The treaty stands, contingent on all of us signing it. I can have the paperwork ready in two days."

"We did it." Wil said. He felt himself deflate. Two weeks of troubled, frustrating, slow negotiations later and they had a working treaty. One that made everyone happy. Or if not happy, then at the very least equally cheated. Wil could hardly believe it.

"We did it!" Syl echoed louder. He drummed his hands on the table obnoxiously, looking around for others to join him. Twist did halfheartedly, Gallath gave a couple of slaps, and Arabella just rolled her eyes. Wil joined the faun enthusiastically before Hugo stopped it.

"Would you knock that off? Yes, yes, we've done it. You have your peace and safety, and we get resources and improve our enchanting. Everyone's happy. Hurray." Hugo couldn't have sounded more petulant if he'd tried.

Wil shook his head at the others and motioned that he'd deal with it. Out loud, he said, "Then I think we might as well leave for the day and let Freddie and Max get it all formally written out. We'll make a big day of it. I think Captain Nesbitt even has a camera, so we can make history!"

"Humans and fae," said Syl, grinning, "friends after all these years!"

"Let's not get ahead of ourselves," said Arabella. "They have a long way to go before we can trust them, but . . . I suppose this is the best start we can hope for."

"I didn't think it would happen," said Timothy Twist. He took off his hat and spun it in his hand. "I thought we'd be locking horns until spring and then we'd just go back home, never to be seen again. This is much . . . preferable." He grimaced.

"Agreed," said Gallath with a rough sigh. "I didn't want war."

Hugo scoffed. "I thought your people love war. You were the ones we would've approached for an alliance early, if you hadn't all decided to die for the others."

All of the goodwill and relaxation evaporated. Gallath's eyes narrowed and his lips pulled back into a silent snarl. "After all that, do you want to start something? My people are good at war and many of them like it, but I'm not one of them. I'd rather spend my days drinking wine and playing music. Wouldn't you?"

"What use do I have for music?" the mage sneered. "And I can drink wine and wage war at the same time. It's easy."

Wil stepped in. "After the past couple of weeks, we're all exhausted and irritable and tense. How about we just drop that for now and come back after the feast to sign the paperwork? No use jeopardizing our efforts over a stupid argument, right?"

Most of them relaxed. "Exactly. Your dedication to sense and peace is, as always, appreciated," said Syl as he stood. "I think that if no one else needs anything from me, I'm going to spread the good news and get good and drunk! Who's with me?"

To no one's surprise, Arabella shot straight up. "Every few thousand words or so, you speak some sense." Arm in arm, they left.

Twist stood as well. The wee man sighed and said, "For all the problems and hiccups, it was a great deal of fun seeing everyone worked up. I'm sad to see that end, but there's still hope yet. Who can irritate you better than your allies and friends?" He threw his hat high and it landed perfectly on his head. The puck didn't walk so much as dance toward the door.

Then it was Gallath's turn. "I'll just . . . be at Bram's if you need me." He looked more satisfied being able to be open with Bram than he was about signing the treaty.

Freddie and Maxwell didn't say anything. At this point, they were well cowed by Hugo's anger anytime they overspoke or interjected anything personal into the mix. They scampered off, leaving Wil and Hugo alone in the small conference room.

"You should be proud," said Wil. "This deal is historic and will go a long way toward making Calipan better. Your name will be remembered forever."

"As someone who accepted a form of surrender," Hugo scoffed, still not looking at him. "Not honorably conquered or subjected. This isn't a victory, this is our glorious and powerful country turning down a fight because we're 'fighting on too many fronts already.' Bah. We have a beeline right to their capital. We could have taken them."

"And now you won't have to," Wil said patiently. "Instead, they'll be giving us resources we can use against Albetosia and Ilianto. The rest of the continent will be ours, and then maybe we can rest and build up what we have. This could herald a new golden age for Calipan. How are you not proud of it?"

Hugo whirled on him, eyes wide and almost desperate. "Because I don't give a damn about any of that! I want to get into Faerie. I want to be back on the mountain, near the leyline. I want to feel that again."

Wil understood and fought back a shudder. As much as he loved Harper Valley, the sense of power and belonging that came from the leyline and Faerie was entrancing. When he told Hugo it was possibly addictive and dangerous, it had been a lie. Now, Wil wasn't so sure.

"You will, soon," he said.

"Soon." Hugo shook his head. "You're so damned naive. We have a working treaty that will carry us for now, but tours and meetings will take a year or more. Soon I'll go back to Cloverton and will have to wait until whenever it's convenient for others to let me through."

Wil had an idea then, yet another he couldn't help but feel was possibly a bad one, but that hadn't stopped him in the past. "If you can curb your talk of war and wanting to dominate them, I might be able to get you in for a single day before you leave for Cloverton. It would be off the record and you would have to be on your best behavior, but I could arrange it. And then maybe we can call me ruining your promotion even." Wil smirked.

Hugo chuckled, and then it turned into a genuine laugh with little of his normal arrogance. "It would take a lot more than that to make us even, McKenzie. I should be an archmage by now. With Master Krine dead, it should've been me replacing him in the Department of War."

That was a thought worth some nightmares. There was no way he could see Hugo thriving in a cabinet position. He didn't voice this. Instead, he offered a lopsided grin and went with the same kind of rural good boy act Hugo expected of him.

"How about you come to my family's Midwinter Feast, then? Half the town's going to be there, and it'll be a nice chance to see the fruits of our work in action as we share them with our new fae friends. We can show you a taste of real Harper Valley hospitality before you go back to Cloverton."

After some thought, Hugo smiled. "I suppose a good meal and sneaking me into Faerie for a day will be enough before I go and get sent to a better, more important place. Maybe then I'll actually get to have some fun and put my skills to good use. I'd say I was wasted on this assignment, but at the very least, I stopped you from giving half the country away."

"That *is* something I was planning on doing," Wil deadpanned. "Good job."

Hugo laughed. "Screw you, McKenzie." He pushed his hair out of his eyes and rose slowly, stretching his back until it popped. "I guess I'll see you tomorrow, then, at your family farm. Just follow the twin stinks of pig shit and ogres, right?"

Laughing again, he left, and Wil took the opportunity to sit in satisfied silence. They'd done it. *He'd* done it. Over a month of traveling, hard work, and dealing with extreme personalities who wanted little to do with each other. Handling Hugo's capricious, cruel nature alone should've earned him a medal.

But Wil would be content with peace. Real peace, cooperation, and community. Both humans and fae had a lot to offer, and just existing near each other and being different would inspire them to be more than they would be on their own. And it was happening because of him.

Only one day left before the Midwinter Feast. It would be the perfect way to celebrate everything going exactly as it should.

CHAPTER 47

Feast Fun

"So there I was in the clearing, storm raging, with a sick dragon who needed my help!" Wil twirled his staff and the large illusion of Skalet curled around the lake came to life. It wasn't to scale, of course, but the gathered children didn't mind. Their eyes lit up with every realistic flash of lightning.

The illusory dragon was about ten feet long, and the miniature Wil was out of proportion so the audience could see him better. Wil had prepared this little show for storytelling shortly after the storm had passed, and the kids never grew tired of it. Mini-Wil raised his hands high and caught lightning as it struck, holding it between his hands.

"I caught the bolt, and I poured all my magic into the curse on the dragon. I made the storm so big it broke and fell apart!" That got him a good gasp. A minor embellishment, but that was just good storytelling. It had felt like he'd held Skalet's power in his hands when he delivered the dragon to safety and saved the town.

Mini-Skalet picked Mini-Wil up in his claws and flew in circles before landing and setting him down in front of the children. He reached up and took off his nose horn and left it behind as he flew away. "And as a thank-you," said Wil, "he gave me the horn I used to make this staff!"

A quick flare of power made lightning race up the staff and crackle dangerously at the horn. One of the kids reached up, awe in his eyes. Wil gently pulled the staff away. "Careful. This is a powerful, dangerous tool. If any of you ever show magic of your own, though, I'll show you how to build one."

"I wanna be a wizard too!" a little girl with missing front teeth cried out.

With a wave of Wil's hand, the illusions disappeared, replaced by a likeness of the girl. The real child gaped at her image and then at Wil.

"You're getting closer and closer to the age I was when my magic came in," Wil said. "It could happen to you. It could happen to *any* of you!"

Of all the things Wil did on festival days, performing for children was his favorite. They were just happy to be there and see what he could do. No one asked what his magic could do for them, they just wanted to be able to see amazing things. He inspired them, and sometimes that was the best thing a person could do.

With one last flourish of his staff, Wil covered the area in pink and blue smoke and let himself disappear with a bang. When the smoke cleared away, the children screamed and looked all over for him. He walked around invisibly for a few minutes, drinking in the festive atmosphere.

The McKenzie farm was no longer recognizable, outside of the barn and original house. Tables and chairs, grown by the fae or shaped by Wil, covered one entire field close to the new lake. Some people even now swam in the warmth of the fae magic, splashing and playing in the middle of winter.

On the two tall tree house towers hung a banner with the words "Midwinter Feast," which could be seen from the drive, just in case anyone missed the thousands of people enjoying themselves and laughing. At times it seemed a little cramped, but almost the entire property was in use.

Wil hadn't quite believed his father when he'd talked about converting the farm, but here he was, seeing it in action. And in that moment, Wil believed. They had their peace treaty, a new friendship with Faerie. Harper Valley was going to have to change drastically, and Bob would be the one to lead the charge.

Wil slipped by a group over to his family's table. Behind it, along all the fences and walls, were large paintings of different types of fae and several of the citizens of Harper Valley. It was the big project that had paired Sarah and Arabella together, who sat one table over, engaged in a three-way conversation with Jeb, who still looked ridiculous in colorful elven festival garb.

"You going to eat that?" Wil asked as he reappeared next to his mother. Sharon jumped in her seat and clutched her chest.

"Why? Why do that?" she asked, laughing breathlessly.

"Well, I gotta have my fun somehow, right?" Wil grabbed a plate and filled it up with mashed potatoes and ham, then a scoop each of bacon-infused green beans and corn. "What kind of son would I be if I didn't pester and scare you?"

"You may be a big powerful wizard, but never forget: I brought you into this world and I can take you out of it! Have you been having a good time?" His mother handed him a bottle of lemonade.

As much as he wanted a stronger drink, Wil had to keep his senses, just in case. He took a sip and grabbed his fork. "Yeah, definitely. I keep worrying about something going wrong, but I'm probably overreacting. I've spent the last two hours just going around, putting on little shows and checking in on Bram and Darlene and Syl and the others. Everything's fine."

With one last pat on his back before she let him go, Sharon said, "Then let it be fine. Don't go looking for trouble where there is none. Let yourself relax and enjoy. You've earned it, don't you think?" She ruffled his hair and left.

Wil looked around. He shared the table with Bob and Jerry, who were chatting animatedly, but they didn't draw him into their conversation. So he did as his mother suggested and ate his meal in relative peace. It was his second helping of the day, and he figured he had one more in him for dessert later.

As the nearby music played and Wil ate, he relaxed a little. And he thought about what had brought him there, who had helped, and how much work there was still to do. It was nice to have a break, but Wil was bad at taking breaks. They were more a time to plan than to truly do nothing.

In this case, at least, the time let him plan who to check in on when he was done. He pushed his mostly empty plate back, downed his lemonade, and went over to the grazing field where Bram and Gallath stood, holding hands and watching a mixed-race group of people playing football.

"Who's winning?" Wil asked as he approached.

"We all are," said Gallath. "Maybe my guys more than yours. Getting tackled by my kind can be painful."

"Our guys are faster, though," Bram added, pointing at a human barely dodging a troll's terrifying attempt to take him down. The human tossed the ball to an elf wearing the same blue armband, who bolted toward the end zone. Bram took his hand back to clap enthusiastically.

"So, no trouble?" Wil pressed.

Gallath shook his head. "A few near misses of hot tempers, but food fixed that."

"Excellent. Well, have fun." Wil threw an arm around each of them awkwardly before moving on to his real dread of the night.

Mayor Sinclair sat at a table with most of the rich and powerful of Harper Valley. Mr. Carrey and Jonjon sat on either side of him, and farther down the table was Old Brown and Judge Caufield, who traveled between cities in and near the Le Guin Basin as needed. He sat next to Frederick, who stared Wil down as he approached. They had a good mix of food, though most of it was hearty human fare.

"Hello, Mr. Mayor," Wil said respectfully. "Has the feast been to your liking?"

Sinclair's eye twitched, but he hid it with an instant smile and laugh. "It has indeed, thank you, Mr. Wizard. You and your family have made for a great celebration, in light of all the hiccups plaguing your efforts."

"Speaking of that, is your house livable, Mr. Carrey?" Wil asked.

Mr. Carrey scowled, but as far as Wil could tell, it was his friendly scowl. "Didn't ask for a business change, but the house is fine. Terrible view now. Just a bunch of beanstalks!"

"You mean you don't want to become the new king of textiles?" Wil joked.

The older man softened. "You're just lucky I have the means to switch my focus like that."

"And how about the rest of you?" Wil asked. "Anything I can get you? Any questions or concerns?"

Old Brown cleared his throat. The brewmaster had largely avoided Wil since he and his friends had started Wiseman Brewing. "Am I to understand that the treaty is going through? What guarantees do you have for us that this won't ruin Harper Valley? Bad enough you're trying to ruin me personally with your business." He laughed and so did those around him, but there was no mirth in it.

"Well, I think that believing anything will ruin Harper Valley is a bit dramatic," said Wil, running his thumb over a groove in his staff. "My dad likes to say that life is change. You can run from it, or you can embrace it."

There was a low mutter and dirty looks at the very idea. Jonjon, of all people, came to his defense.

"There's wisdom in that," he said, laughing his obnoxious laugh. "It's easy to forget, when you're on top, that you gotta be hungry and go for it. We get so used to being on top of the food chain that we forget how to fight. I, for one, see the potential in a new Harper Valley. And anyone else who adopts early will make it big, I'm sure."

That started a heated argument between a couple of the men Wil recognized by sight but not by name. Sheriff Frederick continued to stare daggers his way, so Wil went to his last stop before he returned to putting on illusions.

Hugo and his thralls had an entire table to themselves. It turns out that, despite their broken minds, they very much did need to eat and drink and be taken care of. Most of them. Wil doubted the earth and wind elementals needed much, but the demons and fae did. There were half a dozen of them sitting with Hugo. Seven, if you counted the imp on his shoulder.

"So, enjoying the food and company?" Wil joked. No one else was happy to see the thralls, but a table to themselves proved to be a good compromise that kept them out of the way.

Hugo sipped his beer and said, "I get all the benefits of rural cooking without having to talk to toothless yokels. Honestly, I couldn't have asked for a better spot. You make good beer," he added grudgingly.

Wil shook his head. "That's all Bram. I just fund it and help with the ingredients. I couldn't do this without him and Darlene. Turns out you need fewer helpers when they aren't mindless husks. Do they have enough food?"

Hugo rolled his eyes. "So nice of you to care, but they have enough food, and none of them are capable of being bored. Forget about them. In two weeks we'll be out of your life for good, and I might even write about you favorably in my report."

"That . . . would be nice," said Wil, sighing. "Thank you. Gods, after so much time with the fae, it feels weird to be able to thank someone without it being a huge thing. But I appreciate it."

"It might even keep them from punishing you for rushing off to Faerie without consulting them first," Hugo continued. He smirked as Wil squirmed. "Don't worry, I'll make sure they know it was just excitement and not . . ."

As the mage trailed off, Wilbur got a familiar twisting in his stomach. One look told him Hugo felt it too. And then it came: a wildcat's yowl, piercing and loud. Hugo and Wil dashed to the center of the property, where a six-legged, one-eyed cat grinned at the retreating people.

"Isom? What are you doing here?" Wil asked.

"Wizard!" the wampus cat exclaimed, stalking toward him. "I'm tired of waiting. Today is the day. In front of all these witnesses, I challenge you! TO THE DEATH!"

CHAPTER 48

TO THE DEATH

Wil buried his face in his hands and groaned. "This is just about the worst time you could've picked. Can we do this later? Tomorrow night, maybe?"

A ring of feastgoers had formed around Wil and Isom. Everybody wanted to be close enough to see what was going on, but not too close to the weird mountain lion calling for death. Wil looked around and motioned for people to give them more space.

"No!" Isom let out a loud, theatrical laugh. "You've eluded me long enough, and now, we finish it!"

Hugo came up behind Wil. "What's this, then? You never told me a talking cat was calling for your death. He and I might get along."

Wil took a deep breath. "I didn't tell you because he's kind of a friend—"

"Bitter rival and enemy," Isom corrected. His tail waved behind him.

"—and there's no need for you to step in. This is my problem. Go enjoy some more pie." Wil crooked a finger and his staff jumped from beside the table to his hand. He turned back to Isom.

"There are a lot of innocent people here who could get hurt, and I don't want that. I'm full and not in the mood to fight or make a scene. How about I get you a big plate of meat and we have our big battle to the death in a few days? Please."

Isom growled, making the ring of onlookers take another step back. Notably, very few of the fae stayed close. They knew better. The humans of Harper Valley had so far been spoiled with peaceful fae and didn't know what to make of a talking wildcat threatening their unworried wizard.

"I knew you were a coward, Wilbur, but I never thought you'd be in one in public. If you will not honorably go to your death, then I'll challenge the other wizard! You, with the red hair and face like a weasel! Fight me!"

Wil's eyes widened. "No!"

Hugo lit up with excitement. "Ooh, I think I like him. Which faction is he from?"

"Heartless," Wil said automatically. "Wild fae. Seriously, don't fight him. This is my problem, not yours."

"So no clan? No friends? No one to mind if he doesn't come home? He'd make a perfect addition to my collection." Hugo rubbed his hands together, and so did the imp on his shoulder.

Realizing what would happen if he didn't, Wil stepped in front of Hugo and called out to Isom. "I accept your challenge! Tonight, you go to bed hungry. Forever!"

Isom's vivid green eye sparkled with excitement. He stretched, all six paws digging into the earth, then let out a challenging yowl. His back four legs twitched and bunched up as if he were about to pounce.

Wil held out a hand. "But first! We get out in the open so no one else gets hurt. Understood? Remember your vow."

The wampus cat nodded grudgingly. "You may make your preparations," he said magnanimously. "And in the meantime, can I get some meat?"

While Isom gnawed on a huge hunk of ham, Wil cleared some space in the center of the farm and pounded the earth flat and recessed to make a little arena, partially to limit damage, and partially just because most of his recent fights had been in little arenas and it seemed like the right thing to do.

The sun was setting when they started. Most of the people previously milling around now formed an impressive ring of spectators. Wil's family stood in front, as did Hugo and a few of his bigger, more intimidating thralls. Wil figured the mage needed to feel important at all times, and acting as Wil's backup was as close as he would get.

Isom faced him down, crouched in a ready-to-spring position on his side of the arena. Wil moved a little closer to the center, wanting to give the wampus cat some room to ambush him properly.

"Any last words, Cat?" Wil called out.

"You will be *delicious*," Isom hissed, and then he attacked.

Wil had a theory he hadn't gotten a chance to test out before. As Isom ran forward, he built up enough momentum to spring off the ground. When he was in the air for a second, he disappeared, and Wil threw himself to the side. The wampus cat appeared behind where he'd been standing and pounced on nothing.

Time for the counterattack. Wil lashed out with force and sent Isom rolling along the ground. The cat dug his claws in and went right back for him. "Wizard!" he hissed, feinting. Wil pretended to fall for it, leaping out of the way.

But this time, Isom jumped after. Just as Wil suspected, when the wampus cat was in the air again, he vanished. Wil grinned and held his staff up just in time to block the killer bite as the cat reappeared. The crowd gasped. Two hundred pounds of wildcat knocked the air out of him. Isom gnawed on the staff like a bone, drooling on Wil's face.

Just as Isom extended his claws into Wil's chest, Wil summoned the power of the staff and delivered a nasty but nonlethal shock to the wampus cat. Wil let out a cry as those claws dug in deeper for a second, and then the cat rolled off him, twitching violently.

"No fair," Isom cried out, a foot away from Wil. Then he grinned and blew out a green, noxious breath.

Wil took a quick deep breath and rolled away as fast as he could. Isom followed, slapping the ground with his massive paws every step of the way. When he had the chance to roll to his feet without being pounced on again, Wil felt a surge of odd affection. Then he focused on the ground beneath Isom's feet and launched the cat straight into the air.

Isom let out a distressed yowl as he twisted and flipped in the air to right himself. Wil laughed, and so did the crowd, but Isom teleported right in front of Wil, who stepped backward. The green breath continued to roll in his direction, so Wil spun his staff and sent it away with a gust.

The wampus cat dug his claws into the ground to avoid being blown away, and Wil upped the intensity. It became a battle of wills as Isom hung on and Wil's gusts of wind grew greater and more forceful, until even the spectators got out of the way. It gave Wil a mean idea.

"You can surrender at any time, Isom!" he yelled over the growing roar of the wind.

Isom clung to the earth for dear life. "You haven't done anything to even come close to hurting me!" he hissed.

Wil grinned. "You're right. Bye!" Purple light channeled through his staff. The wind swirled around the wampus cat, forming a small tornado. It ripped Isom from the ground and caught him up in the swirl as Wil sent the twister away from him . . . to his parents' new lake. He released the spell and launched Isom into the water.

The people nearest him laughed and cheered, and Wil took a bow. Isom sputtered and flailed in the shallows. He dragged himself out haltingly. He was soaked, bedraggled, and annoyed. "You've bought your doom, Wizard!"

"I thought I already had!" Wil said, chuckling, but it made him think. Isom was an ambush predator, and this made three times he'd made himself known before attacking. At this point, he wasn't sure that Isom did want to kill him. It made it hard to take this as anything other than a fun show.

Even if Wil *was* bleeding a bit. But that just happened when playing with cats.

Isom blinked forward, hit the ground, and ran. Wil counted to three before the wampus cat blinked out from view again. And then a third time. As he soared straight for Wil with no artistry or deception, Wil saw relaxed joy there.

Wil waited until Isom was at the apex of his jump before turning to advanced earth magic. It was difficult to do, even for Wil, but he focused on Isom's presence and held it in his head from afar. And then he increased the pull of gravity as hard as he could, slamming the cat into the ground.

Isom hit hard with his paws splayed out, as flat as something like him could be. Wil upped the pull and the earth rumbled, burying the wampus cat's six limbs in the dirt before closing around him. No matter how much he struggled, he couldn't get free. When the realization hit him, Isom slumped over.

"I . . . You've bested me," he whimpered, closing his eyes. "Make my death swift."

"Nah." Wil walked up to him. His clothes were a bit torn and his body ached from the wampus cat's one successful pounce, but he was otherwise fine. He bent down on one knee and petted Isom on the head. "I like you too much. So here's what I'm going to do. You surrender, and then I'll let you go back to Faerie."

"No!" Isom growled, snapping fruitlessly at the offending hand. "I'm not going back until one of us is beaten for good!"

"Yeah, that's you."

"Nuh-uh!"

It was an easy decision to not butt his head against a cat. They were stubborn, willful creatures, and Wil had already won. So instead, he stood and stretched. "Then you can take a rest in there for a little bit, and when everyone's gone, we'll try again. Hope you don't have to pee or anything."

"Very funny," Isom growled. "Hey, come back here. Come back here this instant!"

The sun had almost set, and after the short, fun distraction, it was almost time for Sinclair to make his annual speech, and for Bob to announce his candidacy. Wil waved off the crowd, who clapped politely and went back to their meals. Everyone gave the yelling, spitting wampus cat distance. Except for one person.

Wil had already got back to Hugo's table when he realized Hugo wasn't coming. He turned around to see the mage crouched in front of Isom, grinning like a madman. Wil's blood ran cold. He took off, running up to the mage, who had locked his gaze on Isom's one good eye. Hugo whispered a mantra under his breath. His eyes were white. He was already in the wampus cat's mind.

"Hey, stop! Don't do that," Wil said, shaking Hugo out of it.

The color came back to Hugo's eyes. "Stay out of this," he said. "You said you were done with him. Now it's my turn."

"You are *not* adding him to your collection," Wil snapped.

"Aren't I? What are you going to do, pick a fight with me in front of all of these people? All of these witnesses who will be able to say that you turned against your superior?" Hugo scoffed. "If you want that peace treaty, you'll stay out of this."

"Wizard . . ." Isom slurred, slow-blinking at him before Hugo's eyes once more turned white and he locked himself in a battle with the wampus cat.

Wil froze. The right thing to do would be to blast Hugo across the farm and give Isom time to run, but the mage was right. He'd be the one to get in trouble if he struck, and there was a good chance Hugo meant it about tanking the treaty if Wil crossed him. He was just petty enough to do it.

All the tension slowly melted out of Isom's body as Hugo's whispered chant ramped up in intensity. The wampus cat let out a distressed groan before his body collapsed. His eye remained wide open.

If Wil did nothing, then a beautiful predator and a weird sort-of friend would be broken into a shell of his former self. He'd be a mindless thrall, and instead of chasing down his meals, he'd be made into a tool. A killer with no joy in the hunt.

If Wil did do something, there was no telling what Hugo would let happen to both their worlds, just to punish him.

For the rest of his life, Wil would feel shame for taking the easy route. He released Isom from the earth, but at that point, it was already too late. Isom was no longer resisting. And when Hugo's eyes cleared, there was no light left in the predator. The mage rose, and so did the wampus cat.

"Ahh," Hugo sighed contentedly. "Looks like my trip here wasn't a complete bust after all. Isn't that right, Puss?" He scratched behind Isom's ear, chuckling to himself. "Thanks for holding him in one place. He was *feisty*!"

Isom stared ahead into space lifelessly.

CHAPTER 49

A Toast!

Wil couldn't remember a time he had felt enough hate and anger to make him feel physically ill. He stared at Hugo's table from afar, thoughts he didn't care for racing through his head. Most people saw his murderous expression and stayed well away. Darlene did not.

"Stupid question, but are you . . . okay?" she asked, getting close but not touching him. Together, they rested their backs against the fence. Nearby, people were finishing up their meals.

"I want to kill him," said Wil, in a voice he didn't recognize. "I could do it too. Use all the skills he helped teach me and make it look like he choked to death on a hunk of turkey."

"Wil . . ." Darlene shuddered. "Would that free Isom?"

"I don't know," he admitted. "At the very least, it would stop him from being a slave. If I— It's silly, but I like that stupid cat. He and I were just playing. I think he knows he can't beat me without surprising me, but we talked. He's my friend."

Darlene took a chance by putting a hand on his arm. "I know. Can't say I fully get it, but I can see not being threatened by the deadly animal when you're the scarier one. But the rest of us wouldn't be able to stop him if he tried anything."

Wil chuckled and wrapped an arm around Darlene, pulling her close. His throat had a terrible lump in it, and his next sentence made him want to cry. "He wouldn't. He swore a vow to hurt no one but me. I'm . . . I'm going to say something. Do something."

"Whatever you need to. But can I suggest doing it in private, after the speeches?" Darlene asked. "Your dad could probably use your help with that. Why don't we do that?"

Wil closed his eyes, nodding. He breathed evenly for ten seconds and willed himself to be okay. At least for now. They went up to the McKenzie table, now occupied with the whole family, plus Arabella. The elf princess looked about as angry as Wil did and was crushing Jeb's hand in her grip.

"Is it almost time?" Wil asked in a raw voice that surprised him.

Bob saw him, and Wil expected him to ask how he was doing, but his father just nodded and stood.

"It's as good a time as any, I suppose," said Bob. "Everyone's full and fat and relaxed, so we won't be spoiling anyone's meals with talk of politics. I gotta admit, I have a few things in mind, but I didn't write anything down. I feel like I made a pretty big blunder there."

"It's okay," Wil said quietly. "You are always better off the cuff anyway. I can get everyone's attention and boost your voice, if that would help."

"It would. Thank you, son." Bob patted Wil's shoulder, and they stood at the edge of the line of tables. Wil magically pulled a chair over for Bob to stand on, then raised his staff to the sky. One after another, five bolts of color shot into the sky and detonated like fireworks, hissing and crackling in the night sky.

It worked, and a couple thousand people turned his way. Bob cleared his throat and winced hearing his voice echoing and amplified enough so even the farthest feastgoers could hear him.

"Welcome, everyone, and thank you for coming to our Midwinter Feast. With all of the changes and hiccups, I'm glad it's gone this well!"

That got some cheers and applause from the nearest people, but most of the attendees waited indulgently for him to get on with the speech so they could relax once more.

"A lot has changed for us over the last year, and it's got me thinking. Harper Valley has always done well because we've looked out for each other. And in the past, as we built this town up and worked the land, it was easier. The more the years go by, the more things change and it gets harder and harder to keep up.

"I've never minded. I've always enjoyed meeting the challenges and doing what I can to help out my family and neighbors, and I'm so proud to consider that a trait most of us here have. We're helpers and builders, and everything we do is made better together.

"Never have I felt that so acutely as when that massive storm blew in. My son managed to drive off an ailing dragon who almost washed away our town. When the storm was gone and it was time to rebuild, everyone helped out everyone else. We came together as a community.

"And now there's a new complication in our life, one that isn't going away. Our friends from Faerie are here, and it's been my privilege and pleasure to show them what life is like here now, and who we are, and how we can live together in harmony."

Bob took a moment to catch his breath. Those nearest were riveted, waiting for his next words. Wil spotted Syl at his table, waving and showing his support. It was so silent, the only thing that could be heard was the crackle of fires. Bob continued, stronger and more confident.

"Over the last sixteen years, Mayor Bartholomew Sinclair has done a great job of leading this town. But I believe that moving forward, there will be a great many challenges and a lot of changes. Changes we need to embrace if we're not to be left behind. Harper Valley is a sleepy town, but not for long. We're about to get big.

"And that's why I would like to announce my candidacy for mayor. I believe that I have the qualities, temperament, and experience with our community to lead us into the future. A future made from our past as a town full of helpers. A future made of cooperation and embracing new ideas and people. Because when we help each other, we help ourselves. My promise to you is that as your mayor, I will make sure everyone is fed, housed, and taken care of so that when Harper Valley booms, and it will, nobody gets left behind. We'll meet the future together, and be stronger for it. Thank you."

Bob climbed down from the chair. At first, there was nothing, just an odd cough here and there. And then those nearest to him clapped, and more and more people joined in. It wasn't everyone, but it was at least enough to make him a viable threat to Sinclair. The real campaigning would start tomorrow.

Wil gave his dad a one-armed hug and then made his way over to Sinclair, who looked about as livid as could be expected. During his sixteen-year reign, he'd been challenged only twice. Half his run had been uncontested, and he'd gotten too comfortable.

"That's how it is, huh, Mr. Wizard?" Sinclair laughed openly at him, and some of his donors did as well. Most of them looked amused, but a few, like Jonjon, were concerned by the development of a challenger. "We put you through school and you come back, upend the state of things, and then get your daddy to replace me."

Wil smiled, plenty of leftover anger ready to boil over at a moment's notice. He didn't like being this upset, but it came with some advantages. Like being immune to Sinclair's taunts. In a funny way, he had taken a leaf out of Hugo's book and thought of the politician as beneath him.

"Yeah, I'm angering a whole lot of people with everything I do," Wil said. "Comes with having power, I guess." He motioned for the mayor to stand. "If you'd like, I can give you the same boost I gave Dad for a speech of your own. You know, to be fair."

Sinclair sneered at him. "And I know how important it is to you to *always* be fair. So you know what? Sure, I'll take you up on it. Let's make a toast, shall we? This is a special occasion." He reached down to an expensive wooden box on the table and pulled out Syl's gift of special wine.

First, he poured himself a splash, and then he poured for those nearest him, and so on until the bottle was gone and all his supporters and sycophants had raised their cups. One went to sip, but Sinclair cleared his throat. He motioned for Wil to do his thing, and then stood on his chair.

"Greetings, everyone," he said, obviously a little annoyed that he hadn't gotten any fireworks to get their attention. "First of all, I want to thank Bob McKenzie for being so kind as to host this event. It's the first time in years that we haven't used the fairgrounds or Mr. Carrey's farm, and it sure is a novelty to see one of our humble farmers' homes changed to impress. Can we get a round of applause for Bob and Sharon?"

The crowd cheered and clapped enthusiastically. At first, Wil thought it was a mistake, hyping up his newest rival. But then Sinclair continued, and Wil understood.

"They've given so much to this community, and we owe them a great debt for helping raise our fine resident wizard, Wilbur. Without him, we wouldn't be where we are today. He's a great argument for youth and modernity, and constantly moving forward. But it's the moving forward that, I must confess, scares me a little.

"I am happy to greet our fae brothers and sisters, who after some unfortunate fights and misunderstandings are now sharing with us one of our favorite holidays. Having spent time talking to and learning about them, I'm astounded by just how different they can be. Difference can be one of the greatest strengths we have. But it can also get in the way.

"I pride myself on being something of a traditionalist. If something ain't broke, don't fix it, right, people?" He chuckled, and that got a few people around the table nodding in agreement. The richest men in town all had reason to fear change. "And for the last sixteen years, I think I've done a pretty good job of keeping our traditions sacred, and our humble community bustling and in business.

"I heartily welcome a friendly challenge for the office of mayor. Bob is a worthy candidate, with roots in the community and a lot of experience tending to the land. He's the salt of the earth, and exactly what you think of when you think of Harper Valley.

"But . . . ," he added with a chuckle, "I don't mean to sell myself short by any means. With my leadership, I brought the railroad here, I oversaw the education of our first wizard in decades, and I like to believe myself to be good friends with the fine entrepreneurs who keep this town competitive. And it's to them that I want to propose a toast."

He held up his glass of wine and sniffed it, making an appreciative sound. All around the table and across the farm, others raised their drinks. "Here's to old friends and good traditions, leading us to where we need to be when we're ready. Here's to keeping level heads and approaching change with both hope and skepticism. Here's to Harper Valley remaining Harper Valley, no matter what happens. Cheers!"

Wil released the voice amplifying spell and watched as Sinclair and his table all took a sip of the fine satyr wine. He turned around and started back to his table, thinking maybe he'd finally get drunk and burn off some of his anger, but he heard a choking sound behind him, followed by a dozen more. He whirled around and gasped.

Sinclair and the others, everyone at that table, were groaning and gasping and clutching at their faces, screaming silently. Wil's eyes darted around helplessly. He stood, frozen in place, as the entire table began to change.

The mayor's eyes bulged and grew and took up most of his head. His mouth spread into a wide, thin line and his entire body shook and convulsed. He fell out of his chair to the ground. Wil appeared beside him in an instant. But Sinclair wasn't there. A writhing lump in his clothes continued to shrink until the bundle was still.

With a trembling hand, Wil pulled the shirt away. Inside the pants was a fat, warty toad. All around the table, the richest and most powerful men in Harper Valley were now amphibians.

"Reeeeeeb," croaked Sinclair.

CHAPTER 50

Taking Control

Somebody screamed, and then chaos broke out. Wil stood there helplessly as those closest to the table put as much distance between them and it. Frantically, Wil went around, checking. Every single person who'd drunk Syl's wine, from Mayor Sinclair to Sheriff Frederick and Mr. Carrey, had all been turned into toads.

Wil couldn't turn people into toads, or any animals. His transmutation skills were effectively nonexistent, and he didn't think Hugo was much better. Obviously, neither of them had done it, but who did that leave? He didn't like the only answer that remained.

Syl ran across the field, ducking and dodging people heading his way, to get to Wil. "What happened? Why are they toads?"

"I don't know!" Wil said, pulling on his hair. "One second they were toasting and the next they . . . , well, this. What was in that wine?"

"Grapes, mostly," Syl said, looking around wildly. "It's just really good wine, I swear!"

The few people still around turned to him with suspicion. They were mostly the sheriff's recently hired deputies, now scared and confused and without direction from their boss. And then came Hugo and his thralls, closing in as a circle around them. Isom trotted alongside the mage, and Wil had to bite back his disgust.

"Arrest this creature," Hugo barked, pointing at Syl. "Bring him to the jail right away."

The deputies looked between one another, and then at Wil.

"What are you talking about, Hugo? Syl had nothing to do with this. Hold up, fellas." Wil's hands twitched. He and Hugo didn't get along on a good day, but now . . . he had a very bad feeling about this.

Hugo motioned with his hand and the deputies ran forward, tackling and getting ahold of Syl. The faun struggled hard, almost getting free before they pinned him. "H-hey, help! Get off me, I haven't done anything!"

Wil stepped forward, but Hugo put a hand on his chest. He shook his head once. "Don't do it, McKenzie. He's the most likely suspect, and we need to put him away."

"He didn't do anything. Hugo, you can't do this. We might need his help figuring out who did it, and he's *on our side*. C'mon, you've been in meetings with him, and—"

"*Shut it, McKenzie!*" Hugo shouted, suddenly red in the face. "I've had about enough of your moralizing and insistence on putting these creatures over humanity. I am the ranking wizard here and I am taking control. This was an *act of war*. Get that through your skull, Wilbur. Someone just took out your town's leadership on your family's property!"

Wil planted both hands on Hugo's chest and shoved him out of his face. "This may be an act of war, but we need to keep our damned heads on! We need to see if Sinclair and the others are okay."

"Okay? They're a bunch of toads!" Hugo looked ready to throw a punch or spell, but Syl's pained bleating caught their attention.

"I surrender, I surrender! You don't have to hurt me, I'll behave!" Syl looked ready to cry. One of the deputies twisted and wrenched the faun's arm behind his back. That was too much for him, and he flailed more. The grass around their feet grew fast, climbing up and around his attackers' limbs and pulling them off him.

Syl twisted free and took off running. Before he could get far, Hugo's earth elemental grabbed him and squeezed him to its chest.

Syl cried out, struggling to breathe.

"What in the hell is going on here?" Bob demanded as he ran up. He looked between Syl, the tied-up deputies, and Hugo. "You can't just come in here and bark orders. We had an agreement on how we'd handle justice, and this ain't it."

Hugo rubbed his temples. "You McKenzies are getting annoying," he said. "So let me make this clear. We're arresting the goat and confining the fae to the farm while we investigate and find out who's responsible for this. If anyone tries to stop me, I will end them. Is that clear, you fat, ignorant hick?"

As much patience as Wil typically had, there were limits. He gathered up raw force in his hands and slugged Hugo in the nose, discharging the spell. The crack against his knuckles filled him with painful joy as the mage went tumbling backward.

The next thing Wil knew, he was on his back and Isom's jaws were around his throat. He held very still.

Hugo climbed to his feet, cradling a badly bleeding nose. Bob raised a fist. Hugo's devil caught it and placed its bladed tail against his stomach.

"That was stupid, McKenzies. I was going to keep you informed, but now you're going to sit here with the rest of the prisoners until I get to the bottom of this."

"You can't do this, Hugo," Wil said. His heart thundered, and the fangs against his throat filled him with a dread he hadn't known since the storm.

"You have no idea what I can do, Wilbur." Hugo pulled a bloody hand away from his nose. "Some of the cat is still there, you know. Part of him wants to take a bite and eat you. It'd make him a better servant and get you out of my way. Will you fall in line, or should I give Pusspuss a treat?"

To his shame, Wil said nothing at all. He just raised a hand in acceptance.

"That's what I thought. You will remain here. Gather up the mayor and his buddies and keep them safe. Release, Pusspuss."

Isom released Wil and drew back. Wil looked Isom in his blank eye. He pushed his way forward with his mind, but it felt blocked. There was no entering a mind that was only half there. Not while Hugo had control of him.

"I'm sorry," Wil whispered. He carefully sat up and watched as Hugo freed the deputies from their grassy bonds and had them escort the earth elemental off the farm.

"Everyone, stay calm," Hugo's voice boomed. "There has been an attack against Harper Valley by the fae. All denizens of Faerie are hereby confined to the farm until further notice. Any attempts to leave or mingle with the citizenry will be considered attempts at destroying this town. Stay where you are and do not cause trouble. This is your only warning.

"To the humans in the area, I will need volunteers to help keep order and defend the town. We must now consider ourselves under attack and act accordingly. Thank you."

Hugo motioned, and the demon released Bob. "Stay on the farm. Both of you," the mage ordered. He stepped away and his thralls fanned out around him, meeting with the first batch of volunteers.

Wil watched as people he thought had been new friends of the fae signed up to be Hugo's enforcers. Bob came up to him and helped him to his feet.

"Play along for now," whispered Bob. "We'll save him. We'll figure it out, I promise. But for now, we have to play it cool."

"Y-yeah," said Wil, brain tumbling in circles. He couldn't decide whether he wanted to laugh, cry, scream, or launch a full-scale assault on Hugo's stupid face. For now, he took a breath and said, "Do we still have that terrarium from when I was a kid?"

Bob chuckled. "You know your mom doesn't throw anything out."

"Get it for me, please. I . . . I don't know what to do, but the first step is making sure it doesn't get worse, right?" Wil took a deep breath.

Most of the people who came for the feast left the farm. The fae gathered in their trees and largely went inside, save for the small crowd arguing outside. Wil dreaded what they were possibly planning.

Hugo had gotten a few dozen people to help him out. As far as Wil knew, they had gone to the jail with Syl and would likely be armed the next time he saw them.

Before they made it too far, Wil caught all of the toads and placed them in the big glass terrarium he'd gotten on his fourteenth birthday. They fought to get away from him, croaking in distress. The noise quickly grew to be too much.

Once all thirteen toads were together, Wil struggled to make his animal communication spells work. With all the stress, his rustiness, and how different the toads were, it took him nearly ten minutes of trying before he managed to get through.

"Mayor Sinclair? Sheriff? Are you alright?"

The cacophony of distorted croaking voices overwhelmed him.

"Get me back to normal right this instant!"

"I'm hungry. Why am I hungry?"

"What have you done to us?"

"Ahhh! Ahhh! Ahhh!"

The endless screaming among the transformed humans worried Wil a little, but at least their minds were intact. More or less.

"Hey, hey, listen to me," Wil shouted over them. "We'll get you back to normal as soon as we can, I promise. But we're going to need you to hold tight and not freak out. This might take a bit, but we're going to fix this."

One toad in particular stared at him unblinking, judgment and hate in his bulbous eyes. "How do we know you didn't do this to us?" it demanded of him. Wil guessed it was Sinclair.

He sighed and counted to ten. "I can't turn people into toads, you idiot. I could just leave you here if you'd rather. No? Then shut up and hold on." He headed toward his parents' house with the terrarium floating behind him. Once the mayor and others were safe, he could check on the fae.

Together, they would find a way out of this. Even if it meant it was time to cut and run. Maybe Wil would even go with them.

INTERLUDE

Love and War

It was said that an ogre's primary emotion was anger. A sort of permanent, dull resentment for the world. Their home in Faerie was a harsh place of blistering summers and frigid winters, and they were trained to be strong, tough, and ready to fight at a moment's notice. For the most part, Gallath wasn't like that.

Part of it came from being the runt in the family. He was a good foot shorter than most of his kin, and not quite as powerfully built. For some undersized ogres, it meant trying harder and fighting fiercely to prove themselves. For Gallath, raised mostly in Oakheart Spiral with his uncle, it meant finding himself in different ways.

He fell in love more with music than anything else, and he didn't have the same need to fight and prove himself that others did. If he'd been left to his own devices, he would've been completely content to just have a peaceful life, playing his songs.

But his uncle Grimnar didn't allow it. Gallath was put into training and forced to a higher standard. He spent his days drilling and sparring against the other young ogres and trolls, but at least his nights were his own. Even if he had to keep them secret, his flute, drums, and lyre were his heart and soul.

Hot and cool, day by day, produced a young man who was a fine soldier, but not a warrior. Gallath could follow orders and lead a small group of men, but he never thought he'd have the anger and hunger for the violence it took to truly be a threat on the battlefield.

Until now.

"You do *not* get to order us around like children," Gallath growled at the armed man with a silver star on his chest. After the chaos had broken loose, the fae had congregated for safety. They would have even if they hadn't been ordered to. "We are not prisoners here, not for a crime you have no proof any one of us committed!"

The deputy had his hand on a human weapon. Gallath knew how powerful guns could be, but he was confident he was faster if it came down to it. It was dark now and he knew he could see better than humans. The deputy's fear and anger stood out clearly.

"Sure as hell wasn't one of us!" the man snapped. "This is just like what your kind used to do to us when we moved out across the plains."

"Was this before or after all the murder and driving us away?" Gallath scoffed.

"Hey, wait!" Bram came up from the side so fast that the deputy drew his weapon and pointed it at him.

Gallath struck, closing the distance and stunning the human with one punch. He kicked the gun away, glad for the distraction, before grabbing the man and raising him, and roaring in his face.

Other humans approached, drawing weapons. Behind Gallath, the people he swore to protect cowered and hid around their tree. Most of the fae there weren't fighters, just artists and tradespeople and tourists who wanted a taste of their old world in a new way. The stunned man slumped in Gallath's grip, and he let him drop.

"Hold your fire, please," Bram called out, waving his hands. The four men approaching slowed down but didn't stop. "This was a misunderstanding, tempers are high, and—"

"Get down, Stevenson!" one of the men shouted. "Get away from that ogre, it's dangerous!"

It? Of all the insults piled on and on over their time in Calipan, this one made him see red most of all. He stormed forward, drawing his sword. If he died in the attempt, so be it. They had attacked him and his people, and Gallath would take them with him. He never wanted war or violence, no matter what his uncle had demanded of him. It seemed he had little choice now.

Gallath made it four steps before colliding with an unseen force and was sent backward. He rolled along the ground as the energy followed him, finally pinning him against the fallen tree where his people had eaten. Wilbur McKenzie came toward him, pointing his glowing purple staff.

"I've got this," the wizard said to the other men. "Go."

"We had orders to stay on the farm and keep an eye out for—"

Wil's voice burst out of him like a quake cracking the earth. "YOU WILL EITHER LEAVE MY FAMILY'S FARM WILLINGLY OR I WILL PUT YOU INTO A SLEEP THAT WILL LAST THE REST OF YOUR LIFE. YOUR FAMILIES WILL MOURN YOU FOR YEARS, UNABLE TO DO ANYTHING TO SAVE YOU. ALL THE WHILE, YOU'LL BE TRAPPED IN A NIGHTMARE."

They hesitated. One lowered his gun and made the wise decision to clear out. Another joined him, but the two last remained.

"Stand down, McKenzie. You heard Jefferson, they're to . . . to . . ." The man's gun clattered to the ground as he swayed in place. He fell over, curling up into a fetal position. Soon, he was snoring helplessly on the ground.

The last man looked at Gallath, still pinned, and then at Wil. He put his gun away and walked off, obviously doing his best not to look scared.

Bram ran up to him. "Gallath, are you okay? Wil, let him go!" Bram tried to hug him, but Gallath pushed him away.

Wil released him and came up. "I'm sorry about that, Gallath. I was trying to protect you."

Gallath stood, hands twitching. His every instinct told him to attack Wil, but that would upset Bram. Even in the fog of his anger, he recognized that much. Burying as much of his rage as he could, he ground out, "We need to get Syl back and get out of here. We need to get back to Faerie and either seal the way or prepare ourselves for an attack."

"It doesn't have to be like that," said Wil. "We could—"

"Someone sabotaged us, and that bastard mage took Syl!" Gallath bellowed. "Syl's not just your mouthy, horny friend. He is the only child of the king of the Woodlands Association, and if he is not returned, it *will* be war."

Gallath's breathing felt ragged and uneven. As if he couldn't get enough air. It hadn't happened since he was a kid. Everything felt so simple, so black and white, crystal clear. Almost everything was a bad move and would end in war. And maybe it was too late to avoid that.

"Gal, we can get him back. We *will* get him back," said Bram. "There won't be war if we can help it."

"What can you do, Bram? Huh?" Gallath sneered. "You going to try to solve all your problems with beer and potions? You going to get Hugo drunk enough to let this go and not attack us?"

Bram looked like he wanted to cry. It hurt, but the ogre couldn't stop now. "What about you, Wizard? Are you going to do something about the mage, or follow orders? You told us you were different, but you're letting this happen."

Wil flinched. For being such a powerful wizard, he'd never looked so low and pathetic to Gallath before. "I'm going to do something about it. I'm going to get Syl back, and then I'm going to stop Hugo. I don't care if it makes me an enemy of my people. It's the right thing to do, but we have to be smart about it. We can't launch an all-out attack on the jail to get him back. Let me handle that."

Some of Gallath's anger dissipated. It wasn't everything, but it was a start. "And what of your town, your government? What will they do about us when Hugo is taken out and your town leaders are still toads?"

"I . . . I don't know," said Wil, leaning against his staff for support. "If I can, I'm going to close the rift, I guess. We'll get you guys out, and then I'll either close the way or die trying."

It wasn't much, but it was enough for Gallath's resolve. He'd give Wil the chance to do it, but he had orders to follow.

"Fine then," he said. "You get Syl back, and I'll prepare our people to get moving. You'll have as long as I can give you, but my uncle will be angry. There's still a chance this will lead to war."

"I know," said Wil. "But we have to try, right?"

Gallath nodded, and the wizard took off into the night. Bram remained, looking at him with pain and longing in his eyes. His own heart cracked, but he couldn't show weakness now.

"It was nice," he said to Bram. "While it lasted. But we both knew it couldn't be forever. I'm glad I got to know you, Abraham Stevenson. You might want to leave town while you can." It was so much less than he wanted to say but all he could bring himself to get out without breaking down.

"I can't do that, Gal," Bram said. "I can't leave you, or home, or my friends."

"Then you need to prepare yourself for war," said Gallath gently. "I will never willingly hurt you, but I can't guarantee the same for my people. Do not lift a sword or one of your potions against us and you will be spared. Goodbye."

Arabella and Timothy Twist were waiting for him when he went inside the tree. "We're leaving," he said to them. "Pack only what is necessary and be ready to travel light and fast."

"I can't believe this," Arabella seethed. "After all of our efforts, *this* is how it ends?"

"Aye, I'd hoped better from the humans," said Timothy Twist, not trying to hide his mirth. "If nothing else, it proves us right. It's not much in the way of satisfaction, but I'll take what I can get."

Arabella swore and disappeared into her room. Other heads peeked out from their rooms, everyone desperate for more information. Gallath motioned with his head for Twist to follow him into his quarters. Once they were alone, he grabbed the little man by the clothes and shook him.

"Why did you have to do it?" he bellowed. "We were *so* close. Are you happy now? You and my uncle get your damned war, and who knows how many of us will die."

Timothy Twist wasn't bothered or concerned. He just wiped the spittle from his face and grinned. "Oh, it's amazing. What a setup, what a *payoff*. It's one of the happiest memories I'll ever have. All those smug, self-important humans drinking our wine and suddenly in a form far more fitting. Oh, but I outdid myself this time!"

Gallath dropped him, legs turning to rubber. He collapsed on the bed, cradling his head. "I thought we were going to be able to avoid war. I thought I could ignore the orders."

"You thought wrong, Gallath. And now you know what you must do." Twist snapped his fingers until Gallath looked at him. "We'll get Arabella and the others home and then launch our counterattack for this horrible, horrible breach of hospitality. I should go help the wizard, make sure he's where we want him for this."

Gallath let out a helpless, shuddering breath. "How do you live with yourself, Twist? Knowing what's going to happen now?"

"Easily," said the puck. His red eyes glowed in the gloom. "When you're playing a different game from everyone else, it's fun being the only one who knows the rules. You've been a good player, Gallath. Now it's time to end this game and start a new one!"

CHAPTER 51

Bad Bargains

Never before had a walk at night been so nerve-racking. While Frederick had deputized a dozen or so men before his transmogrification, Hugo had managed to instantly revive the rest of the town's dormant neighborhood guardian programs, not in use for the better part of ten years. Things had been too safe to bother, and even the addition of the railroad hadn't changed that.

Now the streets had a guard every hundred yards or so and at every major crossroads. They carried lanterns and torches and often a pitchfork, club, or the occasional hunting rifle. There was no way anyone was going to be able to make it across town in peace unless they could turn invisible.

Wil, Bram, and Darlene stayed close, huddled under a globe of invisibility at the end of Wil's staff. They could see each other, but no one farther than five feet apart would see anything amiss. It didn't stop them from being heard, a fact Wil had to constantly remind Bram.

"There's Joshua. He went on a date with an elf girl. Figures he'd turn like that," Bram muttered, taking every familiar face a lot more personally than either of his friends.

Joshua looked up, holding his torch aloft. Darlene elbowed Bram in the side. Together they held a collective breath as Joshua looked around. Wil sighed and waved his hand. A loud popping sound came from behind him. Joshua whirled around and took off running at the distraction.

The three of them hurried along, crossing the bridge over to downtown Harper Valley. The jail wasn't far now, but there was little time to spare. The crunch of their shoes on snow was deafening in the otherwise quiet night, and Darlene stopped them as they approached city hall.

"Take smaller steps," she whispered. "Unless you can cover the sound?"

Wil shook his head. "Maybe, but adaptable invisibility like this is hard. It takes finesse I'm not sure I have. Smaller steps it is. *Bram.*"

Bram opened his mouth to argue but then thought better of it. They grouped up tightly, trying to step in unison. It helped with the sound, but as they approached the entrance to the jail, they slowed upon seeing two people standing guard outside. The door had been repaired, but if he had to, Wil would knock it down again.

"What're we going to do?" Bram asked, shivering from excitement more than from the cold. "Can you put them to sleep as well?"

"Yeah," said Wil, "but we need to be a bit closer. C'mon."

They inched closer. One of the two guards was sitting in a chair, reading by lantern light. The younger of the two, Arnold, looked around frantically. They stopped, and he looked right where they were.

"Hal?" he said, sounding unsure.

"What is it?" Hal responded without looking up from his book.

"I see something. I think." Arnold leaned closer, raising his torch. "There's tracks leading up here, but then they stop. Right there." He pointed.

Hal groaned and got up, setting his book down on his chair. He raised the lantern and came closer, stopping when he saw it. He shifted the lantern to the other hand and pulled out his pistol. "Show yourselves right now. I know your kind can turn invisible, and I won't hesitate to shoot."

"Y-yeah!" Arnold chimed in, pulling out a short knife.

Wil held a finger to his lips as Darlene and Bram looked to him for an answer. There wasn't much he could do while holding the invisibility, so he let it drop.

The moment they came into sight, Hal aimed. Wil threw up a shield just in time, but the impact knocked him back, flailing. Bram caught him and brought him back to his feet.

"Oh, crap! Mr. Wizard!" Hal looked alarmed by what he'd almost done. And then his alarm turned to suspicion. "You're not supposed to be here! We were warned about you. All three of you."

"Yeah, about that," said Wil. "It doesn't work for me. Get out of my way, Hal. Nobody's going to stop me from doing what I have to."

Hal bit his lip, gun pointed at the ground and trembling.

Darlene tried next, holding up her hands placatingly. "You're doing good, protecting the town, but this is bigger than us. We need to get our friend to safety before something happens that can't be undone."

Hal's gun lowered farther. Just as they thought they were going to get through to him, the door to the jail opened and big Travis Bell came out with a shotgun. From farther off in the distance, there were more gunshots, alerting the entire town.

"Hey," Travis cried, raising his gun.

Wil didn't give him a chance to do anything. He summoned a huge gust of wind that blew the three men back, and kept up the pressure. Snow swirled in violent circles around them, growing in intensity.

"What now?" Bram shouted to be heard over the gusts.

Wil breathed in and out, feeling the magic flow through the air. He circled his staff, increasing the intensity of the small storm, until finally the weapons were ripped from the men's hands. Perfect. Wil thrust the snowstorm forward. Piles of snow crashed against the three men, pinning them against the wall in piles of powder and mud.

Lingering snow continued in through the door and Wil ran forward, shouting, "Give me thirty seconds and follow!"

The second he was in the door, he raised his silver shield. His forward momentum kept multiple gunshots from knocking him on his ass. Wil thrust his staff forward and went with the familiar comfort of earth magic. Four men were in the jail, various distances away. Still close enough. He pulled magnetically, and the guns flew out of their hands.

Wil stepped to the side, ducking one of the guns. He held his staff up and let it flash in quick, rhythmic pulses. One of the deputies immediately charged him but two seconds later slowed to a stop. The flashes picked up in speed and then slowed, back and forth until they were transfixed.

"*Sleep,*" Wil whispered, power in his voice. "*Lie down and go to sleep. Nice and deep.*"

One by one, they crumpled to the ground, not collapsing so much as gently letting themselves get comfortable on the ground. Wil kept it up for another second, pouring more magic into the flashes until he dismissed them. They wouldn't wake until morning, but there were likely people coming shortly.

"Syl!" Wil cried, running over to his cell.

The faun lay in it, staring blearily into space. He looked up at Wil with a severely bruised face, but there was still light in his eyes. "Wil," he slurred, forcing himself to sit up. "Hugo's a jerk."

"Tell me about it," Wil said. "Did he do this to you?"

Syl pointed at the swollen eye, almost completely shut. "His ogre did. So I guess, yes, he did. He . . . You're here to break me out, right? He said he was going to ship me to Cloverton. Some place called the Junk Drawer."

Wil's blood ran cold. "If you had gone there, no one would've ever seen you again." He pointed his staff and blasted the door open. He came in and threw Syl's arm around his shoulder, awkwardly pulling him from the cell. Just as they were out, Bram and Darlene burst in, looking terrified.

"We've got company," Darlene said, running up and pointing at the door. "There's, like, six guys out there, surrounding the jail. Can you make another exit? Blow down a wall and escape that way?"

"Sure, but then we'd still have people chasing after us," said Wil.

Bram moved Wil out of the way and scooped Syl up easily. The faun groaned in pain but reached up and patted Bram's bearded face.

"If I don't make it . . ." Syl started.

"You'll make it!" Bram insisted.

"If I don't make it . . . please shave." The goatman grinned.

"Oh. I could drop you, you know." Bram shook his head fondly.

Wil stepped in front of them, facing the door. "I can fight our way out. Just stay behind me and move only when I tell you. Okay?" He looked over his shoulder.

No one looked happy about being so powerless compared to him, but they nodded. Taking a deep breath, Wil stalked toward the door, staff held out like the weapon it was. Just as he got to the entrance, a high-pitched whistling made him stop. A few seconds later, Timothy Twist came inside.

"Twist?" Wil pulled back. "What're you doing here?"

"Oh, just helping break our playful prince out of here. We need him back in Faerie for an important vote. His vote won't matter, but he needs to be there just the same."

"What are you talking about?" Darlene demanded, but Syl laughed.

"Him. It was him." Syl pointed at the puck. "Wasn't it, Timothy Twist?"

The little man took off his hat and bowed. "Indeed, 'twas I who poisoned the wine! And now, I'm going to take Sylano and get him back home safely. Come along if you like. The humans on the way have been dealt with."

Wil couldn't believe it. Well, he could believe Twist was capable, but it didn't add up. "Why?" he finally asked. "Why would you do all of this? I thought you wanted peace."

"Did I say that? Ever?" Twist laughed merrily. "No, I want *war*, dear boy. War!"

"Again," said Darlene, "*why*? You lost last time. You can't win this time. Not with your numbers depleted and our advanced weapons."

"Oh, do you think so?" Twist challenged. "We've had centuries to replenish our numbers and harbor our grudge. But I can honestly say I don't hold a grudge myself. Not one worth acting on, at least. Do you want to know why I set this up? Why I pushed and teased and poked and made sure there could be no peace? Because it was *boring*." Timothy Twist wiggled his fingers, bursting out laughing once more. "Hundreds of years of peace made us soft! It made us slow and fat and stupid. We're *less* for it. When your reckless antics opened the rift, I finally saw an opportunity. A way to either get us back to the fiery, powerful people we once were, or one final hurrah, one last flash of light before the sun sets on us. Either way, we wouldn't just be sitting around, living out those predictable, safe, boring days without ever growing! You want to know why? Because stagnation is death, and I'm sick of dying. I want to *live*!"

Wil steadied himself, more frustrated. "You mean you were willing to damn your entire people to extinction just because you were sick of sitting around? I'm going to enjoy this. Maybe if I keep you alive and bound, we can still avert this war."

"Hahaha, no," said Twist with a growing grin. "First, I have to deliver on my bargain. Wilbur McKenzie, I know who sent the assassins after you. It was me. I wanted you either gone or tested, and you didn't disappoint. You're powerful, but an empty-headed human idiot, easily led by the nose. Consider yourself filled in and our bargain met."

Wil felt it then. Obligation—the promise he'd made weeks ago to Twist, a medium favor in exchange for knowing more. Gods, he'd been so stupid.

"You think that means anything?" Wil barked. "Not if I take you out first."

Just as Wil pointed his staff, Timothy Twist held up a hand. Wil's brain exploded with pain, like shards of ice piercing his head and burning everything they touched.

"Right! Wilbur, I am calling in the favor you owe me. For the next . . . oh, hour or so, you are to remain inside of this jail and cast no spells. Am I clear?"

"I wo—" Wil screamed and fell to his knees. The shards pierced deeper, and it was then he realized he couldn't refuse. Not without losing a huge piece of himself, or collapsing from the pain. "Yes. Why?" he begged.

Timothy Twist leaned in close. "Because I want you alive to see your precious efforts fall apart. Surprise!" He snapped his fingers and pointed to Bram. "You! Come along, and bring Syl. We've got to get back to Faerie."

"We're not *coming along* with you," Darlene snapped.

Twist just grinned wider. "You are if you want Syl to live. If not, you can all stay here and guarantee he's the first person to die in this war. Honestly, it would make it easier on me, so do what you want. Either way, I'm going to the McKenzie farm and then back up the mountain." He left without another word.

"Wil, are you okay?" Darlene asked, crouching beside him. "What did he do to you?"

"I made a deal I shouldn't have. Bram, go. Get Syl out of here. I'll be fine!"

"And me? I don't want to leave you," Darlene said. "Not if you can't defend yourself!"

"I'll be okay," said Wil, forcing a smile. "The only one allowed to hurt me is Hugo."

A chuckle from above caught their attention. "Isn't that the truth." Hugo's voice came from his ugly, warped little imp, hanging from a ceiling fan. In the commotion, no one had noticed it spying on them.

"I would run away while you can, little girl. You don't want to be there when I arrive."

CHAPTER 52

Bad to Worse

"You need to get out of here, *now*," Wil said, staring at the imp's mocking face.

"I'd listen to him," said Hugo through his puppet. "I'm on my way there now, and I'm more than happy to thank you all personally for this wonderful opportunity."

Wil raised his staff to blast the imp, then remembered he couldn't. No spells for the next fifty-nine minutes and counting. No leaving, no magic—there was no way he could avoid Hugo coming for him.

"We can't just leave you here," said Bram. "Not if he's coming. He might kill you."

"What do you think he'll do to the rest of us?" Syl said weakly. "Let's go."

The look of horror and guilt on Darlene's face threatened to break his heart. "Wil, I—"

"GO!" Wil motioned toward the door. "I'll be fine. He'll want to gloat and taunt me for a while. It'll buy you some time to get to Faerie."

"He's right," said Hugo. "I'm going to have some fun before I get to work."

That did it. Darlene grabbed Bram by the shirt and yanked him forward. He got moving, and she followed. She paused just long enough to throw her arms around Wil and crush him to her, kissing his cheek. "I'm sorry, Wil. We'll get him home safe!"

And then they were all gone, and it was just Wil with the imp, who wasn't moving and was just out of reach for him to poke with the horn on his staff. He couldn't leave, so he decided to make himself comfortable and safe.

The first thing he did was drag the sleeping deputies into the cells and lock them in. Then he went into the bathroom and hid the keys. They'd be able to get out eventually, even if, or when, Hugo killed him. That done, he wiped snow and mud off the sheriff's chair, plopped himself down, and kicked his feet up on the desk.

"You know, I expected you to be a lot more scared, knowing you've just committed treason and are defenseless," Hugo said conversationally. The imp swung forward and caught the edge of overhead fan's blade closest to Wil. It dipped dangerously but held its weight.

Wil grunted his indifference. "You won't kill me. Not like this."

"I won't have to. All I have to do is contain you and bring you to Cloverton. Suddenly, you not being one of our mages will be a good thing, and I'll be the one to have not only delivered justice for an attack against our country but also ensured that a weak-minded traitor wasn't in a position to betray us even worse. You *will* die, eventually. But not for a while." The imp's simian face twisted into a horrible grin, as if it wasn't just Hugo who loved the idea. "First they'll humiliate and break you. You'll be made the poster boy for why we need to go to war with Faerie. You've made it necessary to wipe them out and take their lands. And with that, Calipan will be stronger than ever before!"

As Hugo spoke, Wil's feigned bravery faltered. It was one thing to die by the hand of a bastard like Hugo, it was something else entirely to have a show made of it. Worse than that, what would they do to his family? Every one of them had thrown in their lot with him wholeheartedly, and if the authorities were going to make Wil an example, they would do it to everyone connected to him.

"Ooh, there it is. The realization. You're starting to understand just how bad a decision this was. I love it!" The imp clapped mockingly.

This time, Wil grabbed a baton and flung it at the imp. It connected with a satisfying bonk and the imp fell to the floor, scrabbling against the tile until it crouched on all fours. It still grinned at Wil, but now its mouth bled.

"Look at that, Saint McKenzie taking out his anger on a poor, defenseless, broken creature. It's too bad you couldn't find this kind of coldness in you earlier. You might've been well poised to be one of the most powerful and influential wizards in the country. You would have certainly been promoted to mage, which *is* one step up, no matter what you tell yourself."

"Shut up!" Wil's breathing was harder now. He'd be the first person to admit when he was scared, but he hadn't felt it until just now. It felt like falling into a pit without a bottom. There was always farther to fall, and all hope faded like light as he plummeted deeper.

"Nah." Hugo himself walked through the jail, followed by his ogre and demon thralls. The imp got a running start on all fours and jumped up on the mage's shoulder, tail curling around his neck. "I'm only getting started. We have to give your friends a head start, don't we?"

Wil stood. Fifty more minutes or so until he had his magic back. Not enough time to stop whatever was going to happen to him now. "Why would you give them a head start? Are you just that sadistic?"

"Well, yes," Hugo said, laughing. "But also because I don't want to catch them here in Harper Valley. If I let them go through the rift, then that means I get to follow. And I get to see exactly what that wonderful magic in the air will do to me. If I had to guess, that's why you're stronger than you were. *Oh.* I'm right, aren't I? Fantastic!"

It was a good reminder to Wil that no matter how bad things seemed, they could always get worse. His face fell, which only made the mage laugh harder. That angered Wil enough to cut through his fear and despair, at least.

"So how exactly do you plan on keeping me here? When I get my magic back, I'm going to bust through whatever guards you leave behind and—"

"Oh, I don't plan on leaving any guards," said Hugo with a dismissive wave. "When your time is up, you may follow me. Part of me counts on it. The way I see it, you either come after me and I get to put you down myself, or you lie down and do nothing, and we parade you around Cloverton. Or you run, I suppose, and my newest pet gets to hunt you down. Wouldn't that be a nice treat for him?"

Wil couldn't help himself. One second he was standing there, all but trembling from fear and anger. The next, he launched himself at Hugo, magic or no magic. The ogre flanking Hugo caught Wil by the face. The next thing he knew, he was twisted around and pinned in place.

"Ah, yes. I still owe you for earlier, don't I?" Hugo had cleaned away the blood but the bruising around his eyes and nose was clear. "I'm not usually one to hit people myself, but for you?" Hugo drove his fist into Wil's gut.

Time froze as the air was driven from him with a grunt and the pain caught up a second later. The demon grabbed Wil by his hair and forced him to look up at Hugo. The mage smiled and took a few steps back. From his sleeves, he pulled out an intricate-looking wand. "Unlike you, I'm not willing to damage my hands on your hard head. So . . ."

With a flick of his wrist, Hugo sent a red bolt at Wil. It struck his face and snapped his head back as if he'd been punched. Once, twice, three more times Hugo slapped him around with those flashes of angry red light. It was never enough to be more than a painful insult, but afterward, Wil's head rang and he wanted to cry from the way the pain lingered in his nerves, which had been the real reason for the spell.

The ogre dropped him, and Wil fell to his knees. His skin was on fire and prickled incessantly, and his head throbbed. He stayed there, looking dully up.

"Well, I think that's it. You have your options, McKenzie. Chase me, run away, or stay to die. I'll do you one final kindness. Make the right choice, and I'll make sure your parents are spared."

"Which one is the right choice?" Wil asked, slurring slightly. Thinking was fuzzy and hard.

Hugo shrugged. "Haven't decided yet. Until next time!" Laughing, he left with his thralls.

Wil sat there, mind almost completely blank, save for one endlessly repeating thought: he had failed everyone. All of his best efforts meant nothing, thanks to both Timothy Twist and Hugo. He might've been able to deal with either one on their own, but this perfect firestorm would ignite both worlds, and Wil couldn't do anything about it.

Forty more minutes remained until he could leave or cast any spells. In that time, Hugo would almost certainly take the *Flying Calamity* up to the rift. Would they attack the fae there, or would he just try to fly right through to the other world? Either way, it would be too late.

There was no telling what Hugo would do to his friends, but if he was insistent on inflicting as much pain and humiliation as he could, they might survive for a while until he could do something worse. Time wasn't on his side, but . . .

Wil took a long, shuddering breath. The pain was starting to fade now, but it would probably linger for hours, clinging to his skin like one big, exposed nerve. He couldn't get rid of it or the way he felt, but he could focus. Sitting down cross-legged, he closed his eyes and steadied his breathing.

The conditions of the Obligation stated he couldn't leave or cast spells. It didn't say anything about meditating or drawing in the magic around him. The jail wasn't a happy, familiar, comfortable place. It was just about the worst place for his needs, but though Wil was confined there for the next while, his mind was not.

In and out he breathed, nice and even. He let his senses wander into the land around him, and farther out. There was a leyline, just barely out of reach. Harper Valley had enough good leylines that he sometimes wondered why Cloverton didn't care about them more. Putting that out of his head, he breathed and just took in the land around him.

Downtown Harper Valley was a sign of the city it could one day be. A place where people hustled and bustled and lived, and the echoes of their lives had a power all its own. Even at night, with no one around. The echoes would continue long after the city and people were gone. Wil drew them in and reached, farther and farther. The edges of his senses brushed the nearest leyline, and suddenly it coursed into him.

It was almost too much at first, until he drew back. And then he just breathed it in, let it soothe his mind and his aches and pains. Time stretched and flattened down to something without much meaning. He was keenly aware of how much time passed, and how much faster it seemed, and that calmed him too.

It wasn't too late. It couldn't be. Hugo enjoyed grandstanding too much to make it a quick, clean victory. If he was going to declare war, he'd do it in the grandest possible fashion and make sure there were enough witnesses so no one could deny it. That would slow him down.

Hugo wanted into Faerie, to taste more of the power that had enhanced Wil. It would make him a harder opponent, but he wouldn't have nearly enough time to absorb enough to eclipse Wil in strength. The mage wouldn't be stopped by a magical slugfest, but then, Wil had no plans to take him in an even fight.

It wasn't what Wil was good at, even if he tried to deny or bury it. He didn't think he'd ever crave violence or domination, but this was a valuable lesson. Sometimes, peace wasn't an option. And what was better, to hold onto his ethics and let those around him suffer, or to get it done as quickly and cleanly as possible?

Finally tapped into the leyline, Wil both expanded mentally and went deep into himself, and he planned. As the minutes ticked down faster and faster, he came to know what he would do. His last scuffle with the mage had shown Wil how he could win.

When the time ran out, Wilbur McKenzie stood up and stretched. He grabbed his staff and one of the enchanted sleds he'd donated to the city just before this business with the fae. Once outside, he got on and took one last big breath. This was it. With the power of the leyline charging him, Wil sped over the snow, heading toward the mountains, carrying as much power from the leyline as he could.

One wrong move and those he loved would die and his country would be at war. He was ready for it.

CHAPTER 53

Fire on the Mountain

Wil's sled had never moved so fast, charged by the leyline and his desperation. The cold winter night was soothing on his skin, and part of him relished the rush of moving so fast. The glow of his staff lit his way as he flew over the snow.

Along the way back to his family's farm, Wil saw the unconscious forms of all the guards they'd slipped by that Timothy Twist had later taken out. No one was dead or injured, just asleep or muttering to themselves with a faraway look. He wanted to stop and check on them, but it would cost him time he didn't have. He passed by, silently apologizing for leaving them.

There were still people riled up by Hugo and the events of the day watching over the farm. Two of them waited for Wil at the end of the lane. One raised his weapon, then faltered when he saw who it was.

"OUT OF MY WAY!" Wil boomed at them from afar. "GO HOME IF YOU WANT TO LIVE." And then he increased his speed, heading right for them.

One man looked at the other, then got the hell out of the way. The other waited, looking like he wanted to say something, and Wil blew past him, covering him in snow. He sped straight to the tree houses, where there were still plenty of fae standing around.

"Did Syl and the others come through here?" Wil asked the nearest person, who turned out to be Declan.

The gnome tugged on his beard in distress. "They did," he said. "The representatives took wagons and beasts and went off to the rift in a hurry. They told us to come along, but . . . I'm not abandoning the mission! If we all leave, then we'll look just as guilty as they thought we were."

Others joined in, murmuring their agreement. Wil was surprised. He'd spent so much time thinking of the people of Harper Valley and how they'd need to adjust, and of his immediate friends, that he hadn't thought much about how the rest of their guests felt.

Honestly, he'd imagined they'd all want to go home, but judging from the two dozen or so fae still there, at least some of them liked Harper Valley enough to risk their safety. Wil didn't know if he was impressed or frustrated.

"I don't know if you're making the right choice," said Wil, "given that my people might take it out on you. But Hugo's thrall spied us freeing Syl, and now he's going to assault the rift. Things are about to get a lot worse. Are you capable of defending yourselves?"

"We are," Bob said from behind Wil. He and Sharon had come up when Wil arrived. "We've been discussing what to do about it. With our help, Declan and the others can put a protection spell on the property that should repel for a day or two. But after that, we'd be wide open. Can you fix this in that time?"

Wil didn't have to think about it. "Yes. If I can get up to the peak fast enough, I can stop this. I can stop Hugo and prevent the war, or at least close the way if I have to. But if I do, everyone here will be trapped."

"We know what we're doing," said an older dryad man with ashen skin. "For some of us, it's been several lifetimes since we could come home. I missed it here, even if it's different."

Wil opened his mouth to argue, but a bright light caught his attention. Everyone turned to the west to see bursts of fire in the distance, followed by the muted thunder of cannons. His stomach dropped. Hugo and the rest were there already.

"I need to go," he said. "You all stay here and stay safe. Sarah and Jeb are here, right?"

Sharon laughed. "Sarah is, at least. Jeb went with the princess."

Wil closed his eyes and sighed. That didn't surprise him, but it meant he'd have to bail out his big brother if they hadn't made it through the rift safely by now.

"Alright, thanks. Keep your heads down and look out for each other. And if . . . if I don't come back, you need to run. Abandon the home, because Hugo will come for you next."

Bob shook his head. "You're going to come back. Kick his ass, save the day, and we'll figure out what to do about Sinclair and the others. Make us proud, Wil!"

Wil nodded, then grabbed both of them in a quick hug. With a nod to Declan and the other fae, he went back to his sled and made his way northwest, going down the snowy dirt roads separating swathes of farmland.

Each passing second dug into his nerves. Once he reached the bottom of the mountain, the cannons fired again, flashes of fire and light above him illuminating the *Flying Calamity* in all her menacing glory. It was close now, almost to the summit and closing the distance.

Wil took the familiar path that zigzagged up the mountain, zooming around trees and rocks all the way to the top. Animals of all kinds ran from the noise, crossing his path and sometimes coming too close for comfort. He kept his hands on the twin bars that drove the sled forward, mentally urging it to go even faster.

A malicious red glow waited for him above. When he got close enough, he realized it was because the tree growing on Skalet's Peak was now on fire. As he went up the slope to the clearing, he saw that the tree had several new holes and broken branches, and it was burning brightly. He stopped and hopped off the sled, staff in hand.

The fae guarding the way through turned on him before realizing it was him. "What is going on?" a massive ogre wearing petrified bark armor demanded. "What is the meaning of this? First, the representatives run through without a word, and now we're under attack! What happened?"

Wil shook his head. "Twist betrayed us all and provoked a fight with my people, and now the mage has gone nuts and is trying to get through. We *cannot* let him into Faerie. Are you prepared to fight?"

A gorgeous, lean, sharp-featured elf laughed at him. "I've been waiting for this since this silly trip was planned." A second later her features twisted into fear and she shouted, "Get down!"

Wil looked up to see the flash of cannons again, and then the land around them was torn to pieces. Wil summoned his strongest shield and kept flying dirt and snow from burying him. The barrage ended, but no one seemed hurt. Wil dropped his shield and looked up at the warship. He swore he could feel Hugo's smugness from there.

Maybe he could do something about that. Wil took a deep breath and drew a widening spiral with his staff. The dragon horn glowed, and the clouds blotting out the moon gathered above Wil and the rift. Hugo thought that raw power and domination were the only way to get things done, and that Wil wasn't capable of either. He was wrong.

Between the staff, his power, and the leaking leyline flooding the mountaintop with ambient magic, Wil was plenty equipped for destruction. Flashes of light crackled in the clouds. Electricity arced up the staff in time with the lights above.

"Get back, and get ready for a fight," Wil shouted.

Even at this distance, Wil saw the cannons pulled back, to be reloaded and fired again. Not if he had anything to say about it. In and out he breathed, feeling the storm above and within. Power inside him crackled and burned and itched.

Wil pointed the horn directly at the ship. He put everything he had into it, one good punch to stop the ship from picking off the defenders before the invasion. The clouds lit up the night and lightning crashed down directly onto Wil. It passed through him, collecting inside of him in an agonizing second stretching on forever, before bursting from the end of his staff.

The most powerful magical attack Wil had ever done tore a hole in the hull of the *Flying Calamity*. Wil kept it up until the harnessed lightning burst out the other side. He poured his soul into it until his vision went white and the staff burned his hands. The spell released itself and Wil fell to his knees, breathing hard.

The *Flying Calamity* hung there for a second before it listed to the side. The ship went from parallel to the clearing to slowly swinging its bow their way. Wil realized what was about to happen a few seconds before everyone else.

"Get out of the way," he cried out. "It's coming down!"

The ship crashed a hundred yards away and slid across the ground, hurtling toward him.

CHAPTER 54

Rematch

The *Flying Calamity* came screaming along the ground at them, gouging a gash in the clearing. Wil anchored himself to the earth and threw force against it, but without digging into the leyline, there was only so much he could do. The ship slowed to a stop forty yards away. Crew members slid down the deck, and some hung off the railing, a fifteen-foot drop beneath them.

"You did it," said one of the elves near Wil, gawking. "You brought it down!"

"Yeah," said Wil as he caught his breath, "and now we have to worry about all the soldiers on board. Is anyone here good at shields or warding?"

The one gnome at the camp raised his hand. "That's what I'm here for! I can shield us with some help from the leyline."

"Do it," Wil commanded as he turned back to the ship, which he now saw was on fire. Several people had made their way to the ground, others poured out through the hole in the hull where the cannons used to be. The flickering flames showed them as armed and headed their way.

There was no way Wil could take on an entire crew like that, let alone when Hugo was coming for him. But there was one thing he knew might even things up, or at least buy them time. Once more, he tapped into the leyline. This time it hurt, like the feel of sunlight on a bad burn. He pushed past it and concentrated on one of his greatest strengths.

There were a few dozen fae in the camp, and Wil did his best to account for all of them. The illusion didn't have to be good with this lighting and the chaos that was about to erupt. The camp doubled, and Wil directed the illusions of elves, ogres, hobs, and gnomes to charge across the clearing, screaming with battle fury, their weapons held high.

They were halfway to the clearing when the wards went up. A heaviness settled in the air, along with a compulsion to leave that Wil was decidedly not immune to. He fought it as best as he could, breathing hard as his illusory army charged the Calipan military.

Shots rang out, loud and jarring. They went through the illusions, and some bullets struck the wards, slowing and then dropping to the ground. More and more pops pierced the night until they formed an irregular rhythm, a violent song of battle. When the first illusions passed through them, the soldiers thought they were safe. Then Wil detonated the illusions in an explosion of color and sound.

One by one, they went off in a flash of colors and screams and whistles, anything extreme and distracting. All advances stopped, and several men fell back. Wil pressed forward, passing through the wards. He felt for the earth beneath them and heated it. The snow melted, the ground softened, and one final push turned a fifty-foot circle into a frigid swamp.

The burn was too great and Wil released the leyline, collapsing to the ground. Spots danced in his vision, and he wasn't sure if it was from the strain or afterimages from the light show. His heart skipped every fourth beat, and when he took a step forward, his legs turned to jelly.

"Wizard, are you alright?" An ogre grabbed him from behind and pulled him back through the wards, which set his skin on fire and made his brain scream for him to get out of there.

"Hrng," Wil groaned. He couldn't afford to be weak right now, but this was more magic than he'd moved around in a while.

"Very good, Wilbur!" Hugo's voice came from the ship. "I'm glad you made it. I'll admit, I wasn't expecting you to take out my ship. Or to scare off these pitiful excuses for soldiers. I'll make you an offer right now. A duel between us—winner goes to Faerie. None of my creatures or your fae interfere."

Wil thought about it through the new pounding in his head. This wasn't a fight he was likely to win, after that display. But maybe it didn't have to be. Hugo wouldn't kill him immediately if he lost. That had to count for something. Wil smiled.

"How do I know you'll honor your side of the agreement?"

Hugo's laughter came echoing from everywhere at once. "You don't, but it's either that or I yank these idiots from the mud and we overwhelm you. We've got superior numbers, McKenzie. You want to stand up to me? Let's do it and see what you're made of!"

It didn't matter if Wil did or didn't: Hugo would come through and kill his way to Faerie. In that case, Wil thought he might as well go with the option that could save lives.

"Alright. Then let's do it. Me and you, one last time. And apologies, Captain—I didn't want to have to damage your ship."

"The captain isn't with us at the moment, I'm afraid. He questioned my orders and is taking a bit of a nap." As always, Hugo sounded pleased to be able to flex his power over someone else.

"Are you sure?" the ogre asked Wil. "We could hold them off. Especially if you can blast him with lightning like you did before."

"I can't," said Wil. "That was all I had. Don't worry, I've got this." Wil stood on rubbery legs. He followed the compulsion to leave the safety of the camp, leaning hard on his staff.

Hugo flew out slowly and landed twenty feet away. He had his wand out, pointed at the ground. Isom stalked behind him, and the thralls spread out, moving in unison until they formed a semicircle around Wil. There was nowhere to go but Faerie.

"Anything you wa—" Hugo started.

Wil didn't give him a chance. He pointed his staff and fired a quick bolt of lightning at him, barely anything compared to his ship-killing attack from earlier. The mage blocked it with a slash from his wand, which glowed red.

"Well, that was rude," said Hugo, laughing. "I love it. Try *this*!" He jabbed the wand Wil's way and flicked it in a tight circle. "*Riwg.*"

Much like how Wil had done earlier, Hugo summoned a miniature snowstorm around him. Wet, cold snow blew in his face and against him. Winds picked up and buffeted him, making it impossible to see. He tried to blow it away and blow it past, but Hugo overpowered him, covering him with snow until he cried out, "*D'zooca!*"

The temperature plummeted and all the loose powder on him froze. Wil gasped in pain and shock as half his body burned from the cold. He immediately engulfed himself in heat, amplifying his own for a second before the ice could freeze further and pierce his skin. Wil summoned his own gust of wind outward and the spiky, partially melted ice flew Hugo's way.

The mage flicked his wand and it flew harmlessly over him. He took a step forward and sent three flashes of malevolent red at Wil. Wil stepped to the side and shielded one, while the others whizzed by.

Then it was his turn to press the attack. Through the sluggishness, he tried one of the nastier, more difficult illusions. Wil focused on pure darkness and smothered Hugo's eyes with it. Hugo kept moving forward, a grin on the exposed lower half of his face.

Wil didn't realize what was going on until Hugo disappeared and seemingly reappeared next to him. He'd used his trick against him. The real mage extended his index and pinky fingers and had a charge of electricity of his own. Wil had just enough time to realize how much it was going to hurt before Hugo jabbed two fingers into his side.

The world blanked out for a second. All thought left him and he existed in nothingness for the longest second of his life before he crashed back to awareness on the ground, twitching violently. He wasn't in danger of dying, but his limbs wouldn't answer him. Just like that, it was over.

Hugo and his slaves approached. Wil's fingers clutched at nothing as he worked to get back control. The ogre and the demon each grabbed him by an arm and dragged him to his knees. The thirteen thralls hadn't even been needed in the fight and he'd still lost.

Wil wanted to laugh, but real fear gripped him now. If he was going to survive this, there was only one chance, and it was all based on how much Hugo wanted to gloat. He eyed Isom, full of regret. Not saving him hurt almost as bad as everything else.

"So," said Hugo, twirling his wand between two fingers. "Remember when you said you could beat me in a duel? No."

"Guess not," said Wil, laughing breathlessly. "Shouldn't have downed the ship. Should've saved it all for you."

Hugo nodded, grinning with excitement. He pointed the wand at Wil's forehead, making the end glow. "Do you have any last words before I put you down, Wilbur? Want me to deliver any final words to your girlfriend or parents?"

"Yeah," said Wil. "I do have something to say before you kill me. Something that might change things."

"The suspense is killing me," said Hugo. "What?"

This was it. Wil bared his teeth in a defiant smile. "The leyline ripping open? That was me. I did that. I found out how to change leylines, and as far as I know I'm the only person in the world who does."

Hugo stared at him in silence before laughing. "Yeah, right. You managed to discover something some of our top researchers haven't been able to do for decades."

"Why do you think I made the promise to the fae?" Wil asked. "I knew I could do it. I could close this all behind . . . or open it up wider. And if you kill me, no one will ever know what I know."

The mage looked uncertain now. He lowered his wand. "And you . . . what, want to trade that knowledge for your life? You know we could get it from you after enough interrogation."

"Maybe," said Wil. He paused, and then said, "But wouldn't you rather get that information yourself? Come on in, if you dare."

Again Hugo laughed. He twirled his wand between his fingers, betraying his interest. "Oh, come on. Do you think I'm able to be goaded like a child? Is this your big last-minute play? Have me break into your mind and take the information from you, while you turn the tables on me?"

"Absolutely," said Wil, unable to keep himself from sounding smug.

Hugo put his wand away. "I hate that you're right. Okay, Wilbur. If you want me to tear through your mind and come out with the way to take more from leylines . . . Well, I can hardly refuse, can I? Besides, what a perfect way to beat you in every way imaginable on the same day."

They made eye contact. Pain pierced Wil's brain as Hugo invaded his mind.

CHAPTER 55

Mind Over Matter

Hugo wasn't gentle as he forced his way in, but the pain was the least of Wil's concerns. The change from the real world to being dragged under in his own mind could've been terrifying, but he welcomed the relief from the aches and pains. He wasn't at his best, but now he was in a place where he ruled and the weaknesses of the flesh were left behind.

"Oh my, you've changed the place since I was here last," Hugo called out. He'd landed in downtown Harper Valley, in front of city hall. It was still night, and a full moon loomed overhead. "I guess I shouldn't be surprised that you modeled it after your backwater town. You are a sap, McKenzie. Now, where's the information on leylines?"

"*Why don't you go look?*" Wil shot back, his voice coming from everywhere. His body was nowhere to be seen. He didn't need a body in his mind; he had awareness of everything Hugo said and did. "*You've made a fatal mistake in coming here, Hugo. You've fallen right into my trap!*"

Wil's laughter echoed throughout the mindscape. Hugo scowled and pointed at city hall. Fire burst from his hands, torching the building. It caught instantly and turned into a small inferno. "I'll just have to burn my way through until there's nothing left of your mind. How do you feel about *that*?"

Wil decided not to answer. Hugo scoffed and took a step away from the burning building, tripping over a suddenly upraised stone and falling flat on his face. It wouldn't do more than annoy him, but it made Wil smile.

Hugo stood with a scowl. In response, he tried to torch the rest of the buildings in downtown Harper Valley, but nothing happened. That more than anything annoyed him. "What, so you hid everything essential? You think I won't find how to hurt you?" The mage disappeared from view.

Reappearing on the McKenzie farm, Hugo wasted no time walking up to the house. "There's no way a sentimental sap like you wouldn't keep something important here." He made it to the porch, fire lighting up from his wand.

He wasn't ready for the house to come alive and devour him. As Hugo stepped onto the porch, the front door opened and sucked him in. The house chomped down on the mage, with the nasty crunch of wood splintering and breaking as it chewed viciously.

"Funny thing about mindscapes, Hugo. You deal with a bastard of a teacher like you, you learn to be creative and careful with how you defend yourself. Now you? Your defense is just being willing to overpower anyone who comes knocking. That doesn't work here."

The house spat a bruised and bloodied Hugo out the front door. He skidded across the dirt, coming to a stop. The house laughed in a deep, demonic voice before it returned to normal. The mage picked himself up. Within seconds his wounds closed up, but he was still bruised.

"Okay, I'll play your game. You want to hide? Ready or not, here we come." Hugo made a pulling motion with his hand. Images of his thralls came into existence around him. "Spread out and search!" he commanded. "Destroy anything you find!"

All of them dispersed, spreading to all corners of the mental construct. Wil wasn't the least bit worried. They weren't real, or real enough, anyway. The little slivers of consciousness the thralls had were tied to Hugo, meaning he was splitting his attention fourteen ways. The fool.

The elementals searched the farms, while the ogre and pixie checked the forest. The demon flew up to Skalet Peak, to where they were fighting in the real world. Almost every building and shop and home in town was searched. All but the two places Wil left vulnerable. Everyone was more powerful in their head, but few were as prepared as Wil. Hugo had only himself to blame for how things went.

The elementals found themselves attacked by a Nullbear. *The* Nullbear, still larger than life in Wil's memory. It tore them to shreds. The demon was attacked by Skalet himself, guarding the portal to Faerie. Lightning lit up the town for a second before unmaking the demon. The pixie and ogre were shot by shadows of the sheriff and his deputies.

The previously empty mindscape came to life as shadowy versions of his friends, his neighbors, his nightmares, and his enemies filled the world and swarmed Hugo's minions. Hugo stood in the center of the town, reeling from the systematic destruction of his mental constructs.

"What's wrong, Hugo? Are slaves not doing you any favors in here? I thought you were more powerful than me. Prove it!"

Hugo and his copy of Isom whirled around wildly as if they could fight off the horde of shades charging for them. Hugo hurled bolt after bolt of entropic red energy at the shades, but they passed through them harmlessly. When they washed over Hugo and the wampus cat, they grabbed hold, pulling them down and sinking teeth into them.

This time Hugo screamed in pain as they did no damage but injected a memory into him. The time Wil broke his arm, the way the fight with Jeb had made him feel, the times at the academy he'd nearly quit, and all the times Hugo had slapped him around. The mage experienced them all in first person, sometimes at the same time.

"You know what your problem is? You're not very creative. You're a dumb thug with more muscle than sense. You're strong magically and you've got a decent will, but what does that matter when you've lost control? I can keep this up all night, Hugo. Can you?"

The shades hammered the mage again and again and all Hugo could do was scream. He closed his eyes and centered himself with one of the most basic of meditation techniques. Breathing in and out, Hugo focused and the shades all disappeared. He picked himself up, shaking violently.

"I don't have to. Who cares if you know how to change leylines? If you can do it, then I can do it too. I think I'll just kill you now." Hugo started to withdraw from Wil's mind.

Wil didn't let him. He directed his full mental power toward grabbing hold of Hugo and squeezing him. The mage thrashed around but couldn't get free. Wil could feel the real fear in him. He let his laughter drift in through the wind, echoing louder and smothering his enemy with his disdain.

The moon in the sky shrank as it drifted into the distance. Night turned to day and then twilight as the sun went around. The stars rearranged themselves until they formed an outline of Wil, with the sun and moon as his eyes and a distant galaxy as his mouth.

"Did I say you could leave?" Wil demanded, squeezing until Hugo could hardly breathe. *"I dealt with years of your crap, and now I have you right where I want you. You're not surviving this."*

Hugo's eyes widened in abject terror. "You . . . wouldn't . . ." he wheezed. Wil lightened his grip so he could speak. "You ever have someone die in your mind? A piece of me would be here forever."

The stars twinkled in amusement. *"Do you think I couldn't bury you so deep I'd forget about you? Any final words?"*

Wil was not normally a sadistic person, but he would've been lying if he'd said he wasn't enjoying feeling his enemy, his tormentor, mortally afraid. Mostly though, it was the satisfaction of a plan well executed, and a desire to see it through.

Hugo fought with everything he had, but his strength was flagging. It was his last, desperate burst of strength that freed him from Wil's grasp. He pulled away, struggling to escape. Finally, Wil let him go and followed him.

It was a shame, going from nearly omnipotent in his mind to being a guest in Hugo's, but Wil was more than ready for it. He had a plan and knew where to strike, and the mage was shaken.

The academy grounds were already on high alert. Hugo wasted no time firing up his defenses. Wil hit the ground running and took off down one of the halls as copies of Hugo's thralls appeared around him.

"Catch me if you can!" Wil cried out before disappearing. He reappeared outside of the classroom where Master Krine had taught Hugo and then Hugo had taught Wil. He conjured a ball of shifting colors and hurled it inside the classroom. Flashing, strobing lights made the entire world shake violently.

The imp came screaming toward Wil, and he led it on a merry chase, speeding through Hugo's mind faster than rumors spread on campus. He found the first statue he was looking for. The ogre, one of Hugo's biggest enforcers. Wil touched the statue but didn't let himself get pulled all the way to its consciousness.

He gave it a single command through the connection. Then he tried something he desperately hoped would work. He took a step back and formed a glowing green ball of pulsating energy. His explosively volatile missile was bigger than he'd ever made it in the real world. He slammed it into the statue just as the imp arrived.

The explosion rocked the entire mindscape and sent Wil crashing against a wall. The metaphysical air was knocked from his lungs, but the statue was gone, as well as all senses of the connection. Wil hopped back to his feet, letting out a triumphant whoop.

Hugo appeared beside him, looking haggard. "What the hell have you done?" he demanded.

"Nothing compared to what I'm about to, Hugo," said Wil with a manic grin. "You've dug your own grave." He disappeared again.

The walls came to life, arms reaching out of them, but Wil moved through the mindscape faster, skating by the demon as it tried to slice him open with its tail. He reversed direction and punched the demon, concentrating as he made contact with it. The attack did nothing, but it gave Wil the information he needed.

A second later, he appeared in the academy's drama department, where the demon's statue watched over a ghostly performance. Will didn't hesitate and touched the statue, giving it a command before he blew it apart too. The blast knocked him off the balcony and onto the ground.

Wil launched fireworks above him, loud and flashing, another distraction before he disappeared. He was a man on a mission, and Hugo soon caught up to him, crashing into him from behind. The two rolled along the ground. Wil fought to get free as the mage wrapped his hands around Wil's throat.

It might not have been real, but the panic and sense of not being able to breathe was. Wil struggled, but Hugo was more powerful in his own mind and had anger behind it to make it stick. If he kept it up, Wil would be ejected from his mind again. No way would he let that happen.

A knee into Hugo's crotch was equally unreal, but it mattered as much as the choking. Hugo's grip softened, and Wil slammed his head into Hugo's nose. The two rolled over and Wil covered his face with a hand and cast the highest, shrillest, most obnoxious aural illusion Wil could imagine.

Hugo convulsed and the mindscape roiled. Wil disappeared and reappeared elsewhere, back on his mission to find the other statues. The floor shifted constantly under him, trying to suck him under, and spikes and darts erupted from the walls. Wil twisted and turned, almost serene in his intense focus. None of those mattered. He just needed to find— There! The imp was on the statue in front of the school, where it shouldn't be.

Wil hopped up and gave a different command from the others. Hugo appeared before he destroyed it. He grabbed Wil by the arm and slammed him into it.

"You think I don't know what you're doing to me? Very clever, but it won't be enough. I don't need all my servants to end you, and I'll just get them back when we're done here. You've done *nothing*."

"Yeah? Then why do you sound so scared?" Wil laughed and pulled away, letting his arm rip off. Hugo recoiled with it, looking on in shocked horror. Then Wil blew it up in Hugo's arms, taking out the statue and Hugo as well. The mage disappeared, which gave Wil just a little more time.

His strength was fading now. He'd already been tired, and the brief boost from the fight in his mind helped, but now he was running out of time. One more ought to do it, but which one? Grinning, Wil took a chance. He headed for his old room.

Sure enough, where his bed had been was Isom's statue. The wampus cat was crouched in a dangerous pose, mouth open and showing off his fangs, one of them broken. Wil put his hand on Isom's head and let himself be drawn in.

He saw Hugo's back in real life, just a couple of feet away from Isom. More than that, he felt Isom himself, or what was left of him. His predatory friend still had enough left to mourn what he lost, to buck against the control and want out. He was damaged, but not broken, and Wil's heart sang. Maybe it wasn't too late.

Isom, I'm here. I'll get you out of here. But you need to obey me. I think you'll enjoy this.

Dark mirth answered him, muted but clear. Then Hugo hauled Wil away from the statue and flung him to the ground. Wil landed and found he couldn't move. The ground wrapped around his limbs, and Hugo directed all of his strength to keep Wil there. He couldn't fight it, so he didn't.

"Looks like you got me, Hugo. It was a good try, wasn't it?" Wil laughed weakly. The statue was just a foot away. Would it be enough? Could he pull this off? He wasn't sure if it mattered. He was tired, and his connection to the mindscape was slipping.

"It was especially annoying," said Hugo. "So, well done, I guess. But let this be a reminder: just because you have good mental defenses doesn't mean you were ever suited to assaulting another. You are too weak for that. You always were."

"You're right," said Wil as he laughed one last time. "But guess what?"

Hugo had just enough time to groan as Wil released one final attack. He discharged everything he had, his entire mental construct, overloaded himself, and let the explosion kick him out of Hugo's mind.

The real world was colder than Wil remembered, but that could've been the psychic and magical stress making him weak enough to drop. He did just that, though the demon and ogre were still holding him up.

Hugo recoiled as he, too, came back. Blood poured from his nose and ears, and Wil knew he probably looked just as bad, if not worse.

"A . . . a valiant last-ditch effort," said Hugo. "A lot of big talk. Made it more satisfying at least. Goodbye, Wilbur McKenzie." He raised his wand once more.

The imp crashed into his face, scratching and clawing. Hugo dropped his wand and struggled to pull it off him. He threw it to the ground and kicked it. The imp had gouged out chunks of his cheeks and nose.

"You bastard," he seethed. "You absolute—" The ogre dropped Wil and punched Hugo in the face. The mage tripped over Isom, and then it was over. The demon, ogre, imp, and Isom all turned on the mind mage. Isom purred loudly, stalking forward.

"N-no, no!" Hugo screamed before the wampus cat went in for the kill. Wil collapsed onto the snow, head and body throbbing. The last thing he heard before darkness took him was the sound of eating.

CHAPTER 56

Mutiny on the *Flying Calamity*

Wil wasn't woken so much as booted from unconsciousness. One of the elvish defenders shook him until the heavy darkness lifted and he was, unfortunately, aware once more.

"Wizard! Are you okay?" The elf patted his cheeks until he groaned and waved her off.

"I'll live. Probably." The pain in Wil's head pulsed in time with his heart. There was no way he could do any more mind magic. Possibly any magic at all. Even at the summit with the broken leyline and with Faerie just in his sensory range, he was tapped out. He sat up. "Where's Hugo?"

The elf motioned with her head at a bloody patch of snow just within view. Nine of the mage's thralls stood in the place where they'd been when Wil passed out.

"Eaten by the wampus cat. The cat and three others wandered off when the mage died, but these remained. They're not doing anything, just standing there."

Well, there was a good news/bad news situation if he'd ever heard of one. Isom was free again, and he'd eaten a powerful wizard. Maybe he'd get that fateful duel after all. This was the first time Wil had killed another human being, albeit indirectly. His head hurt too much to worry about it yet.

"What about the soldiers?" Wil pressed. The fire on the ship had been contained, but parts of it still smoldered, a gentle glow in the darkness. "Did they attack?"

"No," said the gnome who warded the area. "That's the damnedest thing. After the other wizard got et, they pulled back and stayed there. I haven't dropped our shields, though. And I'm not going to."

"Good," said Wil. "Smart thinking." He got to his feet and managed to stay upright. If it wasn't for the threat of war still looming, napping right there in camp was tempting. It took a few seconds for his brain to start working again, but when it did, he realized the *Flying Calamity* was possibly an asset.

"Wait here. If I don't come back soon, then . . ." Wil grimaced. "Then we're probably all doomed anyway."

"Do you want an escort? Someone to watch your back?" The elf rested her hands on her twin daggers, and he had no doubt she could use them well.

"Honestly?" Wil chuckled, wincing at the sudden throbbing. "I'd love an escort, but I think I should go this alone for now. If they see you, they might panic." Of course, they might shoot him on sight. If they did, at least the headache would go away.

He lumbered forward on unsteady legs, hands held up to show he wasn't a threat. Not that it meant much, coming from a wizard, but anything to make sure the crew of the *Flying Calamity* gave him a chance. He had gotten within fifty feet of the ship when the first sentry spotted him.

"Halt!" a young man barked. Wil obeyed, staying perfectly still. "The town wizard is here," the sentry called back to his superior officer.

It wasn't Captain Nesbitt but his first mate. She was a canny-looking woman, in her forties, perhaps, with tattoos covering both arms. She wore a simple leather vest with the captain's badge stuck on. She pushed past the crew and stopped a short distance before Wil. She kept her hand on her sidearm but didn't draw it.

"Hello," said Wil, speaking slowly. "Whom do I have the pleasure of addressing?"

She looked at him thoughtfully. "First ma— Ahem. Acting captain Laverne Barclay. Were you the one who blew us out of the sky? Where's Mage Jefferson?"

Wil winced. "Yeah, that was me. I'm sorry about that, by the way. Was anyone hurt?"

Barclay laughed bitterly. "You blew a ten-foot hole in the hull and we crashed. What the hell do you think? No one died, but that crash injured over half our crew and scared the crap out of the rest of us. Jefferson?"

This was the hard part. If he was honest, he was a traitor and they'd be honor-bound to arrest or kill him. If he lied, they might turn on him for that if they found out otherwise. Unless . . . "What happened to Captain Nesbitt?" Wil asked. "Hugo said something happened to him."

The first mate looked like she wanted to hit someone. "Jefferson happened to him. He tried to stop and get confirmation from Cloverton that we were good to, you know, assault another world. Jefferson did something. Now the captain's not dead, but he ain't responding either."

"Would you say that you liked Captain Nesbitt?" Wil chanced. "Obviously you don't need to like him to obey orders, but would I be wrong in saying the crew wasn't happy about what happened?"

Barclay said nothing, which Wil chose to take as a good sign. "Hugo Jefferson attacked your captain, threatened you all, tried to start an illegal war, and then tried to murder me. I held him off until he lost control of his mind-controlled thralls. Mage Jefferson is dead now."

She visibly slumped with relief. "Thank the gods for that, at least," she said. "I'm now stuck here with nearly a hundred injured sailors, an out-of-commission captain, and a ship that's pretty much destroyed. What a *mess*."

Hope shimmered. "You and your crew did nothing wrong. You were threatened into following illegal orders. If you show me your captain, I might be able to help him."

"Well, why didn't you say so?" Acting Captain Barclay grabbed him by the sleeve and jerked him forward.

They avoided the morass Wil had created and went through a makeshift camp of surly sailors, most of whom looked at Wil with a mix of fear and irritation. He could hardly blame them. This close to the ship, Wil had a better chance to look at the damage he'd inflicted. A hole went clean through, and the front of the ship had cracked and splintered upon landing. The vessel lay on its side, with some of the crew working to get supplies out. Other than that, it looked mostly okay.

Captain Nesbitt lay in a sleeping bag in a tent set up for command. His eyes were open but unfocused, and his breathing was uneven. "How long has he been like this?"

"About an hour. They got into a heated argument and then suddenly the captain stopped talking. He collapsed and Jefferson started laughing." Barclay grimaced. "After that, the mage barked orders and only one person dared to defy him. He's in the same condition. Can you do something about it?"

Not with this piercing headache and fatigue. Wil crouched down by the captain and peered into his empty eyes. Pain flared again, but Wil wasn't projecting himself into his mind, just taking a peek.

Unlike most of the thralls, the captain hadn't sustained much damage. Hugo hadn't torn up the captain's mind so much as clubbed him over the head and stuffed him into a closet inside himself. It wouldn't even take much to pull him out of it, but Wil hesitated.

The job was only half done. Hugo was dealt with, but there was still Timothy Twist and Grimnar and that whole headache. The kind thing to do would be to heal the captain and then go to Faerie. But . . . maybe the smart thing would be to leverage it. Wil didn't want to be that manipulative, but lives were at stake. This was bigger than him.

"I can heal him," said Wil, "but not yet. My magic is drained and we're not out of danger. There's still a war to avert, and I might need your help, Captain Barclay."

The woman cringed at the title. "Just Barclay is fine. What do you need from me? If it'll get the captain back on his feet, I'm happy to do it."

There was no time to feel guilty. The only thing he could do was use the advantage. Wil stood and centered himself. "I need to get to Faerie. The fae will let me and a small number of you through, and I'll need a guard as the acting representative of Calipan. I need your legitimacy, you understand?"

She did. Looking back down at Captain Nesbitt, Barclay nodded. "Yeah. If Jefferson's whining was right, you want to prevent war. Yeah, I'll back you. For now. What else?"

Wil tried not to look too relieved. "I need Freddie and Maxwell brought to me, along with the peace treaty we all agreed on."

Barclay looked at him as if he had two heads. "Peace treaty? After all of that, you think the peace treaty is still possible?"

Wil shrugged. "I'm tired, in a lot of pain, and things much bigger than me are getting out of control. It's the only plan I've got, but I think I can make it work with your help. Do that, and as soon as my head clears up, I'll heal Captain Nesbitt's mind. You have my word, Barclay."

"Jefferson hated you," she said. "Called you soft, an idealist, and delusional. I can see two out of three of those. But maybe you gotta have delusions to make your ideals happen. Give me fifteen minutes and you'll have an honor guard and the treaty ready."

Wil bowed his head in gratitude. They left the tent, and he collapsed on a nearby fallen log in front of the fire, along with several members of the crew. A sailor offered Wil his flask. The wizard happily took a swig and gave it back, letting himself rest and enjoy the warmth while the first mate worked.

Freddie and Maxwell looked surprised to be conscripted into the plan, but neither of them were opposed to it. Getting ten sailors to accompany Wil under his command took a bit longer, but they managed to get a group of either uninjured or lightly bruised men and women to protect him and project strength.

On their approach, the fae stood in alarm. Seeing Wil at the head of the group, they didn't immediately attack, but the elf who had woken him called out, "What's the meaning of this?"

"We're going to Faerie," said Wil, "on a mission of peace. I'd humbly like to ask ten of you to join me, to form a coalition of humans and fae working together to stop war. Timothy Twist attacked us and we're going right to the council to talk about it. I ask for some of you to join me, to show our commitment to a better future. Barring that, just let us through. Please."

Pleading was a dangerous prospect, but the situation seemed appropriate. The elf woman looked at him shrewdly. "They were shooting at us just now."

A sailor in Wil's group coughed. "We're really sorry about that," he said, blundering into Obligation. "We want to make up for it."

A mutter arose through the fae. They all looked to the elf for guidance. She pursed her lips and said, "Do I have your word that you will not attack first?"

"You do," said Wil. "I promise that we will only defend ourselves, and anyone who starts something will be dealt with appropriately by me."

The pros and cons warred on her face. Finally, she sighed. "Fine. With your vows, we'll send some people along. If you betray us or make a mistake . . ."

Wil smiled humorlessly. "Then we're all doomed."

CHAPTER 57

A Major Favor

They made sure their elf and ogre guards went through first and announced them. Had Wil simply walked into Faerie with his human crew and immediately gotten peppered with arrows or curses, it would have been a very poor showing. Instead, they stood there for a good five minutes while their vanguard made sure the way was clear, and then through the ring of mushrooms they went.

As much of a relief as it was to be back in Faerie, soaking up the raw magic in the air, the first thing Wil saw was a small army camped out in front of the capital. Fear spiked as he realized just how long in advance Twist and Grimnar must've been planning this. And Wil hadn't seen any of it until people were toads.

"You sure they won't attack us?" one of the sailors whispered to Wil.

Wil shook his head. "Not sure at all, but we don't have many options. Just keep your weapons close and don't point them at anyone unless you have to. Strength, not aggression."

"Yessir, strength it is." They walked through the lush, vibrant meadow, between war parties of all of the fae's strongest fighters. They received curious, sullen stares, but no one attacked them.

Wil stayed in the center as fae preceded him and humans trailed behind and to the side. It wasn't far to the great tree itself, but they maintained a steady, even pace, though Wil's anxiety was screaming at him to run.

They were, naturally, stopped at the opening. "What's the meaning of this?" A surprisingly eloquent troll motioned for others to join him in guarding the doors. "You bring weapons and troops to Faerie!?"

"I do," said Wil, and his entourage parted for him. He stepped forward, leaning heavily on his staff for support. "I am the human representative, and I believe there is a meeting going on that requires my presence."

The troll grunted his disbelief. "We were told by Timothy Twist that—"

"Timothy Twist is trying to start a war," Wil snapped. "And from the looks of it, the rest of you don't seem to mind at all. Well, over my dead body. I'm going to that meeting, and if I have to tear my way through all of you, I'll do so. But I don't want to do that. Please let us through."

The troll grunted. "You alone can go through the portal. I'll not have any more humans in the council room, and certainly not armed soldiers!"

The sailors nearest Wil looked to him for confirmation. He held a hand up, nodding. "That's agreeable. They'll wait outside the portal room, along with some of your men. Is that acceptable? Wait here, gentlemen," Wil directed to the two men from Cloverton. "I'll call you when we need you."

The way to the portal room was as short as Wil remembered, but much better guarded. He had to wait, eating up precious time he didn't have, before they let him through. He went down the spiraling stairs to the basement where the portal waited, ever-shifting images flashing in and out of focus.

For a second, Wil wondered if it could be a trap, another surprise from Twist to stop him from interfering, but nothing happened. He touched the portal and was yanked forward and stretched until he snapped into the council chambers. This time, he didn't scream as much.

Unlike his last several visits to the council chambers, the massive room was full of witnesses. Four of the five fae representatives sat on their thrones, while Twist had the floor and paced back and forth. He stopped upon seeing Wil, shock and a hint of fear on his face.

". . . and so, you can see now why war is inevitable," said Twist, "and our best option is a first strike. Hit them and take Harper Valley before they know what's happening."

"You can't do that!" Wil cried, stepping forward. "It's not too late. We can still prevent war. Where are Bram and Darlene?" He looked around. Hundreds of fae faces gathered around the edges of the room, but no other humans.

"They are safe," Skalet boomed. The dragon sat upright and alert, a world of difference from their last meeting. *"With war possible, we thought it best to secure them elsewhere."*

"You took Bram and Darlene as prisoners? For a war Twist is trying to start?"

"It's a war your people started and we have a chance to finish," said Grimnar, smiling with deep satisfaction. "And now there's nothing to stop us."

"Nothing except a council vote," said Syl pointedly. "You still might fail to get the votes you need."

"Might I?" Twist crowed laughter. "Dear Skalet, have I not convinced you? You know as I do what kind of creatures humans are like. How vengeful and greedy. With this simple, easily reversed prank, they're chomping at the bit to kill us all. Grimnar and I were right about everything."

A pit settled in Wil's stomach. He looked at the dragon, hope in his eyes. "It doesn't have to be that way, King. My friends and I are proof of that. Our town is proof of it. We welcomed people in and showed them a good time. Until this happened—"

"Are you saying there were no problems?" Grimnar scoffed. "No issues that might've gotten worse? Everything was fine?"

"Of course not everything was fine," said Arabella. Wil had never seen her tense before. She looked about as on edge as Syl, who was relatively silent after his rough night.

"There were small issues, but that's diplomacy. We were handling them, and we had a great chance to fix it all. Until you ruined those chances, Twist." Arabella took a deep breath. "War or not, there will be consequences for your actions."

"I'll happily accept," said Twist. "Live, die, we're all in the same boat now!"

"Enough," Skalet growled. *"You have made your point, Twist. You have my deepest regrets, Wizard. While I may hold some respect for you, I do not feel the same about the rest of your kind. What Timothy Twist did was foolish, but it set us on a course I do not believe we can change. On the matter at hand, I vote for war. We must strike first, or else we will surely die when the humans invade."*

"No." Wil's legs turned to rubber. "No, don't do this, there's still time. I can fix this!"

"I think not, Wilbur McKenzie," said Timothy Twist. He climbed back onto his throne with the satisfied smile of a cat with a mouse. "The Wee Folk also vote for war. Win or lose, we'll put this matter to rest and will no longer have to hide from the world we lost."

Gods, this was happening. With Skalet and Timothy Twist, the deciding vote would go to Grimnar. The ogre looked positively ecstatic that he would finally have his war. If Wil did nothing, the vote would go through and who knows what they'd do with him. He had no strength left to fight. He could barely argue.

"Very well," said Grimnar, fingers tapping a tattoo against the arm of his throne. "On the matter of war versus Calipan, I vote—"

Wil breathed in deeply and took in the power of Faerie. Not a lot, just enough to wave his hand and silence Grimnar before he could finish his sentence. Hundreds of faces turned his way, gasping at the interference.

"Wil," Syl warned, shaking his head.

"Wizard, you cannot stop a lawful vote," Skalet chided him.

"I'm not trying to stop it," said Wil, as panic wormed its way through him. If only Twist hadn't gotten there first. All because . . . Wil smiled with the realization. He could call on the connection between himself and Grimnar when he focused on it. There was the answer.

"The vote will go on, but before it does, I am calling in the favor Grimnar owes me. Would anyone here stand in the way of Grimnar fulfilling an Obligation he owes?"

Murmurs passed through the crowd. The story had spread of their fight, but maybe not of the favor. The ogre's orange, rocklike face twisted into a scowl. Wil released the spell, swallowing hard with even that strain.

"And what is it you would have me do, honored foe?" Grimnar said stiffly, irritated he had to go along with it.

Wil smiled. "I want you to vote for peace and trade."

Syl blinked. Arabella looked between him and the ogre, while Twist froze entirely. Grimnar himself barked out derisive laughter.

"Do you think it's that simple? That you can stop this war that way? Our job is done. The war is coming, Wilbur."

"I want you to vote for peace and trade," Wil repeated.

Grimnar took a long, deep breath and continued as if Wil hadn't said anything. "When your government hears of the attack on your town, the fighting will start. Even if you were able to reverse the transformation into toads, do you think those humans would forgive us? They will demand satisfaction."

"Let me worry about them," said Wil, no longer afraid. "I want you to vote for peace and trade. Thrice now I've asked, and now I ask no longer. I demand you vote for peace and the trade agreement we had already settled on before this unfortunate incident. I can smooth it over on the human side. I just need that vote. You owe me, Grimnar. Fulfill your Obligation." Wil smiled as their oath connection coursed powerfully through them. He could see the ogre felt it, too, and wondered if Grimnar could also feel the start of the cost of denying him.

The ogre king slumped. "I'll have your head one day, Wilbur McKenzie," he whispered.

"We've seen how that would play out," Wil said evenly.

Grimnar took a deep breath and announced loudly, "The Ogre Federation votes . . . I vote for peace and trade with the humans."

Arabella wasted no time in continuing. "I vote for peace and trade with the humans," she said. "And I am also in favor of handing Twist over to them if they happen to need a pound of flesh."

And then it was just Syl, looking tired, worn, and beaten all to hell. "After tonight, I can see why people want war," he said, smiling sadly at Wil. "But I could never. If you have a plan you say will fix things, then I trust you. I vote for peace with the humans."

Twist buried his face in his hands, letting out a dramatic moan. "Peace has it. Damn you, McKenzie!"

Skalet growled a low, deep rumble that made Wil's teeth vibrate. *"Now tell us how you plan on stopping the war."*

Wil nodded. "Happy to. But first, I want Bram, Darlene, and the humans I brought. I'm going to need them."

"It will be done," Skalet promised.

This was it. One more major disaster averted, and just one remained. Now, more than ever, Wil knew how close they were to lasting peace.

CHAPTER 58

Peace at Last

"Wil!" Darlene and Bram practically tackled him as they crushed him in a hug. Or Bram crushed both of them. Either way, it was as pleasant as it was painful.

"Hey," he squeaked, tapping out against Bram's shoulder. "What a night, huh?"

"That's what you have to say for yourself?" Darlene pulled away, shaking her head in disbelief. "What happened to Hugo, and Twist, and everything else?"

Wil took a deep breath, opened his mouth, and then paused. "It's a long story and I'll tell it to you when things are calmer. The important thing right now is the treaty, and ramming it through before we have to do even more damage control."

"So it's not too late?" Bram wrung his hands.

"That remains to be seen," said Wil, "but we have to move fast. Where are . . . There. Hold on just a second."

Freddie and Maxwell, the policy advisor and the secretary, stood awkwardly nearby. After the last couple of weeks of being pushed around by Hugo, they were well-trained in silence and staying out of the way. Wil motioned for them to approach.

"Uh, hi," said Freddie, looking nervous. Wil couldn't blame him.

"What can we do to help?" Maxwell was a short, pale, dark-haired man in spectacles who fidgeted constantly.

"I want you to make a couple of quick alterations to the peace treaty, and then we're going to all sign it. You will then record it as legit."

Silence.

Maxwell shifted uncomfortably. "Mage Jefferson is the duly appointed representative of Calipan. Or was. With him out of the way, shouldn't we wire Cloverton with requests for instructions?"

Freddie shook his head vehemently. "We don't have to. If we did, they might just declare war and accept us as casualties. No, I believe that with Hugo out of commission and killed by his own creatures, then clearly there has been no wrongdoing and Master McKenzie would be fit to serve in his place. If he were to declare it time to sign and the others joined in, it would be legitimate."

It was just as Wil had hoped for. "Then all we have to do is make a few tiny adjustments to smooth away the last rough edges and then get them all to sign. Can I trust you gentleman to help me with this?"

Maxwell hesitated, but Freddie nodded. "If it will stop the war and still get Calipan favorable trading conditions, I can make it work," he said. "But if the cabinet members, or even the president, aren't happy with how this plays out, they might do something about it. To you, and possibly even your town."

Bram looked appropriately horrified, but Darlene just became more resolute. "We've got this," she said. "Wil has this."

"Thank you," he said. He turned to the two Cloverton men. "I'll take full responsibility for all of this. Just stay behind me and I'll do the talking."

"Yeah, no problem," Maxwell muttered. "Been doing that all trip anyway."

With that taken care of, Wil led them to the ring before the thrones, where the representatives of Faerie waited. Arabella was excited by this turn of events. Syl dozed, draped over his chair, as the elf princess often was in hers. Grimnar looked defeated, and Timothy Twist, for some reason, looked as pleased as ever.

"Leaders of Faerie, I have our solution," said Wil. "We will proceed with the peace treaty as it was written, with a couple of quick corrections in light of recent events."

Grimnar barked out bitter laughter. "Not enough that you beat me, here come the humiliation and punishments."

"Yes," said Wil honestly. "The mass poisoning of Harper Valley citizens will be forgiven and understood to be a joke in extremely poor taste. However, the perpetrator of the frog prank will step down as leader of the Wee Folk and be subject to whatever justice the updated council sees fit, with the understanding that he is never to have power or be allowed in Calipan again. Is this understood?"

"Aye," said Timothy Twist. "No need to vote on that one. I accept. You got me, Wizard, fair and square."

"Really?" Wil scoffed. "After all the plotting and scheming, you'll go along with it without causing a commotion or mucking things up again? I'm going to want your oath on that."

"You'll have it. You gave me the greatest gift of all, Wilbur: surprise! I was two seconds away from victory, and you snatched it out of the jaws of defeat. Well done!" The little man clapped enthusiastically without a hint of sarcasm or mischief. "I'll resign from the council and accept whatever judgment I get."

"What else, Wizard?" Skalet asked, staring at him with uncomfortable intensity. Wil couldn't tell whether the dragon approved or disapproved, but at least he was listening.

"The same goes for Grimnar," said Wil. "For trying to orchestrate a war against my people and interfering with the diplomatic mission, he's to be removed from his position. He and Twist will sign the treaty and then make way for new leadership. Those are the two biggest changes to the document, but I am adding another one as well.

"All wizards will be prohibited from entering Faerie. Only magic-negative humans will be allowed through, as a matter of safety." He hated that it seemed necessary. After a long night of fighting and pulling miracles out of a hat, the only thing keeping Wil from collapsing from exhaustion was how invigorating just being there was.

"Really?" Darlene asked from behind him. "Even you?"

Wil closed his eyes. "Only by direct invitation can a human wizard enter Faerie. Is that acceptable?"

"I find it acceptable," said Syl. "As far as I'm concerned, you'll have a standing invitation. Others though . . . It's a wise decision."

"Seconded," said Arabella. "I would also like to include allowances for any humans to spend extended time in Faerie when invited by a member of the council." She smiled mischievously.

Wil rolled his eyes. "I don't know what you see in my brother, but you can have him as long as you want. None of us will complain. The final thing is that the people turned into toads will require a bribe as an apology."

"Sure, shake us down for gold and silver while you're at it," grumbled Grimnar.

Skalet growled, and it sounded approving. It reminded Wil of something. "King Skalet," he began, "I have news I think you would like to hear. The wizard who cursed you is dead, and so is his apprentice, who similarly enslaved creatures."

"By your hand?"

Wil paused. "By his slaves' hands, on my order."

The dragon said nothing else, but rumbled louder, and Wil felt that sense of favor, always just barely out of notice, pulsing and warm. Skalet may have voted for war, but he was just as glad to avoid it.

"Then that's it," said Wil. "Tomorrow we'll sign. We're going to usher in a new era of peace, cooperation, and understanding between our people. For now, with your leave . . . I really need to rest."

The quarters Bram and the others had been held in were still free. Wil spent the entire walk there leaning against his best friend, who had no problem keeping the wizard upright. Darlene flanked him on the other side, carrying his staff for him. Wil had just enough energy to make the wall open. They went inside and Wil collapsed on the couch with a groan.

"I can't believe you did it," said Bram as he went to the small kitchen and got them all something to drink.

Darlene sidled up to Wil, setting his staff on the small table nearby. At first, she said nothing, just hugging his arm and enjoying the peace.

"I can't either," said Wil, as he wrapped his arm around her and held her close. "It got bad after you guys brought Syl back. Hugo came, slapped me around, taunted me, and told me he was going to kill my family. When I was able to leave the jail, I made it up the mountain and blasted the *Flying Calamity* out of the sky. It crashed, and then Hugo came for me.

"We fought, and he beat me. He was right about to kill me when I lured him into my mind, slapped *him* around for a change, and then severed his connection to Isom and a few other slaves. Isom ate him. And you know everything that happened after that." He closed his eyes.

He'd just fallen into a light doze when Darlene said, "So what now? When we go back home there's going to be so much damage to smooth over. A lot of fear, panic, and resentment over the toad incident, you know? Let alone *this*. We have a lot of work ahead of us."

"We do," said Bram, coming around with three mugs. He set them down and handed them out. "But for now we have time to toast and let Wil rest. That's a problem for tomorrow."

Wil took his drink and sniffed it. Whatever it was, it was alcoholic, and that was good enough for him. He took a sip and the mix of potent sweetness with a harsh afterbite delighted him.

"No, that's one of the many things I love about Darlene. She's as bad as I am about never shutting off. We do have a lot of work. We've got to cure Sinclair and the others and make it clear that I handled the retribution and they *will* accept it. Or else. If I have to threaten them, I will. We've got to protect the fae on the farm until we can get the story out that the toad thing was a bad prank, and Hugo overreacted and assaulted Faerie. I stopped the fight."

Wil took another sip of his drink and closed his eyes. Consciousness flickered, and he chuckled, raising his mug. "That's a problem for Tomorrow-Wil. For tonight? Here's to us, here's to the future, and here's to a hard-won peace."

They clinked their mugs. "To a hard-won peace."

CHAPTER 59

Warts and All

It took a few days, but the plan worked. For the most part.

The first thing Wil did was sleep a good twelve hours. He woke long enough to devour a platter of food, then napped for another three hours before he got up for the day. As much as he would've loved the chance to rest and let things go on without him, he had Obligations to fulfill. The most important one was time-sensitive.

Captain Nesbitt remained in the same condition Wil had last seen him in: lying down and staring off into space, breathing slowly and calmly. After the past day, the last thing Wil wanted to do was enter someone's mind, but a promise was a promise. It ached, but Wil dropped right in.

Unsurprisingly, the captain's mindscape resembled the *Flying Calamity*, and other flying ships drifted lazily through the clouds around them. They were in port at the newly constructed sky dock at the Hauser Military Base north of Manifee City. A crew of indistinct sailors scrubbed the deck around Wil, while a version of Barclay barked orders. The only thing missing was the captain himself.

Aside from that, Wil didn't detect any lingering damage or intrusion. Hugo hadn't brutalized Nesbitt, he'd simply sucker punched him and had likely been planning on restoring him when he was done, possibly with a few adjustments to his temperament and memories. With that in mind, Wil didn't stress and even enjoyed his tour of the sky dock. After what felt like half an hour and was maybe two minutes in the real world, he sensed the captain.

Wil followed the feel of him, going lower and lower in the ship until he was near the ground level. He found Captain Nesbitt dressed like a low-ranking sailor, working in the laundry room. He had shackles around his wrists and ankles, and a hard-looking, red-faced man was screaming endless abuse at him.

"You aren't worth a dead cow's fart, Nesbitt! Not once in my life have I *ever* seen someone fail as much as you. We gotta put men like you on the front lines. You'd make a fantastic bullet sponge." Nesbitt continued scrubbing shirts against a washboard with everything he had. He had a far-off, glassy look to him.

Wil silenced the shouting man, and Nesbitt visibly relaxed. Wil went up to the captain and put a hand on his shoulder. "You're a talented and well-respected man with a command and the finest ship in the sky."

Nesbitt shuddered. He looked up from his laundry. Recognition dawned in his eyes. He looked down and jerked uncomfortably. The shackles disappeared and his clothes changed back. Wil smiled and withdrew.

Back in the real world, Wil helped the man back to his feet. Barclay let out a relieved gasp and pushed past Wil, tackling the captain.

"Captain, you're okay!" She hugged him tightly. Nesbitt smiled and patted her twice before gently pushing her away.

"Propriety, Barclay. What happened?"

Wil filled him in, sparing a great many of the details and focusing on Hugo's madness and what he now needed from the captain. To his lack of surprise, Nesbitt agreed with Wil's reasoning and the need for everyone to be on the same page. That solved Wil's next few problems.

With the good captain's help, they managed to get Harper Valley under control again and told a censored and cherry-picked version of what happened. It was just a funny misunderstanding and they'd be okay—they shouldn't worry about it. It didn't matter whether people fully believed it, so long as it bought them time to make it true.

Although the fae leadership went back to Faerie to protect Syl, most of the other guests stayed where they were, trusting in Bob and Sharon's hospitality to protect them. Many of them seemed to genuinely believe in the mission itself, which lifted a lot of weight off Wil's shoulders.

The representatives, who now included Declan and Shak among their ranks, returned to the McKenzie farm to stay for the rest of the season and help build up their hub. Arabella directed most of the action, stepping up while Syl recovered and the two new reps adjusted to the new responsibilities and obligations.

"Keep moving, we're almost done for the day!" Arabella called out, clapping her hands. She didn't lift a hand to do any of the work herself, of course, but she was good at making sure the other elves got things done. "The sooner you're done, the sooner we can retire to some wine and song!"

"I envy how easily she gets back to normal," said Darlene, as she and Wil watched the action. Jeb was among the people working at her command, running back and forth with a focused, eager look to him. "We're all working hard and running ourselves to death, and somehow she manages to make bossing others around look like a chore."

Wil nodded along. "It's harder than it looks. She deserves more credit than she gets. And I'm not just saying that because I need her best healers to turn the mayor and the rest back to human. She's doing a good job."

"I know you said you were bad at transmutation," said Darlene, "do many wizards have trouble with it?"

"Ehhh." Wil wiggled a hand indecisively. "Some. For me, it's because it feels like it should be impossible. Turning one thing into another is like . . . It's like forcing something to be what it's not. And we both know I have trouble with *that*."

"Makes sense." Darlene cupped her hands around her mouth. "Hey, Princess! Can we borrow your healers yet?"

Arabella looked down her nose at them. "The potion takes time. It'll be ready when it's ready. Besides, your mayor is better as a toad. Surely we can let that one stick and have Bob as mayor instead."

"Afraid not," said Wil. "As much as I would love to do just that, the terms are clear. We need them to smooth things over." He shrugged helplessly.

The elf sighed. "Marissa, check the potion," she ordered a dark-skinned, blond elf, who had been in the middle of shaping a branch on the tree house.

Marissa dropped to the ground and went through the door. She came back with a glowing pink potion in a glass bottle. "This should do the trick," she said, bringing it over to Wil. "Three drops on each of their heads and they'll turn back to their true form. If any of them are lying about what they are, this will reveal them."

"Ah, so Sheriff Frederick will turn into a walrus," said Darlene, "and Sinclair will remain as he is."

"Yeah, yeah, get it out of your system," Wil said with a chuckle. "We need them to be calm and reasonable, and they've had to spend two days as toads. They're bound to be cranky. Thank you, Marissa, for all the hard work you and your sisters have done."

Marissa's eyes widened and she bowed. "I'm sure I'll find some way you can show your appreciation," she said.

Arabella rolled her eyes. "Don't encourage her. This will go straight to her head and then she'll be unmanageable."

"See you later," said Wil, taking the potion.

The mayor and others were with Doc Hawkins at his clinic. In a warm back room, they sat in tubs of water. Wil wondered if they had been fed yet, and if so, what it had been. Doc Hawkins looked happy to see him.

"This the concoction that's supposed to fix things?" he asked. He took off his glasses and cleaned them on his shirt. "I hope it works. They haven't shut up since we got them in there. I don't know how much of their minds are left in this form."

"Most, I would think," Wil said.

"Then if I had to guess, they've been complaining up a storm this entire time. They're bound to be frustrated, and I can't blame them." Replacing his glasses, Doc Hawkins opened the door and they were immediately assaulted by croaks and chirps.

Wil concentrated and the sounds turned into some form of human speech. He raised his hands. "Alright, everybody, it's time to go back to being human. I'm really sorry about this, but it was a prank gone wrong. I'm going to need you guys to let it go and accept a nice present of gold and an apology, okay?"

"Absolutely not!" one toad cried. "They will pay for this outrage, this insult, this—"

"Yes, that's what I'm talking about," said Wil. "They're going to be giving each of you the equivalent of twenty-five thousand zynce for your troubles, as well as a personal gift. I suggest you take it and not push further."

The mayor hopped his way, vocal sac puffing indignantly. "Are you threatening to leave us this way if we don't go along with your demands? That's low, McKenzie, even for you."

"Everything alright?" Darlene asked, looking around at the dozen toads all getting closer, hopping over one another to get at Wil.

He waved off her concern and addressed the mayor. "It's not a threat, it's advice. My job in this town is to advise on matters regarding magic, magical beings, curses, and the rest. If you all seek satisfaction or retaliate in any way, you'll be picking a fight the rest of us will have to suffer for, and I'm not going to allow that. We'll turn you back, you'll take the apology and gift, and life will move on. If anyone retaliates, I will make life inconvenient for you. I'm tired of tolerating ignorance and disrespect, and I'm *telling* you the matter is over."

The toads fell silent. One with dark, mottled patterns over its mouth spoke up. "You think you're some kind of dictator, Wizard? You don't get to tell the law what to do."

Wil brought out the pink potion and pulled the stopper. "Yes, I do. If only because there's nothing you can do to stop me. I'm trying to do the best thing for everyone, and I would greatly appreciate your cooperation. It might even get rewarded with personal attention, making your lives better."

He dripped three little pink dots onto the toad. The potion was absorbed, and then the toad grew several sizes, rapidly turning back into a human. A very naked, large human. It was a miracle he didn't squash any of the other toads, but Sheriff Frederick soon lay on the floor, panting as if he'd just run a mile.

"Oh, gross!" Darlene made a face and looked away as Frederick picked himself up.

Wil put illusory clothes on him. It was the least he could do. "Doc Hawkins might want to check on you before you go, Sheriff, but you should be in good health. Sorry about what I did to the jail."

Frederick's face turned an ugly shade of red, but Wil had no fear of him anymore. After a brief stare-down with the sheriff, he turned and went to check in with Doc Hawkins.

Darlene looked at Wil, disgusted. "Are they all going to be naked?"

She left him to his work. One by one Wil turned them back, covering them in a light illusion until they fished their clothes out of a box. He personally apologized to each of them and sent them on their way. To his delight, Mr. Carrey was one of the quiet ones. He got up and limped out without a word. Finally, the only person left was Sinclair.

"You're not going to turn me back, are you?" Sinclair groaned. "So much for all those morals you flout."

"Oh, hush," said Wil, pulling up a chair and sitting. "I just wanted to talk with you first. Give you a bit of advice."

The toad said nothing, puffing his vocal sac while he waited.

Wil took it as a good sign and tried his best to reach the man he'd kind of considered an enemy. "I want you to think about walking away," he said to Sinclair. "This isn't a threat but an honest appeal in your best interest. We already signed the peace treaty. Things around here are going to change, and there's no stopping it. If you remain mayor, you'll have to put up with everything you loved turning into something different as we adapt and grow. I think you would be happier if you took a break and focused on enjoying life for a while. No games, no power plays, just appreciating what you have. Doesn't that sound better than losing again and again?"

It felt so much better to be honest and pity the mayor instead of hating him. Sinclair and the sheriff had seemed like such big obstacles in the past, but now Wil realized they had only whatever power Wil gave them. Hugo had been right: wizards could do whatever they wanted. It was on him to make sure he never got out of hand. Wil trusted his gut.

"Just turn me back," Sinclair finally said.

Wil emptied the rest of the bottle onto the mayor's head. He became human once again, complete with illusory clothing. Without saying a word, he walked out the door.

Wil sat there, soaking in the last of his major problems being dealt with. Only one thing remained.

CHAPTER 60

Correspondence

Truth be told, making contact with Cloverton should have been one of the first things Wil did, but he couldn't bring himself to do it until everything else was well in hand. With that out of the way, Wil brought Bram with him to go through Hugo's possessions for the link back to the capital.

"It's weird being on the ship like this when there's a big hole beneath us," said Bram, stepping gingerly as if the deck would collapse beneath him.

The *Flying Calamity* stood upright again, fresh trees having been grown on either side of the ship to hold it steady while the crew and fae alike worked on repairs and enchantments to get it back into the air. First Mate Barclay oversaw the work, nodding at them as they went below decks.

"It's not like we're still flying. Can't crash any more than it has," said Wil. He winced as a nearby sailor shot him a dirty look.

"Yeah, I guess you're right. Are you sure that it's okay for me to come along?" Bram ducked under a low doorway as they approached the mage's quarters.

"Of course," said Wil. "I figured you'd love a chance to get your hands on some of his tools and books. We might not be able to keep it all, but I wanted to share them. And not be alone while I talk with Cloverton."

It was true, but not the entire truth. Since Gallath had stayed behind in Faerie to try to consolidate control of the Ogre Federation and fill in his uncle's considerable shoes, Bram had been despondent. The company was great, but Wil thought that helping himself and a friend out at the same time was fantastic.

Hugo's quarters were luxurious, as far as ships went. That mostly meant the bed looked almost comfortable and the two of them could stand side by side without touching the walls. Shelves stacked one on top of another, all filled with books, wands, potions, crystals, and bottles of liquor. All of those would be interesting to go through, but the real goal was the journal in the little desk nook.

"Oh man, this all looks even more impressive than the stuff at your house!" Bram noticeably lit up, before he realized what he said and chuckled. "No offense, obviously."

"None taken," said Wil. His heart pounded as he read the title. *Hugo Jefferson's Correspondence with Cloverton.* The book was a thick, old-fashioned ledger with an opened lock and a quill in a leather loop.

Wil had one of his own, back in school, though not with the capital. Books like this were linked with a brother, and one could write back and forth with whoever had the other. Taking a deep breath, Wil opened the book and flipped through to the last page. There, he saw messages in two different colors of ink. Hugo's was, naturally, red.

The fae have struck against the town, as I predicted they would. In one fell stroke they took out the leadership and feigned ignorance. Through my spies, I witnessed a conversation between one of the representatives and Master McKenzie, where the fae proudly declared his intent to start a war. I am preparing for a strike upon Skalet Peak, where the rift is, to secure it. Please send reinforcements immediately.

Oh gods. Breathing hard, Wil read the response in blue ink.

Negative, Mage Jefferson. We do not have the troops to move to Harper Valley and will not until spring. You are to secure the fae and hold them on the McKenzie farm and wait for instructions. We do not want any further hostilities at this point. We need more information.

Hugo hadn't responded, and Cloverton had more messages after that. Wil relaxed, exhaling. "Thank the gods, Bram. We should be good."

"Phew," said Bram, setting down the blue star-shaped crystal he'd been holding. "What did you find?"

Wil tapped the journal. "He had explicit instructions to stand down and not escalate things, and he did it anyway. We've got Captain Nesbitt to corroborate it, and the entire crew will tell the same story. I think I can salvage this!"

Bram slapped him on the back. "Fantastic! What do you have to do?"

"I need to respond and tell them what happened, and then . . . I don't know. We'll see what happens." Wil picked up the quill. "Do me a favor? Grab a book and take it to the hallway. Make sure I'm not disturbed."

His friend laughed. "Don't have to tell me twice." Bram scanned the shelves and pulled out a book titled *Entropy Magic and You*. With a friendly salute, he left Wil to the journal.

Mage Jefferson, you have your orders. Respond.

Wil's eyes drifted down the page to the last in a string of demanding messages.

Mage Jefferson, we need to know your current status and that of the situation with Faerie. If you do not respond, we will assume you have gone AWOL and an archmage will be sent to retrieve you.

This was his chance to jump in. Wil focused his magic and channeled it through the quill as he wrote back in green ink.

This is Master Wizard Wilbur McKenzie. Mage Jefferson launched an illegal attack on Faerie, and I stopped it. I then went back into Faerie and managed to gain control of the situation. War was averted, the citizens of Harper Valley were turned back into humans, and the proposed treaty was signed.

Mage Jefferson is dead. While I was in the process of trying to nonlethally stop him, he lost control of his thralls. They turned on him and tore him apart. I take total responsibility for this, but I request a chance to explain myself and my actions in full. Please advise.

Wil knew it was all likely to blow up in his face, but everything else had worked, and he had evidence to back him up. The favorable trade conditions would help.

He didn't have to wait long. Within a minute the blue ink reappeared.

Master McKenzie, your message has been received. Stand by for further instructions.

An hour later, Wil stumbled out of Jefferson's quarters. Bram looked up from his book and grimaced.

"That bad?"

"No," said Wil with a groan, "not quite bad. Not quite good either. The good news is, they believed me, but . . . I'm being summoned to Cloverton. They plan on having a hearing about everything that's happened over the last few months, and they're going to pick at me until there's nothing left."

Bram winced. "That's not ideal. Will you be okay?"

"Probably. And I think they'll honor the treaty we signed."

There was a lot more to it than that, but Bram didn't need to know. As much as his friend was fascinated by magic and wished he was a wizard, he wasn't. The reality was a lot more complicated and, honestly, a pain in Wil's ass. There were many reasons he'd ended up posted in Harper Valley, and not all of them were positive.

It seemed as if all his skeletons were about to vacate the closet. Wil was just glad the instructions were for him to go with only one companion, and it had to be a member of the fae, willing to talk and make contact with the heart of the government. Syl was an obvious choice, if he was willing after all he'd been through.

The hair on the back of Wil's neck rose. "Hold on," he told Bram, and went back on deck just as the first scream sounded.

The crew scrambled to get away from a large six-legged wildcat. Isom's eye was dull, but there was still some awareness to him, something left of the being he used to be. The wampus cat slunk over to Wil, ignoring the gasps and warnings as he went.

Wil stayed perfectly still. He hadn't brought his staff with him, and he wasn't ready for a fight. Isom came right up to him in slow, jerky motions, sniffing him cautiously. When Wil raised a hand, Isom bared his teeth, but there was no growl or sudden movements.

"I'm so sorry for what he's done to you," said Wil, throat tightening. "You kept trying to kill me and showed up at the worst times, but I like you. I'm hoping there's some part of you still in there that can hear me, that I can reach. If so, I can . . ." His head throbbed. "I could try to see if I could fix you."

Isom lay flat on the ground, tense but not attacking. It was good enough. Wil made eye contact and went into his stalker's mind.

CHAPTER 61

My Best Enemy

The first thing Wil noticed was that he was no longer human. He walked around on all fours, tail waving behind him. It wasn't the first time he'd been in feline form, so he wasn't entirely lost. He circled, getting used to the feel of dirt under his paws and the coiled power in his legs.

The mindscape was a savannah, with mountains on one side and rolling hills on the other. Brush and rocks provided plenty of places for the cunning predator to stalk their prey in peace. Wil wasn't alone. His guts screamed about the other cats in the area, all competing for the same prey.

Instinct told him to head toward the water and scout out the land. Wil trotted along, not worried about stealth the way others were. He wanted to be noticed, and something watched him as he went. The feeling of being exposed grew the closer Wil came to the river that split the savannah in two.

Lowering his head, Wil flicked out his tongue. He tasted the seasons and the years passing by—all the creatures Isom had ever seen had left their imprint there. Wil drank in the rabbits and antelope and strange, two-headed beasts with long legs and even longer necks. Each one filled him with the urge to run, the itch to hunt.

Wil followed the inclination, bounding over the hot grasslands. Birds flew up and away from him, but they weren't proper prey. Just a bite or two and then they were done, but it was fun to sneak up on them sometimes. A powerful, musky scent caught his attention. He followed it.

Up and over the rocks and fallen trees littering the land he went, liquid grace and power. His prey came into view, and he put on an extra burst of speed. The young pig squealed in alarm and tried to get away. One pounce later and it was over.

Wil shook his head back and forth in a frenzy until his meal no longer struggled. There was joy in it, a satisfaction that came with fulfilling his purpose, of engaging in the eternal game that ran his life. It was win or starve, and he was more than happy to live life to the fullest.

It was only after he'd consumed half of the memory that Wil calmed down and his sense of self returned. Isom had powerful instincts, but he understood the concept of not killing everything he saw and instead going after the things that made him happy. It was a simple mind, but simple didn't mean stupid.

Wil felt the wampus cat then, strongly, and took off in that direction. The connection was fleeting, and Wil followed it until it flickered out and left him on his own. At this point, he had a good idea of where he was. Off in the distance was an outcropping of rock on the side of a great hill. It looked like home.

The entrance was well hidden, but the hairs on the back of his neck stood straight up. He snuck forward, wary of the bigger cat inside. It took only half a second for his eyes to adjust to the darkness. Isom lay at the back of the cave on his side, broken and bleeding from dozens of tiny wounds.

"Oh no," Wil whispered. "Look what that bastard did to you. I can help, though. I know I can."

Isom let out a weak *mrowl* but otherwise didn't move. Wil crept closer, examining the damage. It was all metaphorical, of course. The important thing was that Hugo had almost broken him. Almost.

As he got closer, Wil returned to his human form, fully clothed and with his staff. He crouched beside Isom and put his hand on the cat's side, just above the middle set of legs. Instantly, he and Isom were connected and Wil felt the cat's pain like his own, blinding and distracting. Wil pushed back against it and focused on his mental stability, blanketing Isom with it.

It was no different from applying pressure to a fresh wound, staunching the bleeding, and stabilizing the subject. Wil had no talent in healing magic. He couldn't close wounds or mend broken bones, but this was in Isom's head. Here, he could piece things together and smooth over the worst of the pain.

On and on Wil worked, and finally, he whispered words of encouragement in Isom's ear. The projection of the wampus cat's body slowly mended back into his normal, ugly, scraggly self. He stood, looking at Wil with a clearer eye.

Wil let himself drift up and outward, keeping a mental hand over Isom's projection. When they parted, it felt as if part of him remained, keeping the damage contained. When the real world came back into existence, Isom stood on all six legs and cocked his head.

"Wiz . . . ard?" the cat croaked. One of the crew drew a pistol and Isom jerked his way, snarling.

Wil held out a hand. "Isom? Are you back with us?"

Wizard.

The thought popped into his head, a purr to it. Wil blinked and motioned for him to continue.

Wizard. I am . . . I am Isom. I am . . . me? A sense of hunger and confusion struck Wil.

"Does your larder have any meat?" Wil asked the first mate.

"Yeah, of course," said Barclay. "Why? You aren't thinking of having us hand over our food to that thing, are you?"

"Yes," said Wil. "Trust me. Beef, if you have it."

Barclay motioned with her hand and two nearby sailors ran below deck. They came out with an entire beef leg. Wil took it from them, gesturing with his hand and sending it floating over to Isom.

The wampus cat dug into it with gusto, making a mess on the deck. A nearby man with a mop sighed. Isom continued until only bone was left. He approached Wil with a renewed light in his eye. "Wizard. Wilbur. I . . ." Isom licked his lips. "I owe you my life."

Obligation hit Wil hard, threatening to bowl him over. It was more than he'd felt from any other oath, save his own promise to close the way between worlds. Isom had said it, and he'd meant it with all his being.

"You don't need to do that," said Wil, horrified by the sense he was getting from the cat.

Isom shook his head. "I owe you my life. Until your end, I will serve you loyally. I pledge my service until my debt is repaid."

The connection in their heads snapped tight, more solid than ever. Wil couldn't read Isom's mind, but he could feel the cat there. The wizard swallowed hard, not sure whether to be honored or scream at the additional complication.

"If you do, then you need to obey me," said Wil. "No matter what I say, with the knowledge that I will not intentionally harm you. Is that understood? Swear to me."

"I understand," said Isom. "I swear obedience, so long as you keep me fed and sheltered. Your enemies will be my enemies, and the fruits of my hunts are yours, until your dying day."

With the oath made, Wil relaxed. He reached out and petted Isom's head, surprised and not sure if he wanted a servant of any kind, even a willing one. The long-lived cat would probably not miss one lifetime with him, but he had places to go. "Then I accept, and . . . welcome to my household."

"You can't be serious," said Bram, coming up beside him. "How many times did he try to kill you?"

"That doesn't matter now," said Wil. "We're friends. Good kitty."

Isom snarled his displeasure, but a second later he began purring anyway.

"Okay, okay," said Bram, holding up the book to shield himself from the cat. "Darlene's not going to be happy, you know."

Wil winced. "Darlene's not going to be happy for a number of reasons. C'mon, let's get back to the farm. I have a lot of explaining to do. And packing."

He motioned with his head and Isom fell into step. Bram took his other side, and they rode the elevator down. Wil looked at the great tree and the ring of mushrooms nearly as tall as him growing in front of it. The way to Oakheart Spiral. He reached out with his magic.

The leyline answered him readily, steadily pouring power into the air like an endless fountain. With his fatigue, it still burned a little, but he didn't draw on its power. So much had changed in the last few months, and now he was going to be apart from it for the first time.

He had a lot of research to do. The fae may not have required him to fix things yet, but he had to try and see if he could do it. If he could be the first man to change leylines and teach others how to do it.

But before all that, he had Cloverton to face.

CHAPTER 62

Farewell but Not Goodbye

Although Wil knew he was being ridiculous, the walk down the mountain felt like the last trip before facing the firing squad. He knew, logically, that things were not likely to be that bad. It wasn't the trip to Cloverton itself—it was once more having to be separated from his family and friends to go on a trip.

"We'll be okay without you," Bram said as they neared the farm.

"Huh?" Wil broke free of his daydreaming.

Bram stopped on the drive leading up to the house. "We'll be okay without you. You've been quiet this entire time. I know you—you're probably worrying up a storm. I would be too, but you shouldn't. We'll be okay for a month or two. Just so long as you come back safely."

"I can't promise that," said Wil. "For all I know, they'll lock me up for the trouble, or decide to junk the treaty. I don't think they will, but it's all I can think about. That and leaving again, and knowing that things are still a bit hot between some of the farmers. There's still so much work to be done."

"And we'll do it," Bram promised. He patted Wil's shoulder and moved on, heading toward the tree house.

Wil walked to his parents' home, taking the time to catch his breath and calm down. He'd sent Isom away until later, so he could explain things to the family. There was just so much to do, and he had maybe a couple of days before he left.

He found his mother in the den, relaxing for a change in her favorite chair, with the radio on. She lit up upon seeing him. "Did you get it done?"

He sank onto the couch with a groan. "Almost. Just one last thing I need to do, but I want to tell everyone at the same time."

Sharon got up immediately. "I'll make lunch, then, and you can call everyone in when it's ready."

Half an hour later, Sharon had turned feast leftovers into a brand-new meal. Even with the major interruption, the Midwinter Feast had left the McKenzie family with a tremendous amount of leftover food. Wil sent up giant glowing letters announcing lunch, and everyone piled in around the kitchen table.

"Thank goodness, I was starving," said Bob, groaning as he got comfortable. "You've got magic all your own, hon."

"Thanks, Ma," said Sarah, picking up her turkey and stuffing sandwich and taking a huge bite. "Arabella and I were going to get to work soon, so this is perfect timing." She sounded so normal and engaged that Wil wondered who had replaced her.

"Yesenia is a great model," Jeb said. "Arabella says I am too, but I don't think—"

"I'm not drawing or painting you. Eww." Sarah gagged and Jeb laughed.

It was so nice, so normal, that Wil couldn't bring himself to interrupt. They had their sandwiches and twice-baked potatoes in peace, chatting and enjoying a moment of ease after so much hard work and chaos. When almost every plate was empty and they had finished off their drinks, Wil spoke.

"So, I spoke to someone in charge, and I need to go to Cloverton to answer some questions," he started. His family looked at him. "I'll be gone for a month or so. Maybe longer. If they let me come back at all. Not to be dramatic or anything."

Sarah was the first one to speak. "But it's *you*. Of course it's dramatic. You'll be fine. You're too soft and sad for them to do anything bad to you."

Jeb, on the other hand, looked appropriately worried. "Do you need any of us to come with you?" he asked, eyes darting over to the front door. "I'd be happy to come along and look after you."

"What do you think you could do to a bunch of government wizards?" Sarah scoffed.

Bob cleared his throat, silencing his children. "We'll be worried about you, but we'll hold the fort in your absence. The last few days, I've been going around and talking to people and clearing up some fears. Fixing up the mayor and others smoothed away the worst of it, but there are still some people spooked. Give us time and your mother and I will take care of that."

"I appreciate it," said Wil. He offered his best smile. "I think that things are likely to go well for me. All the facts are on my side, and as usual, I have a few tricks up my sleeves, but . . . I can't guarantee that things will go our way. So I just wanted to say that I love you all, and I can't say enough how much it means to me that you've all helped out so much. Together, we've changed the world."

"Wow," said Sarah, "you really *can't* resist being dramatic, can you? Yeah, yeah, changed the world, saved Harper Valley again, and blah blah blah. If all goes well, I won't be here when you get back, so get it out of your system now."

Everyone laughed, Wil most of all. He drew himself up and sighed with all the petulance he could muster. "Dearest sister, you I will miss most of all. Please remember me when you're famous and living that art weirdo lifestyle and I am but a lowly local wizard."

Sarah rolled her eyes, but she loved it, he could tell.

"I think I might be heading off for a bit soon too," said Jeb, trying to not sound too pleased with himself. "Bella's going back and forth between here and Faerie and she wants me to come with her. Says she's gonna show me how civilized people live."

"You gonna put up with all the snide insults?" Bob asked. "Don't get me wrong, I like her, but she likes to push buttons."

"So does Jeb," said Sharon.

Jeb just beamed proudly. "I'm gonna be in the middle of her court and embarrass the hell out of her. And then later on—"

"We don't need to know," interrupted Wil. "What about you, Ma? Everyone else has tons of plans, but what are you going to do?"

Sharon ran a hand through her hair, feigning nonchalance. "Well, if your dad's gonna be running around town and all my kids will be gone, then someone's going to have to take care of this place and everyone in it. I swear, just as you kids all grow up, you get me a whole new bunch of people to look after. I'm never gonna have an empty nest."

"Sorry about that," said Wil.

She shook her head. "I love it. There was always going to be work on the farm to do, even if we scaled back to just supporting ourselves without trying to sell. Now I get to scale back early and also focus on our guests."

Bob leaned back, resting his hands on his belly. "All in all, I think everything's going about as well as can be expected. We'll miss you and we'll worry about you, Wil, but not too much. You're more than capable of handling anything the world can throw your way."

Sarah gagged again, making them all laugh. Wil basked in the moment, deeply appreciating how much his family made his increasingly weird life still feel normal. He'd hold on to that when things got tough.

Later, he went to see Syl. The faun had spent the last few days recovering and letting the other representatives handle things. Wil found him in the eatery with a cold drink and a dryad on his lap. Wil sat across from him, not saying anything at first.

"You were so brave, Sylano!" the dryad cooed, running a hand up his chest.

"I was, wasn't I?" Syl's head bobbed with self-satisfaction. His black eye had almost fully healed, and most of the cuts and bruises had faded, leaving only his sunny disposition and playfulness—and maybe a tiny bit of lingering resentment. "The humans are good at giving out a beating, but I held out."

"He's a hero," said Wil, doing his very best to help out. Syl startled and his companion put some distance between her and the faun, slipping into the next seat. "Wouldn't be here if it weren't for him."

"You're going to say that like you haven't been busy stopping every disaster heading our way." Syl laughed and took a long drink. "Wil, this is Kalia. She's been helping nurse me back to health. Unfortunately, I have so many aches and pains, I might need another week of rest."

"Healer's orders," said Kalia, giggling.

"Well, damn," said Wil, grabbing Syl's drink and taking a swig of it. He made a face and returned it. "I kind of need your help for something big. How do you feel about traveling with me to our capital to help give your testimony on how Hugo went crazy?"

The faun blinked. "The capital? I wouldn't be a prisoner, would I?"

"I think you would be part witness, part ambassador," Wil admitted. "It's bound to be stressful and we might encounter trouble."

"Aww, and you thought of me first? I'm touched!" Syl laughed obnoxiously.

"Well, it was either you or Arabella," said Wil, "and between the two of you, I think she would do a much better job here. We could use your charm in Cloverton. If you can, you know, not try to frolic with everything that moves."

"You're no fun." Syl's smirk disappeared. "I'll do it. I know it's important, and we've come this far together, we might as well see it to the end, right? Who else is coming?"

"It's just the two of us . . . and maybe my new cat." Wil grinned.

"Your new cat?" Syl cocked his head to the side. "You don't mean . . . Tell me everything."

A few days later, the repairs to the *Flying Calamity* were complete, and they were due to depart. Bram and Darlene accompanied Wil to the fairgrounds, where the ship waited once more. Unlike the last time he departed, there was no real fanfare, no great expectations. Harper Valley knew he was leaving, but it wasn't the big deal rescuing children from Faerie had been.

Wil preferred it that way. It was hard enough to say goodbye. For some more than others.

"You'd better come back safe!" Bram said, crushing Wil's bones in a tight embrace. "I promise, I'm going to master some new potions so we can focus on the business when we get back."

Wil gently extricated himself from the giant's grasp. "By the time I get back, you're going to be better at alchemy than I am. Take care of yourself first, though. I know you're hurting, but don't throw yourself into your work too hard."

"Oh, like you're one to talk." Darlene had taken the news that he was leaving and could be in trouble harder than most. They had spent the last few days desperately clinging to each other. "I'm surprised a summons is enough to keep you away from work."

"You know, you'd think that, but I desperately need a vacation," said Wil. He took her hands in his. "When I get back, hopefully things will settle down, and we can focus on us. No work for a while."

Darlene rolled her eyes. "There's always more work, and that's okay. I'll take care of your place while you're gone, but only for three months. After that, I'm just stealing it from you."

"Perfectly fair."

Wil felt Isom approaching. Ever since he'd helped mend the wampus cat's sense of self, there had been a new connection between them. Or maybe it had been created when Isom ate Hugo. Wil resolved to ask later. He knew the cat was there for sure when Bram let out a scream.

"STOP DOING THAT," Bram cried out, jumping away from the wampus cat and clutching his chest.

"Why?" Isom loafed on the dirt, a satisfied grin on his face. "You're so much fun to stalk. You look as tasty as a side of beef."

"Wil!"

Wil just shrugged. "Consider it a compliment. He likes and respects cows. Sort of." Isom licked his chops helpfully. Bram turned a funny color, so Wil reassured him. "He's under orders to not hurt anyone who isn't hurting me. You're safe, the worst he can do is surprise you."

"I can't believe you took him in," Darlene muttered. "After all the times he threatened to eat me."

Isom purred loudly.

"Think of it as me keeping him from harming others," said Wil. He looked up at the *Flying Calamity*, restored to its original shape. Then it hit him: he was leaving. He had only a few minutes left.

"If I don't come back—" Wil started.

"Don't," Darlene said. "You're going to come back. We'll take care of things until then, but none of that well-meaning doom-and-gloom preparation crap. Just come home safe."

Wil smiled. "I will. I promise."

Darlene kissed him. Bram courteously gave them privacy. When they parted, she sighed and said, "I love you."

His stomach jolted. They'd never said it before now, but he didn't hesitate. "I love you too. Dinner's on me when I get back."

Wil and Isom took the elevator up to the deck, where Syl was waiting for them already. Captain Nesbitt barked out orders left and right. It was almost time to depart.

"You ready?" Wil asked Syl.

"Of course!" Syl looked around. "Just another exciting adventure, and something to tell my father when I get back. You ready, Cat?"

Isom stretched nonchalantly. "To visit the home of wizards and be unable to eat to my heart's content? If I must."

Wil took a deep breath. "Then this is it."

They cast away from the fairgrounds and rose into the sky. Wil and his fae friends stood at the rail, watching Harper Valley shrink and disappear behind them.

Acknowledgments

Hoo boy, this one was a ride, and it would not have been possible without the love and support of my parents and my partners. I wrote this during a vulnerable, turbulent time, and they all saw me through safely. I love you all.

I'd also like to thank Cass Dolan and Steph VanderMeulen at Podium for their hard work in turning my raw material into the work of a professional. Their patience and helpfulness has helped me grow as an author in ways I'm still figuring out.

And finally, I'd like to thank the Council of the Eternal Hiatus (coteh.carrd.co) Discord community. They're truly the best craft writing environment for hobbyists and professionals alike, and are a huge part of what made me take the leap and just go for it.

About the Author

SmilingSatyr is a millennial bookworm and the author of the Friendly Neighborhood Wizard series, originally released on Royal Road. He writes stories because he's not really equipped to do anything else—them's the breaks!

Podium

DISCOVER
STORIES UNBOUND

PodiumAudio.com

Milton Keynes UK
Ingram Content Group UK Ltd.
UKHW042052130824
446844UK00006B/396

9 781039 454149